Acclaim for **ANDREW VACHSS**'s

SAFE HOUSE

"A cobra's nest of extortionists, neo-Nazis and other assorted freaks."   —*Chicago Tribune*

"With his stripped down, stark prose and darkly evocative sense of place, Vachss introduces us to a world most of us would rather not know about—and then hooks us with a stunning story."   —*Milwaukee Journal*

"Well done and well worth it."   —*Dayton Daily News*

"Vachss's prose is Hammett-tough, and Burke's world is unsettling if not psychologically dangerous for the first-time reader."   —*Huntsville Times* (Alabama)

"Vachss is one of my favorite writers, and I never miss one of his books. He brings incredible passion and flair to the mystery genre. *Safe House* is one of Vachss's very best."   —James Patterson

"*Safe House* comes at you with the speed of a bullet train, a style as spare and stripped down as origami and Andrew Vachss's usual black-as-pitch theme—the abuse of innocence. Yet for all of the their dark modernity, Vachss's novels are inheritors of nineteenth-century social criticism, as much Dickens and Defoe as Hammett and Chandler."   —Martha Grimes

ANDREW VACHSS

SAFE HOUSE

Andrew Vachss has been a federal investigator in sexually transmitted diseases, a social caseworker and a labor organizer, and has directed a maximum-security prison for youthful offenders. Now a lawyer in private practice, he represents children and youth exclusively. He is the author of numerous novels, a collection of short stories, three graphic series, and *Another Chance to Get it Right: A Children's Book for Adults*. His work has appeared in *Parade*, *Antaeus*, *The New York Times*, and many other forums. He lives in New York City.

The dedicated Web site for Vachss and his work is www.vachss.com

Books by ANDREW VACHSS

SAFE HOUSE

SAFE HOUSE

ANDREW VACHSS

VINTAGE CRIME/BLACK LIZARD

Vintage Books • A Division of Random House, Inc. • New York

FIRST VINTAGE CRIME/BLACK LIZARD EDITION, APRIL 1999

Copyright © 1998 by Andrew Vachss
Excerpt from Choice of Evil copyright © 1999 by Andrew Vachss

All rights reserved under International and Pan-American Copyright Conventions. Published in the United States by Vintage Books, a division of Random House, Inc., New York. Originally published in hardcover in the United States by Alfred. A. Knopf, Inc., New York, in 1998.

Vintage Books, Vintage Crime/Black Lizard, and colophon are trademarks of Random House, Inc.

The Library of Congress has cataloged the Knopf edition as follows:
Vachss, Andrew H.
Safe house / Andrew Vachss.—1st ed.
p. cm.
ISBN 0-375-40084-2
I. Title.
PS3572.A33S25   1998
813'.54—dc21   97-50557
CIP

Vintage ISBN: 0-375-70074-9

www.randomhouse.com/vintage

Printed in the United States of America
10   9   8

for the grief we have harvested
from the evil you have sown
jackals will forever call you coward
and vultures refuse your bones

—family curse

SAFE HOUSE

SAFE HOUSE

Vyra twisted her body to catch the pale mid-afternoon light purring against the white mesh curtains in the window of the downtown hotel room. She was nude except for a pair of sheer stockings and sunburst-yellow spike heels with black ankle straps. Posing, she stood in front of me, one foot on a straight chair she'd pulled away from the desk, watching me over one shoulder, wheat-colored hair hanging straight down her back. As she slowly turned to face me, her enormous breasts came into view, appearing even more massive on her thin, curveless frame. She raised her hands high above her head, looking down.

"Aren't they just perfect?" she asked.

"Absolutely," I assured her.

"They're so beautiful, I just hate to take them off."

"They won't get in the way," I said.

Vyra's idea of foreplay is putting on a fashion show. But she makes up for it—a couple of cigarettes is about all the afterplay she ever has time for.

Me too.

I'd known Vyra for years—I wasn't the only key that had ever fit her lock. But my timing was good. Her husband did something that brought in beaucoup bucks. Or his people left him a bundle, I could never remember. Vyra changed her stories about as often as her shoes, but she loved them both. All I really knew about her husband was how he worshipped those humongous, incongruous breasts. That's why she kept them, she said, just for him. They strained her scrawny frame, hurt her back. The heavy underwire bra she had to wear cut harsh marks into her pale skin. Her body looked like a cartoon drawn by a fetishist.

Vyra had a sweet, lonely heart. And a deep borderline's void. When she got bored, she shopped. And volunteered for all kinds of organizations. Suicide hot lines, animal shelters, like that.

Vyra doesn't know what I do, but she knows I'm not an accountant. She gets nosy every once in a while—just to keep in practice, I think. But she doesn't push, and it never comes to anything.

Vyra knows where to find me. Or where to leave word, anyway. She never calls unless she's already got a hotel room. And if I'm around when she calls, we get together and do what we do.

But only if I'm around when she calls. I never think about what she does when I'm not.

I sat up slightly, reached down and tangled her hair in my hand. Pulled gently. She kept her mouth locked around my cock, shook her head no. I pulled harder, warning her. She stayed where she was, making little grunting sounds until it was over.

After a minute or two, she slithered up my body, her breasts trailing against my stomach, stopping at my chest. She looked down.

"Is it different when a woman does it?"

"What?"

"Blows you. If your eyes are closed, does it make any difference?"

"I don't know," I said.

"But you were . . . in prison, weren't you?"

She brings that up a lot. I don't know why—it's important to her in some way she never explained. And I never asked.

"Yeah. So?"

"Were you in a long time?"

"What's a long time, little girl?" I asked her gently, running my thumb over her sticky mouth.

"More than . . . I don't know, a year?"

"Sure."

"So what did you do for . . . sex?"

"Went steady with my fist."

"But I heard . . . I mean, if you have sex in prison, it doesn't make you gay."

"So?"

"Is that true?"

"Prison's like the rest of the world. All kinds in there."

"Is that why you never did it? In there? Because you hate them?"

"Hate who?"

"Gay people?"

I slid my right hand around to the back of her neck. She smiled down at me. I suddenly twisted my hand, shoving her face down into the mattress. I moved to one side, held her down with my right hand while I pressed my left thumb into the base of her spine, hard. I leaned down and put my lips to her ear.

"You like this?" I said softly.

"*No!* Let me—"

"Rape is rape," I whispered. "It's not gay, it's not straight. I don't give a good goddamn how people fuck, long as it's what they *want* to do, understand?"

"Yes."

I let her go. She popped up on one elbow. "I didn't mean anything, honey," she said, a fake-contrite tone in her voice. "I was just curious."

"You've got a sweet little nose," I told her. "Just watch where you stick it, okay?"

"*You* watch," she giggled.

I pulled away from the hotel an hour later. Winter was against the ropes bleeding, but it refused to go down for the count. That gray day in March, spring was still a whore's promise—nylons whispering, but no real juice waiting.

I cursed the cold as the Plymouth slid around another corner.

its wipers all but surrendering to the leaden sleet sneering down from a sullen sky. The anemic sun had vanished along with Vyra.

The Plymouth was an anonymous drab shark in an ocean of quicker, brighter little fish—all of them darting about, secure in their front-wheel drive, ABS-equipped, foglight-blazing perkiness—at war with glowering pedestrians, all engaged in a mutual ignorance pact when it came to traffic signals. I feathered the throttle, knowing the Plymouth's stump-puller motor could break the fat rear tires loose in a heartbeat, wishing the guy who had built what he thought was going to be the ultimate New York City taxicab had lived to finish the job.

The meet was set for just off Frankfort Street, under the Brooklyn Bridge. The downtown subway system was a disease incubator in winter, and I'd be damned if I was going to walk in the miserable weather. I hadn't set the meet up, and I couldn't change it. When I'd called in, Mama had given me the done-deal message.

"Man call. Say name. Herk Kew Leeze. Say friend. From Upstate."

Hercules. Big strong good-looking kid. I'd done time with him, years ago. Solid as a railroad spike. And just about as shrewd. He was stand-up all the way. Dead reliable. Inside, those two words intersect a lot. But we couldn't let him crew up with us on the bricks. The Prof had cast the veto. "Boy can't go pro," the little man told us. "Heart don't count the same as smart." I'd heard Hercules was heavy-lifting for hire. Not a made man, not even part of an organization. He was a disposable samurai, and whatever he wanted to tell me wouldn't be good news.

"What did he say, Mama?"

"Say meet. Second shift. Butcher Block. Okay?"

Meaning: did I understand what he meant?—because Mama sure as hell didn't.

"Sure. It's all right. I'll take care of it."

"You need Max?"

"No, Mama. He's a friend."

"I not know him?"

"No."

"Sure," Mama said, cutting the connection. I wondered what I'd done this time.

The second shift meant prison time—three in the afternoon to eleven at night. When you set up a must-come meet the way Hercules had, you always give the other guy a wide margin for showing up. The Butcher Block is an abandoned loading dock under the Brooklyn Bridge. It got its name because thieves used to meet there to cut up the swag from the trucks in the nearby Fulton Fish Market. Hercules didn't know where I lived. Guy like him knows that, he drops by one day, just to say hello. Maybe brings a six-pack. Or the cops.

I slid the Plymouth to a stop on Broadway, just across from the outdoor homeless shelter the politicians call City Hall Park. In another few seconds, the passenger door popped open and the Prof climbed in.

"If it's Herk's game, you know it's lame. Gonna be some motherfucking sorryass shame," the little man greeted me, his voice sour with disgust.

"You want to pass?" I asked him.

"You know I can't do that, Schoolboy. Man was with us, right? He took the weight, we got to pay the freight."

That said it all. We'd hold up our end. Obligation and honor, same thing. But that was no middle-class citizen's one-way street. What drove us was the certain knowledge that, if we called Hercules from a pay phone in Hell, he'd drop right in.

You can't buy loyalty like that. But you have to pay what it costs. In installments.

"Where's Clarence?" I asked him.

"Clarence? That boy don't have nothing to do with this, whatever it is. He don't owe, so he don't go."

"Fair enough," I told him, meaning it.

I hooked left just before Vesey Street, doubled back up Park Row, ignored the entrance to the bridge and forked to the right, staying low like I was heading for the FDR. When I spotted the opening, I nosed the Plymouth inside, peering through the windshield.

"I got him," the Prof said. "Over there."

A man was approaching the car. A big man with long dark hair, looking even bigger in an ankle-length yellow slicker like traffic cops wear. The Prof jumped out and slipped into the back seat, leaving the front door open, a clear invite. The big man piled in, shaking himself like a damn Saint Bernard, showering me with icy water.

"Burke!" he said, extending his hand to shake.

"Herk," I greeted him back, my voice low, sending him a message. Which he promptly ignored as soon as he spotted who was in the back seat.

"Prof! Hey, this is great!"

"Be cool, fool," the Prof told him. "This ain't no reunion. You got business, right?"

The big man shook his head again. Hard, like he was trying to remember something. Something important. "I'm up against it," he finally said.

"Spell it out," I told him.

"There was this girl. . . ."

"God*damn* it, Schoolboy. What'd I tell you? This chump is a bull, and gash is the pull."

"Easy, Prof. Whatever it is . . ." I let the sentence trail away, turned to Herk, opened my hands in a "Tell-me" gesture.

"There was this girl," he said again, like he was starting the tape from the beginning. "She was getting . . . stalked, like. You know what I mean?"

"No," I said, edging my voice just enough to tell him to get on with it.

"Okay. Her boyfriend used to beat on her. All the time. For nothing. Then he'd say he was sorry and she'd take him back. Finally, he puts her in the hospital. Not just the E-Ward, like he did before—they had to operate. On her face. I guess she was too fucked up from the drugs they gave her to cover for him, I don't know. Anyway, the rollers took him down. He went easy," Herk said, his voice veined with a hard-core convict's contempt for anyone who doesn't automatically resist arrest. "Anyway, she says she ain't gonna press charges, and you know what the Man said?

You ain't gonna believe this, Burke. They don't *need* her—they could just go ahead and lumber him anyway, no matter what she wants. I mean, they could *make* her come to court. Jesus."

I took a pack of cigarettes off the dashboard, offered one to Herk. He shook his head. Same way he was in the joint. A *serious* bodybuilder, the only drug Herk would play with was Dianabol, and he'd stopped the red-zone steroids when we'd pulled his coat to the cold light at the end of that tunnel. But the Prof snatched the butt out of my hand before I could light it. I heard a match snap into flame behind me. "Thanks, bro," he said sarcastically. I lit another one for myself. "What's the rest?" I asked the big man.

"He gets some bullshit baby-time. Six months on the Rock, out in four. She gets one of them Orders of Protection, you know what I mean?"

"Yeah."

"But that don't mean nothing. He calls her. Right from the House, calls her. Collect, okay? After a while, she don't take the calls. Even changes her number. So he writes her letters. Real weird shit—like he loves her and he had a dream that he sliced her face into ribbons."

"He's still locked up when he does this?" the Prof asked.

"Yeah."

"She show them to the cops?" I wanted to know.

"Sure. But dig this: there's nothing they can do, right? I mean, this time she *wants* to prosecute his ass, and they don't do nothing. They told her those letters, they wasn't threats, just talking about his dreams and stuff. Stupid mother—"

"—and then he gets out . . . ," I prompted, cutting off the flow.

"Uh-huh. And he starts it right back again. Calling her on her job, leaving notes in her mailbox, all like that. He's got her scared now—"

"And you're dipping your sorry wick, right, sucker?" the Prof stuck in.

"No, Prof. I swear," Herk said in a hurt tone of voice. "I mean, I never even *met* her, okay? It wasn't like that."

"So what *was* it like?" I asked him.

"You know Porkpie?"

"Yeah," I told him, nervous now. Porkpie was a minor-league

fringe-player. One of those maybe-Jewish, maybe-Italian, Brooklyn-edge boys. He didn't have muscle or balls or brains, so he played the middleman role. A halfass tipster and two-bit tout—he wouldn't touch anything with his own hands, but he always knew a guy who would. Or so he said. He wasn't mobbed up. Didn't have a crew, worked out of pay phones and the trunk of his car. Only a citizen or a stone rookie would do any business with him.

Herk wasn't either one, but he was just thick enough so it didn't matter.

"Okay, so Porkpie tells me about it," he continued. "The job, I mean. He says they need someone to lean on this guy, give him the word, tell him to get in the wind, let the broad alone, understand?"

"Sure."

"A grand for a few minutes' work, that's what he told me."

"You was gonna move on this guy, do work on him, let them turn the key for one lousy G?" the Prof snarled. "What the fuck's wrong with you, boy? You been down twice. You can't ride that train—it ain't nothing but pain. You go bone-busting, you get called to the Walls. *That's* your idea of good pay for a few minutes' work?"

"It wasn't that, Prof. Honest. Porkpie said the guy was a stone pussy, okay? All I hadda do was muscle up on him, maybe bitch-slap him once. Porkpie said he'd give it up in a minute, kinda guy beats a woman. . . ."

"All *kinds* of fucking guys beat on women," the Prof told him. "That don't tell you nothing. You been enough places to know that, Herk."

"It don't matter now," the big man said sadly.

"Bottom line," I said. "Let's get to it. Come on."

"Porkpie gives me a picture, okay? What the guy looks like and all. And he drives me to the spot where the guy gets off work."

"You braced him in daylight?" I asked, already shuddering at his stupidity.

"Nah, Burke. He's a security guard, like. Gets off after midnight. In this big building on Wall Street. He has to go right through this alley to where they park their cars. Porkpie said I could grab him there."

"And . . . ?"

"I snatch him, okay? I slam him up against the wall, tell him I'm the girl's cousin. Porkpie told me to say that, so he'd know I was serious and all. He tries to talk to me, but I'm not playing. I told him, he wants to get down, let's do it. Right there. He drops his hands, puts his head down. I figure that's it. . . . Then he comes out with a piece. I didn't . . . think about it, man. I just plunged him."

"You shanked the motherfucker?" the Prof asked quietly, leaning forward over the back of the front seat.

"Right in the gut," Herk said. "I didn't mean to, but . . . once I stuck him, I knew he was gone. I could see it in his face, like when the light goes out, you know? He was off the count."

"Anybody see you?" I asked. It was business now.

"I don't think so. I don't know. Porkpie said he didn't see nobody."

"When was this?"

"Two nights ago. I mean, it'll *be* two nights when it gets dark."

"What do you need, Herk?" I asked him.

"I need a stake, Burke. I got to get outa here. Outa this city."

Herk couldn't say it, but he could feel it. He was a mine-shaft canary, just beginning to smell the fumes, fluttering his wings against the cage. I looked back at the Prof. He nodded.

"I'm gonna take you someplace," I told him. "You'll be okay there. Meanwhile, I'll see what's going on, okay?"

"Sure, Burke," he said, smiling. A big, sweet, dumb kid.

"This one ain't no Fourteenth Amendment citizen, is he?" the voice on the phone said.

"He's the same fucking citizen I am," I said, keeping my voice down to a jailhouse whisper—soft with threat.

"No offense, man," the voice said quickly. "But you know how I have to play it. I mean . . ."

"No offense. A yard a day, right?"

"Right. Ten-day minimum."

"He'll have it with him."

checked on the wire. The police had it down as a mugging that went wrong. At least Herk had been smart enough to grab the dead man's watch and wallet. And toss them into the nearest Dumpster, where some foraging wino was sure to pick them up. He'd never touched the dead man's pistol, leaving it where it was. The cops had no suspects.

But I did. Herk was the third day into his hideout before we found Porkpie. He was coming out of a dive in Red Hook, wearing a snazzy dark overcoat and his trademark little hat with a fat little white feather sticking up from the band. A zircon glistened on his hand, bloodshot from a faded red neon sign in the window of the bar.

"Hey, Porkpie!" I yelled at him, closing the distance between us, hands empty at my sides.

He stopped in his tracks, making up his mind. Before he finished, Max had him.

One good thing about Red Hook, you never have to go far to find some privacy. I docked the dark-green Volvo sedan next to one of the piers, backing in carefully so I could spot any visitors. I didn't expect cops—even when the weather is warm and the piers are crawling with longshoremen, the rollers working the pad know the money men only come out in daylight.

Porkpie was in the front bucket seat, Max right behind him, one hand on the weasel's neck. Max's hands are hard autobiographies: big leather-colored maps of seamed scar tissue with callused ridges of horn along the knife-edges—flesh-and-bone sledgehammers with bolt-cutters for fingers. Porkpie couldn't see the hand, but he could feel it, the fingers pressing his carotid artery, thumb hooked just under his Adam's apple. What he could see was the pistol in my gloved left hand, held at my waist, pointed at his crotch.

"Open the glove compartment," I told him softly.

"Burke, I . . ."

"Open it, Porkpie."

He pushed the button and the door came down. In the light from the tiny bulb he could see the coil of piano wire. And the barber's straight razor with its mother-of-pearl handle.

"We wrap your hands and your ankles in the wire," I told him. "We got a couple of car batteries in the trunk for the weight. Then I take the razor and open you up so you don't float, understand?"

"Jesus! Don't . . ."

"It's a hell of a way to die," I said. "But you tell us quick, I'll do you a solid, okay? I'll put a slug in your head first, so you don't feel nothing."

His stink filled the front seat.

"There's only one way out," I said, breathing through my mouth.

"Anything," he blubbered. "Just tell me, I'll—"

"You got Hercules to do a job for you. The girl, the one this guy was threatening, she yours?"

"No. No, man. I don't know her. I ain't never even *seen* her."

"So somebody paid you, right?"

"Right. It was just—"

"Shut up, punk. Just answer what I ask you. Who paid you? And what was the job?"

"I don't know her name. Honest to God, Burke! She found me in Rollo's. Said it was her sister, that girl. The one this guy was—"

"Don't make me tell you again," I said. "I don't want to hear your stories. How much was the job?"

He hesitated. I nodded to Max. Porkpie spasmed in his seat, his spinal fluid turned to liquid pain. "I don't like this part," I told him. "I'd rather ice you right now than keep hurting you, understand?"

"Yesss . . ."

"How much was the job?"

"Five grand."

"And you were supposed to do . . . what?"

"Just scare the guy. Like, spook him, you know? Run him off."

"Not total him?"

"You crazy? I ain't no hit man."

"That's right, punk: *you* ain't."

"Burke, listen to me. Please. If I was gonna have Herk do him, would I go along? I didn't know nothing until he comes charging back to the car. I . . ."

"That's enough," I told him. The smell of truth came right through the stench. Porkpie didn't have the *cojones* to be anywhere within a mile of a killing, even as the wheelman. "Describe her."

"I *told* you—I never even seen her, not once."

"The woman who paid you, Porkpie. Her."

"Oh. She's some kinda Chink."

"Chinese?"

"I don't fucking know, man. Something like that. Small. She had a hat on, with one of them veil things, black, like they wear at funerals."

"What did she call herself?"

"She didn't say no name, man. Just asked me, could I get it done? I told her the price. She paid me. That's all. I never seen her again."

"But she gave you a phone number."

"No, I swear it! Nothing. I didn't need to talk to her—she paid me the whole thing up front."

"So how come you didn't stiff her? Just take the cash and walk?"

"She said she could find me again. I . . . believed her, like."

"You believe *I* can find you again, Porkpie?"

"Yeah. I know your rep."

"You know who's holding your neck? That's Max the Silent. You know *his* rep?" I asked him gently.

He shuddered a reply.

"I'm gonna trust you," I lied. "We're gonna let you slide on this. You take the car. Drive it anywhere you want and leave it there. But don't fuck around with it—it's hot. Understand?"

"Sure. I mean—"

"Ssssh," I said, holding my right finger to my lips. "You get popped dumping the car, that's your problem. I can find you in jail, Porkpie. You know I can. You'd be easy in there. This is your last chance. That woman calls you, you call me. And if you're holding anything back, you're landfill, understand?"

"I'm not! I—"

I nodded to Max. He released his grip, slid out of the back seat, quiet as Ebola. I opened the car door and backed out, still pointing the pistol at Porkpie.

Max and I faded back into the shadow of the pier. In a minute, we heard the Volvo start up. We watched Porkpie pull away fast, the rear wheels spinning on the slick pavement.

Clarence pulled up at the wheel of my Plymouth and we all went back across the border.

I worked the relay over the pay phones, got the word to Hercules: Stay put.

And hoped the Prof wasn't right about him.

D ays passed. I vacuumed the newspapers, listened to the radio, even watched some TV. Nothing about the homicide. There was no outcry, no pressure. It would probably disappear into the black hole the cops called Unsolved. It wouldn't be the first time— not all floaters go into the water.

There was a cop I could ask, a cop who owed me, but that would be the same thing as telling him I was connected in some way. Even if you trust a man not to play certain cards, there's no point in dealing them to him.

Time was on our side. But the statute of limitations wasn't. So I went to see a lawyer. Davidson's a hard-nosed criminal-defense guy, but he passed for honest in our world. He might jug you a little on the fee, but he wouldn't favor-trade with the DA, and he wouldn't sell a client for some favorable press ink, the way some of the others do.

H is office is in midtown, just one good-sized room with a secretary's station outside. At one time, he had a big joint with a bunch of associates, but he went lean-and-mean a few years ago.

His office is furnished in early Salvation Army—all the money's in technology. And in the heavy cork paneling. In Davidson's business, traveling sound can get you killed.

"Feels like a decent justification defense to me," he said, puffing appreciatively on one of the mondo-expensive Expatriados cigars I'd brought him. "Where'd you get these?" he asked.

"An old pal of mine makes them down in Honduras. Cuban seeds, Cuban artisans, but he says Cuban soil is all played out. These are better."

"Sure are," Davidson said, holding the dark cylinder at arm's length to admire the shape. Then he got back to work. "One guy pulls a gun, the other one pulls a knife. One gets a jury trial, the other gets an autopsy. Self-defense. It happened in a bar, we walk. But your guy, his story's shaky. He was just strolling through the alley at that hour, minding his own business . . . ? I don't *think* so."

"And we don't know if the other guy's pistol was still there when the EMS crew arrived," I told him.

"Yeah," he agreed, nodding his head. "We'd get that on discovery, but if it comes up blank . . ."

"Anyone could have picked up the piece and walked off with it," I told him. Thinking of the dead man's wallet and watch.

"Forensics?" Davidson asked. Meaning: fingerprints, blood splatters . . . anything the police-lab vultures could vacuum from a corpse.

I flashed on what the Prof had said about that same question: "Blood don't tell no more, Schoolboy. We ain't gotta worry about that. A good shyster can always O.J. the DNA." I scratched my temple, like I was thinking about it. "Nothing," I told him.

"It's still dicey," Davidson said.

"So you advise—what?" I asked.

"Your guy got a sheet?"

"Long one."

"For this kind of thing?"

"Oh yeah."

"He a predicate?"

"Twice over."

"So he couldn't take even a Man Two," Davidson mused. "No way to bring him in and make a deal."

I didn't say anything. Manslaughter Second Degree is a Class C Felony in New York. Even if Davidson could sweet-plea his way past the life sentence a Habitual Offender tag would bring, Herk was looking at seven and a half to fifteen.

"You got any more cards?" Davidson asked.

"A witness," I told him. "He's not a hitter, but he's no citizen either."

"Would he roll?"

Would Porkpie turn informant? It wasn't even a question. The Prof had dismissed any other possibility with a contemptuous snort: "That punk ain't no real thief, chief. You know the way he play—don't do the crime if you can't drop a dime." He was right: give Porkpie a pass on one of his own cases, he'd sell his mother.

Then again, so would I.

But I'd never sell my family.

"Sure," I replied.

"Well," Davidson said, switching to self-protective legalese, "given the facts of the hypothetical with which you've presented me, I would advise absolute discretion."

Meaning: Herk couldn't come in.

Only two ways to tap Porkpie's home phone—take a major risk or use up a major favor. And even if he *had* a phone in that pesthole he lived in, he probably wouldn't use it for business. He was a weasel, but not a stupid one. "Got to send Clarence in," I told the Prof.

"No way, Schoolboy. I told you true—my boy don't work for Herk."

"Look, Prof. The only place we know we can possibly get to this girl Porkpie told us about is at Rollo's, right? If Porkpie's there, he spots me in a second. You too. Max can't negotiate. Who's that leave us?"

"I don't feature no undercover crap," the little man said, giving ground grudgingly.

"Clarence goes in, he hangs around, okay?" I said, pleading my case. "He spots Porkpie talking to the girl . . . spots *any* girl who matches the description . . . he steps back, makes a call. The rest is ours."

"The whole motherfucking thing should be ours."

"What's the problem?" I pressed him.

"Bad juju, youngblood. We ain't fucking *detectives*," he said, jeering the last word. "We don't solve crimes—we do 'em. Maybe Herk should just relocate his dumb ass to some fresh green grass."

"What good's that gonna do? He tries to make a connect on strange turf, he's just gonna end up back in jail."

"But no fear if he stays here?" the little man challenged.

"Okay," I said, throwing up my hands in surrender. "Fuck him. Let him fall."

The Prof looked at me a long quiet minute. Then he said: "Guess I taught you even better than I thought, son. Two weeks, all right? We put it together by then, good. If not, Herk's gotta walk his own way."

I bowed my head in agreement.

"Rollo's is an old-time thief's bar," I told Clarence. We were sitting in my booth at Mama's a little before midnight, drawing the diagrams. "I been in there a few times over the years. Little round tables in the middle, booths against the wall. Lousy food, watered booze. The tables are for bragging and bullshitting, the booths are for deals. You got something you want to buy or sell, you take a booth. Waitress comes over, you order food, she's gonna tell you the booth's reserved. You get stupid, say you wanna eat there anyway, guy they call T.B. comes over. I don't think that's his initials—man's bad enough to be named after a disease, you don't mess with him. Tall, slim build. Nice looking kid, long knife-scar across his face below the left eye. He's a kenpo man, snap you like a twig without breaking a sweat. So no Bogarting in there, got it?"

"Yes, mahn. It is clear."

"But if you ask the waitress, 'Where's Mimi tonight?' she'll just walk away, no problem. Then you'll get Mimi. A real pretty Latina. Watch her hands: long nails with black polish, gold wedding ring. You tell her what you want, just work around the edges, you don't have to come right out with it. No drugs, but anything else is all right. She says okay, you give her a hundred. That's the rental."

"I tell her firearms, mahn. I am known for this a bit. From when I was with Jacques."

That's when I first met Clarence, a long time ago. When he was a young tiger working for a Jake gun-runner in Brooklyn. He hadn't come up with the rest of us, but he'd been forged just as hard in another fire.

"That'll do," I assured him. "I got a crate of AK's I been holding back to sting one of those dumb-fuck gangbangers, so we could show the goods if anybody wanted a checkout. Now what you gotta do is dance, brother. Make sure you string it out, stay as long as you can, set it up so you come back a couple of times, right?"

"I have it," the young man said. He was wearing a black jacket—looked like a regular suit coat, but it came down almost to his knees—over a pale-violet silk shirt buttoned at the neck. Clarence doesn't really peacock it up until the warm weather hits, clothes blooming with the foliage.

"You know who to look for?"

"Porkpie, you already described him, mahn. And a Chinese girl with one of those pillbox hats, like. And a veil."

"She may not be Chinese, not Chinese like Mama, anyway. Oriental, though, if Porkpie was right. And we don't know if that outfit is a trademark or she just wanted to hide her face. Porkpie's the key. No way he stays away from Rollo's for long. You got any questions?"

"Who will watch my ride, mahn? I do not like to leave her alone in some nasty parking lot, you know?"

"We'll cover her," I promised. Clarence's beloved British Racing Green 1967 Rover 2000 TC was his prize. He took it for granted that we'd have his back at Rollo's, but his car was a separate commitment. "We can't go inside, but the parking lot's no problem."

I lit a cigarette and smoked in silence, thinking it through. Rollo's wasn't a dangerous place. They had to keep it under control to do their business. But still . . .

"Want the Mole to go along?" I asked Clarence. "Porkpie's never seen him, and he could—"

"Oh, that's quick, Slick," the Prof snarled. "What's that maniac gonna do if something jumps off, blow the place up?"

"Mole's smart," I defended him.

"Smart? Man's a motherfucking genius!" the Prof shot back. "Did I say no? But he ain't smart like *people*, you understand? I don't want none of his science shit around my boy, see? We be right outside, laying in the cut. One tap on the cellular and we Rambo the joint, we have to, okay? Ain't no need to go nuclear."

"I was just—"

"Nix that," the Prof cut me off, any concern for Clarence's safety quickly overridden by even the slightest implication that the kid wasn't competent to handle the job. "Clarence walks point, we cover the joint. Our dice, loaded nice—it's all on ice."

But our dice didn't make one good pass all night. A five-hour investment drew nothing but blanks. "I didn't see no Chinese woman, mahn," Clarence said during debriefing. "And never this Porkpie guy either."

"It worked like I said? With the booth?"

"Yeah, mahn. *Just* like that. Only two nibbles on the pieces, though."

"Sound legit?" I asked him, leaning close. In our world, when we're dealing guns, "legit" means criminal. And "crooked" means the goddamned ATF.

"I think so," Clarence said. "Hard to tell with those boys. We just . . . talked around it, like. He want to know what I got. I want to know what he want. You know. . . ."

"Yeah. You said two, right?"

"Oh, the second guy, mahn, he was nothing. A kid. One of those European guys from the Bronx, maybe. I could not tell for sure. He wanted a pistol. Just one pistol. It felt like personal, not professional. I blew him off."

A European guy from the Bronx was Clarence-speak for Armenian. There's supposed to be a whole tribe of them up there, gunfighters, every one. "He cop an attitude?" I asked.

"Nah, mahn. Nothing like that. I told him bulk only, and he didn't push. He had his boys with him, over to the side. I think he was just profiling, maybe. Young stupid boy. Probably throw the piece away when the clip get empty."

If that was so, the kid sure wasn't Armenian, I thought. "You up for another round?" I asked Clarence.

"I go the distance, mahn."

The next night was the same. "Place is nasty, brother," Clarence said afterwards, a disgusted look on his face. "I keep this up, I have a big dry-cleaning bill for sure." He grimaced, examining the sleeve of his plum-colored worsted sport coat as though it contained the answer to some important question.

"The buyer come back?" I asked.

"I didn't see him, mahn. But I told him next week, right? He was gonna speak to some people, you know how that go."

"Yeah."

I gave it some thought, turned to the Prof. "You think we need a different player? Porkpie, he'd take a booth and just open up shop. He's a middleman. Whatever you want, he could find it for you. Maybe that's the kind of guy we need. Clarence set himself up as an arms dealer. This Chinese woman, she's only looking for muscle, maybe?"

"Or maybe she already found it," the little man replied. "And she's not coming back, Jack."

I wasn't ready to let go of it. "One more time," I said. Clarence nodded.

From our vantage point deep in the parking lot, we watched from the front seat of the Plymouth as cars came and went all night long. No way to tell who was inside. Sometimes the cars parked, sometimes they just dropped someone off. The weather was too cold and ugly to make a solid ID, everyone wearing coats, all bundled up. A lot of them had hats too. With the lousy light and the slanted sight-lines, I couldn't tell Chinese from Swedish. But I'd know Porkpie—and he didn't show.

The Prof and I talked each new sighting over anyway, just to keep the time moving. It was bone-deep cold in the car. Still, we didn't want to run the heater. Nobody was cruising the lot peering into car windows, but a plume of smoke from the exhaust would mark us even from a distance.

The cell phone in my pocket buzzed once. Twice. I didn't touch it. In about ten seconds, it did the same thing again.

"He's got her," I said to the Prof. It was one buzz for Porkpie, two for the Chinese woman, three for both. "Check to be sure."

The Prof pulled his own cell phone, punched in a speed-dial number, let it ring a few times, then cut the connection. I lit a cigarette, waiting. The Prof's phone buzzed, then went dead. Same again. One more time.

Max was on Porkpie. We'd had the little ferret on full-shadow ever since we started this piece. Max can't hear, but the Mole had fixed him up with a vibrating pager set to go off if we dialed a certain number. The instant callback meant he had Porkpie in his sights. And a single ring meant the weasel was nowhere near Rollo's.

Like they say in the S&M clubs . . . time to role-play.

I opened the door to Rollo's and walked in. Caught Clarence's eye. He climbed out of his booth and went toward the bathroom in the back. The only way out is through the kitchen, and that isn't open to customers. He'd stay back there for a few minutes, checking for traps while I set mine.

I was wearing an old leather jacket over a heavy black sweatshirt, jeans and steel-toed work boots. They kept the joint hot enough to make a nun work topless, steam hissing from the industrial radiators lining the windowless walls. I took off my jacket, sat there a few minutes, getting my eyes adjusted to the haze from the low-lying smog. Clarence walked past me to my left, heading for the door. I got up and took an empty booth, jacket over one shoulder.

The place looked like a Southern juke joint, only bigger and without the music. Ramshackle, thrown-together furniture, a big red-and-white Coke sign behind the wood plank bar, yellowing posters on the walls—looked like they'd been swiped from a Medicaid dentist's office. The low ceiling trapped a heavy, multi-tone hum of voices, keeping the heat close to the floor. Somebody had nailed a THANK YOU FOR NOT SMOKING sign to the side wall. The floor was a giant ashtray.

I eye-swept the big room, watching the criminal food chain draped over the landscape, everything from bottom-feeders to land sharks. I scanned quickly, looking for familiar faces. Nothing.

At one of the tables a teenager with an Arabic face watched intently as an older man from a similar tribe demonstrated some three-card-monte moves, doing it slow enough so the kid could follow, talking a blue streak in a low voice. Teacher and student.

Right across from them, a skinny blonde woman was getting histrionic with three heavy-bodied, stoic-faced men with identical slicked-back black hair. They looked enough alike to be brothers—Greeks, I thought. All watching quietly as the skinny blonde waved her hands around, contorting her face to make a point.

An old man with a thick shock of graying hair sat alone at a table, a heavy gold watch on each of his broad wrists. People stopped by his table, bent over and said something in his ear. Nobody sat down. Odessa Beach godfather, maybe.

In one corner sat a smooth-bodied man with plain round glasses, dark hair cut right to the scalp. He was big, six six at least, had to weigh in over two fifty. He had a bemused expression on his face, a drawing tablet open before him, right hand sculpting.

One of the Greeks spotted what he was doing, started to stand up. The big guy didn't move, didn't take his eyes off the drawing tablet. An island of quiet popped up out of the ocean of noise. The old Russian got up, walked over to the big guy's table, put his hand on the big guy's shoulder as he looked closely at the drawing. A giant diamond on his hand sparkled—the real thing. The old Russian nodded approval, went back to his table. One of the Greek's brothers whispered something to him—I didn't need a translator: "Sit still!" The ocean swallowed the island again. Maybe the Greeks were really Russians. Or just guys who knew the score. Whoever the big guy with the drawing tablet was, he was nobody to fuck with.

The waitress strolled over, a stone-faced woman in her forties. "What'll it be?" Her voice made her face look inviting.

"Mimi around?" I asked.

"I'll check," she said, and walked off.

I cracked a wooden match into flame, but I didn't even have it to the tip of my cigarette when she materialized at the booth.

"You looking for me?" Mimi asked, a friendly smile on her classic Aztec face. Her skin had a lovely pale-bronze glow. Highlights glinted in her long raven hair. But her eyes were as flat as a cadaver's heart monitor.

"Actually," I said, "I was looking for some work."

"What kind of work do you do?"

"Body work," I told her, softly.

Her obsidian eyes ran over my torso appraisingly. "You work with your hands?" she asked, showing me hers. Her fingernails were long black-lacquered talons.

"I do heavy work," I said, meeting her gaze.

I didn't know where Mimi had been raised, but she recognized the jailhouse stare quick enough. "We don't vouch for anyone here," she said. There wasn't a trace of accent in her voice. Just a warning.

"I got it," I told her. Handed her a hundred-dollar bill. It disappeared—she had fast hands.

"You want something while you're waiting?"

"Rye and ginger. Don't mix them, okay?"

The waitress brought me the shot glass of what they said was rye and a taller glass with a small bottle of off-brand ginger ale. "Seven-fifty," was all she said. I gave her a ten. She took it and walked away again. Rollo's ran like city buses: Exact Change, No Refunds.

Moved just about as fast too. I sat there by myself for a good while. Poured ginger ale into the tall glass and drank most of it off. Then I dumped in the shot and let it sit there melting into the ice cubes until the glass was a quarter full. The waitress came over, asked me if I wanted another one. I told her "Sure," nodding at the tall glass. She took it away, brought me the same setup, pocketed another ten.

I couldn't spot the Chinese woman, but the cell phone in my pocket hadn't gone off, so she hadn't left. If she was the right one, we had her boxed.

An argument broke out at one of the little round tables. Man and a woman. He grabbed her hair and slapped her a couple of times. Back and forth. Slow. Showing her how things were between them. I couldn't hear what he was saying to her, but he was talking all the time he was slapping her. The bouncer—the one they call T.B.—glided over, hands empty at his sides. He spread his arms wide, saying something peaceful. The guy dropped the woman's hair and jumped to his feet. T.B. stepped back. Encouraged, the guy came out with a knife, flicking it open with his thumb as he went into a crouch. A grin split T.B.'s face, twisting the scar under his left eye. I didn't see his foot move, but the guy's knee went out. T.B. hit him once, just under the heart, as he was falling. The guy stayed where he was. The girl was on her feet then, but Mimi was behind her, hands on the girl's wrists, locking her in. The girl said something I couldn't make out.

"As if!" Mimi laughed, letting the girl go, giving her the shot if she wanted to take it.

The girl kept her hands down. Eyes too.

T.B. put his finger to his lips. The girl helped the guy up. They went out together—she was walking, he was leaning on her. T.B. went back someplace into the shadows. Mimi pulled a rag out of her waistband and started swabbing up the table.

Then the Chinese woman sat down in my booth.

Only she wasn't Chinese. Her face was too square, especially around the jawline. And her complexion was a dusky rose, with a gold underbase. Her eyes were a pale-almond color, and they lacked the Oriental fold at the corners. Her hair was a red so dark that the color kept shifting in the reflected light, with a distinct curl as it fell to her shoulders. Her mouth was wide and full, slightly turned down at the corners. A faint spray of freckles broke across her wide flat nose. Along the L-line on her right jaw was a dark undulating streak, as though an artist had inked it in for emphasis.

"Trying to guess?" she asked me. Her voice was husky, cigarette-burnished. Musical, but not Top Forty.

"Yeah, I was," I admitted.

"I'm half Inuit, half Irish."

"Whatever the mix, it worked great."

"Thank you," she said, flashing a smile. Her teeth were so white, tiny and square they looked fake, like a mouthful of miniature Chiclets.

"You, uh, want something done?" I said.

"What are you?" she asked suddenly.

"Me? I'm just a guy who—"

"No. I mean, what *are* you. I told you what I was."

"Oh. Truth is, I don't know."

"You were adopted?"

"Abandoned," I told her, watching her face.

Her almond eyes darkened. "But somebody had to raise you. Didn't they . . . ?"

"The State raised me," I told her. Telling it all, if she knew anything.

"What's your name?"

"Burke," I told her. If she was a cop, she already knew. And even if she wasn't, those almond eyes had photographed me good enough to guide a police sketch artist's hand right to my mug shot anyway.

"Mine's Crystal Beth."

"Your parents were bikers?" I laughed.

"No," she said, smiling. "Hippies. At least my father was. He met my mother up north, and they came back to Oregon together. Where I was raised."

Rollo's wasn't a singles bar. And I didn't even know for sure if she was the same woman who'd hired Porkpie. I was there on business. But I felt the current pulling me and I went with it.

"In a commune?" I asked her.

"Yes. It was a lovely place, but it's all gone now. All the old ways, gone." She might have been a Plains Indian talking about another century for all the sadness in her voice.

"You want something to drink?" I asked her. Once someone in a booth attracted a visitor, the waitress would stay away unless you signaled her over.

"You drink the stuff they serve here?" she asked. A slight smile played around her lips, but the corners of her mouth stayed turned down. Genetics, then, not an expression.

"I got a strong stomach," I assured her.

"Umm. Then maybe you'd like a job . . . ?"

"I might. What have you got in mind?"

"My . . ." She hesitated just a heartbeat, but I caught it. ". . . cousin's having trouble. With her boyfriend. Her *ex*-boyfriend. Only *he* doesn't think so. Do you . . . ?"

"Sure. Some guys don't get the message the first time."

"And sometimes it depends on the messenger."

"Yeah. You need a messenger?"

"That's exactly what I need."

"Uh-huh. You know this guy?"

"I don't *know* him, I know *about* him, okay?"

"Just what you've been told?"

"No. I mean, I met him. Once. But . . ."

". . . you have all the information about him?"

"Yes."

"And you just want the problem solved, right? Not the details?"

"Yes. I thought it best to leave that to . . . professionals."

"Professionals get paid," I reminded her.

"I grok that. I don't ask strangers for favors. And I'm guessing you don't work on a sliding scale either."

"Right. I don't. But I'm sure I can fix whatever your . . . cousin's problem is."

"Yes? And how much would it cost to do that?"

"Depends on how . . . permanently you want the problem solved."

"You mean . . . what?"

"I mean, for some people, it's personal, you know? They get it into their heads that a certain person belongs to them, and they won't let go unless . . . Other people, they're just bullies."

"Bullies are easier?" she asked, leaning closer to me across the table.

"Bullies are very easy," I said, holding her eyes. Or maybe hers were holding mine.

"The bigger they are . . ."

". . . the more they cost to fix," I finished for her.

She looked at the pack of cigarettes I'd left on the tabletop, raised her eyebrows in a question. I lifted it up, held it out to her. She took one. I fired a wooden match. She didn't bring her face down to the flame like I'd expected. Just sat there watching my hand from under her long dark lashes. The flame burned, slow and steady in the musty joint's dead air. I stayed on her eyes, feeling the increasing heat against my fingers. She leaned forward and blew out the flame, her breath so gentle it barely got the job done.

"Your hand is very steady," she said.

"A jeweler needs good eyesight." I shrugged. "You changed your mind about the cigarette?"

"Sometimes, if I really want something, I make myself wait. Then it's sweeter when I finally have it. You understand?"

"I understand the waiting part."

"You're good at waiting?"

"I'm the best," I told her. "It's my specialty."

"You're not like . . . the others." It was a flat statement. Her judgment, not a question.

"The others?"

"I've talked to a . . . number of people. About my cousin. You're different from them."

"You try any of them?" I asked.

"Try?"

"On your cousin's problem?"

"No. Not yet. It's a delicate thing. My cousin wants it to be over, that's true. But she wants magic, you know? Wants it all to . . . disappear. And that's hard."

"That's real hard. Real expensive too."

"How expensive?"

"Depends."

She glanced at her wristwatch: big black-and-white dial on a thick black rubber band. "This is taking longer than I thought," she said. "I have to meet somebody. But I want to . . . talk to you again. Is there a way . . . ?"

"Sure," I told her. "I could give you a number to call."

"That would be great," she said, flashing another quick smile.

I gave her a number in Brooklyn. It's on permanent bounce— the only place it would ring aloud would be one of the pay phones at Mama's. The woman didn't write it down, repeating it a couple of times just under her breath. The dark streak at her jawline moved along with her lips. She nodded, like she was agreeing with herself, and started to get up. I didn't move. She sat down again, put her hands flat on the table. "Can I do something with you? Just an old hippie thing. It would make me feel better . . . even if you laugh."

"What?"

"Can I read your palm?"

I put my hands on the table between us, palms up. "I don't know. Can you?"

"Watch," she said softly, taking my right hand in both of hers, bending her face forward to study.

I let my hand go limp as she turned it in hers. A couple of minutes passed. "Can you strike a match with one hand?" she asked, holding on to my right hand, making the message clear.

I took out a wooden match with my left hand, snapped it along my jaw. It flared right up. When I was a kid, that used to impress girls. That was a long time ago—on both counts. "Hold it close," she said.

I held the match just over my open palm, lighting her way. It only took her another couple of seconds after that. She blew the match out for me, closed my palm into a fist, squeezed it quick and then let go. "Thank you," she said. "I'll call you."

I gave her a good thirty-minute start, just in case she was hanging around outside, planning on the same thing I was. When I finally walked through the exit, the sky was clear and the air was sharp. But the ground was wet, like there'd been a light rainfall during the past couple of hours.

Clarence's Rover was missing. So was the Prof. I cranked the Plymouth over and pulled out of the pitch-black parking lot, heading for Mama's. On the drive over, I used the vibrating pager to call Max back in.

The Chinatown alleys are never really deserted, but they get quiet in the late-late hours. I docked the Plymouth under the white rectangle with Max's chop painted inside and slapped my hand against the slab-faced steel door at the back of the restaurant; one of Mama's so-called waiters let me in. After he scanned my face close. And put the pistol back inside his white coat.

It was almost three in the morning, but Mama was at the register in the front like she was expecting customers any minute. A tureen of hot-and-sour soup was at my elbow even before she made her way to my booth in the back. I surprised her by standing up and reaching for the tureen to serve her a bowl, but she waved me back down, an impatient look on her face. Then she ladled out a small bowl for me, the way she'd done it for years. To Mama, progress is a crack in the wall of civilization.

I sipped the soup, making the required sounds of deep appreciation. Mama nodded acceptance, played with her soup while I finished the first small bowl, and then filled it up again. Once, I'd asked her why I had to have at least three bowls at every sitting. "Bowl small," is all she said, and I haven't questioned her since.

"Max around?" I finally asked her.

"Basement," she said. "You find girl?"

So Max had brought her up to date. No surprise. Even the Chinaboy gangsters, with their merciless eyes and ready guns, who dot the viper-twisted back streets around the restaurant like clots in the community's bloodstream, step aside when Max walks . . . but he obeys Mama like a dutiful son.

Nobody knows why. Nobody ever asks.

"I think so, Mama," I said. "I can't be sure."

"Girl Chinese?"

"No. But she'd look Chinese if you didn't know, maybe."

Mama grunted, letting it pass. Years ago, she would have called a woman like Crystal Beth a bar girl, her shorthand for half-breed. But Immaculata had cured that. Immaculata was Max's woman, part Vietnamese, part American soldier—whatever. And when their baby, Flower, was born, Mama proclaimed the newborn both her grandchild and pure hundred-generation Mandarin Chinese in the same breath.

Nobody argued with her.

I was halfway through a dish of braised beef tips on a bed of fluffy brown rice with scallions and shiitake mushrooms when Max came upstairs. He sat quietly with Mama until I was finished, then I hand-signaled what had happened with the woman between sips of ice water as the silent warrior watched.

His turn: He took me through Porkpie's night—mimed putting quarters in pay-phone slots, cupped one hand over the side of his mouth to show whispered conversations. Grubbing, hustling—no scores. Porkpie had never gone anywhere near Rollo's. Finally, Max put his hands together against one cheek, tilted his head and closed his eyes. Porkpie was back inside his crib, presumably asleep, dreaming of nickel-and-dime hustles.

"Mama," I asked her, "you know anything about palm reading?" I put a finger to my own palm, tracing the lines so Max would understand what I was saying.

"Gypsy? That just—"

"No. For real. You ever hear of—?"

"Sure. Chinese invent first. Very good."

Naturally. Far as Mama was concerned, Galileo was Chinese. Noah too. Only he took some of the wrong animals on that ark.

"You really think some people can foretell the future?"

"Not future. Past. Which palm look at?"

"Uh, my right hand."

"Yes! Work hand, right? Hand show what you do. What you *do*, what you *are*, see?"

"No."

"Some men farmers, some make shoes, right? Work with hands, leave marks. Like tracks."

"It only works on men?" I asked her, smiling to show her I was joking.

Big mistake. "Women do *all* work. Work in factory, come home, clean house, take care of baby, plant garden. Man do only one thing. Woman hand tell nothing."

"Where do you look, then, Mama?"

"Look in eyes," she said, looking deep into mine.

"The eyes tell lies," the Prof said, right behind my shoulder. I hadn't heard him come in. "What you do, that's what's true," he finished, echoing Mama's wisdom of a few minutes ago.

I moved over to make room for him and Clarence. "How'd you make out?" I asked him.

"We lost her, bro. Bitch vanished like cash in a whorehouse."

I raised an eyebrow, not saying anything. There had to be more—losing the Prof in city streets would be harder than confusing a London cabdriver.

"She comes out the joint," Clarence explained. "Pulls this parka-thing over her head so she is all in black. Then she walks around the back, right past where we are waiting. We do not see her after that, but there is no other way out of the parking lot, so we are patient. All of a sudden, mahn, we hear this *roar*, and she comes flying past us. On a *motorcycle*, mahn. A black one. Small. Japanese, I think, but she was moving too quick. By the time I get the Rover into gear, she is *gone*. I hear the bike, and I follow the sound. Catch a glimpse of her going around a corner. No taillight, couldn't see a license. And that was it. We box it around, trying to pick her up at an intersection, but it is no good. That woman is a fine rider, mahn. Hard to make time on those slick streets."

Nothing to do now but wait for a call.

I t came the next day. The cell phone I was using that week chirped on the table I use as a desk, startling Pansy into some semblance of activity. The massive Neapolitan raised her huge head and glared in the direction of the noise. She's gotten more conservative as she ages—anything new is viewed with baleful suspicion. Anything old she's already intimidated.

"What?" I said into the mouthpiece. The Mole had some sort of portable encryption chip he planted in all the cell phones we used, switching it every time we recloned to new numbers. Anyone listening who didn't have the right chip would only pick up gibberish, but old habits hadn't died, and I always used the damn things as if everything was being recorded.

"Girl call. I tell her you outside, be back in half an hour, okay?"

"Good. I'm rolling."

"Hey!"

"What?" Mama had my same habits, wouldn't use my name on a cell phone. Fact is, I was surprised she wanted to stay on the line for anything at all.

"Girl not Chinese."

"Uh . . . right."

I walked down the back stairs to the garage I'd built into a narrow slot on the first floor of the old factory building I lived in. The landlord had converted it to lofts years ago, but the trust-fund twits who lived there never knew about the extra unit on the top floor. They think it's crawl space. And even if they got curious about anything more than the bulk price of Hawaiian hemp, the triple-braced steel door would be more than enough to discourage them.

And past that, there was Pansy.

The landlord's not my pal. We have a business relationship. I

don't pay rent. And I don't talk either, so his firstborn is safe in the
Witness Protection Program. The kid was a rat's rat, informing for
the fun of it. When I ran across the new identity the *federales* had
rewarded him with, I'd found the key to my apartment. It's still
good after all these years. The Mole has me wired into the electricity downstairs, so I don't show up on any Con Ed meter. I cook on
a hot plate, and I heat the place with a couple of pipes tapped into
an old cast-iron radiator. It's not real well insulated, and the windows don't seal so good, but I have a pair of electric space heaters
that take the chill off when it gets too icy-ugly outside.

It's only two rooms, but a pre-Shah Persian rug that covers one
wall makes it seem like there's another room behind it. That was
for when I used the place as an office. I haven't done that for years.
The Mole rigged me a stand-up shower and a sink with a mirror
over it. Stainless steel, just like the State gave me on my last bit. I
have an extension phone on the ones they use in the loft below me,
but I only use it for emergencies. Fact is, I haven't used it at all since
we found a way to code-grab cellular numbers off the airwaves. We
change the cloned number every week or so, but one thing stays
the same—when I make a call, someone else gets the bill.

I fired up the Plymouth, used the periscope to check the empty
street and carefully inched my way out. By the time the pay phone
at Mama's rang for me, I'd been sitting in my booth for ten minutes.

"**G**ardens," Mama answered, using a heavy Mandarin accent.
She's got a lot of them. Mama cocked her head, signaling to me
she was listening, then said, "Oh sure. Right here. Just come back. I
get him, okay?" into the phone, and handed it to me.

"Yeah?"

"Burke? Is that you?"

"Sure."

"It's Crystal Beth. From—"

"I remember," I said, neutral-voiced.

"Can we meet someplace?"

"Sure."

"You don't talk much on the phone," she said, a teasing undertone to her husky voice.

"Neither should you," I told her.

"Why? I'm not ... Oh, never mind. Do you know a good place?"

I thought it over fast. She didn't want to show me her cards. I could understand that. I balanced the safety of meeting her at Mama's with letting her see where I worked. But too many people around me had died over the years, and some of my secrets along with them. The local cops knew about Mama's; so did the feds. A low-tier nothing like Porkpie wouldn't know, but even he could find out if he put some money out on the street. "Yeah, I know a place," I said. "How about if I buy you dinner? Tonight?"

"I'd like that."

"It's a deal," I said. And gave her Mama's address.

"**Y**ou sure *you* killed him?" I asked Herk. I didn't bother to watch his eyes—the big dope couldn't lie any better than he could steal.

"I got under the ribs, Burke. The light went out. Soon as I stuck him. You could see it."

We were sitting in the front seat of my Plymouth, just inside the fence of a junkyard in South Ozone Park. I know the owner. We could sit there for hours without a problem. Except for the cold. I was trying to put it together. The way I figured it, it wasn't ever meant to be a warning, it was a setup hit. Somebody knew how the mark was going to react when he was braced, especially by a guy Herk's size. Somebody knew the mark would go for his gun.

Herk hadn't known that. Maybe the woman hadn't either. Maybe Porkpie . . .

"And then you ran for the car?" I asked.

"Right. Porkpie had the engine running and we just—"

"And there was *nobody* else around, Herk? You're sure?"

"Oh man, yes! I checked the alley on foot first, before the punk even came out. Burke, when am I gonna raise on outa here? All you can do is watch that little TV in my room all day. Like being in the hole. No guys to hang out with, no weight room, no nothing."

"You want some stuff to read?"

"Yeah! Can you get me some comics?"

"What kind? Like *Batman* and stuff?"

"No, man. Batman's a slug. That stuff ain't no fun. Get me something like this," he said, pulling a rolled-up comic book out of his coat."

"*Hardboiled?*" I asked, looking at a comic cover as intricate as an ancient tapestry.

"Yeah! This guy rules! I love his stuff."

"Which guy?"

"The *artist*, man. Look!"

I saw the name in tiny letters. Geof Darrow. "This is him?"

"Look at the *pictures*, Burke. He's got the magic, bro."

I lit a smoke and thumbed through the book. Thinking Herk was right. I never saw drawings like that. They vibrated like liquid poetry—the deeper you looked, the more there was to see.

"You're right, brother," I told him. "Okay, anything else?"

"Yeah. Anything by Alan Grant, okay?"

"Alan Grant, he's an artist too?"

"No, man," Herk said scornfully. "Don't you know nothing? He's a writer. A *great* writer. Check out *Lobo*. And *Anderson: Psi-Judge*—that's like a British one, but they got it at any decent store."

"I will," I promised him. "Just stay put, all right? We're working on it."

"I wish *I* was working," the big man said.

"There'll be work soon enough," I told him.

"Not that work," he said, dismissing my whole life. "*Real* work. A job, like."

"A citizen job?"

"Yeah. That's right," the big man said, rolling his shoulders like he was expecting a fight. "A square job. With a paycheck."

"You wanna work on the docks? Kick back to the foreman every shape-up? Drive a cab and eat shit all day from the fares? What?"

"I heard all that," Herk said. "I been hearing it all my life, okay? What're you asking me? Do I wanna kiss ass? There's gotta be another way."

"I guess. But if you don't know what you wanna do . . ."

"I fucking *do* know," he said quietly. "You remember Dante? From Inside?"

"The old Italian guy? The one who—?"

"Yeah, the guy who had that big garden? Remember? He had all them plants—tomatoes and cucumbers and radishes and carrots and everything? He showed me how to do some . . . stuff. I really liked that, Burke. It was . . . I dunno. . . . I can't explain it."

"That's what you want to be, a gardener?"

"That's right," he said, chin out-thrust, an undertone of aggressiveness in his voice. "Dante said there's lotsa jobs like that. Gardening. Landscaping. That's real work. Not being no coolie or wetback, working for yourself. Inside, even, if you want. In greenhouses and stuff. There's money in it too, he said. If you know how to do it good. If you really care about it."

"So why can't you—?"

"Sure," he said, just this side of a snarl. "Where am I gonna find somebody to give me a chance? With my record and all? I know I ain't no genius. But old Dante wasn't no genius either. And he could make stuff grow like nobody else, right?"

"Right."

"Another chance," Herk said softly, all the aggression gone from his voice. "I guess that's what I really want. Another chance."

"That was Number One on the Jailhouse Hit Parade," I told him. "Everybody sung it."

"Yeah, I know," he said sorrowfully. "The punk was gone, Burke. Soon as I stuck him. I gotta do something soon. I'm telling you, this place's worse than the fucking joint."

"No, it isn't," I said quietly, reminding him.

Herk nodded, done arguing.

"I need to look at an autopsy report," I told the man on the phone.

"You need a copy?" the man said, the Ibo accent thick in his voice. "They are very strict about this ever since—"

"Not a copy. Just a look."

"I do not forget my debts. And a debt of my sister is a debt of mine, I know this. But this is a fine job I have now. And it is—"

"Okay," I told him, getting to what I wanted in the first place. "I'll settle for this. You pull it and read it to me. Over the phone, all right? Nothing more."

"I can do that," he promised. "Give me the name."

Four hours later, I rang him back. Soon as he heard my voice, he started talking, the influence of the British colonialists clear in his precise voice.

"Single puncture wound, left ventricle. That's all?" I asked him.

"Yes."

"That's the cause of death?"

"Yes."

"No other intrusions?"

"No. Nothing. All the other organs were normal. Lungs clear. Toxicology was negative too."

"Tell Comfort we're square," I said, and hung up.

She was right on time, crossing the threshold at eight on the dot. She stopped by Mama's register at the front. I couldn't hear what they were saying. Finally, she disengaged herself and walked back to my booth.

This time her dark reddish hair was in two thick braids on either side of her head, tied at their tips with plain strips of rawhide. She was wearing a long red wool coat with a shawl hood. When I stood to help her off with it, I noticed it was all black on the inside. Reversible. No amateur, this one—the motorcycle hadn't been some hippie's idea of fun in the snow. Under the coat she had a thick goldenrod-yellow turtleneck sweater over tailored black wool slacks and short, crumple-top leather boots the same color as the sweater.

"They don't have a menu here," I told her. "Just tell them what you want." Actually, they do have menus. But they're plastic-coated and fly-specked, as disgusting-looking as the so-called food they serve citizens dumb enough to wander in here. None of those ever come back.

"Couldn't you just order for us?"

"Sure," I said, looking around for a waiter. The place was empty. I figured one of Mama's thugs had already slipped around to the front and put the CLOSED sign up on the door. Then he'd arrange the dragon tapestries in the streaked window so that the red one was showing, telling the rest of the crew all they needed to know. The blue dragon meant cops, the red one meant danger. White was all-clear, but this didn't qualify. The risk was mine. Mama's too, but she was a volunteer. No point in giving Crystal Beth a free look at the rest of us.

Mama ambled over, snapping her fingers sharply as she moved. A waiter came out of the back with some ice water—the blue glasses were so clean they looked new.

"Can you recommend something?" I asked Mama, straight-faced.

"Recommend? You want food?"

"Yes. Food."

"Okay. Food coming," she said to me, barking something in waterfront Cantonese over her shoulder at the waiter.

We didn't get the hot-and-sour soup—that was only for family. But one of the waiters unfolded a fresh white linen tablecloth over the corroded Formica, then set the table with ultra-modern Danish stainless cutlery, gleaming like it just came out of the tissue paper.

Mama checked the setup, nodded approval. The waiter brought a wild assortment of dim sum, plus some spring rolls so light the crackle of the skin was a surprise. Next there was beef in oyster sauce with disks of bok choy, some kind of lemon chicken with snow-pea pods, and fried rice with hefty chunks of crabmeat. All beautifully presented on ice-blue dishes. Mama even found a deep-purple orchid and placed it in a translucent white vase shaped like a genie's bottle.

"It's wonderful!" Crystal Beth exclaimed after quickly nibbling at a half-dozen different dishes.

Mama bowed, just the ghost of a smile around her mouth.

"What's in these?" Crystal Beth asked her, holding up a half-eaten piece of spring roll.

"Big secret," Mama said gravely. "Everything here big secret."

"I'd keep it a secret too," Crystal Beth assured her.

Mama bowed again, and went back to her register. The lights in the restaurant dimmed. A waiter came out and put what looked like a blue hurricane candle on the table, close to the wall. He lit the candle with a long red paper match, studying the flame until he was satisfied.

Crystal Beth chewed her food slowly, eyes on my face all the while. She didn't say anything. The candle flickered to her left, so the dark line along her jawbone was hard to see clearly. I tried not to stare at it.

I guess that didn't work. "It's a tattoo," she finally said. "You want to see it up close?"

"Yes," I told her, surprised at my own honesty.

She turned her face all the way to her left. I moved the candle toward the center of the table and leaned over. The line came fairly straight down her jawbone, then formed a curlicue before it continued on around toward her square little chin. At the very tip it ended in what looked like a tiny crude arrowhead. I wanted to touch it, but I kept my hands flat on the tabletop.

"It looks . . . tribal," I said.

"It is. It means I have a purpose."

"But they did it when you were a girl, right?"

"Yes. How did you know?"

"I just . . . How could they know your purpose when you were a child?"

"They didn't. But . . . they knew I would have one."

"And that was true?"

"Oh yes. Very true."

I returned the candle to its place near the wall. Her hands were small, the nails cut short and straight across, clear polish gleaming in the flickering light. Her face was fresh, free of makeup, deep-black pupils in her almond eyes. If she was uncomfortable not talking while she ate, she didn't show it.

A waiter cleared the plates, slowly and ceremoniously. I didn't know any of Mama's people could do either one. Then he brought us each an egg cup of lemon sorbet and a small silver spoon.

"No fortune cookies?" she asked the waiter.

He gave her a blank look. That's one thing Mama's people were real good at.

"They don't speak English," I told her.

"I'm surprised this place isn't jammed," she said. "The food is unbelievable."

"It's . . . erratic," I told her. "Cooks come and go pretty quick. This is more like a . . . school. If they get really good, they move on to one of the upscale places. Some nights, you could eat here and go right to the Emergency Room."

That was the truth, but it had nothing to do with the food. Every once in a while some outsider checks out the hole-in-the-wall location and decides Mama's would be a good place for a robbery. I was there when it happened the last time. A kid came in the front door holding an Intratec Scorpion, the favorite of homicidal triggerboys throughout the city—the gun's a piece of garbage, but they love the look. The kid had mastered the urban-punk killing machine's pose—he had his wrist turned so he was sighting down the back of his hand, the side of the pistol parallel to the ground. Just like in the movies. A genius move with a semi-auto—it guarantees the spent cartridges are going to fly right up in your face. But the triggerboy never got the chance to find that out. His body went into a Chinatown Dumpster. I don't know what happened to it after that.

The waiter took the egg cups, put a large blue glass ashtray precisely between us. I took out my cigarettes, offered her one. "No thank you," she said politely. "I have my own."

She took a pack of rolling papers from her purse, tapped out some dark rough-cut tobacco from a green-and-white tin and expertly assembled the cigarette. She ran the trailing edge of the paper over the tip of her tongue and sealed the package, then rapped it against a thumbnail to tamp it down. I held a wooden match for her. She inhaled deeply, blowing the smoke out her broad flat nose.

"About my cousin," she said.

I waited a few beats. Saw she wasn't going to say anything more. Some kind of dance rules I didn't understand. I tried to pick up the slack.

"Yeah. . . ?" I prompted her.

"What do you know about them, Burke?"

I liked that she said "Burke," not "Mr. Burke" the way most people did. She never asked me whether it was my first or last name, just used what I gave her.

"Who's *them?*" I asked her.

"Stalkers."

I shrugged. "There's all kinds."

"That's what I thought too. Once. But I don't think so anymore. They're all the same. They get to make the choices. All the choices. That's the most important thing to them. It's all about power."

What do you know about power, little girl? I thought to myself. *What do you know about when the Beast gets loose? And loves the taste? Like in Rwanda. Or Bosnia. Or in some families.* "Yeah," I said aloud. "But—"

"Do you think an ex-boyfriend is so different from an obsessed fan of a movie star?"

"Sure. The ex-boyfriend, he's got a history. Or what he thinks is a history, anyway. He had it, once. The fan never had it."

"That's very rational," she said, her voice just this side of frosty. "But rational doesn't count. All that counts is pressure. The more obsessed they are, the more power they have. They can concentrate—focus their energy like no normal person ever could. They're like heat-seeking missiles, homing in on the signal. And if you're alive, you give off *some* signal. No matter how carefully you refuse to engage with them, no matter how much security you can buy. Strippers get them. So do college professors. Anyone who's ever written a book or appeared on a talk show is a potential target. It's like sexual harassment cranked up to the nth degree."

"Sexual?"

"Of course it's sexual. They call it a lot of things, but it all comes out the same. Stalkers are rapists. They try and take by force what they can't have by consent. That's all those anti-choice people are, every one."

"Anti-choice?"

"That's what they *really* are, those so-called pro-lifers. *They* get to make the choice; that's what they want, not to save some fetus. If a woman is raped and they force her to carry that vicious animal's child to term, what is that but more rape? Self-righteous rapists, that's them. All of them."

"But if they—"

"Maybe you think it's funny, a man like you," she said. Her nostrils were flared, almond eyes crackling with anger. A vein throbbed in her throat.

"Funny? Why would I—?"

"People *do*, don't they? There's whole sitcoms based on it now. And movies. Stalking as a hobby. Isn't that hilarious? Of course, that's *women* doing the stalking. When it's—"

"—your cousin . . ." I prompted, trying to bring her back.

"My cousin?" She caught a breath, eyes focusing like they'd just caught her own reflection in a mirror. "Oh. Yes. He's just . . . *hounding* her. He calls up and cancels her credit cards. Steals her mail. He bribed somebody at the phone company to get her unlisted number and he *calls* . . . hundreds of times a day, but he never speaks. You know what he told her? She's going to die. He's going to kill her, and then himself. So he won't even be punished. He couldn't stand going to jail, because then he wouldn't be in power anymore. He's going to do it."

"She go to the cops?"

"Sure," she laughed, a dry, brittle sound in the empty restaurant. "You think life is like the movies? Some cop's going to fall in love with her, devote all his off-duty time to watching her house?"

"So she wants . . . what?"

The woman who called herself Crystal Beth ground out her cigarette, not saying anything, eyes downcast.

It was a long minute before she looked up at me. "Help," she said.

I sat there by myself for a long time after she left. If she had the motorcycle again, there wasn't much point in trying to follow her. We didn't have the personnel for a three-car box. Clarence was good, but the Prof couldn't drive at all. Max piloted a car with all the finesse of a bull rhino. And compared to the Mole, he was a surgeon. But if we could score a license number . . .

Clarence was the first one back. He greeted Mama, then came back to where I was sitting. I waited patiently for him to have the first cup of soup—Mama was watching.

"The bike was parked two blocks over, mahn. I got the number." He handed me a piece of paper torn from a small spiral notebook.

"Good," I told him. "It'll probably dead-end, but it's worth a look. Any problems?"

"Could have *been* a problem, mahn. Maybe a big one. She had the bike chained up tight to a parking meter, so it took a long time to get it unhitched. Couple of young boys said something to her. She gave them something back. I think they were drunk. They came across the street like they were going to . . . I don't know, make trouble, maybe. Then they saw Max, standing over to the side. So they turned around and split."

"Did she see him?"

"No, mahn. Not a chance. I had her eyeballed the whole time."

"What color coat was she wearing?" I asked him.

"Black, mahn. All black. With a hood."

When Max came in, Mama sat down with us. She stared at Max's face for a long moment, then said to me: "That girl, she same as Max."

"Same as . . . ?"

"Not Chinese," Mama said.

Then I got it. Max wasn't Chinese either. He was a Mongol. From Tibet. I dimly remembered reading something about Eskimos when I was in prison. Weren't the Inuits originally a Mongol tribe? I couldn't pull it up on my screen. When I was locked down, I read everything I could get my hands on, telling myself you never knew what you could use on the streets. But that wasn't the real reason I spent so much time reading. I was trying to get *out*. Any way I could. And, sometimes, for a few hours, it worked. Now part of my mind is like some crazy trivia game—I know all kinds of things, but I can't always connect the dots.

"I think you're right," I told her. Naturally, Mama took that as an insult.

Nobody asked me what the woman had wanted until the Prof made the scene. Then I ran it down, simultaneously gesturing for Max. "It's all here," I said, tapping a sheaf of photocopy paper. "Got his name, address, phone numbers, photographs. Got everything on her too. The woman Crystal Beth says is her cousin."

"She wants the guy whacked?" the Prof asked, getting right to it.

"No. Not a chance. She wants it to stop, doesn't much care how it gets done. But I don't think she was looking for a hit man when she met Porkpie that time."

"Maybe so," the Prof said. "But no way the bitch has *two* relatives with this kinda problem."

"There's that," I acknowledged. "And she didn't blink when I told her it'd be twenty large to make it stop. Guaranteed."

"She had that much cash with her, mahn?" Clarence asked.

"I don't know. She didn't flash it. But she did have five. And she put it up."

Max pointed at me, made a face.

I shook my head no. Five up front hadn't been my idea. She'd negotiated it. Like she'd done it before. Which meant maybe she still owed Porkpie some money. And if the little weasel had lied about that . . .

"What you gonna do, Schoolboy?" the Prof asked.

I fanned the money out on the table. Circled my fingers around my eyes to make the sign for glasses, then gestured like I was pulling a satchel off the ground. I cut a thousand out of the pot and set it aside. Money for the Mole. The Prof took a thousand for himself. Then Clarence did the same. Then Max.

All in.

Mama watched silently. But she didn't protest when we each pulled two hundred off our shares and handed it over to her.

"First thing," I told them, "I go and talk to this cousin of hers."

The apartment building was on the West Side, just off Amsterdam, a few blocks south of Ninety-sixth. Soot-gray stone, six stories, faded gilt numbers just above the smudged glass doors. I stepped into the lobby and almost broke my neck sliding on the throw rug of leaflets scattered all over the tile floor. Take-out restaurants, sex-phone services, stereo repair. Armies of off-the-books humans sweep through the city every day, carpet-bombing neighborhoods with their load of useless paper like it was propaganda for invaders. It makes every citizen mad, but petitioning that coalition of pathological slugs they call the City Council would be like trying to get a hooker to take an IOU.

No doorman in this place. Probably one of those rent-controlled joints the landlord's trying to empty out. Uptown, they'd let the rats and roaches run wild, not repair the plumbing, have a super with a felony record who kept in practice on the tenants. They wouldn't have to get so intense in this neighborhood—probably most of the building had gone co-op during the boom a dozen years ago.

I hit the button for 4-C. Waited for a count of ten. No response. Maybe the buzzer didn't work. I tried it again, being careful to press the button with a short, respectful tap. Crystal Beth told me I'd be expected, but if the woman upstairs was listening, she'd *still* be scared. They all get that way after a while.

I saw a dim shape on the other side of the glass. Couldn't make out if it was a man or a woman. I moved closer to the glass, keep-

ing my shoulders slumped and face bland. I was wearing a char-
coal suit with a faint pinstripe over a white shirt and burnt-orange
tie, all visible under the camel's-hair overcoat I got for a song from
a busted-out gambler a couple of years ago. My shoes were plain
black lace-ups, polished but not gleaming. My hair was cut
medium-length and neatly combed. But I couldn't do anything
about my face.

The shape coalesced. A woman. Hard to tell her age. Dark hair,
pale face. Wearing some kind of white housecoat. I stepped closer.
So did she. But she didn't move her hands, just stood there. Only
the French doors between us—two wide panes of glass separated
by two narrow panels of wood. Even an amateur could kick
through it before she had a chance to run. I held out my hand so
she could see the white business card I was holding. She still
didn't move. I slipped it between the flimsy doors the same way
any fool could have used a credit card to loid the cheap snap-lock.
She reached out and took it, stepped back to peer at it closely. I
mimed for her to turn it over. On the back was a note from Crystal
Beth in her own handwriting.

The woman took a deep breath, then reached forward and
opened the doors, eyes darting as though she wanted to see
around me, make sure I was alone. I stood to the side, letting her
have a better view.

"You're . . ."

"From Crystal Beth," I finished for her.

She turned her back on me and started for the stairs. I stayed
behind, not close enough to spook her. As she climbed, I could see
the housecoat was really a lab gown of some kind. White low-cut
shoes on her feet. A nurse, maybe?

The stairs were dirty, but not outstandingly so for New York.
No discarded condoms, no live vermin, no graffiti. Still, she kept
carefully away from the walls. "I never know what's worse," she
said over her shoulder. "The stairs or the elevator. He could be . . .
anywhere."

"Why don't you let me walk up ahead of you?" I asked her
gently.

"I . . . okay," she said, stepping aside for me to pass.

We came up the rest of the way in silence. "This is it," she said from behind me, stepping past me to open a door to the fourth floor.

"I never know how to do this," she said, moving down the hall over a carpet runner the exact color of slag. "When I go downstairs to get something. If I lock up behind me, he won't be able to get in my apartment. But then, if he's in the building, I won't have time to unlock everything before he gets me. But if I don't lock up, he can be inside. Waiting for me. That would be . . . worse, I think."

She pulled a ring of keys from the lab coat. One lock was above the doorknob, another was set higher, a big deadbolt with a heavy strike-plate around it. She opened them both, pushed the door aside to let me pass.

The apartment opened into the living room. "Please sit down," she said, gesturing toward a futon couch covered in plain white canvas. "Can I take your coat?"

"That's all right," I told her, slipping it off, folding it over my forearm and dropping it next to me as I sat down.

"Would you like some coffee?"

"No, thank you."

"I . . . I'm not sure where to begin." She walked in a little circle, then abruptly sat down on a straight chair made out of a single piece of white molded plastic. She tugged at the hem of her lab coat, pulling it down across her knees as she looked across at me. Her eyes were scars.

"Pardon the cliché," I said gently, "but at the beginning is always best."

Her dull mouth twisted in what might have been a smile. "I'm sure. I expected . . . I don't know. Someone who . . ."

"Some kind of thug?"

"No! I mean, Crystal Beth said you would be . . . I guess I just don't have any . . . image of this. It all seems so . . . insane anyway."

"I'm sure it does," I said soothingly. "Still . . ."

"Yes. Still. It *is* happening, insane or not. And I need . . ."

"I know. Just tell me, all right?"

"Are you sure you don't want any coffee?"

"I'm sure."

"Do you mind if I . . . ?"

"Of course not," I said politely, staying in that role, balm to her fear.

She got up quickly, left the room. I heard kitchen sounds. I glanced around the room. One empty white wall was dominated by a huge framed poster of the *QE II*, flags flying, just about to leave port. A set of shelves loaded with what looked like textbooks. One of those high-end mini-stereos—I recognized the distinct Bose wave shape. The floors were highly polished hardwood, the windows framed with mauve muslin curtains, pulled fully open. On an upended white plastic milk crate stood an elaborate phone-and-answering-machine, set up to work cordless as well. The plastic and canvas stuff wasn't to save money—it was just her taste.

She came back into the living room, a steaming dark-brown mug in her hands. Took the seat she had before.

"This goes back almost three years," she said. "To when I was a resident."

A doctor, then, not a nurse.

"I met him about where you'd expect. In a bar. Only a few blocks from here. You don't get much time for dating in medical school. You don't get much time for anything, actually. Most of the other women were married. Or engaged. Or . . . connected in some way. I was . . . lonely. Not so much for a lover, for companionship. There were so many good things in my life, so much to look forward to. And nobody to share them with."

As if on cue, a magnificent seal-point Siamese cat pranced into the room. It slinked over to her chair, rubbed against her leg. "Well, not *nobody*," she said. "Isn't that right, Orion?"

The cat purred.

"It's funny," she said. "Orion is so jealous. You'd think I'd be used to it. . . ."

Her voice trailed away into silence. I let it go for a few seconds, then I prodded her with: "He was jealous . . . ?"

"Not at first. I mean, it didn't come up. Not really. He didn't want me to see other men, but that wasn't exactly a big problem," she said ruefully. "It was kind of . . . sweet that he was so possessive.

I *wanted* to be possessed, I thought. Treasured. Cherished. At first, that's how it felt."

"What does he do?" I asked her.

"To me? He . . . Oh, you mean work, right?"

"Yes."

"He's a stockbroker. No, that's not right. A . . . portfolio manager. A 'player,' that's what he always called himself. He would always say he was 'making a play' instead of buying something. For a client. He had only a small number of clients. He wasn't one of those cold-callers, you know, the . . ."

"Salesmen?"

"Yes. He made that very clear. It was so important to him. He was a player, not a salesman. He had to study the . . . charts, he called them. Like a gambler betting on a horse. He said there was *always* money. The same amount of money. Nobody really *makes* money, that's what he said. It's the same money, it just changes hands. Some people win, some people lose."

"Did you ever invest money with him?"

"Oh no. I mean, he never asked me. It wasn't like that. He did help me with it, though. Money, I mean. Do you know what a SEP is?"

"No," I lied.

"It's a pension plan for the self-employed. It's really a wonderful deal. One of the few breaks the IRS still gives. I didn't have one, and he showed me how to set one up."

"With his brokerage house?"

"No," she said, an annoyed tone to her voice. "Stan wasn't after my money. He has plenty of his own. He's *very* successful in his business."

"I'm sorry," I apologized.

"He spent more on me than I was making," she said, the defensive tone still in her voice. "When we went on vacation, he insisted he pay for everything. He was old-fashioned, he said. The man should always pay."

"When did it start to go wrong?"

"The first time he hit me," she said, looking down at her hands.

"Which was . . . ?"

"Right after we had sex."

"He was—?"

"No!" she interrupted me. "I'm telling it all wrong. It wasn't a . . . sexual thing. He didn't hit me after we . . . made love. Or before it either. I just meant, he never hit me all the time we were dating. He didn't start until we became . . . intimate."

"And then it was . . . ?"

"He . . . We had an argument. Over something silly. I don't even remember what it was about. But I remember we were in his apartment. He has a condo. In TriBeCa. Right near the—"

"What did he do?" I cut her off. She was going to skirt the edges, and I needed her near the center.

"He just . . . shoved me, I guess. And shook me. He was yelling at me and suddenly he grabbed me by the shoulders and . . . I was terrified."

"So he stopped?"

"Yes. He did stop. And he apologized too. It was the stress of his job. He's responsible for tens of millions of dollars every day. It's very intense work, and he has to be in control every minute. His job is a pressure cooker."

"And he had to blow off steam every once in a while?"

"That's right. That's what he—"

"But it escalated?"

"Yes. Of course. I'm sure you've heard this a thousand times in your line of work."

Seeing as she'd been nice enough to upgrade me from thug to psychologist—or downgrade me to lawyer, I couldn't tell which— I decided to let that one pass.

"It wasn't really the . . . violence," she finally said. "He did hit me, eventually. Even punched me in the face, once. I didn't have to go to the hospital . . . and didn't *want* to, all right?" she continued. "It was . . . humiliating. I had told the other residents that we were . . . together. They don't train you to ask for help, they train you to give it. And to stay . . . detached."

"Okay."

"No, it *wasn't* okay. I should have stopped it earlier. But . . . I just didn't. Do you know what a cancer is, Mr. . . . ?"

"Smith."

"Of course," she said, in that self-hating tone. Why should this hard-faced man tell her the truth? He wasn't there to help her. He didn't care about her. He just wanted the money. "Smith. Do you know what a cancer is, Mr. Smith?"

"Not medically."

"Cancer is simply unregulated growth. That's all it is. The human body has mechanisms within it to regulate growth. When they malfunction, the cancer starts to work. If you don't stop its growth, it eats the host. That's what my . . . relationship was. Unregulated growth. He got more . . . controlling every day. At first I . . . liked it. Then I didn't know how to stop it. It was . . . swallowing me. There wouldn't have been anything of me left."

"The police . . . ?"

"It wasn't the violence!" she said sharply. "Not the *physical* violence. He could stop that. He even . . . did, sometimes. It was the . . . picking away at me. Eating my . . . self. I was too fat. So I lost weight. I was too rotten a dancer. So I took lessons. I always said the wrong thing. I was always . . . embarrassing him, he said. I didn't really love him, he said that too. So I did . . . whatever he wanted. To prove it to him. I made myself into exactly what he wanted." She took a deep breath, holding it for a few seconds before she let it out. "And then I didn't want to be what I was. But he wouldn't let me go."

"He threatened to hurt you?"

"Hurt me? Yes, that's about right. Not kill me. That wouldn't be his style. You can't totally dominate a dead person."

This wasn't the story Crystal Beth had told me, but I kept my face bland, asked: "How would he hurt you, then?"

"He has . . . pictures of me. They weren't a secret. I mean, I knew he was taking them. But . . . you can't imagine. The things I did. For him, I thought. So I could prove I really loved him."

"Still or video?" I said, getting down to business.

"What?"

"The pictures. Polaroids, transparencies, black-and-whites, eight-millimeter, camcorder . . . what?"

"Oh. Both. I mean, he had a regular camera, and a video camera too."

"Okay. What else?"

"What *else?*"

"Yeah, what else? So he's got some sexy pictures of you. Maybe that would upset your parents or something, but there's nothing illegal—"

"I wrote some prescriptions," she said, looking down.

"For . . . ?"

"For him. Oh! I see what you . . . For tranquilizers."

"So . . . ?"

"And amphetamines. And painkillers."

"So . . . ?"

"I wrote the prescriptions for . . . people who don't exist. Just . . . names he gave me."

"How often—"

"I did it *all* the time," she said quietly. "He needed them for . . . clients, he said. Part of the entertainment package, he called it."

"And he'd go to the law? That'd drop his anchor too."

"His name isn't on any of them," she said. "I could lose my license. . . ."

"Are you sure he'd do it?"

"He would do anything," she said, her voice tense with the calm certainty of the doomed. "Anything at all."

"Like cancel your credit cards? Or steal your mail?"

"He never did that," she said, a puzzled tone to her voice.

"Your cousin said that—"

"My cousin? I don't have a cousin? Who . . . ?"

"Crystal Beth."

"Crystal *Beth?* She's not my cousin. I met her when I was volunteering at the center. And when the same thing started to happen to me, I . . ."

"Yeah, I guess it's just a word she uses. 'Cousin.' Like 'sister,' you know? It doesn't mean anything," I said quickly. "What you want is for him to stop, right?"

"Yes!"

"You understand, there's probably no way to get the pictures back. Not all of them. They could be anywhere."

"I know."

"And the scrips. You already wrote them. There's already a

record. The best you can get is that he goes away, leaves you alone. That's enough?"

"I told Crystal Beth. I already made all my mistakes. All I want is for him to leave my life."

"Give me what you have on him," I said.

She had a lot, but it wasn't much. Volume, not substance. The photos were a help, but she didn't have a spare set of keys to his apartment. Or his car.

What she had was mostly "Dating Game" keepsakes. Only thing, she finally figured out, she *was* the game.

Like the pimps say, it's *all* game.

She gave me the letters too. At first they were lovely little hollow things. On creamy stationery with his name embossed in florid script. Handwritten with a fountain pen in a self-assured flowing hand. Bullshit homilies. Talk-show clichés. Recycled garbage.

The philosophers say "Whatever will be, will be." My darling, all I know is that we will be. Together.

But the temperature dropped as he got closer to what he was. The last one was computer-font typed on plain paper. Using what the chump probably thought was an untraceable laser printer.

Broken promises make broken people, you dirty miserable fucking lousy bitch.

All you ever need to scan someone who plays above ground is the usual registration paper. A Social Security number can do it. Or a driver's license. Or whatever. It's easy. Some of that government ID stuff. And some cash.

Wolfe pulled the records for me in forty-eight hours, sneering "amateur" as she handed them over. I asked her, since I was protecting a battered woman and all, if she didn't want to cut me some slack on the fee. She didn't, but she threw me one of her beautiful smiles as a bonus.

The ex-boyfriend looked good on paper. Went a little deep into his platinum AmEx every once in a while, but nothing radical. He'd overpaid for his condo like every yuppie twerp who bought before 1988 and his BMW M3 was leased, but he was pulling a heavy salary and a yearly six-figure bonus too; so, even with semi-annual runs to St. Bart's, Armani on his back, Patek Philippe on his wrist, regular heavy restaurant tabs and the occasional limo down to Atlantic City, he was well inside the margin.

On paper, anyway.

Sometimes you get lucky. Like if a mark has a Jones for strippers and he puts all the lap-dances on his credit card so he can take his fun as a tax deduction. Or if you find big holes in the financial records—the kind of holes coke eats in your nose after a while. Nothing like that with this boy, though.

Doesn't matter. When you're looking to hack somebody up, a machete works as good as a modem.

A few more days, and we had him boxed. He left his BMW in the condo's garage and took a cab to work every day. Nobody else lived in his apartment. No girlfriend. No roommate. No out-of-town guests staying over. No dog.

"I work alone, home," the Prof said sharply. "No way I'm taking that maniac with."

"Mole's no maniac," I told him.

He gave me a look of profound pity.

I switched gears, looking for traction. "Look, Prof, the Mole's the only one who can rig the guy's machinery, you know that."

"That's us today, the fucking IRA?" he asked sarcastically. "We don't need to make his room go boom, right? You wanna ice the motherfucker, we could just give the job to your boy Hercules, get *some* use outa that chump."

"I'm not talking about blowing him up," I said quietly, ignoring the jab. "This is gonna be . . . subtle, okay?"

"The Mole ain't . . . mobile, brother. We run into some shit, he's gonna still be there when it's over."

"Max'll go in with you."

"And I will be outside, Father," Clarence put in.

"No you won't," the little man snapped. "I told you—"

"Yes, you have told me many things," the young gunslinger said calmly. "And I have always listened. With love and respect."

"Ahhh . . ." the Prof surrendered.

I plugged the cellular phone into the scrambler box sitting on the Plymouth's front seat. Gave the "Go" to the crew as I watched the mark climb out of the yellow cab in front of the World Trade Center, where he had his office. I lit a cigarette and waited, giving him time to get to his desk, to his direct line. By the time he sat down, his life would be invaded.

"Anytime I want, Stanley," I hissed into the cell phone when he picked up, my whisper-of-the-grave voice on full menace.

"What? Who is—?"

"It don't matter, Stanley. You been fucking with the wrong people. You been a problem, punk. The people I work for, they don't like problems."

"Look, whoever you—"

"Keep quiet, Stanley. Keep *real* quiet. You know how it is. Something's wrong with you, you see a doctor, right? And the doctor writes you a prescription. Me, I'm the prescription now, understand?"

"If that little—"

"Stanley, don't make me tell you again. It's over. That's the message. There's no more. You got no motherfucking idea how bad a mistake you made. You got one chance. Real simple choice. Go fucking *away*, got it? No phone calls, no letters, no nothing. You do anything, anything at all, we do *you*. You got twenty-four hours, Stanley. Then it's over. Or you are."

"That's one sick motherfucker," the Prof said, handing over a little wooden box of six-month recovery medals from AA. Now I knew where the player met his prey—he was a Twelve Step stalker, a shark in a pool of victims. I wondered what Crystal Beth's client had never told her. Or Crystal Beth never told me.

"You get the—?"

The Prof pulled a white leather photo album with thick padded covers from under his long coat without a word.

"Find any scrips?" I asked him, not looking inside the white covers.

"Only a few. But he had a heavy pill stash. It was all like you called, Schoolboy."

"You switch the pills?"

"One for one. Perfect match."

"Righteous. The Mole get his work done?"

"Oh yeah. Only took a few minutes. Soon as that piece of shit opens the line, it's Nightmare Time."

By the next day, it was over. A private courier had come to the woman's apartment. I'd left Max on watch just in case Stanley wanted more than a package delivered, but the courier handed it over without protest once I calmly explained to him that I was the doctor's "representative." He asked me for a signature on his receipt form. I looked at him until he stuffed it back in his pocket and walked away.

We opened the package inside a box the Mole has for stuff like that, using a computer-controlled robot arm to do the work. No explosive surprises. I kept one piece out, reassembled the rest and gave it to Clarence to drop off.

Back in my office, I opened the secrets of the white leather album with a surgeon's scalpel. The negatives were just where I thought they'd be, inside the cover, repasted so fine you'd never spot the seam if you weren't looking for it. The pictures were all of the woman. And him, I guess, from the waist down. About what you'd expect. Weren't worth much unless her next fiancé wanted to marry a virgin. Not even erotic, unless you liked ropes and ball-gags and mirrors. Just trophies from an ugly hunt. I placed them flat on a piece of thick glass, used a box-cutter to shred them down, made a little bonfire in a stone jar, lighting a cigarette from the flames licking over the open top. It tasted good. The negatives needed something better, and I'd take care of it soon. I know a guy who works in a crematorium. Nights.

"It was all here," she said on the phone when I called later, a wave of happiness bubbling under the surprise in her voice. "Every-thing. My letters. The . . . gifts I'd given him. Even the last of the . . ."

"I know. The one he hadn't used yet."

"Yes! Everything except . . ."

"The pictures?"

"Yes."

"They're gone," I told her. "I watched them go."

"Oh God."

"Sure."

"There was a letter. Should I . . . ?"

"Read it to me," I told her.

"It just says: 'You already got the rest. There is nothing more between us. Please leave me alone.' Can you imagine? Like I was terrorizing *him.*"

"Doesn't matter, right?"

"Yes, you're right. I don't know what to say."

"Let it sit for a while. Don't do anything. If he ever shows up again, tell your friend, okay?"

"Yes. Thank you! I—"

I clicked off the cellular.

Impossible to know which buttons would drop his elevator, so we'd pushed them all. Maybe it was the high-pitched sound blast ripping his ear when he picked up his home phone. Maybe it was the message on his computer screen when he fired it up, black-bordered like an obituary:

> **REMEMBER TO BACK UP
> ALL YOUR DATA, STANLEY**
>
> **WE DID**

Maybe knowing we had copies of everything he'd stored on his hard drive made him real nervous and he popped a Valium. Big mistake—the perfect-match lookalike pills we substituted would give him bad enough stomach cramps to make him think he'd been poisoned. And if he tried to drive himself to the Emergency Room, the air bag exploding into his face when he turned the ignition key in the BMW wouldn't calm him down much.

And after what we left in his bed, somebody was going to get a great condo at a bargain price. Kind of a pre-fire sale.

"**H**arriet told me what happened," Crystal Beth said to me. "Well, I guess, she didn't actually *know* what happened. But he's gone. Really gone, she thinks."

"If she doesn't call him," I said, nothing in my voice but the words.

We were at a small table by ourselves, seated next to the palm-print-smeared window of a coffeehouse on the Lower East Side. Some residents call it the East Village, part of the neighborhood-renaming frenzy that hit the city during the co-op boom. They tried other names for it too—Alphabet City, Loisaida—anything that would make it sound sweeter than it is. Lots of new names came to Manhattan for different pieces. "SoHo." "TriBeCa." Even Hell's Kitchen became "Clinton." I've known that sorry game since I was a little kid. When they put me in a POW camp and called it a foster home.

Crystal Beth had picked the place. With a day's notice, I'd sent

Clarence over to check it out. "Big nothing, mahn," he said. "No action."

The street outside was covered in a thin film of the gray filth that passes for snowfall down here. She took a long hit off one of her hand-rolled cigarettes, letting the smoke bubble slowly from her broad nose, wafting up past her almond eyes. "I should be angry at that," she said.

"At what?"

"At your . . . assumptions. That women ask for it."

"I never make assumptions," I lied. All of us, all the Children of the Secret, we all make assumptions. We assume you're going to hurt us. Use us. Betray our love and violate our trust. We all lie too. You taught us that.

"So why would you say Harriet would ever call him?" she challenged.

"I don't know Harriet. I know the . . . dynamic."

"Yeah," she said, sadly acknowledging. "I do too. I hope she never—"

"Her choice," I said. "At least she's got one now."

"Choices aren't cheap," Crystal Beth replied. "Are they?"

"I paid heavy for mine," I told her. Thinking about when I was too small to know what it cost. Or to steal the price. But while I was learning, a *lot* of people paid. Mostly the wrong ones.

I love it when citizens talk about hard choices. Where I live, you don't get many. And the ones you do get are *all* hard.

"Speaking of which—" She started to reach in her purse.

"Not here," I cut her off. "You don't flash cash in a joint like this."

"I know better than that," she came back, insulted.

"Oh. You did this before?"

Her face turned to her left, the tattoo clear in the feeble afternoon sunlight. "Why would you . . . ?"

"Porkpie ever come back for his money?" I asked her, trying to catch those almond eyes.

"Porkpie?"

"It was five K, right?" Then I told her enough of what I knew to show her there was more.

As soon as I was finished talking, she went into herself. Deep. I know what it looks like. What it feels like too. Her eyes were open but unfocused, her breathing was so shallow I couldn't see her chest move. Her hands were gently folded on the table between us.

I left her there, undisturbed. Sat waiting, not smoking or sipping my hot chocolate. Table sounds all around us, but she was safe in her capsule, untouched.

I knew what she was doing. She wasn't in shock, she was looking for answers. I could walk down the same path, but I couldn't join her, so I stayed where I was.

Time passed. Prison-slow.

Her eyes refocused. "Want to take a walk with me?" she asked suddenly, her mouth straight and serious, the corners turned down slightly.

"In this weather?"

"It's not far."

"Okay."

I left a ten-dollar bill on the table. Figured it was more than enough to cover my hot chocolate and Crystal Beth's mint tea. But she tossed another bill on top as we were getting up—I couldn't see what it was. She wasn't doing some feminism number—the joint was a dive, but it was probably chic enough to charge uptown prices.

On the street, she flicked the hood up over her shiny hair, tucked her hands into the pockets of her long red coat. I put on a pair of leather gloves, zipped my jacket to the neck, turned the collar up. The wind cut at us with ice-edged neutral hostility. Nothing personal—city winter hates everyone. Crystal Beth stuffed her hands into black mittens, inhaled a deep breath through her flat nose.

"This way," she said, bumping her hip against me to move us to the right.

At the corner, she waited for the light to change even though traffic was so light we could have slipped across easily. We were heading east, the Bowery somewhere just behind us. The streets narrowed. We passed an open strip of vacant lot, its ground cover of broken glass sparkling in the lousy sunlight that followed the dirty sleet. Splattered across the dead-eyed wall of a semi-abandoned building in huge jagged letters was a troubadour's message:

SMACK IS BACK!

As if anyone needed a reminder that the privileged princes and princesses of Generation X had rebelled against their elders by rejecting cocaine. And embracing heroin, snorting it in the deep delusion that only the needle could bring death.

Poor little rich kids. Never learned how to act. The FDA doesn't regulate street drugs. The same fifty bucks that bought you a mild buzz on Friday night will buy you a quiet ride down to the Zero the next weekend.

Crystal Beth reached over and took my hand, held it like a trusting child. A trusting bossy child. She never looked at me, just tugged slightly when she wanted me to cross another street. We were walking down a long block, all by ourselves. Crystal Beth pulled her hand free, put it in her mouth and pulled the mitten off with her teeth. Then she wrapped her small hand around one of my fingers and gently tugged at the glove until it came off. She handed it to me without a word. I put it in my pocket. She took my hand again, swinging it slightly between us.

Three men came out of a bar down the street. They turned in our direction and started moving toward us in a tight triangle. I tried to pull my left hand away from Crystal Beth. She held it tighter.

"Drop it," I told her, cold, eyes on the men.

She did. I put the glove back on, unzipped my jacket so I could reach inside, stepped forward quickly, putting her a half-pace behind me. I followed the rules for dealing with a pack—take the alpha first. The lead man in the triangle was a Latino, shorter than me but thicker in the body. Our eyes touched, dropped at the same time. The triangle moved past us. I reached over for Crystal Beth's hand, but she yanked it away, making a snorting sound through her broad little nose.

We turned left at the end of the block. "What was that all about?" she asked me.

"I needed my hands free," I told her.

"For what?"

"For whatever. If those guys got stupid, I'm holding your hand, I might as well have been wearing handcuffs."

"They didn't do anything."

"I'm not a fucking fortune-teller," I said.

"Are you always this suspicious?"

"Yeah. Are you always this not?"

"I wasn't raised to be paranoid," she said, looking at me for the first time.

"Where I was raised, it was the best way to be."

"Where . . . ?"

"Inside," I said. "Surrounded. You understand?"

"I . . . don't know."

"You want to give me your hand again?"

"Why? Did you like it?"

"Yeah. I did."

She was quiet a minute, walking next to me now, stride for stride. "Me too," she finally said. And put her hand back in mine.

She led me into an alley just barely wide enough for a garbage truck. Didn't look like one had tried that for quite a while. She turned right, stopping before a chain-link fence secured by a rubber-covered padlock that spanned a narrow opening in the alley wall. A metal sign wired to the gate said: BEWARE OF THE . . . The rest of the sign was a jagged edge from where it had been ripped apart.

Inside the chain-link, a back door was positioned between a pair of windows covered with thick wire mesh. The door itself was encased behind a security gate, a heavy lock anchoring it to a steel frame. She took her hand from mine, pulled a Medeco key from her coat pocket and turned the lock. The security door pulled out. Behind it was another, this one painted a light blue. Crystal Beth used the same key on another lock, and we were inside.

"Come on," she said, starting up a flight of metal stairs.

The staircase was almost pitch-dark, the dim light flowing from somewhere above us too faint to do anything but cast murky shadows. Crystal Beth climbed as confidently as a Sherpa. I followed a couple of steps behind her, not questioning. Only myself for going along with this.

At the landing, she turned and walked toward what had to be the front of the building. We passed a few doors—all closed. At the end of the corridor was a pair of blacked-out windows. The floor looked deserted. Crystal Beth walked past the windows without a glance and started up the next flight, still not saying a word. I went along, following.

On the next floor a pair of long fluorescent tubes cast a yellowish light down from the ceiling. One door stood halfway open. Crystal Beth stepped through it. Over her shoulder I saw a whole wall of exposed brick and a tall woman with a clipboard in one hand. The woman looked past Crystal Beth to where I was standing, said, "Who the fuck is this?" in a voice as warm as a microchip.

"He's helping me with something," Crystal Beth told her, not moving.

"No outsiders," the woman said, holding the clipboard like it was a cross and I was a vampire. A chocolate-colored cat stuck its narrow head around the corner of her room, regarding me with that "What's-in-it-for-me?" stare they all have.

"Stop making rules, Lorraine," Crystal Beth told her. "We're going to my place. I just wanted you to know we were in the building."

"I—"

"Come on," Crystal Beth told me again, turning on her heel and walking away. I followed her again, not looking back, feeling the tall woman's glare on my back like a laser-dot from a sniper's rifle.

We walked quickly past the next floor. All closed doors, but I could hear music playing behind one of them.

"This is mine," Crystal Beth said when we finally reached what I guessed was the top floor. She opened a door and walked in.

As soon as I saw the skylight overhead, I knew I'd been right about it being the top floor. The room was spartan—a mattress on the floor with neatly tucked blankets on top, an ancient leather easy chair patched with multi-colored scraps sitting under an old-fashioned floor lamp with a parchment shade; next to it, an empty orange crate held a large handmade clay ashtray and a box of kitchen matches. A wood desk was against the far wall, bracketed by some army-surplus filing cabinets. The only modern furnishings were a laptop computer with a row of wire-connected peripherals and a radio–CD–cassette-tape combo with bookend speakers sitting proudly on bookshelves made from long planks set on cinderblocks. I glimpsed what might be a kitchen to my left. Closed door to my right was probably a bathroom. The other door was a closet, maybe? Thick-cored gray radiators sat between the windows and against a side wall. The windows were heavy-coated with the same blackout paint they had downstairs. On the sill next to one of them was a green Micata cordless electric drill, a long narrow bit already fitted.

"You into carpentry?" I asked her.

"I'm into self-defense," she said firmly, picking up the drill and pulling the trigger. The bit whirred. Up close, it would make a knife look friendly.

Crystal Beth replaced the drill—crossed over to the easy chair, flicked on the floor lamp. It glowed faintly yellow through the parchment shade. "Give me your jacket," she said. Hers was already off, folded over her arm.

She opened one of the closed doors. Hung up our coats on a single hanger, mine over hers. Said "Have a seat," pointing to the easy chair.

Then she took a beige metal chair from where it had been lying folded against the wall, unsnapped it and put it next to the easy chair. She sat down.

"I'm going on my instincts," she said. "Letting go of my fear. Do you understand?"

I nodded like I did, but the whole idea was insane to me. The best thing you can do with fear is use it, not lose it.

"You know what this is?" she asked, making a sweeping gesture with one hand.

"Squatter's roost?"

"No. It just looks abandoned. We did that on purpose. It's mine. I own it. This is a safehouse."

"For . . . ?"

"Victims," she said quietly. "Victims who are tired of the role."

"Where do I . . . ?"

She smiled and handed me my own pack of cigarettes. Must have taken them from my jacket when she hung it up, searching with her fingers. I lit one with a kitchen match from the box sitting on the orange crate, blew smoke at the ceiling to tell her I was still waiting for the answer.

"Do you want to hear my story?" she asked. "Or just the bottom line?"

Without taking my eyes off hers, I reached up and pulled the cord on the floor lamp so I wouldn't feel like I was in an interrogation cell. The room darkened. "Tell me your story," I said.

"All communes get runaways," Crystal Beth said. "Throwaways too. Good ones and bad ones. The communes, not the runaways. And they all make newcomers live by their rules if they want to join. For some of the communes, that means practicing their religion. For others, it means turning tricks. Or selling drugs.

With us, it was they had to live in peace. Peace and love. Sounds stupid to you, maybe?"

"No. Not stupid. Just . . . hard."

"Yes! Sometimes it was very hard. They didn't all make it. Some were running away just for the adventure. Some because they were scared. Or lost themselves. There were outlaws too, looking for a place to hole up. And some, they thought they could . . . take over, I guess. Be in charge. We never had anyone in charge. We never did that. They—the elders—started the commune to be free of violence. They had all felt violence in their lives, and they all had moved away from it in their spirits. What they wanted was a place where anyone could do that."

She stopped talking then. Got up and walked around in a little circle. Came back and took her seat again.

"Her name was Starr," she said. "Good name for a little hippie, wasn't it? When she came to us she was maybe fourteen. . . . Nobody really knew. And we never asked." She took a breath. Then she said, "Everything was fine until they came for her."

I knew better than to hold her eyes all through whatever story she wanted to tell, so I focused on the tattoo, not even sure if I was actually seeing it in the darkness, just knowing it was there, moving as she spoke.

"Who came for her?" I asked.

"Bikers. A whole pack of them. They said she was their property, and they wanted her back."

"Were they flying colors?"

"What difference does it . . . ? Oh, I know what you mean. I'm not being fair. With the story, I'm not being fair. We knew a lot of bikers. They had their own communes, just like we did, only they lived in cities. They were nice, most of them. Friendly to the big people, sweet to the children. I remember one of them—Romance, his name was, I'll never forget that. He had a great flaming red beard, like a Viking. I used to go for rides on the back of his motorcycle all the time. Not off the grounds—my mother wouldn't let me do that—but we had plenty of land."

She was rambling. I threw out a line. "He was the one who taught you to ride?"

"No, that was Roxanne. She had this old Indian, a big huge black thing with a white stripe on the tank. It had a foot clutch. She had to work it for me while I sat in front of her. She was . . . How do you know I ride?"

"Just a guess," I told her, straight-faced. "So these bikers—the ones who came for Starr—you didn't know them?"

"None of us knew them. They were from downstate somewhere. California, I think. But I don't know. I don't remember much about them except . . . my father wouldn't let them take her. Starr. He was very gentle with them. He explained it. Nobody is property. No person can own another. That's wrong. It's against nature. Starr was scared. She said she would go with them, but my father said she didn't have to go if she didn't want to. I remember it like it was an hour ago. Three of the bikers, aimed like an arrowhead. Straddling the motorcycles, the leader in front. Telling my father that Starr was their property. She even had their brand on her. They told my father to make her strip, take a look for himself. . . ."

Crystal Beth started to go somewhere else, like she had earlier, in the café. "What happened?" I asked her, trying to bring her back.

"They killed him," she said in a flat, detached voice. "The leader did it. He just took out a pistol. A big chrome one. I remember it gleaming in the sun. I thought it was pretty. He shot my father in the chest. He was standing so close blood flew out of my father's back. Then they turned around and rode off."

"What did—?"

"Nobody did *anything*. We were in shock. The sun disappeared. I don't even remember the rest of that day. The police were there. It was a death. Not just the death of my father, the death of everything."

"Did they ever catch—?"

"The killers? They left Starr there. She knew who they were, but she wouldn't tell."

"If—"

"She wouldn't tell the police. But she told my mother. It was a few weeks later when she told. That's when she left."

"Starr?"

"My mother," Crystal Beth said, a sadness in her voice as long and deep as thigh-bone marrow. "My father was a brave man, but he was a hippie in his heart. Gentle and sweet. A poet in his soul. But my mother, she was just *with* him, you understand? She loved him, so she lived his life. But that wasn't her, not in her spirit. She was a warrior."

"So she went after them?"

"She told me goodbye. She told me she was going to be with my father. I was grown then, almost sixteen. My mother had money. We weren't supposed to have money. Not individual money, you know? But she had some, and she told me where it was. And some other things. That's when I got my markings," she said, touching her jaw. "My mother did that. Herself. Her mother's mother taught her, she told me. But she never did her art on anyone else, not in all the time I knew her."

"And she just left then?"

"There was a ceremony. I don't know if I could explain it to you. It was . . . just me and my mother, alone. When I got my markings. She took Starr with her and they left in the pickup truck we had."

"And you never heard from her again?"

"In a way I did. There was a . . . network. In a little book my father had. I went to the different places. Traveling. Not just here—I went to Europe too. There was a passport in the stuff my mother left me. I'd never known I had one. Never thought I'd ever leave the commune. . . .

"I was looking for my purpose," she said. "Like my mother wanted. One of the families I stayed with told me—I don't know how they knew. When I came back to America, I went to the library, and I found it in the newspapers."

"What happened?"

"Happened? Nothing happened. My mother went to be with my father, like she said she would. As she had vowed. My father, he wasn't always a man of peace. I don't know why he left Ireland, but I know he had to. He always kept a chest, like a captain's chest? My mother emptied it out before she left. She gave me my father's poems, and she took the other stuff."

"He had—?"

"I don't know what he had. All I know is that my mother took whatever it was. To their clubhouse, that's what the newspapers called it. She walked in there with a knapsack on her back. And while she was inside, the place blew up. Seven of them died. My mother too."

"Damn."

"I started walking then," Crystal Beth said. "And I didn't stop until I found my purpose."

She sat there in silence after that. Not inside herself, just watching. And waiting.

I did that too.

It was a few minutes before she spoke. "Does my story make you . . . feel anything?"

"Yeah," I told her true. "Jealous."

She nodded like that made perfect sense to her. Didn't say anything else.

"Was this your purpose?" I asked her finally. "This . . . shelter?"

"Not a place," she said softly. "A place is never a purpose. I knew my purpose was to protect. Like my father did Starr."

"Like your mother did . . . ?"

"Me? Maybe. I didn't think so at first. I thought it was just revenge. My mother believed in balance. Natural balance. The others, they never really understood that. Oh, they *said* they did. Hippies worship anything 'native,' even though they don't get it. Not really. They used to argue with my mother sometimes. About hunting, that was one. My mother never argued back, but my father did. Oh, he *loved* to argue, my father. But he would always do it with a smile, with a joke. I remember once, he asked some of the others if they thought my mother's people should be farmers instead of hunters. 'Should they grow wheat on the bloody tundra, then?' I remember him saying. I don't know why my mother did . . . what she did. All she ever told me was she was going to be with him. And I know she is."

"But sixteen, that was a . . ."

"Long time ago?" Her smile flashed in the darkness. "Sure. I'm not a girl anymore. It took me a long time to find . . . this. I wandered for a while. Tried other communes. Looking for the music. But there were always too many chemicals in the mix. I wasn't at home there. Then I went to school."

"High school?"

"College. I was schooled on the commune. We had so many people there who could teach. There was this place, not far from where I was raised. A place for girls who had been abused. I wasn't abused, so I never lived there. But I was friends with one of the girls, and she took me to her counselor, her education counselor. And he told me how I could get advanced-placement credit by taking exams. CLEP exams, they were called. I was almost twenty when I started, but I went right into my junior year."

"For what?"

"To get an—oh, you mean, what did I study? Just a bunch of different stuff. Looking for the blend. Science and math, history and literature. Even philosophy . . . although I never liked that stuff much. I was trying to get . . ."

". . . closer to your parents?"

"Yes! How did you . . . ?"

"The courses—the ones you studied—the mix sounds like them."

"I guess it was. But the truth is, or it *was*, anyway, that it didn't work. The books always seemed so hollow. If there was anything valuable in them, it was in a vacuum, kind of. Not connected to anything. The way I was . . ."

I waited a few minutes after her voice trailed off. Until I could see there wasn't going to be any more. "What then?" I prompted her.

"I thought about the Peace Corps, but . . . I remembered my mother telling me about the missionaries who came to her village, and I crossed that one off. So I became a VISTA volunteer. In Appalachia. I didn't like the trainers much. They kept giving us a whole bunch of long stupid speeches about 'shedding our middle-class attitudes' and stuff like that. I didn't *have* any middle-class attitudes. *They* did. It was mostly the males. White males. Just another way of asserting dominance. Pressuring the women. For sex, mostly.

"But once I got out into the field, it was great. Just like it should be, I thought. I taught and I learned. I just didn't learn enough, so I moved on. That's when I came to my first shelter."

"For the homeless?"

"For battered women," she said. "I never realized how ... frightened people could be until I worked there. They were so helpless. Nobody would listen unless they were half-killed. Even then, sometimes. And I had trouble fitting in. The director, she wanted to do therapy all the time. For the men, mostly. The perpetrators, the ones who needed all the 'understanding' so they could 'break their patterns,'" Crystal Beth said, her voice heavy with scorn.

"And the director liked to give speeches too," she went on. "Fund-raising. She *worshipped* the media. Any reporter who wanted to talk to the women, that was okay. There was no ... privacy for anyone."

"Like on the commune?"

"No! You don't understand. We didn't have private *property*, that isn't the same thing. But you could be by yourself. The others would always respect that. In that shelter where I worked, even your thoughts weren't your own. Everything had to be ... examined. Talked about. That's what it was. *All* it was. Talking, not fighting."

"Who did you want to fight?"

"Not who, what. The ... Beast. The Stalking Beast. There's a legend ... Never mind, now isn't the time to tell it. I left there with a couple of the other women. We wanted to start our own place. I thought ... runaways. That's where it started for me anyway. Not just girls, we took in boys too. Most of them were prostituting themselves for—"

"Them*selves*?"

"Okay, you're right. That's what I thought too. At first. People call them child prostitutes, but they're not. They're prostituted children. The girls, anyway."

"Why just the girls?"

"Some of the boys, they went into business for themselves. They didn't have pimps."

"Sure. I get it. Just ran away from a nice home where everybody treated them good and started peddling their bodies for cash to buy clothes and CDs, huh?"

"I didn't mean that. I know they were mistreated at home. Just—"

"You ever read about the cops busting a whole whorehouse full of girls from another country?"

"Yes. Just last week. On the West Coast. All the girls were from Thailand."

"Sure. Eighteen, nineteen, twenty years old, right? At least that's what they told the cops. You think that was the first time they turned a trick?"

"No. I'm sure they started . . . Oh, I see."

"Sorry I interrupted you."

"That's all right. I mean, *you're* right. I should have said—"

"It doesn't matter. Tell me what happened next."

"They closed it down. The pimps. They just closed it down. They hung around outside. They dropped on the girls like hawks as soon as they left the place. A couple of them even came inside. By the time the police got there, they were always gone."

"And some of the girls recruited for the pimps themselves."

"Yes," she said softly. "You know about that too. Some of them did that. We weren't . . . prepared for it. We thought we could all stand together, but some of them, they *wanted* to—"

"You can't want something else unless you believe something else really exists."

"*We* really existed. We were really there."

"You're not there now."

"I know," she said. Not ashamed, just stating a fact. "It didn't work. It wasn't my . . . purpose. But this is. This truly is."

"This is a shelter too?"

"Yes. But not for battered women. Or prostitutes. Or runaways. It's a safehouse from the Beast. From stalkers."

"What's the difference?"

"Maybe it's just the degree, I'm not sure. But some men, no

matter how ugly they were in the . . . relationship, when it's over, they let it go. And some women, they aren't afraid enough. Or they still think things can be fixed. I'm not a psychologist. I couldn't give you a name for the difference. But we know it when we see it."

"So where do I come in?" I finally asked her.

"It's too dark in here now," Crystal Beth said by way of reply. She stood up, walked over to the desk, took out a candle, held a match to the bottom until it was soft, then jammed it against the desktop and lit the wick. The flame was faint, but it bathed her in a red-yellow glow.

Then she studied me. Or my face, anyway. If it was a patience test, she was playing with a pro. I let her do it, not challenging, just waiting.

"You're here because now I have one too," she finally said.

"One what?"

She didn't say anything more. I went back to waiting.

"You never stared at my body," she said suddenly.

"What?"

"My body. My chest. My legs. My hips. You never stared. Not once."

"You sure?"

"Yes, I'm sure. *Look* isn't the same as *stare*. I meant, oh, *leering*, I guess. You know what I'm talking about. Some men are more subtle about it than others, but a woman can always tell when they're doing it."

"You don't exactly . . . display yourself."

"No, I don't. But that wouldn't matter. That only . . . frustrates some men, doesn't it?"

"I guess so. What I don't get is the point."

"You're not gay," she said. A flat statement, not a question.

"If I was, I wouldn't score any style points for not checking you out?"

"No, I don't mean that. Gay men do that too. Especially your butt, for some reason."

"Where are you going with this, Crystal Beth?"

"You like my name, don't you? Most men don't. They always call me 'Crystal,' like that's easier for their tongues. Do you know why?"

"No."

"Neither do I," she said, getting to her feet. "You're very into self-control, aren't you?"

"I'm not saying."

It got me the laugh I was playing for. "You don't drink, right?" she asked. "Or take drugs?"

"No. Unless you count nicotine."

"I'm not a hypocrite," she said, nodding her head toward her own cigarette makings. "I know it's a drug. But that's not what I mean. About self-control. I'll bet I could come and sit on your lap and we could talk. Just talk. Comfortable. What do you think?"

"Depends on how much you weigh," I told her.

She chuckled, a deep, chesty sound. Then stood up, turned her back and sat down, saying "Let's see, okay?"

Crystal Beth was warm on my lap. Rounded and dense, heavier than she looked. Her hair smelled of rich tobacco and bitter oranges. Her solid thighs were across my knees, her bottom off to the side, crammed against the arm of the easy chair, right arm around my neck. The candle's flame lit the tattoo along her right jaw, the arrow of her purpose still against her silence, poised and ready. She leaned back against me, closed her eyes, made a little sound I didn't understand—I'd never heard it before.

"There's only three women staying here now," she said after a while. "One got an Order of Protection after her husband beat her too many times. It said he had to keep away from her. She stayed in the house. He came over one night and did it again. He tore up the Order of Protection. Then he made her eat it. Then he raped her. When the police came, it was too late."

"Too late for what? They could still lock him up on her say-so."

"He was educated. Somebody taught him. He beat her with an open palm against the top of her head. She thought her brain was going to fracture from the pain. He was wearing gloves. Doctor's gloves. When he raped her, he wore a condom. And he had an iron-clad alibi. Four other men, all playing cards at one of their houses. He told her. About being educated. That was the word he used: 'educated.' And he told her it was going to happen again and again. Anytime he wanted."

I rested my right hand on top of her thigh, balancing her weight, smelling her scent. Waiting.

"Another woman, she's a young one. Do you know what 'R and R' is?"

"Military? Like Rest and Recreation?"

"Were you a soldier?" she asked, shifting her weight slightly.

"I was never in the army," I told her, dodging the question.

"Ummm," she said. Letting it hang there. Then: "It means something different now. To some . . . people. R and R, it stands for Rope and Rape."

"Kidnappers?"

"Not the way you think. Not for ransom either. 'Rope' is Rohypnol. The 'date-rape drug.' A cute name for the Devil's own brew, isn't it? Rohypnol is a potent tranquilizer, ten times more powerful than Valium. And it has no taste. Slip it into a woman's drink and she comes around a few hours later. While she's down, you can do whatever you want."

"Like a Mickey Finn . . . ?"

"No, not like chloral hydrate. It's not knockout drops, it's a paralytic agent. The victim is semi-conscious. When they come out of it, they know *something* happened, they just can't be . . . sure."

"And they can't testify?"

"That's right. It's legal in Europe. They use it to pre-tranq a patient before major surgery. Supposed to work very well. But now it's a big black-market drug over here. They sell it in the original packaging and everything. Little white pills, two to a pack. Clear plastic."

"They got bathtub versions of that too," I told her.

"Bathtub versions . . . ?

"Home brew," I said. "GHB. Gamma hydroxybutyrate. There's no legal version of it, like what you're talking about. Any freak can mix it up. It's got a lot of street names: Liquid X, Gook, Gamma 10 . . . It all works the same."

"Oh," she said, sad-quiet.

I tightened my hold on her waist, not asking her how she could describe the drug so accurately. Maybe not wanting to know. Feeling an old friend wrap its comforting cloak around my shoulders. It's been with me almost as long as Fear, that friend.

Hate.

"There's no defense against it," she said quietly.

"Seems like there could be," I told her, keeping my voice level. "It's a chemical, right? So what you need is a reagent. Some other drug that would react with it, turn it a distinctive color. Like the DEA uses to field-test cocaine."

"Oh God, that makes so much *sense*," she gasped, squirming in my lap. "Is that what you . . . really do?"

"You mean, am I a chemist?"

"No. I know you're not. I mean . . . solve problems. Figure things out."

"Some things," I said, letting an undertone of warning into my voice.

"That's what . . . Anyway, this young woman, the man who did it to her wasn't a stranger, it was her boyfriend. Her ex-boyfriend. After they broke up. He talked her into having a last drink together. In a public bar. All she remembers is getting sick, him helping her out of there. When she came to, she was in his apartment. Naked. And it was hours later. She called the police too. But when they came, he told them they made love. *Love*," she said, her voice trembling with something I thought I recognized. Somebody had told her that same lie, once.

"So why is she hiding out?" I asked.

"Because he took her mind. She believes he can do it again. Maybe not with a drink . . . with food, or air particles. Or whatever. She's quite . . . insane now. But she feels safe here. That's why the doors are always closed downstairs. If she knew there was a man here, any man, she'd be sure you were with . . . him."

"And the last woman?"

"You *are* a good listener," she said, nuzzling against my neck.

"The third woman isn't really here. I mean, she's *been* here, but she's not here now. We have her someplace . . . else. And she doesn't have one stalker, she has two."

"Are they together?"

"One of them thinks so," she said cryptically. "Do you know what a falconer is?"

"Yeah."

"Well, then you'll understand. Two stalkers. One's a falcon, one's a falconer, see?"

"No."

"That's all right," she said, slipping her left hand inside my sweatshirt, short fingernails scraping my chest. Carefully, like she was drawing a map. "Do you think I'm a mystery?" she whispered.

"You're a woman," I said.

"What a careful man you are." She chuckled. "And not very aggressive."

"I'm a pussycat," I assured her.

"A tomcat, more likely."

"When I was young."

"You're not so old."

"I want to *get* old," I said, slipping the warning tone in again.

"So . . . you want to know why you're here?"

"Yeah."

"You want to know why you? Why I chose you?"

"Yeah."

"And you want to get paid too."

"Sure."

She leaned close to my ear, speaking so softly I could barely make it out. "Do you like secrets?"

"No," I told her, more harshly than I'd intended. Thinking of my childhood. Or what should have been my childhood.

"Not those kind of secrets," she said, catching my thoughts from my tone, her voice still soft as gossamer. "Sweet secrets. Shared."

"I don't know about those kind," I said.

"I'm going to tell you a secret," Crystal Beth said. "Then I'll show you one. And, if they come together, I'll do both. All right?"

"First tell me," I said.

"The last woman I told you about. The one with two stalkers? Well, one of them's stalking me too."

I didn't react, just let her nestle against me. Thinking how it's always personal with some people. And how, every time I had let it be that way with me, somebody died. I felt the warmth of her cheek against mine, the woman-weight of her body . . . and reached for the comfort of the ice inside me. "An old boyfriend?" I asked her, wondering if I was being groomed as the replacement. And whose life it would cost to buy that ticket . . .

I haven't played that game since I was a teenager, but I still remember how it felt. To be lying on the ground, bleeding, watching the fire-starter walk off with the guy I had fought, swinging her hips like she was slapping my face. The hardest lesson I ever had to learn was not to make the next girl pay for what the last one took.

I'd ended up doing time with a lot of men who hadn't learned that one.

"Not even a friend," she said quickly, slowing my train of thought before it ran off the tracks. "An enemy, in fact. He doesn't want me, he wants me to *do* something. And I won't."

"Wants you to . . . ?" I asked, leading her into it, fire-bursts flaring under my skin. Arson in readiness, distrust standing by for the accelerant.

"Betray a trust. Sell someone out. Give them up."

"And if you don't?"

"Then it all comes down. Not just me. The network. My whole . . . purpose."

"I still don't know what that means."

"And you still don't know why you, yes?"

"Yes."

She got to her feet. Bent forward at the waist and kissed me on the side of my mouth. "Another walk," she said. "A much shorter one this time, okay?" And held out her hand.

I took it and got to my feet.

"What about my jacket?" I asked her.

"We'll be back," she said.

Still holding on to my hand, Crystal Beth blew out the candle, leaving the room almost black. She made her way over to the door as if she'd memorized the place in the dark. Once it was open, there was enough light to see by. She trailed one hand behind her, keeping me connected as she descended the stairs.

The second door from the staircase was painted black. Against the dull white walls, it looked like a cave opening. Crystal Beth rapped sharply. I couldn't hear anyone approach from the other side, but the sound of a bolt snapping open was clear in the silence. The door opened to a wash of pinkish light. Crystal Beth stepped aside, nudging me forward with a hip. A woman was seated on a padded stool aimed right at us, back-lit. I couldn't make out her face—all I could see was a pair of nylon-sheathed legs crossed at the knee, one foot dangling as though to better display a brilliant turquoise spike-heeled shoe.

"Long time no see," Vyra said.

I felt Crystal Beth behind me, so close her breasts pushed against my back. Vyra's heavy perfume filled the little room. It stunk like a trap.

"What *is* this?" I asked her, keeping my voice relaxed, my hands on my belt buckle in case my nose was sharper than my eyes.

"Don't be mad," Vyra said. "This was my idea, not Crystal's."

"What idea is that?" I asked her.

"Bringing you in."

"You're . . . being stalked?"

"Not me," Vyra said. "The others. I . . . support this place. Crystal and I, we're . . . close."

"Why didn't you just—?"

"Because you wouldn't take me seriously," she interrupted. "You never have. Never had a reason to, I mean. I thought, if Crystal told you about the . . . situation, you'd help."

"You're in over your head," I told her flatly.

"But *you* wouldn't be. We agreed, Crystal and me. She'd tell you the first part. Then I'd explain how she came to you. Then we'd both tell you what—"

"Maybe I need to tell *you* what," I said.

"Burke, please don't be mad at me. I couldn't stand that. Can't you just listen for a few minutes?"

"I've *been* listening. And for more than a few minutes."

"I know. I'm sorry. Maybe this was the wrong way, okay? If I screwed it up, I'll take whatever's coming to me. But it isn't Crystal's fault. Don't punish her for what I did. Please . . ."

I stepped away from Crystal Beth, my eyes acclimating to the pinkish light. The room was bare except for the vanity mirror and the stool. Not even a closet. "Go ahead," I said quietly. "Say what you want."

"Can't we go upstairs?" Crystal Beth asked. "It's more . . . peaceful up there."

"Go ahead," I told Vyra again.

She took that for agreement, got off the stool and squeezed past me. I felt silk against my hand. She went out the door. I didn't move. Crystal Beth tugged at my hand. I pulled it away from her. "You need both your hands," I told her.

"For what?" she whispered behind Vyra's back.

"To put all your cards on the table," I told her.

Vyra went first, snake-hipping her way up the stairs, silk rustling, spike heels flashing, perfume trailing. Crystal Beth was next, walking strong and carefully, like a warrior to battle.

At the top of the last flight, Vyra marched into Crystal Beth's room as though she'd been there before . . . and owned the joint. She had the candle lit by the time I stepped inside, leaving the door open. I took the easy chair. Vyra grabbed the metal chair, crossed her legs again and went back to admiring her shoes. Crystal Beth dropped to her knees without making a sound, positioning herself between us to my right, leaving me a clear sight line to the door.

"Anytime you're ready," I said, to neither of them in particular.

"I met Crystal a couple of years ago," Vyra said, talking over the other woman's kneeling form like there was no doubt who I was going to listen to. "I was volunteering at a shelter. On the phone, mostly. Crystal was a . . . visitor. Not a client. When I found out what she was up to, I said I'd help out. And it just . . . grew on me, I guess. When she finally was ready to start this place, I put up some of the financing. It's a 5o1(c)(3) corporation, so my . . ."

She didn't say "husband," just let her voice trail away. I didn't fill the silence.

"It's tax-deductible," she finished lamely. "When Crystal started to have this . . . problem, she tried to figure out who could help. I told her I knew someone, but she was stubborn. Sure she could do it herself. Once she realized she couldn't, then she said she'd listen to me," Vyra finished smugly. "That's when I told her about you."

"You don't know me," I said. Flat, no room for argument, denying her credentials.

"I know enough," she responded, a pout in her voice. "I know you could do something if you wanted to. And I know you work for money. What could it hurt to listen?"

"I don't like that kind of game—closing my eyes and guessing if it's gonna hurt."

"Why do you have to be so hostile?" Vyra asked. "Crystal's my friend. Friends exchange . . . information, don't they? If she asked me did I know a good mechanic, or a compassionate gynecologist, or whatever, why wouldn't I tell her?"

"I don't know why you'd do anything," I said, staying inside myself. The danger-jolts crackling around my nerve endings weren't from physical fear. By then, my crew was in place. Somewhere outside, not far away. The store-bought locks these women had on their doors wouldn't keep the Prof out. And nothing they had behind those doors would stop Max, if it came to that. But they had plans, Crystal Beth and Vyra. And I don't like being in people's plans.

"Burke, *please*. Come on," Vyra said. "It's a . . . job, right? You do jobs."

"You're guessing," I told her.

"You must do *something*, right? I'm not asking you what that is, okay? But anyone can listen, can't they? You can never get hurt just listening."

I ignored that. If she'd been raised like I was, she wouldn't talk so stupid.

"If he doesn't want to . . ." Crystal Beth said, like I wasn't in the room.

I turned to her. "Don't lie," I said.

She refused to take offense at what I said. Played it for a green light instead, said: "It started when—"

"Tell him about the—" Vyra interrupted.

"That's enough," I cut her off. "This isn't a movie. You're not the director. And I can't listen in stereo anyway."

Vyra snorted through her tiny custom-built nose, tried to fold her arms over her huge chest, gave it up in frustration. Sat quiet for a long few seconds. Then Crystal Beth started again:

"Marla—that's her name—she's one of those girls everybody says doesn't know any better, do you understand? She got married when she was barely seventeen. It was better than where she was, she thought. That happens a lot—we see it all the time. He's a lot older than she is. She said it wasn't all that bad at first. Oh, he hit her and everything, but she was used to that. Her father had . . . been that way, so it wasn't a . . . surprise, I guess."

She watched my face for a few seconds, waiting for a reaction—didn't get one, so she went back to her story.

"No matter what Marla did, it didn't make any difference. He never stopped. It took her a while, but she finally figured it out. He liked to do it. As simple as that."

I said nothing, waiting.

"I know what you're thinking," she said, accusingly. "Why didn't she just leave, right?"

"Or stab him in his sleep," I offered. "Or poison his food, or—"

"You could never understand," she cut in. "How could you—?"

"—or hire a hit man," I went on like she hadn't spoken.

That stopped her. The room went silent. "She was afraid," Vyra finally said in a pious tone. "Do you know what it means to be afraid? Really afraid?"

"Better than you ever will, you stupid, spoiled bitch," I told her, a trigger-pull away from being done with them all. "Save it for the proposal-writing, okay? You want to tell me a story, tell it. You want to give lectures, find someone who wants to get in your pants bad enough to pretend like they're interested."

Vyra jumped to her feet, stepped toward me, hand raised like she was going to slap with it. The move was so natural I knew she'd done it before.

"Don't even think about it," I told her. "I'm not your husband."

"You . . ." She couldn't find the rest of the words. Crystal Beth put her arm around her waist, push-pulled her back to the chair, saying something so softly I couldn't hear it.

"Let's be calm," Crystal Beth said like she was proposing an activity we might all enjoy. "Maybe we're just all . . . combustible. A bad combination. Would you like it better if we talked alone, just the two of us?" she asked me.

"It doesn't matter," I said. "If you two trusted each other, you wouldn't both be here anyway."

Neither of them said anything to that, but Vyra's face flamed under her makeup.

"If this is a story, you're a long way from the end," I told them. "It's getting late, and I got work to do."

"What work is that?" Vyra sneered.

"Work I get paid for," I said. "You wouldn't understand."

"Bastard," she said. No more emotion there, just stating a fact.

Crystal Beth dropped to her knees between us, stretched out her hands. Vyra took one. I didn't. She put that empty hand on my knee like an acupuncture anchor, maintaining the current. She stayed there like that for a long moment, eyes closed. At least she wasn't chanting.

"She was afraid," Crystal Beth said quietly. "Or she was used to it. Or she didn't know any way out. It doesn't matter. Because once she got pregnant, everything changed."

"He stopped belting her around?" I asked sarcastically.

"Yes, he did," Crystal Beth said, surprising me. "He stopped punching her and kicking her, anyway. He just found . . . other things to do to her."

"You trying to tell me he wanted the baby?"

"Oh yes," Crystal Beth said. "He wanted the baby very badly. That's when she found out the . . . rest about him."

"Which was?"

"He wanted the baby for the race," she said. "The white race. Do you know what I mean?"

"Sure. Pure stock, right? What was he? One of those halfass Nazi geeks?"

"He's an Aryan," Crystal Beth said. "In his mind, a true Aryan."

"And you're one of the mud people, right?" I asked her. "And she's a Jew," I said, nodding at Vyra, maybe getting the connect between them for the first time.

"Yes. But he doesn't know us. We're not in it that way."

"Isn't there some shortcut on this road?" I asked her. I didn't have much more patience. If these women thought all White Night followers were the same, they were too dumb to keep walking where they'd stepped.

"We're being calm," Crystal Beth reminded me. "If you listen too fast, you miss some of the words. He kept . . . hurting her. Burning her with cigarettes, making her . . . do things. Degrading her in front of other people. Before she got pregnant, he told her if she ever tried to leave him he'd kill her. Not shoot her, torture her to death. He liked to talk about that. He even had films of it. Torture tapes. Videos. I guess they were acting, I never saw one. But Marla said they looked so real, she couldn't tell. He made her watch them. She said it didn't change until he told her he was going to have his son watch them too. So he'd be ready."

"What changed?" I asked her.

"That's when Marla knew she was going to leave. She started to feel it when she was deep in pregnancy. Maybe her seventh month, she doesn't know for sure. She told me she knew they—

her husband and his friends—would take her baby. The baby would be one of them. She couldn't bear the thought of her son torturing one of those women like they were in those videos. She couldn't bear to kill the baby either. . . . That's what killing herself would mean. She knew she couldn't wait until she went into the hospital—she'd be lost then. So she ran away. And she found us."

"How did she know she was going to have a son?" I asked her. "This happened before she gave birth, you said."

"Sonogram," Vyra put in. "Everybody does them now."

"We have lawyers who advise us," Crystal Beth said. "They told us Marla would get custody, no contest, but he'd get visitation. Some kind of visitation. Probably even unsupervised, sooner or later. That would be enough. He could just take the child and disappear into the underground. She'd never see him again. One of the other women—'breeders,' he called them—would raise the baby. Raise him to be them."

"So she's gonna disappear?"

"No. She doesn't have the resources. It will take time before she learns enough skills to support herself and the baby. And if she took Welfare, it would be easy enough to track her. We came up with a better way. When she left, she took a lot of his stuff. He kept . . . records of what he did. Him and his friends. There's enough there to put him away for a long time. It's all set up. She had him served with papers. Legal papers. At the place where he works. He has to come to court. She's suing him for a divorce. And child support."

"How's that going to—?"

"When he shows up, he's going to be arrested. And they're going to hold him without bail. A . . . what do they call it?"

"Remand," I supplied.

"Yes, that's right! Remand. They set it up perfectly. She called him a couple of times when she was on the run. They have it on tape, him saying what he was going to do to her. To scare her, he reminded her of some other stuff he did. To other people. Him and his friends. They have that evidence too."

"How do you know you're not being hosed?" I asked her.

"What's 'hosed'?" Crystal Beth asked.

"Tricked. Scammed. Hornswoggled. Whatever you want to call it. To really set this guy up, you'd need more than a friendly cop, you'd need a DA."

"We have that," Crystal Beth said. "Guaranteed."

"So who's the Man?" I asked her.

"Not a man," she said with a gentle smile. "A woman. Her name is Wolfe."

ood thing I hadn't taken Crystal Beth's hand. A lifetime of practice could keep my face flat, but she would have felt my pulse jump at the name. Wolfe. Former boss of City-Wide Special Victims, a sex-crimes prosecutor so intense one newspaper said she drank blood for breakfast. She spent years on the front lines slugging it out with every verminous predator they threw at her— rapists, child molesters, kidnap gangs, it didn't matter. She was a warrior woman, at her loveliest doing her work, a sleek mongoose who could clean out a nest of cobras without breaking a sweat. But a politically greasy DA took her down, sacrificed her to the only god humans like him worship.

When Wolfe had been on the job, we'd bumped paths a few times. She wouldn't go an inch over the line, but she'd tightrope it pretty good if it meant dropping a freak. When they fired her, she went outlaw. At least that's what the whisper-stream that runs under the city said. She ramrods a private intelligence cell. Does it for the money, the way it's told. But Crystal Beth was doing some telling of her own. And it looked like Wolfe couldn't stay away from the war.

Wolfe could get it done, I knew. There were still some prosecutors who stayed true to what she'd stood for. Not in City-Wide— that whole crowd had all rolled over like the knee-pad wearers they were. But there were other bureaus, other operations. And some of them would still work with Wolfe. They couldn't bring her into the courtroom, but they could bring her information there. And use it.

She knew cops too. Good, tough old-school cops, most of them members of the KMA—"I already got enough time in to retire, Lieutenant, so Kiss My Ass"—Club and all too clean to be intimidated out of meeting with her. Cops she'd worked cases with for years before they took her off the beat. Wolfe had handled mostly sex crimes, but some of the freaks touched other nerves too: Homicide. Narcotics. Anything gang-related. So she knew cops from all over the city, in every bureau.

Yeah, Wolfe could get it done.

I took a shallow breath, thinking that all through in less time than it took to exhale fully. "Okay," I said to Crystal Beth, "you've got him, right? He comes in, he goes down. What's the problem?"

"There's another man," she said. "Like I told you. The falconer. And he's after me too."

A ll I could see of Vyra's face was a pale oval in the dim light. Her chest was easier to focus on—whiter because of the blouse she wore, bigger because of what filled it. But she was quiet, holding Crystal Beth's hand, waiting.

I waited too.

"I know this is complicated," Crystal Beth finally said. "But I don't know a simpler way to tell it."

"This other man?" I prompted. "He's with Marla's husband? One of the Nazi crew?"

"The opposite," she said, a tremor in her voice telling me she wasn't as sure of that as she tried to sound. "He's a hunter."

"After Marla's husband . . . ?"

"Lothar, that's his name. Well, not truly, I guess. His real name is Larry, but he changed it. He said Larry sounded Jewish. Anyway, he's not really after Lothar either. He's . . . Oh, I'm not *sure*, okay? I just don't know."

"You know he's after you, though?"

"Yes! That didn't take any guesswork. He told me—"

"Who told you?" I interrupted her.

"The man. Mr. Pryce. Pryce with a "y," not an "i"—that's the name he said to call him."

"Pryce is the one after you?"

"Yes!" she snapped impatiently. "Just let me . . ." She stopped herself, pulled a deep centering breath through her nose. Her hand on my knee went limp. Then she spoke slowly, being clear with herself more than with me. "This Pryce said he knew about the plan. To bring Lothar into court. He said we couldn't do it. We could either call it off, or he could stop us, whatever we wanted. 'It's your choice,' is what he said. But there isn't a choice."

"There's always a choice," Vyra piped up.

"Save it for something you know," I told her. "This isn't about shoes."

I felt the jolt pass from her all the way through Crystal Beth to me, but she stayed quiet.

"Vyra's in this too," Crystal Beth said, her tone both defending and defensive. "If we go ahead with the plan, he's going to hurt her too."

"How'd he say he was going to do that?"

"With . . . information," Crystal Beth said. "That's what he has, information. Secret information. When I first heard his voice, it was on the phone. On a special line I keep. Unlisted, in someone else's name. It doesn't connect to me in any way. We use it for . . . business. He knew my voice. Said he had listened to it on tape enough times to recognize me easily."

"So he got a phone number. Pulled a wiretap. That don't make him James Bond."

"He has it *all*, Burke. Everything. He knows things about my own father that I never knew. About what happened with my mother. Even Starr's name. He knows how we run our operation, who owns this place. And some things I . . . did. A long time ago. He could close us up, make everything disappear."

"He's just trying to spook you. What would he get out of—"

"It's not just me," Crystal Beth whispered urgently. "He could put Lorraine in prison. And he could hurt Vyra too."

"How?"

"With my husband," Vyra said, her voice dead.

"I thought he didn't care about . . ." I said. Vyra had told me plenty of times that her husband thought it was fun that she slept around. All he wanted to do was listen to the details, take topless photos of her, lick her shoes and pay the bills.

"He'd care about this," Vyra said in the same tone.

I waited, but she wasn't coming off anything more.

"Okay, this Pryce guy could take it all down. Fine. What does he care?"

"Care?"

"About this Lothar geek. Why does he want to protect him so bad?"

"We don't know," Crystal Beth said, flat-voiced. "That's the job. The one Vyra said you could do."

I was in a room with two women. Within the last few days, one had held my hand in the street, sat on my lap and told me secrets. The other had paraded around in her new shoes and sucked my cock. Now they were together, and they wanted me to do something.

It wasn't easy, telling them that I had to get paid for what they wanted.

So I stalled.

"I don't know if I could do it or not," I told them. "I'm not even sure something can be done. There's no schematic for a thing like this."

"Will you at least talk to him?" Vyra asked.

"This guy, he's an information-freak, right? Got stuff on both of you, on other people. That's his weapon. Me, I'd be going in there without one. And maybe, he gets a look at me, I go on his list."

"You scared of him?" It was Vyra talking, but I'd heard that kind of thing from women all my life. And from girls before them. I have the scars to prove it—ones you don't need a Ph.D. to see.

"Damn right," I said. "Add it up. You got some Nazi loon who wants his kid to help seed the Master Race. And you got somebody else running interference for him. Somebody who knows a lot he shouldn't know. And you want me to 'talk' to him. How about spelling that one out?"

"You know what we want," Vyra said.

"No you don't," Crystal Beth corrected her, standing up and bending toward me. "Remember what you did for Harriet? Well, maybe something like that. But not . . .".

There it was. "I got paid for Harriet," I reminded her. "And there wasn't any major risk in it. At least, not like this."

"I have money," Vyra said.

Crystal Beth rolled herself a cigarette. When she got it burning, she held it out to Vyra . . . who took one short drag and handed it back. Now they were waiting.

"How do I find this Pryce?" I asked. Thinking, if he's as good as they were saying, he probably already knew about me.

"I have to call this number," Crystal Beth said. "Tonight. Before midnight. Then he'll call back. I'll tell him then. And I'll call you."

She left Vyra where she was, took me down the stairs to the back door. Stood on her toes, her lips next to my ear. "I'll tell you everything soon," she promised, holding on to the front of my belt with two fingers, keeping me close so I'd listen.

I stepped into the biting-cold night, eyes on the clear sky. And walked away slowly, the weight of treachery yoking my shoulders.

It was almost nine when Clarence's Rover swooped down, plucking me off the corner. I climbed into the front. The Prof's hand dropped onto my shoulder.

"You was a long time in there, Schoolboy. You get enough of a look to pull Herk off the hook?"

"It was never about Herk," I told him. "He was never the game. The poor bastard just stumbled in."

"Figures," the little man said acidly. "So we're out?"

"I'm not," I told him.

And then I told him the rest.

"**Y**ou can never shed a street-brand, honey," Michelle said. Sitting in my booth at Mama's—next to the Prof, facing me and Clarence. She was perfectly coiffed, wearing a red satin jumpsuit with a wide black belt, her lovely face slathered in full war-paint, getting ready to work. I'd asked her once why she dressed up just to work the phones. "It's all feeling, baby. If you *feel* it, you can *be* it."

Michelle does tele-sex. She's the best at it. If you could run fiber-optic cable under a glacier, her honey-silk voice would melt it. And she's the finest natural hustler I've ever known.

Michelle is my sister. No biology there, something closer to the root. We had the same father and the same bond: the State and our hate. She'd been born a toy. By the time she knew the medical term for what she was—a transsexual—her freakish family had found a dozen ways to use her. So she ran. Headlong, like a man jumping off the top of a blazing oil rig into the black ocean water below, knowing whatever was down there couldn't be worse.

She'd known she was a woman trapped in a man's body even before puberty tortured her from both sides of that twisted line. In the bent-sex underground where Michelle survived, the sadistic trick nature played on her raised the price of the tricks she turned. She climbed into the front seat of cars and dropped to the floor, each time wondering if the driver would be that life-taking psychopath all hookers know is out there somewhere. *Always* out there, his pounding blood seeking another's.

Michelle stole whatever she could, and lived the same way. She kept trying do-it-yourself to make things right. Almost destroyed her body with back-alley implants and black-market hormones. Always saying she was going to get it done—be herself. Be*come* herself. "Going to Denmark, honey. Real soon," she used to tell me every time our paths crossed.

I knew Michelle loved me. She'd proved it too many times to doubt—not with conversation, with the way you prove things in the street. But we were never really family until the night I pulled a little kid away from a pimp in Times Square. That wasn't the job

I was hired for, but I couldn't just leave the kid there—I owed Hate that much. I was going to get him to a shelter or something, but Michelle took him for herself, right then and there. She made me bring him to the Mole's junkyard. Her baby. Terry, she named him. And she and the Mole raised him, the two of them. They were still doing it.

It had been a loose network before. Steel mesh ever since. Michelle always told people the AIDS plague drove her off the streets, but that was a lie. It was Terry. Her boy.

It was Terry who finally took her over the line too. Not to Denmark, to Colorado. But she got it done. A citizen might call her a post-op transsexual. To me, she was as much woman as there could be on this earth. My sister. Terry's mother.

What we all wondered was . . . would she ever be the Mole's wife?

"You think that's what they're playing for?" I asked her. "They want somebody done?"

"What else could it be?" she snapped back at me, angry and impatient with my slowness. "Those two bitches have a problem, right? Some man. Some men. Whatever. They just want it to go away. I know how that feels."

"You scan it different than Schoolboy does?" the Prof asked. To him Michelle was a kid—that's the way he saw everyone—but he had an awesome respect for her criminal mind. More than he had for mine, that's for sure—it wouldn't take much for him to toss out any analysis I tried to offer.

"This girl—Crystal Beth, what a name, puh-leeze—she went to that little skeeve Porkpie first, didn't she?" Michelle answered him. "Nobody'd hire Porkpie to middle up a scam. You know how he profiles, like he can get heavy work done. He's selling muscle, not brains . . . like he's got any of either."

"She couldn't have known that guy was going to go down," I told Michelle. "Best she could have hoped for was Porkpie would get him fucked up, scare him off. She wasn't buying a hit, not for five grand."

"Unless Porkpie was lying," she put in tartly. "Remember the first rule, honey—deviates never deviate."

"He wasn't lying," I said. "Max was there with me when I talked to him."

Michelle nodded, dropping the argument. Nobody lied when Max had them in his hands.

"So how about she knows another way?" Michelle proposed.

"Knows what?" I asked her.

"The street-brand, baby. You've had the hit-man tag on you ever since . . ."

She didn't finish the sentence. Didn't have to. We'd all been there when it started. Except Clarence. And he was there when it got added to. Once it was a mosaic, a landscape dotted with truth if you knew where to look. Now it was a miasma, a junkyard so full of discards you couldn't find the truth with a microscope.

But the cops had tried. More than once. In our world, homicide happens . . . so the police are always around. But they never press all that hard. You listen to the PR guys at One Police Plaza, you'd believe the Man takes it just as seriously when someone from our world goes down as they would a citizen.

Sure.

I picked up the hit-man label a long time ago. When some Sicilians got into a range war. One of the dons hired a guy I'd come up with. An ice-man so laser-locked to his work that predators cringed in the shadows every time the whisper-stream passed the word that he was coming.

A man who stood alone, as emotionless as the death he dealt. "Nobody knows where he's going," the Prof said once, "but everybody knows where he's been."

A man everyone feared. In our world, that passed for respect.

A man I wanted to be, once.

The don double-crossed the ice-man, and the killer did what he was. The Sicilians starting dropping—some alone, some in bunches. Finally, the don came to me. He said he wanted me to talk the killer into a truce. Call it off, go back to the way things had been.

But if I'd gone to him with a message from the don, the killer would have taken me out too.

The don thought he had me in a box, but it was only a bottleneck . . . still a narrow bit of exit road left. I took it. And the don's life paid the tolls.

But it was too late then. The wheels had come off.

The perfect killer was gone now. He went out with a sheaf of dynamite sticks wrapped in duct tape held high in his cold hand, standing like a homicidal Statue of Liberty just before the blast took him away. He took a whole mess of citizens with him for company. And left a note warning the cops not to follow him into whatever lesser Hell awaited.

I have that note. It was his last gift to me, a Get Out of Jail Free card, if I played it right. But the only place to play it was from Death Row.

So he's gone now. And I talk to him sometimes. In my mind. The only place any of us ever say his name.

Wesley.

I knew what Michelle meant. The whisper-stream flows everywhere, a toxic blend of rumor, legend and lies—but it always carries a current of truth too. It said there were only two pro snipers working the city—Wesley and El Cañonero. But El Cañonero only worked for the Independentistas, a man with a cause, a soldier under the flag of Puerto Rican liberation. Wesley worked for whoever paid him. A long time ago, I faced some men in a parking lot. One of them was a *karateka* called Mortay, a death-match fighter who wanted Max. And threatened his baby daughter to bring the Mongolian into the ring. One of the men died in that parking lot, picked off from the nearby rooftop. The whisper-stream said it was Wesley, working for me. It wasn't. It was El Cañonero, but that's what the whisper-stream does with the truth.

Crystal Beth might have tapped into it, thought I was the man for the job. Maybe it was me she'd been looking for all along.

"But Herk's the wild card," I protested. "He doesn't run with us."

"He did," the Prof reminded me.

"That was Inside," I told him. "No way that hippie chick has those kind of wires."

"The other bitch, she knows your business?" the Prof asked.

I didn't take offense. We don't talk to outsiders, and I'd had all the lessons, but tight pussy makes loose lips sometimes, and the Prof was within his rights to ask.

"Nothing," I said. "Zero. I'm a slumming fuck for her, that's all. But who knows what kind of bullshit she's cooked up in her head."

"That's the place for it, all right," he agreed.

"What do *you* think, sweetie?" Michelle asked Clarence. That was her way, always. To build us up, all of us, spread the respect. If she hadn't asked, Clarence would never have volunteered an opinion.

"I do not know," he said carefully, uncomfortable on center stage. "But it seems to me, if this woman—the one who hired you, my brother—" he said aside to me, "if she somehow knew Hercules would be the one Porkpie would select for the job, she would still have to know it would end . . . as it did. And she could not know this. Nobody could know. It was not the plan. What if Hercules did not have his knife? Or if he was not so quick?"

The young West Indian slid out of the booth, stood on his feet, addressing us like a doctoral candidate at his orals, glad for the chance and nervous at the same time.

"If she was running a . . . If it is murder she wanted, why would she have been so satisfied when you did the work on that other man? Scaring him off, *that* is what she wanted, yes? I believe that is all she asked Porkpie for too."

"So it was an accident that she grabbed me at Rollo's?" I asked him.

"You do not go there enough," he replied, more confident now. "It is not our place. I think, maybe, she was just . . . looking. And when she told the other one—"

"Vyra," Michelle said. Like you'd say "maggot."

"Yes, Vyra. When she told her, then this Vyra, she said, maybe, 'I know that man.' And then, perhaps, it all came together."

"So, if Porkpie had passed the test, she would have brought him into it?"

"Ah, I do not know this girl, mahn. But she seems too clever for that. She must know the difference between a contractor and the hired help, yes?"

"Yeah, I think so too."

"That goes together like barbed wire and panty hose," Michelle said, venom dripping from her candy tongue. "Little sister don't think so."

"Little sister?" Clarence said, puzzled.

"Me, honey," Michelle cooed at him. "I'm your little sister, aren't I?"

"I . . . mean, if you—"

"You don't see me as your *big* sister, do you, baby?" Michelle asked him, sugar-voiced, but the Prof knew better. He shot Clarence a warning glance.

Too late. "Not a sister, no," Clarence said. "I mean, you know how I love you and respect you. But I always think of you as like my—"

"What?" Michelle asked, still sweet.

Oh Jesus . . . , I thought to myself, catching the Prof's eye.

"Like my auntie. A sister to my—"

If Clarence hadn't been honed to a lifetime of quickness, the flying bowl of fried rice would have cracked his skull.

It took us a good half-hour to get Michelle calmed down. That crazy, all-class broad would catch a bullet for Clarence as casually as she'd touch up her lipstick, but her self-image was baby sister—bossy baby sister, maybe, but not *anybody's* aunt. While the Prof crooned confection into her ear, I grabbed Clarence and poured some survival truth into his.

I don't know where he got them at that hour, but the armful of orchids—I warned him not even to *think* about some chump-change Reverend Moon roses—he came back with went a long way toward banking the fire.

Mama watched all this impassively. Treat *her* like she was younger than you and she'd show you where the "chop" in chop suey came from. And she thinks losing your temper is an Occidental thing anyway.

Hours to go yet. No point in leaving—the restaurant was the

only number Crystal Beth had. I told Mama I needed Max, then I went to the bank of pay phones and started to work.

"**A**llo?" A young woman's voice, distinctive French accent.

"Is Wolfe around?" I asked.

"Pretty late at night to be calling, chief." Pepper's voice, the accent gone. She'd recognized me, though. I didn't know she did voices, but I could see why Wolfe's crew could use that skill.

"Yeah, I know," I told her. "I didn't expect to catch her in. Can I leave word?"

"Sure."

"Just ask her to call me."

"Is this hot?"

"No. But it's not social either."

"Okeydokey." She laughed. And hung up.

Last time I saw Pepper she was in Grand Army Plaza dressed in a pair of baggy striped clown pants, teaching a whole pack of little kids some kind of gymnastics. And walking point for Wolfe to set up a meet. Wolfe told me once Pepper was some kind of actress, but I'd never paid much attention. I guess she was, though. A real good one.

As soon as I put down the phone, Max was at my shoulder. I hadn't heard him come up, but that's nothing new—they don't call him Max the Silent just because he doesn't speak. As soon as he finished his soup, we went down to the basement. Mama keeps a long table set out there. "For counting," she'd explained when I'd first asked her why.

I went through all of it. Slowly. Not because Max couldn't follow otherwise, but so I was sure I had it straight in my own mind. Max shook his head impatiently, interrupting my hand signals. He got up, went over to a black lacquer cabinet in a dark corner of the basement, opened a drawer and came back with some sheets of cream-colored origami paper. Then he gestured for me to start over.

Every time I came to a name, I'd spell the sound out with my lips. And Max would fold paper. By the time I was done with the first pass, Max had a table-full of distinctive little paper sculptures. He had me say each name again. And for each one he held up one of the sculptures . . . until we were on the same wavelength.

And then he gestured for me to start again.

HERCULES

ME

PORKPIE

CRYSTAL BETH

HARRIET

VYRA

WOLFE

PRYCE

Max looked at the neat row he had fashioned. Then looked at me and held up the Vyra sculpture, reached over, and touched my watch.

I held up three fingers on each hand. It was maybe about six when I knew Vyra was in the safehouse.

Max shook his head no hard, looked another question at me.

I didn't get it. Told him so.

He got up, went upstairs. He was back in a minute, with one of those cheapo calendars insurance agents send to everyone on the planet. He placed it carefully between us, held up the Vyra sculpture in one hand, probed his finger at this month's calendar page with the other.

"When's the last time I saw her before tonight?" I asked him, words and gestures together.

He nodded yes.

I showed him. Max switched the order, now placing Vyra first.

Then it was my turn to shake my head no. I made the sign of talking into a telephone, made the gesture for Mama so he'd know the call came in here, and picked up the Hercules sculpture. Then I touched another day on the calendar—one just before when I'd been with Vyra at the hotel. Herk had called the night before and left word about the meet.

Max's face went into repose. But his hands were busy, fingers flying now. He was creating more sculptures, duplicates of the ones he'd already made, as precise as a cookie-cutter. If I hadn't seen him do this before, when he made an entire origami chess set for his daughter, Flower, I would have been astounded. Even so, I had to shake my head in wonderment.

Max was like the rest of us. He had so many gifts. So many skills. He could have been anything. Should have been . . .

I felt his hand on mine, looked up and snapped out of wherever I'd been going. Max made the sign of a man being stabbed, showed me the sculpture he'd fashioned to represent the guy Herk had taken down. Then he made the sign of a frightened man— Harriet's stalker. Showed me that sculpture too. Then he laid out a new configuration of the players:

CRYSTAL BETH	VYRA	CRYSTAL BETH	WOLFE
PORKPIE	ME	ME	PRYCE
HERCULES	HERCULES	VYRA	
DEAD MAN	PORKPIE		
	CRYSTAL BETH		
	HARRIET		
	SCARED MAN		

I nodded that he was right, then held up three fingers, pointing at the stack of unused origami paper. Three more players. I went through it slowly, Max making the new pieces as I talked. I took them from him, placed them on the table so it looked like this:

CRYSTAL BETH	VYRA	CRYSTAL BETH	PRYCE
PORKPIE	ME	ME	LOTHAR
HERCULES	HERCULES	LORRAINE	
DEAD MAN	PORKPIE	VYRA	
	CRYSTAL BETH	MARLA	
	HARRIET	LOTHAR	
	SCARED MAN	WOLFE	

And then I started to see it.

Max took the sculptures for Vyra and Crystal Beth, moved them back and forth in his hands, eyebrows raised in question.

I told him I didn't know. Didn't know who came first, who started it, who was in charge.

He did the same with Lothar and Pryce. I gave him the same answer.

Finally he pulled the Pryce sculpture from the layout, placed it way off to the side. All by itself.

It was almost one the next morning when the phone rang.

"He called," Crystal Beth said as soon as she heard my voice.

"And . . . ?"

"And I told him there was someone I . . . wanted him to meet."

"That's all you told him?"

"No."

"What else?"

"Your name."

"He didn't ask any more questions?"

"No."

"Didn't ask who I was to you?"

"No."

"Didn't ask why you wanted me to meet him?"

"No. Nothing." Her voice was . . . something. Sad maybe, I couldn't tell.

"And he said . . . what?" I asked her.

"That it was okay. That he would do it. Tomorrow. At three-thirty." Then she named a midtown deli on the East Side.

"All right," I told her. "Let's do it. You know the Barnes and Noble bookstore on Astor Place?"

"Yes."

"I'll meet you there at two, okay? In the café."

"Vyra—"

"Isn't coming," I said.

I hung up on her silence.

I slept until almost ten the next morning. When I used the cellular to check with Mama, she told me Wolfe had called. There wasn't any point calling back—when Wolfe went outlaw, she'd adopted a series of phone cutouts, same way all of us did. Pepper would catch the calls. And you could catch Pepper, if you could make the connections and move fast enough. But Wolfe would never be in that net. I decided to let it ride for now.

And do some riding myself.

I slammed a new tape into the cassette player, letting the blues take me to the Chicago stop on that deep dark tributary reverse-flowing out of the Mississippi Delta, carrying players and poets in its lush stream. Junior Wells doing Little Walter's "Key to the Highway," paying homage, father to son. Mighty Joe Young's sub-dued, pain-seared version of "The Things I Used To Do." Luther Allison and Otis Rush and J.B. Hutto chasing both Sonny Boys. Howlin' Wolf and Muddy Waters. And the next wave. Dave Spector's "That's How Strong My Love Is" following the blood-spoor of Delbert McClinton as the Texas troubadour breached another border behind Lightnin' Hopkins. Paul Butterfield lurking out-side "Yonders Wall." Charlie Musselwhite barking out "Early in the Morning." Buddy Guy coaxing witchfire from a slide guitar. Hoochie-coochie through the back doors. Jailhouses and grave-yards. Part-time jobs and part-time women. Grown-up schoolgirls and black Cadillacs not every man could ride. All of them on Robert Johnson's don't-mind-dying hellhound trail.

When I'd had enough I switched to my girl. Judy Henske. Lit-tle Miss Magic, all six feet plus of her. Judy can bring it back from places the other torch singers couldn't go at all.

I don't share my music with citizens. They never get it. One time I was waiting in this joint for a guy who said he was a buyer to show up when I overheard some earnest dweeb talking about how "profound" the Beatles are . . . if you just *listen* to them. That's when I started wishing bars had metal detectors.

That poor chump would never get it—you can't get jellyroll from a white-bread bakery.

Just over the Brooklyn line, a guy in a red Jeep Cherokee cut me off. One of those deep-dish-overcooked fools who believed four-wheel drive would give you traction on ice. I tapped the brakes, let him slide by. He stuck a fist out the window, waving a kid's baseball bat, screaming something I couldn't hear before he sped away. I got a glimpse of his tags. Handicapped plates. I didn't have to guess what his was.

Herk's room was prison-clean. That's one of the things you do Inside. Scrub every surface. Slow. Taking time the way the State took yours. And making some little space more your own. Inside, nobody calls it their cell. "My house" is what you say. And keeping it clean means keeping more than just the roaches and the mice at bay.

"Thanks for the books, brother," he greeted me. "Sure helps."

"It won't be much longer," I promised him.

"Burke, I could do . . . something, right? I don't dig all this sitting around."

"You got to lay in the cut until we scope what's out there," I told him.

"Yeah, I know. But I been reading the papers. Every day. And listening to this here radio. They ain't got nothing on the . . . guy. I think I'm in the clear."

"You could be," I said. Thinking, if it wasn't for the connect to Crystal Beth, he probably was. "But let's play it this way for a bit longer, okay?"

"Your call," he agreed. "But . . . if I'm gonna do more time here, you think you could get me some more books?"

"More of the same?" I asked him.

"Yeah. I heard about a new one too. *Mercedes*, it's called. And *Jonah Hex*. Hell, *anything* by Joe Lansdale."

"He's a writer, right?" I said, into his rhythm.

"Oh yeah," Herk said fervently.

"**Y**ou can*not* overdress for a first meeting," Michelle informed me in her "don't-argue-with-me" voice. "It's so true what they say about first impressions."

"You want me to rent a tux?" I asked her.

"What I want is for you to be quiet long enough for me to coordinate. And tell that heinous hound of yours to stop following me around—this place isn't big enough for me to use an assistant."

I made the silent command for "Place" and Pansy trotted obediently into her corner just to the side of the door, arranging herself on the thick sheepskin rug I'd gotten her to take the chill off the floor in the winter. "Good *girl!*" I told her, reaching into the refrigerator and coming out with a handful of raw hamburger. I patted it into the shape of a baseball, held it up to get her attention, and tossed it underhand. Pansy snapped it out of the air like it was a dog biscuit.

"It's amazing she doesn't weigh five hundred pounds, the way you feed her," Michelle said over her shoulder, her face buried in the steel locker I use as a closet.

"She works it off," I said defensively. Truth is, Pansy's maybe thirty pounds heavier than she was at her peak. She's almost fifteen now, and I don't know how much longer she's going to be with me. Neapolitan mastiffs are long-lived. And I never thought I'd be here longer than her anyway. Things didn't work out like I thought. Some people died—friends and enemies both—but not me. Every time I think about Pansy going first, I can't stand it. She's been with me since she was born. I weaned her myself. She'd die for me. What I should do is put her on a strict diet, grind a few more months of life out of whatever allotment she has left. But she loves food so and I want her to have a . . .

"What *is* this junk?" Michelle snarled, her hands full of my clothes. "This is *so* not now. Where're the suits I bought you?"

Bought me? Michelle picked them out all right, but it was me that paid. Through the nose, if I remember right.

"In the other locker," I told her, not self-destructive enough to voice my thoughts.

Michelle rummaged around, finally hauled out a handful of black wool. "Oh, Burke, this is a genuine Hayakawa, for Susan's sake. Eighteen hundred dollars—and that was a *bargain*—and you have it stuffed in there like it was polyester."

"Sorry," I said lamely.

"Never mind. We'll steam it in the shower and I'll press it—that's why you buy the best goods, they always come back."

"Right."

Michelle found a heavy silk cream-colored shirt and a black silk tie that flashed blue when the light caught it. "The alligator boots," she pronounced. "That will tie it together perfectly. I wish you had time to get a haircut."

"I just *got* a haircut," I reminded her.

"Yes, and it shows. What did you pay for that masterpiece, anyway?"

"Six bucks," I told her.

"Including tip?"

"Hey, it's good enough."

"I suppose," she said reluctantly. "Now, where did you put your good watch?"

I showed her.

"At least we can do something about your nails. I brought my kit."

"Michelle . . ."

"Thank Susan you don't chew them," she said, ignoring my tone.

It was almost one in the afternoon by the time she was done. "Now give us a spin," she said.

"I'm not—"

"Oh, never mind," she snapped, taking a quick stroll around me. "This is cashmere," she said lovingly, patting the sleeve of the black overcoat. "It *reeks* class. Camel's hair is so totally yesterday, but *black* . . . that has to carry itself. See how it's so completely unstructured. Without the belt, it just lies there. But when you pull it tight . . ."

"Yeah, it's fucking lovely," I said, thinking about how much damn money it cost and here I was wearing it for the first time.

"You're not getting on the subway like this, are you?"

"I'm gonna drive to Mama's. Clarence'll pick me up there. I'll drop you anywhere you want."

"Perfect."

"Uh, Michelle . . ."

"What, baby?"

"Thanks."

She gave me a kiss. Then she whipped out a towelette and wiped off the lipstick.

Crystal Beth was already seated when I got to the bookstore. I spotted her as I went through the turnstile. The uniformed guy standing there nodded respectfully, crossing me off his potential-booster list. Maybe I should wear cashmere more often.

Places I go most of the time, maybe I should just paint a fucking bull's-eye on my back too.

"You look . . . amazing," she said as I slipped the coat off my shoulders to sit down.

"You too," I replied.

It was true. She was wearing a pale-blue jersey turtleneck top over an ankle-length black skirt, just the tips of oxblood boots peeking out beneath. Her hair was in pigtails, blue ribbons the same color as her top tied to each end. Dark-red lipstick. The tattoo glistened on the side of her face.

"Thank you . . . for doing this," she said quietly.

"We have a deal."

"I know. But still . . ."

A waitress came over. Crystal Beth ordered some complicated espresso junk; I had hot chocolate. With whipped cream.

"You like sweets?" she asked me.

"Some sweets."

"Burke . . ."

"What?"

"I'm scared."

"Of this guy Pryce?"

"Yes. Not just him. The whole thing."

There was nothing to say to that. It could mean anything. And it wasn't the time for exploring—I needed her mind to be right for the meet. I sipped the hot chocolate, idly watching the customers come and go. Nobody seemed in a hurry. Lots of posing going on at the tables. See and Be Seen. Whoever came up with the idea of a café inside a bookstore was an entrepreneurial genius—you can't go wrong opening a singles bar in a city where so many people do their time in solitary.

Whoever picked their playlist was righteous too. I couldn't spot the speakers, but the whole joint was filled with music. No elevator stuff either: Son Seals wailing "Going Back Home," Marcia Ball's beautiful "Another Man's Woman," Bazza's hardcore "Ghost," Little Charlie and the Nightcats doing "Rain". . . even Fats Domino's version of "One Night With You"—the one that puts Elvis on the trailer every time I hear it. I've heard that music everywhere from juke joints to late-night FM, but never expected it to wash over a place like this. If my head was different, I would have taken it for an omen. Being me, I just let myself get lost in the blues for a bit, going away to be with myself. When they switched to some softer stuff, I came back to where I was . . . and what I was there for.

"How'd you get here?" I finally asked her.

"I walked. It isn't that far, really. I'm used to walking. And the weather has been—"

"I've got a car waiting," I told her. "You ready?"

"I . . . guess so."

"No, you're not," I said, leaning forward, dropping my voice. "You're not ready at all. Whoever this Pryce is, he's a bad guy, understand?"

"Yes," she replied, almond eyes calm.

"Me too. Not you. Understand that?"

"I . . . think so."

"You hired me to do something, right?"

"Yes."

"Because I can get it done. And you can't, right?"

"Yes," she said, annoyed now, and showing it.

"So you're gonna do it the way I say, right?"

"All *right*."

"Let me tell you something about players," I said. "They think everybody else is playing. A pro would, anyway. My name wasn't in this. You brought it in. I gave you the okay to do that, I'm not complaining. But if this doesn't work out, if I walk away, this guy Pryce, he's not gonna buy that. For him, I'm *still* in it, no matter what, understand?"

"That you're at risk?"

"Yeah. That I'm at risk. So what I get to do is minimize that risk. And that means you do what I tell you."

She swallowed that a lot harder than she had the espresso, but she seemed to keep it down. She went quiet then. I went back to watching "The Dating Game."

"What does it mean?" she asked sullenly. "Do what you say?"

"I don't know this guy. I don't know if he's alone, if he's got a crew, if he's working free-lance, if he's with the government . . . nothing. But he has my name. And if he's connected, he'll have stuff to go with that, I don't know how much. He's gonna know, for me to be in it, it's either money or blood. Depending on how it goes down, maybe it's better if he thinks it's personal instead."

"Personal?"

"That I'm your man."

"Oh."

"You can do that, right? Maybe you can sit on my lap when we talk."

Her face burned. One corner of her wide mouth twitched. "You think—?"

"Me, I don't think anything. Just guesses. You talked it over with your pal Vyra. She told you sex wouldn't make it happen—I only work for money. But you thought maybe you'd prove her wrong. . . ."

"So I'm a whore?" she said quietly, tendrils of rage webbing her voice.

"I wouldn't know that," I said calmly. "Only you know."

"Didn't you ever make a split-second decision? Just to . . . trust someone?"

"I'm going to tell you the truth," I told her. "You know those silent whistles, the ones only dogs can hear? People got them too. Certain people. You hear it, you know it."

"You heard that from me? That you could trust me?"

"Mine doesn't work like that," I told her. "It works the opposite. Like a burglar alarm. I know when someone's trying to break in."

"And you think I was?"

"Yeah. The only thing I don't know is what you wanted—to look around, or to take something."

The back seat of Clarence's beloved Rover is small, just a pair of black leather buckets separated by a center armrest. He pulled smoothly away from the downtown curb, heading for First Avenue.

Crystal Beth reached over and took my hand. I looked at her.

"Just practicing," she said.

I pulled my hand away, grasped her wrist, moved it around. Showed her the difference between connection and control. She didn't resist. "Practice *that*," I told her.

Clarence let us off four blocks from the meet—three streets and one avenue. The afternoon sun was a sociopath's smile, brilliant without warmth. I put Crystal Beth's right hand on my left forearm, stuffed my left hand into my pocket and started to walk.

"I've never—"

"Don't talk," I told her. "Don't say anything. If he asks you anything, just look over at me, understand?"

"Yes, master."

I stopped walking suddenly. She lurched a step ahead, stopped and turned to face me. "This isn't about politics," I told her, letting her hear the tension in my voice. "You hired a guide. Like you're on a jungle safari, okay? I know the trails. You don't, and you could get lost. I know the animals. You don't, and you could get hurt. You don't want to listen to me, you don't want to do what I say, you can have your deposit back, lady. Just go on in there and tell the man I changed my mind."

"I'm sorry," she said, stepping close to me, putting her hand back on my forearm.

I searched her face for more sarcasm. Couldn't find any. And I couldn't read her almond eyes.

That's him," she whispered as soon as we walked in the door. He was seated at a café-style table, alone. The table was alone too, standing isolated between two rows of booths against the windows, an island in empty space. I'd been in the joint before. And the Prof had visited yesterday too. No way that table was part of the usual decor—midtown space is way too expensive to set up a restaurant like that. Either he was connected deep or he paid heavy.

Not good news.

Four chairs at the little round table. He was occupying one, a colorless human in a G-man suit. A khaki raincoat with a dark brown zip-in liner was draped over one of the chairs.

We walked over. I took Crystal Beth's coat off her shoulders, tossed it on top of his. Held out a chair for her. I took my own coat off, carefully draped it over Crystal Beth's and sat down.

His face was bony and angular, but the flesh around his eyes was pouchy, dark half-moons under each one. His mouth was so thin you had to look twice to see it. Indoor skin. Or a night worker's.

"You have something for me?" he said to Crystal Beth, somewhere between a question and a command.

"That's why I'm here," I told him.

He shifted his head a few micrometers. The pupils of his eyes were a muddy brown, running at the edges like imperfect yolks. "Mr. Burke," he said.

"And you are . . . ?"

"Mr. Pryce."

Nobody's hands moved.

"She," I said, nodding my head in Crystal Beth's direction without dropping my eyes, "says you have a problem with something she wants to do."

"Something she can't do," Pryce said, nothing in his voice.

"Because . . . ?"

"We've been through this," he said. "If you're here for muscle, you're wasting your time."

"Why would you think that?" I asked him. "I'm not muscle. That's not what I do. There's a problem. I thought maybe I could . . . add some perspective."

"Yes?"

"She has a client who needs to do something about your . . . client?"

"Not my client," he said, voice still empty.

"But someone you need to protect?"

"Not that either."

"I'm not following you," I said.

"Do you know why I picked this place?" he asked.

"It wasn't for the service," I said. Telling him I'd noticed that the waiter was giving the little table a wide berth.

"No. It was for the view. I don't know your relationship to this . . . situation. You talked about a problem. I understand that I'm that problem to . . . her," he said, nodding at Crystal Beth the same way I'd done. "And I wanted to be sure you weren't hired to solve that problem."

"I wasn't hired," I told him. "She's in it, I'm in it."

"If you say so," he said indifferently. "But the problem could still get solved the same way."

"Which is?"

He drummed his fingers on the tabletop. I noticed the fingers were all flesh-webbed—deep, right up to the first set of knuckles. A muscle twitched under his right eye. "Do you want me to talk in front of her?" he asked.

I could feel the heat from Crystal Beth next to me, but she didn't move. "Sure," I said, noncommittal.

He mimed opening a notebook, read from its imaginary pages. "Baby Boy Burke," he said softly. "That's what the birth certificate reads. Father unknown. Mother was sixteen at the time of your birth. Or so she told the hospital. A working prostitute . . ." He paused, but I didn't react. Calling my mother a whore was nothing to me. I'd never met her.

"Baby Boy Burke was left in the hospital. Mother walked out. Presumed missing . . .

"Child was institutionally raised. Four foster homes. Removed from the third one following an investigation into . . . does it matter?"

"Not to me," I said. Meaning: not anymore.

"Chronic runaway. Three placements. Same pattern. Returned to foster care. The last foster home was closed when it burned to the ground. Arson. Perpetrator never apprehended."

Again he looked up. Again he saw me looking back.

"First conviction for gang-fighting," he continued. "Age thirteen. Last placement as a youthful offender was for attempted murder with a handgun. Subsequent adult prison sentences for armed robbery, hijacking, and assault with intent. No current parole holds."

I made the face of a man desperately trying to look mildly interested. Anyone with access to the computers could get everything he'd spit out so far.

"Employed as a mercenary by a rebel faction inside the Federal Republic of Nigeria between 1968 and 1969," he said, raising his eyebrows.

"It wasn't a rebel faction," I told him. "It was a country. Its name was Biafra. And I was a relief worker, not a mercenary."

"Yes. With the Red Cross, no doubt," he said, lifting an eyebrow just a fraction.

I didn't say anything. The man knew his business. That tribalistic insanity in Africa was the first time in history a Red Cross plane had ever been shot right out of the skies. Up to then, the Red Cross symbol had been a guarantee of safe passage, universally respected. That's all changed now. . . . Ask anyone in Bosnia.

"Evacuated right near the end," Pryce continued, "whereabouts unknown for several months. Since then, worked variously as a salesman of various products. No known affiliation with organized crime."

He was wandering off the track now, mixing rumors with truth. Big deal.

"Listed as suspect in several apparently unrelated homicides over a period of a dozen years. Seven arrests, on a variety of charges, during that period. No convictions."

I watched him roam through his invisible notebook, reading yesterday's headlines. He wasn't close.

"Also known as Arnold Haines. And Juan Rodriguez."

Ah, *that* was bad. The Arnold Haines ID was a throwaway, good enough for renting cars and buying airline tickets. It was the name I used on the visiting lists at prisons where I still had contacts too. But Juan Rodriguez *was* me. My driver's license, Social Security, everything. Juan was an employee of a junkyard in the South Bronx. Only I really owned the place. The manager wrote me a regular paycheck, did all the withholding and everything. I cashed it and kicked back a piece, but it squared me with IRS. It's not illegal to use another identity, so long as there's no intent to defraud.

My whole life was an intent to defraud. And now a carefully

constructed piece of it was shot to hell. I kept my face bland, waiting for the rest.

"Known associates include . . ." He looked up at me, held my eyes. And said Wesley's name out loud.

"Go fix your makeup," I told Crystal Beth out of the side of my mouth.

As she started to stand up, Pryce made a "sit-down" gesture with his hand. She ignored him.

He pushed his chair back a few inches, looked around the restaurant. "I don't like that," he said. The muscle under his right eye jumped again, harder than before. When he interlocked his fingers, the webbing closed, forming a solid mass of pale flesh.

"You think Wesley's dead?" I asked him, a threat so subtle only a guy who really knew the score would get it.

"Accounts vary," he said evenly, not telling me if he'd missed it or if it didn't faze him.

"She's not your problem," I told him, moving my head in Crystal Beth's direction. "Me neither. I got no little notebook on *you*. When she comes back, we walk out of here. Out of your life, okay? Find another way."

"There *is* no other way," he said, putting his elbows on the table.

But not his cards.

"This guy, Lothar. The one you don't want busted. He's not yours, right?"

"That's right."

"And the people he's with, you're not with them?"

"No, Mr. Burke. I *want* them."

"But when you get them, old Lothar walks away, right?" I said, getting it. Finally.

"That's the deal," he said. Flat-out, no more playing.

"He get the kid too?"

Pryce shrugged. He was a player all right. And the rest of us were nothing but chips.

"You're by yourself," I said. Not a question.

He didn't react. Even the muscle under his eye was quiet.

"I'm not," I told him. "Look in that notebook of yours—see what it says about who's with me. All you can do is protect your boy Lothar from the law. Not from me. You're worried about what I'm going to do? Think about it—why would I do it to *you*?"

"What are you saying?"

"Me? I'm not saying anything for your little tape recorder. All you got is this tired old 'rogue-agent' routine. And a bunch of half-ass 'info' any cybergeek could vacuum. The only one committing crimes here is you, threatening a helpless woman to drop charges so some fucking Nazi can keep doing what he does. Promising him a baby as a booby prize. But if something happens to old Lothar, the game's over, right?"

"Nothing is going to happen to Lothar."

"I didn't say it was. I'm just . . . theorizing, okay? What you're doing, it's a game. You say 'Or else.' Now I get to say 'Or else, what?'"

"It's not you that gets to say that, Mr. Burke."

"The bitch will do what I tell her," I promised him.

"She might," he agreed, lipless mouth reluctantly releasing the words. "But she's not the only one who gets a vote."

"Intelligence," I told him. "It's a commodity. Like dope or diamonds. A thing people buy and sell, right?"

"Yes."

"Sometimes they trade things too."

"And you have something to trade?"

"You got to bring some to get some," I said. "What you brought, it's nothing. And you know it. Just showmanship. Flash and splash. If you're telling the truth, there's only one reason why you're covering Lothar's play. Maybe I could do something, get you what you want some other way."

"Provided . . . ?"

"Provided you leave the baby. With the woman. The baby's out."

"He won't—"

"And provided I get paid."

"What possible guarantees could you—?"

"None right now. I have to see about some things first. Then we meet. You and me. Alone. Anywhere you say. Then we both ante up. Deal?"

"There isn't much time."

"Don't spread it on so thick," I told him. "There's always some slack in the rope in these matrimonial things. We can stall the divorce papers, put the whole thing on hold."

"That's not the only—"

"Forty-eight hours. A little more if you want the meet to be after dark."

His neck stiffened. I glanced behind him. Crystal Beth was approaching, slowly. I waved her over. She took her seat meekly, eyes downcast.

"Call her," I said, jerking my head briefly in Crystal Beth's direction. "Just tell her the place and the time. I'll be there. And then you'll decide."

"All right," he said.

"Can I drop the act now?" she asked, walking next to me in the street.

I reached behind her, grabbed one of her pigtails, pulled it sharply. She let out a little gasp. "You know who's watching?" I asked her.

"No."

"That's your answer," I said.

"Do you know why women always used to walk three paces behind their men?" Crystal Beth asked me as she pulled the jersey turtleneck over her head.

"Because they were property?" I offered, watching the black bra standing sharp against her dusky-rose skin.

"No. And not because they were submissive either. My mother

explained it to me. Her people, the ones who didn't go to the cities, they still do it that way."

She untied the drawstring at the waist of the long skirt, let it fall to the floor. Then she hooked her thumbs in the top of the black tights and pulled them down. The black panties and bra looked like a modest bathing suit. "They usually had a child between them," she said. "It was to make a box, to protect the child. If the woman turned around, they would be back-to-back, do you see?"

"Yeah. Like walking point and drag."

"I don't know what that is."

"In the jungle, military, you walk a column. The trails aren't wide enough for more. You put the sharp man ahead, to watch. But you put the heavy firepower at the end, in case they close up behind you."

"The woman had the harder job," she said. "Looking behind you is always hardest."

"Maybe you're right."

"I am right," she said, reaching behind her to unhook the bra. Her breasts were wide and round, not sticking out much. The small nipples were dark in the candlelight.

"If I get you a nice hanger, will you take off that beautiful suit?" she asked, walking over to where I was sitting.

She kept the black panties on until right near the end. Moving so slow, kissing and whispering, never impatient, holding my cock like she was taking its temperature, waiting for the right time.

"Can you hear that whistle now?" she whispered against my face.

I entered her then. Or maybe she took me in.

"Did I do it right?" she asked me later, propped on one elbow, looking down at my face, fire-specks of light from the candle playing across her tiny teeth.

"There is no 'right,'" I told her, wishing women wouldn't always pull that number when sex was done.

"Not . . . that." She laughed deep in her throat. "I could tell about that. I knew it even . . . before."

"Before . . . ?"

"Before you did," she said, flashing a smile. "I meant with Pryce. In the restaurant."

"Yeah, you did fine."

"He's a scary man."

"There's two pieces to that," I said. "There's the gun. And there's pulling the trigger, understand?"

"I think so. I thought about that too. What good would it do him to . . . ruin people? It would be too late to stop us—we'd have already *done* it, right?"

"You know what loan sharks are?" I asked her.

"Sure," she replied, cocking her head with a question she didn't ask.

"You know why they break legs?"

"So people will pay."

"What if the borrower's broke? I mean, dry-well broke. Tap City. Nobody to touch, nothing to borrow against, nothing for the pawn shops. Every bridge burned. Say he's already crippled from the last beating. Maybe got cancer too, okay? Maybe he's ashamed of himself, for what he did to his family. Maybe the only thing he's got left is some life-insurance policy. Maybe he *wants* to die and just doesn't have the guts to do it himself. Any reason to kill him *then*?"

"Of course not. What good would it—?"

"It's good for the reputation," I said quietly. "Word gets out they totaled a guy for not coming up with the cash, it makes all the others pay attention. One killing is worth a lot of beatings, see?"

"So you think he . . . would do it anyway?"

"I don't know him. But that's the way he comes off. No way this is the only time he's done this. Every working extortionist needs a head on a stake once in a while. It's good advertising."

"Oh."

"Yeah. You know why he wanted that meet out in public?"

"No. I met him before, and he wasn't—"

"He thought maybe you were gonna solve your problem."

"I don't—"

"Cut him down," I said softly. "Take him out. He goes away, your problems go away too, right?"

"*Kill* him?"

"Sure."

"I wouldn't—"

"He doesn't know that. I didn't either, until we met. He's an info-player, stacking up his chips. That's one he doesn't have."

"But . . ."

"He's going to call you. Then you're going to call me. I'm going to meet him. And then we're going to decide, you and me."

"Decide what?"

"If there's a way out," I told her. "A way you can live with."

Early the next morning I stood on the paved area just off the Hudson River across from Riverside Drive, the hood up on my Plymouth like I was having engine trouble. The sun was just making its move. Light downtown-bound commuter traffic flowed past on the West Side Highway. Summertime, this spot would be crowded: guys fishing, working on their cars, chilling with blunt-and-brew combos. But now it was deserted. The radio said it was fifty-four degrees, but it didn't feel that warm to me.

I was lighting a cigarette when a street-hammered old Audi sedan pulled in a few spaces away. The driver's door opened and she got out. Wolfe. I'd know her at a hundred yards, the long glossy dark hair with the two white wings standing out so clear. I knew the dark blot that filled the passenger's window too. Bruiser. A killer rottweiler who had been going to work with Wolfe ever since he was a puppy. He used to lie under her desk when she ran City-Wide. Now he rides shotgun, making the transition from law enforcement to outlaw as smoothly as Wolfe had. I didn't close the gap between us, letting her come to me—Wolfe never locks her car and I could see the passenger window was down.

She was wearing a quilted orange car coat that came down past her knees, walking with a free and easy stride, like it was a country lane instead of garbage-strewn asphalt.

"Pepper said you wanted to see me," she said by way of greeting.

"You want to sit in the car?" I asked her.

"No, it's nice outside today. Makes me think spring's almost here."

She was being guarded, but that was her usual style. I got right to it: "You know a guy named Pryce?"

"Yes," she said, no hesitation.

"I may be . . . in something with him."

"*With* him?"

"No."

"You want what I know, what I can find out . . . what?"

"Same menu?"

Wolfe gave me her enchantress smile. The same one that had lulled a decade of defense attorneys to their doom. "These are inflationary times," she said.

"How much for what you know?"

"I know a lot," she said.

"Figured you might. How much?"

"Five thousand dollars."

"*What?*"

"Or," she went on like she hadn't heard me, "we could trade."

"What have I got that you want?"

"I don't know," she said. "Not for sure. But you want the information for a reason. Something's going on. Or something's going to happen. Something with Pryce. That's what I'll trade you for."

What do you know, you beautiful warrior-girl? I thought to myself. Wolfe already knew about the stalker—Crystal Beth had told me she was part of the plan. But had Crystal Beth ever mentioned Pryce to her?

"Even up?" I offered, nothing on my face.

"A thousand for what I have. Then you fill me in. And keep me updated."

"How come you—?"

"Come *on*." She smiled again. "You want to pay for that too?"

"They're so lucky," Wolfe said, looking out at a tanker going up the Hudson.

"People with jobs?"

"No." She laughed. "People who get to be on the water all the time."

"You like that stuff?"

"I love it," she said quietly. "If I had my way, I think I'd live on a boat."

"Like a cruise ship?"

"No, a sailboat. A nice three-master that I could sail with a small crew."

"*You* could sail it?"

"Sure." She grinned. "I captained a ship from Bermuda all the way back to Cape Cod once."

"By yourself?"

"There were other people on board, but I was in charge."

"Where'd you learn to do that?"

"I was a Sea Scout."

"A what?"

"A Sea Scout. Like a Girl Scout, only we went out on boats instead of camping."

"I'd be scared to death," I told her. "The water . . ."

"You don't know how to swim?"

"No. I mean, I guess I wouldn't sink. We used to jump off piers when I was a kid. But it's so, I don't know . . . I mean, you don't know what's out there."

"There's worse things on land," she said.

I knew she was right, but it didn't make any difference. Once, when I was small, I went down to the river to see what I could hustle up. It was night—I always felt safer at night. A boat was there. Not a big one, some kind of sport-fishing rig. They had a shark up on a hoist. It was twitching, like it was going to break loose. The men were laughing, drunk, celebrating their conquest. I looked out at the black water. I thought about more sharks being down there. Men hunt them for fun. I wondered if the other sharks wanted revenge.

"Sure," I said, getting back to it. "This Pryce, is he one of them? Those worse things?"

"I've run across his trail a few times over the years. Only met him once face-to-face. He said he was with Justice then, but when I tried a trace, it got lost in the maze they have down there. By the time I worked it through, he was gone. He tells people he's with the Company sometimes. Or DEA, ATF, whatever. And by the time anyone can check, he's moved on."

"Transferred, maybe?"

"Not a chance. I think he's sanctioned, but he's on permanent-disavowal status."

"What the hell is that?"

"Pretty much what it sounds like," she said, combing both hands through her thick mane of dark hair as a river breeze came up. "He does contract jobs, but he works for cash, not on the books."

"Active work?"

"I don't think so. He's an information guy, not hands-on. What he is, I think, is kind of a bounty hunter. A bounty spotter, if there's any such thing. He doesn't make collars, he doesn't do wet stuff. He works the edges, tracking. And he manipulates situations. There's no holds on him—he doesn't have to play by the rules."

"Could he get favors done?"

"From the feds? Probably. At least he could from certain agents he's bird-dogging for."

"And he doesn't play for headlines?"

"I remember one thing he said to me. 'I never take credit. Only cash.' I think that about sums him up."

"You had a beef with him?"

"Not at all. He was very polite, very respectful. Said he knew about a pedophile ring. A new twist—on-line molestation in real time."

"Huh?"

"One of the freaks would get the little girl—they only used girls in this one—in his studio. Then he'd set up the cameras, notify the rest of them and flash her image over their modems.

They could tell him what they wanted him to do to the little girl, and they could all watch as he did it."

"And Pryce knew this how?"

"He didn't say. But I got the impression that he had reached one of the freaks. Had him in his pocket."

"Was he trying to make a deal, have this one guy roll over on the rest in exchange for a walk-away?"

"No. He doesn't work for defense attorneys. It wasn't anything like that. As near as I could tell, he was willing to let his own guy go down with the rest."

"So what was the problem?"

"He wanted to get paid. Not a favor, cash."

"How much did he want?"

"He didn't say exactly. Six figures, anyway."

"And you wouldn't go for it?"

"No. I couldn't. We don't have a budget for things like that. Nobody posts a reward until there's a victim, right?"

"Yeah. And nobody knew—?"

"Nobody knew anything. This was the first I'd heard of it. I tried to put some pressure on him. Told him, if he didn't turn over the information, not only was that one little girl going to continue to be gang-raped over the Internet, there had to be others too. He said that should make it worth more. I tried to spook him about 'withholding information' and he just laughed. I never saw him again."

"So it just went on?"

"Actually, it didn't. A week later there was a big bust. Federal. The FBI vamped on the whole operation, took it down in one fell swoop. A beautiful case: even the first one to roll got major time."

"You think Pryce sold it to the Gee?"

"There's no way to know. I asked a friend over there how they got the case, and he just said it started with a CI, that was all he knew."

"But he didn't mean Pryce was the Confidential Informant?"

"No. But he could have been running the CI, whoever he was. Or it all could have been bogus, a setup to justify the search warrant."

"You got anything else?" I asked her.

"No, that's it. But if I hear anything, I'll call you."

"Okay."

"Your turn," she said, giving me another deadly smile.

I was telling Wolfe the story, spooling it out in bits and pieces, not going anywhere near Hercules. We both played outside the lines now, but we didn't play the same. I trusted her, but Wolfe was a cop in her heart. A rule-busting cop, sure, but that doesn't tell the whole story. There's a hell of a difference between concocting probable cause to take bad guys down and taking money from them. The only difference between Wolfe's operation and a vigilante team was that Wolfe's crew got paid. She still made her living busting crime—I still made mine committing it.

We were standing against my car, talking quietly, all by ourselves on that isolated patch of ground. Years ago, I used to think things could be . . . different between us. Not thinking, really—wanting. She drew the line. Once in a while we got to hold hands over it, but I couldn't pull her to me, and she'd never tried to pull me to her.

Wolfe took a photograph out of her pocket. Not a mug shot, some kind of surveillance photo. "Is this him?" she asked me.

It was murky, indistinct. "I got a flashlight in the trunk," I told her.

She was standing by herself between the Plymouth's dead headlights when the egg-yolk-yellow Pathfinder rolled into the parking lot. No music coming from it. Bad sign. I looked up as it slid within ten feet of Wolfe. A young guy bounced out: shirt to his knees, sleeves past his knuckles, worn over baggy pants ending at half-laced ultra sneakers endorsed by some role-model basketball star and made in some sweatshop in Southeast Asia, black knit watch cap with White Sox logo turned sideways, representing. Hip-hopper or wigger—I couldn't tell his color in the early light.

"Yo *bitch!*" he shouted at her.

I came around the back of the Plymouth with the tire iron in my hand. The guy said "Oh shit!" and piled back into the Pathfinder. It took off, grinding its chunky tires against the crusty blacktop.

"Bruiser, *out!*" Wolfe yelled. That's when I saw the rottweiler, closing ground like Judgment Day wrapped in black fur.

"**W**ho knows what that was really about," Wolfe said to me, leaning on the Plymouth's hood, smoking one of my cigarettes, the rottweiler sitting next to her, calm now. "They could have been after anything from a hassle to a rape. There's something about being in a car that gives punks courage."

"It isn't the car," I told her. "It's the gang. And a woman alone."

"I guess."

"And don't call it courage," I said. "Your dog, he's the one with the balls."

"Don't remind me," Wolfe chuckled, reaching in her pocket and pulling out a disgusting-looking length of what looked like dark-red sinew. The rottie watched it, eyes narrowed in. But he didn't move a muscle. "Bruiser, okay!" Wolfe said, handing it over. The beast immediately snatched it, lay down, grasped the prize in his front paws and started tearing into it. The sounds he made would have scared a forest ranger.

"What is that you gave him?" I asked her.

"It's a dried beef tendon," she said. "One of his favorites. Next to fresh pineapple. But I can't carry that around with me."

"Well, he earned it," I said. "I never saw a dog that big move so fast. He ever bite anybody?"

"Sure," Wolfe said, grinning at the stupid question.

I hefted the tire iron, feeling foolish. I don't carry a gun anymore. Don't keep one in the car either. It's got nothing to do with search warrants or being an ex-con. I'm just . . . careful. Ever since I tried to kill my childhood and killed a child instead.

"I don't know what's going down with this Pryce guy," I lied, playing the flashlight over the photograph Wolfe had. It was him all right. "Maybe nothing. I'll let you know."

"Either way," she said, pulling a promise with the words.

"Either way," I agreed.

I rolled the Plymouth onto the highway, merging with the traffic, blending back in. A lot of stops to make that day, but I couldn't really get started until the comic shops opened. The rest of what I needed for Herk was already stashed in the trunk.

Which is where Pryce could end up if he played me wrong.

It was after dark by the time I got back from meeting with Hercules. When I cruised by Mama's, the white-dragon tapestry was in the front window. All clear.

But as soon as I came out of the kitchen into the main room I knew something was up. Mama wasn't at her register—she was on her feet, hands on hips, waiting for something. Max was sitting at one of the tables, eyes closed the way he gets just before he has to work, a violence machine with its battery on trickle-charge.

At another table, three young Orientals, all dressed in identical black leather dusters and red silk shirts buttoned to the neck. They were all razor-built, with long glossy black hair and delicate features. They didn't look like brothers, but the tribal relationship was stamped deep . . . the kind of deep only the crucible creates.

And in a booth, an elderly Chinese woman, bird-faced and stick-thin, wrapped in a heavy dark-green shawl, eyes aimed at the floor.

Mama gestured for me to come over to my booth. She sat down across from me. No soup this time.

"Tigers have her nephew," she said, voice low-pitched, head cocked slightly to indicate the old woman. "He owe big money. Thirty thousand."

I didn't need a translator. The nephew was an illegal, smuggled in by one of the gang operations that supply so much of the cheap labor in Chinatown. The family back home picks the youngest, strongest one to go first. When that one works off the debt in the sweatshops, they can send another.

That's one of the reasons you see guys making a couple of bucks an hour off the books get so deep into gambling. Their families back home encourage it, especially those relatives far down in the next-to-go chain. It's the only way to pay off the transporters quick. In the sweatshops, thirty grand would take a decade, minimum.

"Kuan Li old friend. From home. Everything set, okay?" Then she told me the plan.

The squat Chinese who opened the door had a cop's nightstick in his right hand, the leather thong wrapped around his wrist. The brutish expression on his face didn't change until he saw that the three young men in their matching black coats also had matching black semi-autos, each one aimed at a different part of his body, as professional as it gets. He moved his hands away from his sides, the nightstick dangling loose and useless, eyes only on me.

One of the young men stayed with him, the other two came along as I moved down a passage so narrow it was more like a tunnel than a hall.

The basement was divided into wire-mesh cages, Bowery flophouse–style. Maybe thirty, forty illegals slept there. One toilet, one shower—just a rusty nozzle poking out of the wall with a drain underneath. A hundred bucks a month apiece. Overheated from human cargo, it stank like the hold of a slave ship.

I swept my eye through the cages. Third from left, lowest tier, Mama had said. Her description of the nephew was photo-perfect. I pointed at his face. One of the young men showed him his pistol, said something to him in bad-accent Cantonese. The nephew said something back. The gunman chopped at his face with the pistol. The nephew came along, hands at his sides, head down.

We walked out into the afternoon. The gunman shoved the

nephew into the back seat of a Chinatown war wagon, an old Buick four-door sedan with welded-up fake plates. The other two piled in right behind him. The car took off. The squat doorman poked his head outside. Max came up behind him and did something to his neck. The doorman crumpled to the ground. I stepped into a fog-gray Lincoln that had pulled to the curb. One of Mama's cooks was at the wheel.

The street vibrated the way it always did, no change.

"Not like old ways," Mama told me back in the restaurant. "Tigers not with the Tongs. Nephew go someplace else, they never find."

"They're supposed to think I had a beef with him, hired those other guys to take him out of there?"

"Yes, maybe think so." Mama shrugged.

"Won't the Tigers look for their money from the guys who took him?"

"What guys?" Mama smiled.

"The Chinese guys. The young ones in the jackets."

"Not Chinese," Mama said. "Cambodia. How old you think?"

"Twenty, twenty-five?"

"Fifteen," Mama said. "Oldest, fifteen. Khmer not kill, Tigers not kill either."

"Jesus. They're operating down here now too?"

"Sure," Mama said.

I played cards with Max until early the next morning. We used to play gin rummy, a life-sentence game we'd started years ago—keeping score, but agreeing that we wouldn't settle up until we both crossed over. Figuring that, if it was divided up like people say it is, we'd both end up on the same side of the line.

Max had owed me a fortune until he'd tapped into that perfect vein of gold all gamblers dream of—the Prime Roll. It only lasted a few hours, but Max was unbelievably unbeatable. Every card fell for him. He was a rampaging tsunami—I was a balsa-wood beach house. I survived, but I was barely on the plus side when the wave passed. Ever since, he'd refused to return to gin, knowing he'd never see a run like that again in life. So we switched to casino. He doesn't play that game any better, and I had his debt back into six figures.

Mama continued to monitor just about every hand in her self-appointed role as Max's adviser. She was lousy at it. Even worse than at gin—at least she knew how to play gin, casino was a total mystery to her. Mama speaks a half-dozen languages, including math, but any form of gambling got her blood up and made her forget the odds, so she never indulged. Didn't mind helping Max out, though.

She tapped Max's shoulder, nodded her head, grinned as he tossed the four of clubs on the four of hearts, building eights against the one he held in his hand instead of just taking one four with another. I slapped the deuce of spades on top of his build, against the ten of diamonds I held. I knew Max didn't hold any tens—the other three had already been played. The diamond card is the Big Ten in casino—the only one worth two points. The deuce of spades was another point card. . . . A lovely score. Max scowled. Mama's face indicated that the whole thing was his own fault.

The pay phone in the back rang. I looked at my watch—it was just past two in the morning. Mama got up, walked to the back, grabbed the receiver, said something . . . listened. Then she came back to our booth.

"Girl. Name Vyra."

"Tell her I'm not here," I said.

Mama nodded, nothing on her face.

I went back to my office, let Pansy use her roof, watched some early-morning TV with her after she polished off a quart of some stuff Mama put together—mostly beef chunks in oyster sauce.

Then I slept.

Once I got up, I started rolling. Spent the next twenty-four checking on leads, just in case Pryce went for what I was going to offer him. But the paths were too twisted—I couldn't pipeline down to a core truth strong enough to bank on. The White Night underground is a poisonous brew, fed by rumors and driven by psychos. American-born Nazis working as mercenaries in Croatia, slaughtering Serbs, cleansing the ethnic cleansers, the whole operation set up by fascist groups in Germany who had fond World War II memories of the Croats helping out; a range war between two Hitler-loving crews—mostly a talk war over the shortwave bands—one leader saying the head of the rival crew was gay, that guy saying his opposite number was a crypto-Jew; the tax resisters and the do-it-yourself litigation clubs; virulent anti-Semites calling themselves the true Israelites; one-member fascist organizations blindly cyber-groping with anti-IRA skinheads in England and transplanted American biker gangs in Denmark . . . all riddled with undercover agents and free-lance informants and ready-to-roll rats.

Not a network, threads. Some of them as unanchored as the lunatics who tried to grab on and pull themselves up to the Fourth Reich. Just outside Chicago, one of those deadly defectives gunned down a plastic surgeon, convinced the doctor was giving non-whites an "Aryan" look. Maybe he was following the footprints of the white supremacist on the coast who blew away a beautician years ago because he heard she was bleaching Jewess hair.

More Führers than storm troopers, sure. But any one of them strong enough to lift a suitcase can level a building now.

The reason the media never gets it right is that the media lives on spokesman interviews, and nobody could ever speak for that collection. How do you speak for a congregation that screams the Holocaust never happened while it prays for it to happen again? You think if you assembled a hundred rapists they'd all tell you they rape for the same reason? "Their rap don't mean crap, honeyboy," the Prof had told me once. "Their trail always tells the tale." On the prison yard, a hundred years ago. I was full of questions then.

I've been dealing with the hyper-whites for years, selling and scamming. They've got no loyalty, so they're easy. But mining their ranks for truth is like looking for a congressman's ethics.

But I asked around anyway. Working the edges, careful like always. Keeping a flat face as they flashed their self-awarded decorations, tattoos: the "88"—for "Heil Hitler," the eighth letter of the alphabet being "H," borrowed from the way the bikers used to wear the number "13" on their denims . . . "M" for "marijuana." And the spiderwebs on their elbows, meaning they killed for the race . . . although most of them upgraded any two-bit assault to that status. Skinhead sheep with red laces on their Doc Martens and Iron Crosses around their necks, certain they were the vanguard to Valhalla. A Mafia don's *omertà*, an emir's jihad, or a Führer's race war, it's always the same—only the congregation sees the prison cells or catches the bullets, never the preachers.

I heard all about how only the NRA was standing up to ZOG—Zionist Occupation Government in Nazi-speak—and how gun control was just the prelude to registration of all citizens. Saw enough copies of *The Turner Diaries* in grungy furnished rooms to crack a best-seller list. Tapped into some of the fax chains. Read the luno-newsletters. Listened to the Ballad of Ruby Ridge and what *really* happened at Waco. Heard a half-dozen different accounts of why the Swiss banks kept looted Jewish gold in their vaults all these years, waiting for that cable from Paraguay to release the assets. And how Hitler was ordained, a minister of Jehovah, sent by God to punish the Jews for killing His son. Watched self-proclaimed "constitutionalists" applauding more marches through Skokie, this time on the Internet. Even sat with a Mossad agent the Mole brought me to, an Arabic-looking man with pianist's hands and slot-machine eyes.

I listened to it all. But when it came to anyone named Lothar operating in New York, I drew a handful of blanks.

"I always wore clothes when I was a child," Crystal Beth said. She was lying on the mattress on her belly, nude, smoking one of her hand-rolled cigarettes, candle-flicker shadows dancing over the perfect parabolic curve of her bottom before disappearing into the blackness around her thick thighs.

I didn't say anything, watching her.

"A lot of the kids didn't," she said. "On the Farm. That's what we called it mostly, the Farm. Their parents thought children should be free, not have to wear clothing until they were older. My mother didn't believe in that."

"Were there fights about it?" I asked her.

"Fights? Nobody fought. It was a commune, but it wasn't a *government* commune. There were no laws from on high, that isn't the way we did it. A parent could raise a child any way they wanted."

"Could they hit their kids?"

"You mean like spank them?"

"Whatever you call it."

"Burke," she said softly. "What's the matter?"

"Nothing's the matter. I was just making conversation."

"Your face . . . Oh, you're going to think I'm a ditz."

"You're losing me," I told her.

"Come over here, okay? Just lie down next to me for a minute."

I did that.

She stubbed out her cigarette, rolled over on her side to look at me. "Your aura changed," she said. "Please don't laugh. It's not some New Age thing. People do have auras. Not everyone. At least not powerful ones, ones that you can see. Do you think that's crazy?"

"No," I said, not lying. Martial artists call it *ki*. They don't talk about seeing it, just feeling it, but it's really the same: a force field. When I was young, before I learned to make my temper go the same place as my pain, when the rage in me built high enough I could move people out of a room without saying anything. A long time later, when Max explained it to me, he used his hands to indicate waves coming off me. I don't know where Max got his knowledge, but it wasn't from books. And it wasn't new.

The only thing is, *ki* doesn't work on everyone. Some people aren't tuned to the signal. That's why a street punk will try you when a pro would give you a pass.

"When you asked about . . . hitting children, your aura turned . . ."

"Dark?"

"No. It's always dark. This was like . . . Did you ever see heat lightning? It doesn't make a sound, just kind of . . . flashes?"

"Yeah."

"Like that. Did . . . people hit you when you were a child?"

"People did everything to me when I was a child," I told her.

She reached over, took my hand, put it on her proud soft breast. "Feel my heart," she said.

"**N**obody ever hit children there," she said about an hour later. "What?"

"On the Farm. Remember, you asked me? Nobody ever did that. Once I came inside from playing and my mother and father were there. They didn't see me at first. My mother was cleaning the table. My father walked behind her and gave her a slap on the bottom. A hard slap, I could hear it crack. I got angry and I started to run to her, to protect her. Then I heard her . . . not laugh, or even giggle . . . some kind of sweet sound. I was so confused I started to cry. Then they saw me. My father tried to get me to sit on his lap, the way he did when he explained things to me. But I wouldn't do it.

"My mother took me for a walk. She told me my father was just playing. It didn't hurt her at all. I asked her if all men played like that, and she told me they didn't. But she also told me it didn't matter how men played. All that mattered was how the women wanted them to play. Men should never play any way women didn't want.

"A couple of days later, I remember asking my father if he wanted to smack me on the bottom, like he did my mother. He got very upset. My father was a very dramatic man. My mother had to calm him down. You know how she always did that?"

"No."

"Like this," Crystal Beth said, planting her broad little nose in my chest and pushing so hard with her head that I had to grab her and brace myself to keep from staggering backward. "See how it works?" she whispered, nuzzling me, her hands locked together behind my back.

"Yeah."

She kept pushing until I felt the easy chair against the back of my legs. I sat down, pulling her with me. She snuggled into my lap, gave me a quick nip on the neck.

"It was so easy when my mother explained it," she said softly. "There are things a man does with a woman that he doesn't do with a child. Not his child, not any child. She said someday a man would do things with me. I asked her what things. And she told me. Some of them, anyway. That's how I learned about sex. My mother knew when it was time. My father, he never would have known."

"You really loved him, huh?"

"My father? I *adored* him."

"So you're doing his work?"

"His work? My father was a—"

"Protector, right?"

"Oh. Yes. I never thought about that. It's my . . . purpose. Like my mother told me. I didn't think it was . . ."

"Ah, what do I know?" I said.

"Burke?"

"What, girl?"

"It must have been so hard. Not to have even . . . known your father."

"You think they're all alike, fathers?"

"No. I just—"

"I didn't miss a fucking thing," I told her.

The phone rang. Crystal Beth got off my lap and padded over to a far corner in her bare feet. She pulled some papers off the top of a two-drawer file cabinet and picked up the receiver lying underneath.

"Hello."

She listened, cocking one hip the way Mama had cocked her head—I guess all women listen differently. Then she said: "Yes, I understand. All the way in the back. All right."

And hung up.

"That was him," she said. "He says to meet him in the Delta parking lot at La Guardia. All the way in the back, against the fence. He'll be in a white Taurus sedan."

"When?"

"Now. He said he'll give you an hour."

"Okay," I said, climbing into my clothes.

"An hour isn't—"

"This time of night? No problem," I assured her.

She knelt at my feet, carefully threaded the laces of my work boots, tied each one precisely. "Burke, he didn't say anything about calling you. He had to know you were here."

"He's calling from the meeting place," I told her. "He's already there. Probably been there for hours. In a war zone, names don't matter, just addresses. It's the only way he can be sure I don't fill the parking lot with my own people. He's not watching outside— he was just guessing about me being here. Not a bad guess anyway, right? I told him I was your man, remember? Or maybe he thought you could find me on the phone right away."

"Or maybe he has people of his own," she whispered.

"Maybe."

She stood against me in the dark. Her skin was silky, warm with the blood beneath it. I kissed her tattoo and left her there.

took the Brooklyn Bridge to the BQE, the Plymouth gobbling ground effortlessly. It was still cold out, but the pavement was dry and traction was no problem. I kept near the speed limit until a bright-orange Mustang with a huge rear wing shot by me, a white Camaro with a broad red racing stripe in close pursuit. They were doing at least a hundred. Not racing—just screwing around, pushing each other. The BQE isn't a race road—too many giant potholes, too many reverse-graded curves. When the dragsters want to really throw down, they go over to Rockaway or work the deep end of Woodhaven Boulevard in Queens. But those fools were all the interference I'd ever need on the off-chance some highway cop was lurking in the night. Which I'd never seen on the BQE in my entire life anyway.

As I went by the McGinnis Boulevard cutoff, the back of the rear seat popped out and Max emerged from the trunk. He climbed into the front seat, dressed in full night-runner gear—a modified ninja outfit, light-eating black, complete with hood and face mask. I handed him the key and he opened the glove compartment. Took out a little square box made out of gunmetal-gray Lexan with a row of tiny Braille-style dots across the top. Max tripped the switch and the dots flashed in sequence before they settled down to only one glowing steady. Green. Pryce didn't have a tracking device planted anywhere on the Plymouth—the Mole's technology was as good as anything the government had. Better, probably. Underground research is pure Darwinism—no grants, no bureaucracy, no politics. It works or it dies.

I checked the rearview mirror. Empty. I rolled over the Kosciuszko Bridge and pulled up on the shoulder just past the LIE turnoff, playing it safe, watching the sparse traffic roll by.

Nothing.

Max kept watch as I sketched a rough map of what I wanted. He took one quick look, nodded okay—he'd been there before. I put the Plymouth in gear and pulled back on the highway. Max tore the hand-drawn map into tiny pieces, let them trail from his hand out the open window.

Plenty of time. I turned off the BQE to the Grand Central, followed it to Ninety-fourth Street, exited and ran parallel to the highway through East Elmhurst until I was well past the airport. I doubled back through the interchange at Northern Boulevard and grabbed the Grand Central again, heading back toward Manhattan. I kept sliding right until I picked up the service road that leads to a highway gas station. I pulled over just before I reached it. There's a small parking area there. Limo drivers use it when they have a long wait for a flight—they're not allowed in the taxi line.

At almost one in the morning, the lot was deserted—La Guardia doesn't handle international flights and it's usually out of business by midnight. I let Max off. Checked my watch. I still had almost twenty minutes.

I punched Crystal Beth's number into the cell phone.

It rang a dozen times. No answer.

I smoked a cigarette. Slowly, all the way through. Then I went to meet whatever was waiting.

The Delta lot is all the way at the east end of La Guardia, the last piece of solid ground before the whole place turns to swamp. I pulled a ticket from the automatic vending machine and the gate lifted to let me in. The lot was sporadically dotted with cars, almost all of them clustered near the exit to the terminal, probably airline personnel. In the warm weather, some people use this lot as a four-dollar-an-hour motel, a Lovers' Lane where you don't have to worry about prowlers. But in the winter, it's all business. I let the Plymouth poke along between the rows of parked cars, feathering the throttle, watching. Halfway through the lot, it turned empty. Except for a white Taurus sedan standing all by itself against the back fence, front end aimed in my direction.

I docked the Plymouth about five car-widths away, stepped out and walked to the Taurus. Saw it was a SHO model, about thirty-five grand worth of high-speed anonymity. Quick enough for pursuit work, generic enough for shadowing, comfortable for stakeouts. A pro's choice, even the color—more white cars than any other out there now. The windows were deep-tinted—couldn't see inside. But I figured he could see out, so I just stood there, looking at the windshield, holding my hands far away from my body, my jacket zipped up tight.

Nothing.

I heard pebbles crunch, sensed movement behind me. Not stealthy—letting me know he was coming. I turned around slowly.

Pryce was walking toward me from the corner of the lot, hands as empty as mine.

I wondered if his heart was too.

"Sorry," he said as he got close enough to speak. "I had to take a leak."

I spread my arms wider, going for a Christ-on-the cross position. "Let's get this part over with quick," I said. "It's too cold to be standing around playing games."

He stood there looking at me, his featureless face calm. "I couldn't do an adequate job out here," he said. "You know that."

"Then do what I'm gonna do," I told him.

"Which is?"

"Don't say anything you don't want on tape."

He nodded. "Fair enough. You want to talk in the car?"

"Sure."

In the silver leather passenger seat, I turned my right shoulder to the windshield so that I was almost facing him. "Okay if I smoke?" I asked him.

He turned the ignition key, hit the switch for the power windows. The glass behind me whispered down. Step one. He shifted position so that he was facing me. Two. "I've got an idea," I told him. "But first I have to know some stuff."

"Ask your questions," he said.

"It all comes down to this," I started, exhaling a heavy puff of clove-cigarette smoke in his direction. His expression didn't change, but he pushed the switch, taking his own window down. Three. "Is this Lothar guy the whole machine, or just a tool?" I finished.

"He's a tool," Pryce said without hesitation.

"Tell me what you're willing to," I said. "If there's blanks, then I'll ask, okay?"

He scratched absently at the tip of his nose. Phantom itch? Like you get from an amputated limb. Or plastic surgery. The tip of the nose changes the face radically, a doctor told me once. "Larry James Bretton," he said. "Now known as Lothar Bucholtz. He changed it legally. I don't believe his wife knows about the surname, but he's been calling himself Lothar publicly for some time now. General failure. Trained as a printer, but fired from three straight jobs for using company facilities to put out various propaganda sheets for extremist groups. He doesn't write the stuff himself—he hasn't got brains enough even for the intellectual challenge of using 'nigger' and 'kike' in the same sentence. But he's a true-believer all the way. You know the party line: If the government can be destabilized, if the artificial restraints come off, the streets will run with blood. Knock ZOG off and the kikes won't be able to stop the niggers from slaughtering them. Muscle beats brains in the short run, the way they figure it. Of course, the niggers won't be able to run a government. . . . That's when the true Aryans come in, the race warriors. With the weapons they've been hoarding, they'll be able to carve out a few states as their own."

"Your basic Helter Skelter scenario," I said. "A Charlie Manson update."

"Right. Not many of them acknowledge it, but he's their visionary all right. Okay, next they'll get foreign aid from wealthy countries who support their mission, especially the Arabs—after all, exterminating Jews should give them perfect credentials." He waved a hand dismissively, anticipating me. "Yes, I know, the A-rabs are mud people too. But that's just the first step in the master plan. After they ship all the niggers back to Africa—the ones they don't just outright kill in the camps with the kikes—they'll run the show here. The Day of the Rope will eliminate all the race-traitor whites. Next step is acquisition of nuclear weapons," he said, face flat but his voice loaded with sneer, "and then it's time for the A-rabs to pay the piper. Finally, there'll be a natural link between all the North European tribes—the Aryans, right?—and the true Americans, their descendants. Not the Indians, of course . . .

"Lothar's people are divided as to the next step. Some of them want to retain all the mud people in South America and Africa and Asia as slave labor. Some want to just kill them all—you know, nerve gas, poison the water supply, the ovens . . . the usual."

"Sure."

"Anyway, when they're not hyping up some of those retarded skinheads into bashing cruising gays or mixed-race couples with baseball bats—or recruiting on military bases—they're sitting around plotting how to make Oklahoma City look like a pipe bomb in a bus-station locker. And my boy Lothar is a real live member of an action cell."

"Bombers?"

"Oh yes. *Major* bombers. Domino bombing—you know what that is?"

"No."

"A couple of dozen targets. Virtually *simultaneous* targets. Congress. The FBI. Post offices. Communications centers. Airports. Train stations. The whole infrastructure. That's Phase One."

"And Phase Two?"

"The way they figure it, the military *has* to respond. National Guard first, but soon there'll be warplanes in the air. And where are they going to respond to? Wherever there's riots. Whoever starts the looting. And they know who that's going to be. With the communications cut, it's all going to be word of mouth. They don't have the troops for guerrilla warfare, but they have the weapons. *Lots* of weapons. They've been stockpiling for years."

"That plan is Swiss cheese," I told him.

"It is," he agreed. "But it's going to be America that gets the holes punched in it."

I felt a chill on the back of my neck. Probably the night air. I wondered if Pryce was feeling it too. I lit another nasty clove cigarette from the stub of the last one just in case he was thinking about zipping up his window.

"And Lothar's yours?" I asked him.

"All mine," he said. "But if he's taken out of the play, it won't work."

"What won't work?"

"ZOG likes to play dominoes too," Pryce said, the muscle under his right eye jumping hard.

I worked it around in my head for a minute. And it didn't add up. Not for what I needed. "You're not telling me Lothar's a government agent," I said flatly.

"No. *He's* not," Pryce replied.

I passed up the invitation. "But he's not gonna roll either," I said, no trace of a question in my voice.

"Why do you say that?"

"Couple of reasons. If he rolls, the best he can hope for is immunity. And that means the Witness Protection Program. Okay for some guys, maybe. But he's not gonna be able to do his Master Race crap there. And he's not gonna get his son either. Even if you could find a bent judge to give him custody, the media would have you for breakfast."

"He's not going to get immunity," Pryce said. "He's not going to testify at all. When the bust goes down, he's going to slip through the net. Go into the underground. The sole survivor. He'll be a hero. And he'll have his son with him."

"He's stupid enough to buy that?"

"He's stupid all right, but it's the truth. It's already set up. He'll leave the country. England first, then Germany. They'll take him in, never fear."

"And you'll keep working him, right? He changes his mind, you've got the hammer over his head."

"That's right," Pryce said, refrigerator-voiced.

"And he keeps his kid?"

"That's the part I thought we were going to negotiate. That's all you want, isn't it? Believe me, there's no way he's going to bother his wife ever again. He's going to vanish. New name, new face, the whole works."

"They're going to do plastic surgery on the boy too?"

"It's been done," he said calmly. "The pedophile rings have been doing it to kidnapped children for years. But I believe you already know about that . . . ?"

I ignored the opening. It hadn't really been a question anyway, just bait. Any pro interrogator knows that trick—you make the subject think you approve of whatever he did, show some empathy, get him bragging about it . . . and you've got him locked. He probably knew about some of the things I'd done in the past, had me tapped as a vigilante. Maybe he thought I'd welcome the chance to unburden myself to a kindred spirit.

Or maybe it was *his* chance—to show off, the info-warrior flexing his muscles.

"How come you don't just tell him not to show up for the divorce thing? That it's a trap?" I asked, like I'd never heard him mention pedophiles.

"I don't have complete . . . control," Pryce said. "His son has always been part of the deal. I told him we might be able to . . . obtain the child at a later date, but he's afraid his wife will just vanish. There's more than one underground operating in America. His Nazi friends don't have the resources to find one woman and one child in some safehouse. I don't even know where the woman is now. Only your . . . friend knows that."

"So it's her you threaten?"

He shrugged, dismissing the accusation. "The only thing holding his wife close is legal jurisdiction," he said. "She has to bring the divorce and the custody in New York, where they both live. She won't run until that's over with. But he doesn't have everything I . . . need yet. Do you understand my dilemma?"

"What if you had another man in there?" I asked, flipping my trump card on the table. "Someone who could get you the information?"

"Forget it," he said. "Believe me, you are quite well known to those people, Mr. Burke. They don't have my sources, and they certainly don't have the . . . extent of my information. You may have some . . . credentials that they would respect. But this isn't some racist prison gang we're talking about. If one of them you've . . . done business with recognized you, you'd be dead. Right then. And so would the man who brought you into the group."

"I've never done business with—"

"Don't insult me," Pryce said softly. "You sold a bunch of original tapes of one of Hitler's early speeches to some idiot Nazis a number of years ago, remember?"

"No."

"That was a long time ago, before you became so . . . sophisticated in your operations," he said, ignoring my denial like I'd never spoken. "It was very easy to trace. How do you think those morons felt when they learned what those original, authentic tapes really were? Oh, they were revolutionary speeches, all right. A call for armed resistance in support of the homeland. Only it was Menachem Begin, exhorting the Irgun to violence."

I had to laugh. Couldn't help it. Yiddish sounds like German if you don't speak either language. I used to do a lot of stuff like that. Not for politics, for the easy score. Freaks are always easy. And they never go to the law.

"I doubt they'd see the humor," Pryce said dryly. "There's also the little matter of selling them a few crates of machine guns. Funny how the ATF showed up a few minutes after the money changed hands. And after you'd left."

I didn't laugh at that one. And if he said anything about some fake mercenary recruiters who ended up dead in a shabby little Manhattan office, I was going to take something besides tobacco out of the pack of cigarettes I'd left on the dash after I'd smoked the last one.

"There's a long list," he said ambiguously, letting me wonder what else he knew. "Anyway, it doesn't matter. It wouldn't work."

"I didn't mean me," I told him. "I got somebody else. Somebody perfect."

He sat quietly, wrapped around himself. If he was thinking, it didn't show on his face.

" 'Perfect' is a big word," he finally said.

"Let's leave that for a minute," I told him. "Say I'm right. Say I've got a man you could put in there. That means Lothar goes too, you care about that?"

"No."

"And this other guy, he gets the same deal?"

"If he's not involved with the . . . if he's only going in to pipe-line back to me, he wouldn't need the same deal."

"New face, new ID, full immunity," I said like I hadn't heard him.

"Immunity for what? For whatever he had to do to prove himself to the cell?"

"*Full* immunity. Not 'use' immunity, not 'transactional' immunity. No-testimony, walk-away-clear, no-arrest, no-prosecute, dis-a-fucking-*peer* immunity. You can do that?"

"Yes," he said, like I'd asked him a stupid question.

"And you can make this Lothar bring someone in? Even this late?"

"If that person had the right bona fides. But they'd have to be good."

"How much time are they looking at?" I asked him, thinking about how even a double-crossed Lothar could be out in a few years. And go looking for his son.

Pryce held up his webbed hands, ticking off the counts on his fingers. "Conspiracy to commit mass murder, possession of the means to do it, dozens of assorted felonies—mostly armed robbery—in furtherance," he said. "Plus a load of individual crimes committed by individual members for which they've never been arrested. Yet. Homicides, rapes, firebombings . . .

"A couple of thousand years apiece," Pryce concluded. "Enough to make any of them resist arrest."

"Okay. This Lothar, he's not the only one you got, right?"

"I'm not sure what you mean. The only what?"

"The only Nazi. No way you just stumbled on him blind. You're running some others, maybe in different spots around the country."

"And if I was?"

"You wanted a credential. I'm gonna give you one. The best. Gilt-edged. Can you get word of a contract put out on someone? Call him a race-mixer, a closet Jew . . . I don't give a damn."

"A contract?"

"Don't be cute," I told him. "We're both over the line now. Don't worry. Your guy doesn't have to *do* anything. Just say he heard about this contract, that's all."

"When would that have to start?"

"A few weeks ago."

"I don't under——"

"Something already . . . happened, okay? Let's say this guy I'm talking about, he's gonna say *he* did it. If he did it off a contract, if he whacked someone for the cause, that'd ace him up, right?"

"Yes," he said, nodding at the truth. "That would do it."

"And you can put that together?"

"I can. But I'm still not——"

"I got two things that'll convince you," I said. "Number one: You get to meet the guy. Face-to-face. Ask him any questions you want. Satisfy yourself. You like it, he goes in. Deal?"

"You said two things," he reminded me.

"You think you know me," I said, my voice as intimate as a caress. "You parked this big white target of a Taurus out here, all by itself. And then you stood aside, waiting in the shadows. Just in case I decided to lob a bazooka round into it, right? One big bang, you're gone and the problem's solved. That's why you wanted me to get in this car with you. You're a puppeteer, Pryce. Information is your strings. Before you pull them, you better be sure they're connected."

"Which means what?" he said, only boredom in his voice.

I tapped the pack of cigarettes to take one out. A tiny black cylinder fell into my hand. "This is a flashlight," I said in the same gentle tone of voice I'd been using. "If I had taken it out, shined it in your face at any time, we'd be done talking."

"Nobody's that good a shot," he said. "Even with the window—"

I touched the flashlight, but I didn't aim it at his face. A tiny dot of red light showed in the windshield. And then Max the Silent touched the back of his neck.

"Don't turn around," I told him. "Don't do anything stupid. You're not gonna get hurt, understand?"

"Yes," he said, holding his head rigid.

"It wouldn't take a bullet," I said. "And it wouldn't have to make any noise. Or it could make a *lot* of noise. But one thing would always be the same. You know what that would be?"

"No."

"You'd never see it coming," I told him.

He sat there without moving for a couple of minutes after Max pulled his hands away and went back into the night.

"This is a battlefield friendship," I said quietly. "You and me. Your enemies are my enemies, that makes us friends, right? Or allies, anyway."

"Yes."

"I'm going to do my piece. Do it right. Like I promised. You too. No more threats. You already did your threats, and you're gonna get what you want. Don't do them anymore, okay?"

"Yes."

"We're going to have to meet again. You're going to need to see the man I have. You're going to have to know some things about him. That's the only way we can play this, you and me. Together. The way I scan it, you're a lone wolf. Whatever you know, you're the only one. Is that right?"

"Yes."

"Let's be clear. You want this cell. Lothar's a chip. You're going to ante that chip. I'm going to put up my man. He goes in. Lothar *brings* him in. You take care of that. I take care of getting you the information. I make sure the information is right. I guarantee you keep getting it even if Lothar turns unreliable. Information, that's what you get from me. You cash that information when they all go. That about cover it?"

"Yes."

"And when you get paid, I get paid."

That got his attention. He shifted position for the first time since Max took hold of him, his lipless mouth twitching to match the muscle under his eye. "We never discussed that," he said.

"Yeah we did. In the restaurant. Only thing we didn't agree on was the price. How much is ZOG paying for hard-core terrorist cells these days?"

"It . . . depends. On a number of factors out of my control."

"Sure. Look, I know we're not fifty-fifty on this. All I could do is take a wild guess. And I'm not gonna do that. But I don't think I'd be much off if I was thinking seven figures. . . ."

"That's—"

"Sure, I know. Let's just pretend I'm an agent. Your agent. Agents get a cut. Ten percent, right?"

"You want a hundred thousand dollars?"

"Yeah."

"Done," he said, no expression on his face.

I handed the parking ticket to the drone at the gate. He made an impatient gesture, waving his hands in aggravation. A small TV set flicked in his booth.

"What?" I asked him. Not friendly—people tend to remember anything unusual.

He pointed at a slot on the outside of the booth. I fed the ticket into the slot. A panel lit up: $4.00. I handed him a five-dollar bill. He managed to overcome his annoyance at me not having exact change long enough to hand me a single. Compared to him, the toll-takers on the bridges were complex mathematicians.

I exited the airport, taking the highway east toward Long Island. Did the same double-back I'd done coming in and picked Max up where I'd dropped him off.

On the way back, he made a series of gestures I hadn't seen before. It took me a few tries before I got what he was telling me.

In the country, the morning sound of early spring is birds calling. Down here, it's car alarms screaming their impotence. In either place, only the tourists pay attention.

The sun was bright and strong when I got up, spring's promise closer to truth now. The refrigerator was empty, so I trudged over to one of those all-night Korean bodegas that pop up so often down here. They usually close just as quick, soon as they find out all the working people disappear after dark. Even the strip bars do most of their business in daylight.

I loaded up heavy on provisions, but Pansy scarfed most of it in one sitting.

When I called in, Mama said, "Girl call. Late." Meaning earlier that morning.

"Vyra?"

"No. Other girl."

"Okay. She say what she wanted?"

"Talk to you."

"**D**id it go all right?" Crystal Beth asked as soon as she heard my voice on the phone.

"I'll tell you all about it. Later, okay?"

"When later?"

"Tonight. Around . . . nine?"

"Good. Are you—?"

"You got room there?"

"Room?"

"For a . . . guest. Part of what we're doing."

"Sure. As long as she's—"

"See you then," I said, thumbing the cellular into silence.

"**Y**ou wanted another chance," I told him. "This is it."

"Be a rat? *That's* your fucking idea of another chance?"

"This isn't being a rat, Herk. It's like being a . . ." I searched for the word ". . . spy. Like behind enemy lines, during a war."

"Dropping a dime is still—"

"This *isn't* dropping a dime, okay? What we got is a bunch of lunatic motherfuckers planning to blow up some buildings, kill a whole bunch of people. The Man *already* knows about them. They been penetrated to the max. The Man *already* has a guy inside. Only thing is, he's one of them, see?"

"One of who?" Herk asked. A reasonable question.

"One of the Nazis. Now, *he's* a rat, see what I'm saying? Those are *his* boys. And he's gonna dime them, just like you said. You know how it works. The Man's gonna give him a free pass. New face, new ID, new everything. We play this right, that's yours. Instead of his, yours."

"Oh man, I ain't doing no Witness Protection—"

"You're not gonna *be* a witness, Herk. This isn't about testimony. And you're not gonna be in the Program either. You're not gonna have a PO, nobody to report to. You get all the new stuff, a little bit of cash to get you started, and then you're on your own."

"What about the guy I—?"

"Forget that. It's gonna be covered, all right? The Man won't be looking for you. Not for Hercules, not for the new guy, whoever that's gonna be. You, I mean."

"Burke, I dunno. . . ."

"Listen, Herk. This all started with . . . you know. Okay, let's say you slide on that beef. So what? Where are you? Back where you was, right? Nowhere. This here is what you said you wanted. Another chance. What you got going here that's so fucking great?"

"Nothing, I guess. But . . ."

"You're going back to the joint," I told him. "Sure as hell, that's where you're going. You got no job, no trade, a long record. What do you know how to do except fuck people up? And you don't even like to do that. You go back to the street, the wiseguys are gonna use you until the Man takes you down. You pull this off, you can be a gardener, right? Find yourself a greenhouse somewhere out west maybe. Start fucking *over*."

He paced the little room, listening to me. Then he finally snapped to what he was doing—practicing for his next bit, already boxed up in an eight-by-ten in his mind. When he looked over at me, I said: "It's a dice-roll, partner. You throw a few naturals, you make your point and catch it, you're golden. You're crap out, and it's over. One way or the other, you go into this, you don't come out the same."

"Those books you gave me? The last time you was here? I gotta, like, memorize all that?"

"No. Not word for word. But you heard it all before, right?"

"I guess. . . ."

"Sure you did," I encouraged him. "Inside. Plenty of guys were into that."

"And I gotta cut my hair?"

"Why?"

"Look like one of them skinhead motherfuckers, right?"

"Nah. You go in the way you are, Herk. You look like a fucking Viking anyway—it'll be perfect."

"You'd be like . . . around?"

"Not in there with you. But I'd be like your . . . coach, okay? There's stuff we have to find out first, but we don't have much time, Herk. If you don't wanna do it, that's okay. I got some cash here. Right with me. Say the word and you're in the wind."

"Burke . . ."

"What?"

"You're right, bro. Fuck it, I ain't goin' back Inside. Let's do it."

I parked Herk in Mama's. The Prof was already there. He'd handle the first round of coaching. Pryce was going to call Crystal Beth around midnight, so I fired up the Plymouth and headed over there.

But I didn't go straight to the Lower East Side. First I had to stop in the South Bronx. At the Mole's bunker, where I said the magic words to him—the only words absolutely guaranteed to ring his bell.

Nazis in the house.

I rapped on her back door at nine. She opened it immediately, like she'd been waiting.

"What happened?" she greeted me.

I just pointed to the staircase, then swept my arm like an usher to indicate she should go first.

She threw me a look over her shoulder, but she went up the stairs without another word.

Inside her room, she bent to light the candle. I stood there, watching, unzipped my jacket. She came over to where I was standing, put her arms around my neck. I reached behind her, grabbed her bottom through the loose cotton slacks and pinched with both hands, hard.

"Ow! What was that for?" she squeaked.

"I just wanted to see if you were sore," I told her, leaving my hands where they were.

"I am *now*," she said, pulling her hands down from my neck and trying to rub her bottom. My hands stayed in the way, keeping her from doing it. I pinched her again for emphasis.

"Burke, stop it!" she yelped, trying to wiggle free. "What are you talking about?"

"I thought that fat butt of yours might be a bit tender," I said in her ear. "Riding a motorcycle over that rough terrain in the middle of the night and all."

She stopped struggling. "I was just—"

"Spying," I said. "Or playing some game I'm not in on. You tell me."

"I didn't think you saw me following you," she said, no repentance in her voice. "I ran the whole way without lights."

"What's the deal, Crystal Beth? You weren't close enough to listen."

"I wasn't trying to listen. I was just . . . afraid."

"Of what?"

"Not *of* anything. I was afraid for you."

"So you were gonna protect me?"

"Yes!" she said defiantly.

"With what?"

"I don't *know*," she almost moaned. "I just . . . He's a very bad man. I thought, if he had other people there, I could ride up and . . ."

"What? Have me jump on the bike so we could make a getaway?"

"All right, I didn't know. I didn't have a plan. But I had a . . ."

"Purpose?"

"Yes. Go on, mock me. There wasn't anything I could do . . . here. Just sitting and waiting. I got you into this and . . ."

"It's okay," I said, patting her where I'd pinched. "But why didn't you tell me?"

"Would you have let me go?"

"No."

"That's why," she said, flashing her smile. "I know what men are like."

"You don't have a clue," I told her.

"I know what my father was like," she said. "He never would have let my—"

"I'm not your father, little girl."

"I know. I didn't mean—"

"Never mind."

"Burke, I'm sorry, okay? I'll—"

"I thought we had a deal," I told her. "You were going to do what I told you."

"I *did*."

"Not just in the damn restaurant, Crystal Beth. Until this is done. Until it's over."

"And then?"

"Then you can do what you want."

"What*ever* I want?" She smiled.

"Don't press your luck," I said.

She put her nose in my chest and rubbed like she had before. It worked. I sat in the easy chair and she plopped herself in my lap. Then I told her a pretty close version of my conversation with Pryce. Everything but the money part.

"Are you really going to . . . put somebody in there? With Lothar?" she asked when I was done.

"Yeah."

"When?"

"Pryce is going to call here tonight. He's going to want another meet. I figure he'll do it the same way. You know, he'll already be in place. We'll have to leave right away."

"We? You mean you want me to—?"

"No. I mean me and the guy I'm putting in. He's going be here later. Around eleven-thirty. And he's got to stay here until we move him out."

"Stay here? A man?"

"Yeah. Pryce won't give me time to go and pick him up. And I already moved him out of where we had him staying. It'll just be for a day or two."

"I can't let him. . . . There's no men living here."

"You got a basement, right?"

"Yes. But it's not really set up for living. There's no—"

"It doesn't matter. He's stayed in worse. We can fix it up easy enough. All right?"

She didn't say anything, one fingernail idly scratching the back of my neck.

"All right?" I asked her again.

"All right," she agreed.

She was quiet for a few minutes after that. Then she shifted her weight so her hips were resting on the arm of the easy chair. "I'll bet I'm bruised," she said on the wings of a soft breath. "From where you pinched me."

"It wasn't that hard," I said.

"Yes it was," she said. "There's bruises. Big ones, I'm sure of it. You better take a look."

We waited downstairs together. Eleven-thirty sharp, knuckles hit the outside door. I motioned Crystal Beth to one side and opened it. Herk and Clarence stood there. And the Mole, an indistinct blob in his dirt-colored jumpsuit, a toolbox in his right hand.

I waved them in. "This is Hercules," I said to Crystal Beth.

"I'm glad to meet you," she said, holding out her hand for him to shake.

"You're goddamn gorgeous!" Herk said, staring. He can do that—say something like that to women without a trace of a leer or a sneer—I've seen him do it before.

Crystal Beth flushed, mumbled something under her breath.

"And this is Clarence," I told her.

"I am honored to meet you," the West Indian said in his formal voice.

"The honor is mine," she replied, on safer ground now.

"That's the basement?" I asked, pointing to my left.

"Yes."

The Mole walked past us without a word and disappeared down the dark stairs, Clarence right behind him, trusting the Mole to see in the dark. Crystal Beth gave me a look. I ignored it. "Let's talk upstairs," I said.

She started up the steps. I elbowed Herk out of the way before he could tell her what a beautiful butt she had and fell in right behind her, leaving him to follow.

In her room, Crystal Beth hit a switch and three separate lamps snapped into light. The place looked different in artificial light. Colder, more efficient.

"It's gonna be tonight," I told Herk. "This guy, Pryce, he'll call here. And we'll go to the meet. You'll stay here until he has it set up."

"Here?" Herk asked, smiling at Crystal Beth.

"In the basement," I told him. "We're gonna rig something down there."

"There's a toilet," Crystal Beth said helpfully. "I think it works. And there's a sink, and a—"

"Whatever," I cut her off. "We'll make it work. It won't be for more than a couple of days, max." Then I turned to Hercules. "You can't come upstairs," I told him. "Not for nothing, period. This is supposed to be an all-women's joint, understand? Nobody else can see you. Got it?"

"I got it," he replied, not bitching.

"We'll take my car to the meet. Pryce has already seen it. And I'll bring you back. By then, the guys will have it set up downstairs, okay?"

"Sure, Burke. Like you said."

"You've been reading that stuff I left with you?"

"Yeah. It ain't all that complicated. Just . . . stupid, like."

"What do you mean?"

"The Jews run everything, right? That's what the books said. They run the government, the newspapers, the TV, everything, okay?"

"Okay . . ."

"And these guys, they fucking *hate* the Jews, and . . . Ah, excuse me, miss. I didn't mean to . . . curse, like. I'm an ignorant asshole sometimes."

Crystal Beth's laugh was a merry sound in the room. "That's all right," she said.

Goddamn Hercules. He probably could have been the world's greatest pimp if he didn't love women so much.

"Go ahead," I prompted him.

"Okay, so I'm the Jews, right? And I got all this power, right? And these Nazis or whatever, they wanna wipe me out, right? So how come I don't just wipe *them* out?"

"Good question," I told him. "But not a question you want to ask these guys you'll be with."

"Oh yeah, I know. I was just—"

"Herk, this is no game. Don't be wondering *anything*. No talking, all listening, got it?"

"I got it."

The phone rang. Crystal Beth walked over to pick it up. Hercules watched her like a kid in an ice-cream forest.

"Hello."

There was a long pause as she listened, brushing away her hair to get the receiver right against her ear.

After a minute or so, she said: "I understand. Nine-E as in 'Edward,' right? I'll tell him."

She hung up. Gave me an address on the East Side in the Seventies. "He said to ask for Mr. White," she said.

"When?"

"Right now, if you want. Or anytime between now and four in the morning, that's what he said."

So Pryce didn't know I had Herk with me, was giving me time to pick him up. Good.

I turned to Crystal Beth. "If I so much as *hear* a motorcycle . . ."

"I got enough bruises for one night," she said softly, stepping close to me, sticking her nose into my chest. "Anyway, you have to bring . . . Hercules back, don't you?"

"Stay put," I told her, the warning still in my voice.

We all came downstairs together, walking silently past the closed doors on the second and third floors. Lights were on in the basement. We went down the stairs and saw an army cot with a full bedroll all set up. A folding table and matching chair were in place, plus a small TV set, a radio with a cassette player, a little cube of a refrigerator, a hot plate and a bunch of books . . . race-hate literature to comics. Herk's duffel bag was standing next to the cot. Looked like my place.

"It's great!" Hercules said.

I held out my hand to the Mole, palmed what he had in his. We all walked upstairs together, then out the back door. Crystal Beth closed it behind us.

"You got those keys made fast, Mole," I told him in the street, slipping them into my pocket.

"Where are the Nazis?" was all he wanted to know.

The apartment building had a circular driveway in front with a drop-off area protected by a canopy. I cruised past it twice, just checking. Then I found a parking place about a block away and we walked back together.

The uniformed doorman wasn't asleep. A bad sign, made me edgy. I told him we were there to see Mr. White in 9-E. He raised an eyebrow. I didn't respond.

"Two gentlemen to see you, sir," he said into the house phone, eyes never leaving my face. He was a tallish man in his fifties, built blocky, like an ex-athlete who hadn't kept up the training regimen. His hair was buzz-cut, gone mostly gray. His eyes were small, porno-movie blue. They didn't blink.

He listened, no expression on his face. "Go on up," he said. "Last elevator on your left."

The walls of the elevator car were mirrored, with rows of tiny lights inset into the ceiling. A bell in the control panel pinged a greeting when the car reached the ninth floor.

The door to 9-E was right across from the elevator. It opened before I could knock.

"Come on in," Pryce said, stepping to one side so we could.

Just past the foyer, there was an oversized living room with a broad expanse of glass facing east. Might have been a river view behind it but I couldn't tell from where I was standing. The main furniture was one of those sectional leather sofa-chair combos, muted ecru, extending in a J-curve toward the window. A pair of complicated-looking chairs were positioned right across from it, strips of tan leather pulled taut over black wrought iron. A free-form glass coffee table sat between them, all set off nicely by the thick wine-colored carpet. The walls were bare except for some old movie posters from the Forties, framed in chrome.

Pryce waved his hand toward the sectional, taking one of the suspension chairs for himself. Herk and I sat down. I slid over a few feet so that Pryce couldn't watch us both without turning his head a bit.

"This is your man?" he asked without preamble.

"This is Hercules," I said.

He swiveled his head to Herk. "And you're a Nazi?" he asked suddenly.

"I'm an Aryan warrior," Herk said, no hesitation. I was proud of him.

"What does *that* mean?" Pryce stayed on him.

"It means I love my race. I would die for my people. And kill for them too."

"Your . . . race?"

"The white race," Herk said, trying to keep his voice calm like I'd schooled him, but unable to keep the juice bubbling out—he was proud of himself, a kid eager to show he'd learned his ABCs.

"Define 'white,' " Pryce said.

"Huh? What's so fucking hard? White."

"So not blacks and . . . ?"

"And not browns and not yellows and not reds and not no other fucking *shade*, okay?" Herk told him, a step shy of aggressive.

"And Jews?"

"Jews? They ain't white people. They ain't people at all."

Pryce went "Ummm . . ." like he was considering this newly presented wisdom. "Tell me about the man you killed," he said finally.

"I don't know nothin' about no—"

"You first," I interrupted, holding Pryce's eyes.

"This is a leaderless cell," Pryce said, like he'd never asked the homicide question. "A super-cell, in point of fact. It's been in place just a few months. There are only a half-dozen or so members, and they all have conventional lives. Relatively conventional. The meetings are in various places, but they use a bookstore in lower Manhattan for an information drop. They're only in New York until—"

"What's a super-cell?" I asked him.

He nodded like a college professor who got asked a moderately intelligent question—one that showed the students were paying attention. Finally. "Each of them is a . . . representative," he said. "From one of the original leaderless cells scattered throughout the country. Eventually, each of them will return to his base area to a pre-determined residence and await contact. Their home cells may have changed composition or personnel by then. Or they may have disappeared. But if they *are* contacted when they return, each member of the super-cell passes the word. The date for the unified action."

"And you don't know that date?"

"No. I don't believe it *is* known. Yet."

"Or the target list?"

"There's no way to know that at all. Each of the local cells has that. The way it's set up, the member they detached to the super-cell doesn't know it either."

"Why can't you just shadow each of them when they split?"

"Do you know the kind of surveillance effort that would require? And without tipping them off? No, we need the date. Anything else we get would be gravy."

I raised my eyebrows at the mention of gravy. If he noticed, Pryce gave no sign.

"Up to now, they've been taking their cues from the newspapers. The church arsons, that's an example. One cell just goes out and commits an . . . action, they call it. Another reads about it, does the same thing. There's no communication between them. None at all. But this one's different."

I looked around for an ashtray. Couldn't see one. Lit a cigarette with a wooden match. A real one this time, no damn cloves. I watched Pryce's face. Nothing. Okay. I took out a small metal box, the kind some cough drops come in, and opened it up. Pryce nodded approvingly. Good. Let him get used to me taking things out of my pockets.

"You telling me *each* of them has a home cell?"

"Yes."

"So where's Lothar's?"

"Right here," Pryce said. "New York City."

"And he's gonna give them up too?"

"He already has," the colorless man replied, the muscle jumping under his eye.

"So they're being watched?"

"He has no contact with them, I told you. And we don't have the resources to do that anyway."

I wondered who "we" was in that sentence. Whoever it was, it wasn't the FBI. It has enough damn "resources" to watch anyone. Could they already be in custody?

I dragged on my cigarette, thinking. The whole thing was as snaky-shaky as a politician's promise.

"Herk's gotta be a *member*, right?" I put it to him. "Not some free-lance assassin—a card-carrying, true-believing member. He's gotta be inside."

"That's true."

"And his credential is that he did some . . . job for them, right?"

"Yes."

"And you can cover that?"

"Yes."

I got it then. "So Herk was in Lothar's cell? From the jump, right?"

"Right."

"And the guy he . . . took care of, that guy was in the cell too?"

"Yes."

"An informant?"

"No!" he said sharply. "There can't even be the *hint* of such a thing. They would instantly disband if they had any reason to believe they'd been infiltrated. Just fold their tents and go."

"But not drop the plan?"

"Of course not. But there'd be no way to pick them up again."

A thought crossed my mind. Something I'd never asked. But it could blow the whole thing higher than Timothy Leary. "This guy you . . ." I asked Herk. "He was white?"

"Uh, yeah," Herk said. He hadn't thought about it either.

"No he wasn't," I said leaning forward, flushed with relief. Elbows on knees, looking only at Herk, shutting Pryce out of my vision. "He was a Jew. His mother, or his grandmother, whatever, was a Jew. That makes *him* a Jew. That's the way they do it in Israel. He'd changed his name, but the cell discovered it. That's when you got the word to—"

"That's when you *volunteered*," Pryce interjected, with me now.

I shifted my eyes back to the colorless man. "They have some kind of mail drop?" I asked him. "I know they can't contact the old cell, but is there some way for the cells to reach out to them?"

"Yes. They use a P.O. box on—"

"Okay." I spun it out. "Lothar gets word that . . . one of his cell buddies was rotten, okay? Now listen, he *tells* the other guys in his unit that he got this word. He can get the details, but, to do it, he's gotta meet with someone from his old cell. That's Herk."

"They might panic and—"

"And that's the game," I said flatly. "If they run, they run. But if they want to hear what really happened, calm themselves down, make a decision whether to abort or not, they have to meet with Herk. And once they meet with him, he's gotta *stay* with them until it's over, right?"

"Yes," Pryce said slowly. "That's the way they would behave. Once he was there, he couldn't go back. But it's a risk. . . ."

"Any other bullshit way you try and stick Herk in there is a risk too. Only question is, who takes the risk? And here's the answer: it's not gonna be us."

"It's my decision," Pryce said. "Not yours." He scratched the tip of his nose with his index fingernail. "Unless you can guarantee that this divorce business will be dropped."

"I can't do that," I told him. "My way's the only way. You can get a meet with Lothar, right? That's when he meets Herk. He wouldn't necessarily know all his cell buddies that good anyway. This is the way to do it, and you know it."

"We'll need good information, *very* good information about the . . . Jew."

"I can get all that," I promised him.

"How fast?"

"Twenty-four hours, max."

He took a shallow breath. "You have complete control? Of that woman?"

I knew who he meant. "Total," I promised him.

"Get the information," he said. "We don't have much time. You two stay together. Wait for my call. I'll call her. Two, three days at the most."

"Done," I said. To remind him about the money.

I called Crystal Beth on the cellular to tell her we were on our way. As soon as I tapped lightly on her back door, it popped open. If she wondered how I could get past the padlock on the outside gate, she kept it to herself.

"Everything went fine," I said to her. "Let me get Herk established in the basement and I'll come back here and tell you about it."

"I'll help," she said, starting to go downstairs.

"Go on up," I said. "I'll be there in a few minutes."

"I'll wait here," she said firmly. "If you don't want me to go downstairs, I'll wait right here. You can't wander around upstairs by yourself. If Lorraine saw you, it would be—"

"Okay," I agreed, cutting off the speech.

In the basement, I went over everything with Herk again. Then I palmed the cellular and left a message for Wolfe.

As Crystal Beth and I walked past the doors, I noticed one of them was open just a crack, a yellow band of light outlining the frame. Lorraine's room?

"Tell me," she said as soon as we got into her room.

"There isn't a lot to tell. We're going to try to do it. Depends on a bunch of things that have to happen in the next day or so. Pryce, he's going to call here. You reach out for me and—"

"You're not going to be here?"

"Not twenty-four/seven. There's people I have to see."

"I could come with you."

"No. You couldn't."

"Because—?"

"Because I fucking said so," I told her, my voice as tired as I felt.

"You don't have to snap at me."

"And you don't have to pout like a spoiled brat," I told her. "This is business. My business, not your business."

"I thought you trusted me."

"I do trust you, bitch. That's *my* risk. I don't make my people take my risks, understand?"

She didn't say anything, just stood there facing me squarely, one hand pulling idly at her hair. Then she said, "Why do you use that word like that?"

"What?"

"'Bitch.' You say it like some other man would say 'honey' or something."

"I don't know. I just—"

"You *do* know," she said. "People know why they do things, if they would just think about them."

"Okay, I guess I never thought about—"

"Do it," she said. Then gave me a sweet smile. "Please."

I sat down in the easy chair and closed my eyes. Crystal Beth came around behind me, put her hands over my eyes. Little hands. Soft. Smelled like purple lilacs and dark tobacco. Her nose nuzzled gently against the back of my head. I let myself go into it.

"When I was a kid, I had a dog," I said, thinking and talking to her at the same time. "A fox terrier. A walking death warrant for rats. She was my great pal. I loved her. When I went to one of those foster homes, they took her away from me. I never saw her again."

"Why wouldn't they let you take your dog?" she asked, more anger than sadness in her voice.

"I'm sure they had their reasons. Reasons that looked good on paper. But I knew what it really was. They wanted to hurt me. They all did."

"But . . ."

"I was right," I told her, cutting that off before the feelings came back too strong. "I always swore I would have a dog someday. My own dog. In the juvie joint, the fucking 'reform school,' other guys dreamed of cars. Mostly cars. Where I came from, nobody thought about having a house, so it was cars we dreamed about. Fantasies, I guess they were."

"You didn't fantasize about girls?" she asked, her voice more flirtatious than teasing.

"I meant fantasies you could talk about," I told her. "Out loud. Girls, the play was you *already* had them, see?" *And mothers too,* I thought to myself, remembering how kids in the joint would fight to the death if you called their mother a name . . . even if that mother was a drunken whore who never showed up on visiting day.

"And you could talk about them? About girls?"

"Lie about them mostly," I told her, keeping my voice light. Thinking of the boys in there who were already talking about girls they hadn't met . . . and what they were going to do to them when they did. "But me, my fantasy, my dream was to have a dog."

"Did you ever get one?"

"I got the best dog in the world," I said. "Her name is Pansy. She's a Neapolitan mastiff. One of the original war dogs. They came over the Alps with Hannibal. Marco Polo took one to China."

"Are they smart?"

"Smart? I don't know. In some ways, I guess. But that's not her big thing. Pansy would die for me. She's not some *pet*," I said scornfully, "like a tropical fish. Or one of those damn cats."

"What do you have against cats?" she asked. "Lorraine has one, and it's—"

"Cats are the lap-dancers of the animal world," I told her. "Soon as you stop shelling out, they move on, find another lap. They're furry little sociopaths. Pretty and slick—in love with themselves. When's the last time you saw a seeing-eye cat?"

Crystal Beth took her hands away from my eyes and walked around the chair. She knelt in front of me, hunched forward, almond eyes widening, not listening so much as opening herself, as if to make her body understand me too.

"But when I come back to . . . where I live," I went on, "Pansy's always glad to see me. It doesn't matter what I look like. It doesn't matter whether I'm a success or a failure. Or even whether I have food for her. She's so . . . loyal. Loyal and true."

"And she's a bitch?"

"And she's a bitch. Maybe that's it. I'm not sure. We get the words all wrong. A man steps out on a woman, he gets called a dog. But if the woman's ugly, *she* gets called a dog."

"I know. And if the girl's pretty, she gets called something like 'kitten,' yes?"

"Yeah," I said.

"Burke?"

"What?"

"It shifted again. Your aura."

I didn't need her to tell me that. I could feel the blue in the room. A mist rising from my . . . I don't know what. "Kitten." When I was a young man, I called a lot of girls that. They always liked it. I did it so I wouldn't blow my cover, call one of them by the wrong name. I had a lot of girls then.

"Had." Looking back, I know I never understood what that meant. But I remember the last one. Ruth. The more she loved me, the more I knew I had to go away. Before Ruth, it was all game. I knew what they wanted. They knew what I wanted. Fire-dancing, seeing which one of us would tumble in first . . . and get burned. It was never me. You can't lose what you don't ante up.

The only thing I knew for sure about myself back then was that I was no good. Ruth wasn't like any of the other girls I'd been with. She didn't want me stealing to buy her jewels, didn't shake her ass in the street and then come running to me because some clown noticed it, demanding I defend her "honor" . . . be a man. I thought I knew what that meant too, back then—cause pain, and never show any.

Ruth wanted to be married. Have children. A house. She wanted me to have a job. Be a citizen. Her eyes were the color of nightclub smoke.

She came from the same place I did, but she wasn't going to stay there. And she'd wait for me to join her, however long it took.

I knew how long it was going to take. And I felt so bad about it I had to go.

But I couldn't make her see it. When I told her we were done, she said maybe someday I'd understand that she had true love for me and I'd want her back. And she'd come, she said. All I had to do was leave a notice in the paper. People did that then—before the personals columns got degenerate the way they are now—left messages for someone they actually knew.

"Just say 'kitten,'" she told me. "And I'll know it's you."

"But I wouldn't know it was you," I said. And told her how I used that name. How it was nothing special.

I told myself I was just being honest, squaring up with her like she deserved. But I saw something die in her eyes right then.

Every once in a while, I would feel that again. First time I heard Barbara Lynn singing "You'll Lose a Good Thing," I felt that way. Sorry. For me. A lot of things happened since then. I never broke up with a woman for her own good again.

No, they went away from me. Or died.

When I thought about that, only Hate kept me from drowning.

Crystal Beth stood up. Held out her hand. Then she pulled me in.

The Plymouth swam over the Manhattan Bridge, dwarfed by the Brooklyn-bound trucks. It rolled past the car-repair shops and topless bars on Flatbush, me safe inside, listening to the truth girl-growling out of my cassette player, Magic Judy warning her sisters everywhere—if you're dumb enough to brag about your man to your girlfriends, they'll double-cross you every time.

Ten in the morning on a weekday, the Plymouth was invisible in the moderate traffic. I crossed Atlantic, hooked the first sharp left and motored a couple of blocks past the abandoned *Daily News* printing plant—they do all the work in Jersey now—looking for a place to park.

I found one close enough. Got out and walked back to the bridge over the railroad yards. Wolfe was standing there, waiting. At the curb across from her a dark-green Lexus GS sedan stood idling—I could see smoke from the exhausts. Pepper waved at me merrily from the driver's seat, a small, pretty dark-haired girl with an electric smile. I could make out a much larger shape in the back seat. Not the rottweiler, a human shape.

I lit a smoke, cupping my hands against a nonexistent wind so I could glance over my left shoulder. Sure enough: a young woman with long winter-blond hair in a bright-orange jogging outfit strolled by past the entrance to the bridge behind me, walking like she was cooling down from a long run. I knew who that was. Chiara, one of Wolfe's crew. I remembered her from our last meeting; her and that honey-colored pit bull she had on a short leash. They both stopped walking and watched me, making no secret of it.

A lot of security for Wolfe to bring to a meet with me. Or maybe it was just the neighborhood . . . ?

A pair of Puerto Rican kids ambled up the block, approaching Chiara. One of them was holding a spike-collared pit bull of his own on a bicycle chain wrapped around his wrist. The dog was a big, chesty beast, caramel-colored and shovel-headed. He was out of one of the classic red-nose lines, and his strut was pure testosterone. He stopped suddenly and growled something at Honey, tugging at the bicycle chain. Didn't sound like a threat . . . more like pit-bull–speak for "What's your sign, baby?"

Honey snarled something back. Easy enough to translate that too: "Skull and crossbones, sucker! Want to play?"

The big pit didn't back off, but he stopped tugging. And he

didn't protest when the Puerto Rican kids took off, eyes glancing at me over their shoulders. Like their dog, they'd figured out something was going on . . . and they wanted no part of it, whatever it was.

Chiara just stood there, calm and watchful. She had a cellular phone in a leather holster over one shoulder. At least that was what was in the holster the last time I'd seen her.

I turned back toward where Wolfe was waiting across from the Lexus, walked over and handed her a newspaper clipping about the guy Herk did in that alley. Seemed like a long time since that happened. "This guy," I said, "I need anything you can get me on him."

"The victim?" she asked, quickly scanning the news clip.

"The dead guy," I said.

"Oh," she responded, getting it right away. "This is an Unsolved?" she asked.

"Yeah."

"And you're looking to—"

"Find out everything I can on the dead guy."

"You got a TPO. Wouldn't the cops—?"

TPO. Time and Place of Occurrence. Enough of a locate key for any cop who could tap into the computer. "I don't want to ask them," I said. "And I wouldn't want you to either."

She nodded. An amateur might have been confused, but for Wolfe it was a large-scale road map—with the route I wanted to travel etched in neon.

"I don't care about the . . . about what happened," I told her, drawing the boundaries. "I'm looking for background. As deep as you can go. His mother's maiden name, where he went to school, military, if he did time . . ."

"It says here he was a security guard."

"So that means he never did time?"

Wolfe chuckled at that. "No, I just want to know if you want his employment record too."

"Everything."

"You mind telling me what you're looking for?" she asked. "It might narrow the search, make it quicker. You *do* need it quick, right?"

"Real quick," I acknowledged. "I'm looking for a Jew," I said.

Wolfe's map-of-Israel face hardened. "Any particular Jew?"

"I'm *not* particular," I said, so she'd get it clear. "What I need is some Jew in his background. A female relative. His mother would be perfect, but if you can't do that, then—"

"So you think one of those Nazi groups did—?" Wolfe interrupted.

"Yeah," I said, planting the lie. Wolfe traffics in information. She wouldn't shop me, but she might peddle something she picked up while she was working. And if she did that this time, it would blend seamlessly into the whisper-stream. Right where I wanted it.

"If it was one of them who did the job, you're looking at an ex-con," she said quietly.

"Why would you say that?" I asked her, alarm bells ringing all around me.

Her gray eyes were clear, not a hint of guile in them. "A knife, that's a jailhouse weapon. It takes a different head to stab than to shoot. Those misfits running around cross-dressing in swastikas, they don't like to work close-up."

"Skinheads don't seem to mind," I told her.

"But this was a one-on-one, right?" She dismissed me. Wolfe was too experienced to be played off—every act of skinhead violence law enforcement ever heard about was always a group activity. If you wanted to earn your spiderweb tattoo, you needed a witness, for authentication. "It was me," she said, "I'd look for someone who was a member of a Nazi prison gang. Probably AB."

AB. The Aryan Brotherhood. I flashed on my old pal Silver, buried for life Upstate. I didn't want Wolfe nosing around there. "That's my piece," I told her. "You work the opposite end of the tunnel."

"And stay out of yours?"

"Yeah."

"Okay," she agreed. Too easily? I let it pass. "The security-guard thing should make it simple," she said. "They'll have his Social Security, date of birth, all that. Give me . . . how long?"

"Can you get it today?"

She raised her eyebrows, but didn't say anything, just nodded.

"One more thing," I said, handing her a sealed white #10 envelope, the kind you can buy in any stationery store. "You have any men in your crew?"

"I'm not running a sperm bank," she said, smiling to take the sting off. "Why would I need any men?"

"I know *you* don't need any, Xena," I told her. "But I do. To deliver this," pointing at the envelope she was holding.

"It has to be a man?" she asked, smiling at the gibe. Wolfe was a warrior princess way before any writer's wet dream came to life on TV.

"An observant man," I emphasized. "All he has to do is take this to a certain address, ask for a certain person, go up to his apartment and put it in his hand."

"Anything else?"

"He has to wear a suit, carry an attaché case, look like a businessman, the whole bit. And he has to put it in the man's hands personally, not leave it with a doorman." Then I gave her the details.

"I can get that done," Wolfe said. "No risk, right?"

"No risk," I promised. Thinking maybe the form in the back seat of the Lexus was Pepper's man, Mick. I'd only seen him once—big guy, long hair, athlete's build. Max had made him for a fighter, but we'd never needed to find out.

"The parking lot across from Criminal Court," Wolfe said. "Same time tomorrow?"

"Thanks," I said, handing her another envelope. She slipped it into her purse without looking. Then she walked across the road and got into the passenger seat of the Lexus. It pulled away with a cheerful chirp from the rear tires, Pepper driving like she talked.

"Put it right over the heart," I told the old man. We were in the back room of a tailor shop in the Bronx, just off the Grand Concourse. The narrow storefront was surrounded on all sides by members of that heavily armed tribe of *bodegueros* who operate trading posts in hostile territory throughout the city's pocket ghettos, selling overpriced Pampers and yesterday's milk and loose cigarettes for a quarter apiece in a can on the counter. There was also a sprinkling of liquor stores that looked like the inside of Brink's vans, and a solitary dump that pretended to sell used furniture but whose only real business was exchanging food stamps for cash at a deep discount. The front room of the tailor shop was lined with fabric samples and suits on hooks. A three-sided mirror stood against one wall. Even the dust looked clean.

The old man looked over at the Mole, who said something to him in Yiddish. Or Hebrew—I couldn't tell the difference. The Mole told me once that the young Israelis spoke Hebrew and the older European Jews spoke Yiddish, but it wasn't a rule or anything.

Hercules was sitting in what looked like a barber chair, bare-chested, his upper body as deeply ripped as when he'd been Inside and hoisting iron every day. The old man held the tattoo needle steady as he created a black swastika on Herk's left pectoral, just under the nipple. I watched his hands as they worked. Watched the faint blue row of numbers tattooed on the inside of his forearm in the harshly focused light from the lamp.

"Two days," he said, covering the fresh tattoo with a clean bandage. "Then it will look old, like it was done a long time ago."

I thought of what it must have taken for a man who'd been tattooed in a concentration camp to copy the oppressor's symbol onto living flesh. Then the Mole said something to the old man again, touching Hercules on the shoulder. The old man kissed Hercules on the cheek. Not a mob kiss—gently, as he would kiss a beloved son. "*Sei gesund!*" he said.

And then I knew what the Mole must have told him.

"Lorraine isn't on the run from . . . them," Crystal Beth said to me. Talking softly, her breasts mashed against my chest, face in my neck.

I didn't say anything, just rubbed my palm in tender circles right above her bottom, wondering why she was telling me about the harsh-faced woman with the clipboard and the Siamese cat.

"She's much older than most of us," Crystal Beth said. "A different underground. She's one of the last ones left."

"What is she, an ROTC bomber?"

"Something like that," Crystal Beth said. "It doesn't matter anymore. For Lorraine, it's all merged."

"Into what?"

"Men. She's very bitter at how weak they all were. They weren't true, she always says."

"I guess most of the women in here would say that."

"No, not what you think. Not true to their ideals."

"Some are."

"You?"

"I don't have any," I said. "All I'm trying to do is get through this."

"This . . . ?"

". . . life," I finished for her. Leaving out the last word I always spoke in my mind: "sentence." A life sentence. That's what I got. Some liberal wet-brain once told me, "We're *all* doing life." I guess that was supposed to be some startling insight, make me see we were all brothers. He was some halfass religion-peddling do-gooder. A missionary to a country where he didn't speak the language, talking to cannibals who'd feast on his flesh if he spent the night with them. I was only sixteen years old then, locked up. But I knew he wasn't doing *my* life.

"I like that," Crystal Beth said.

"What?"

"You . . . stroking me like that."

I dropped my hand lower. "You like this too?"

"It's better than being pinched," she cooed.

I slapped her bottom, lightly. "Shut up, girl."

She giggled. "I got that from my mother."

"What?"

"A big rear end," she said. "It's genetic."

"It's a gift," I told her.

"It could be," she whispered, her right hand dropping to the outside of my thigh.

The door opened. A woman walked into the room. Even without

the outrageous silhouette, I knew who it was by the click of the spike heels.

"Can I play too?" Vyra asked.

In the frozen moment, my cock deflated and my eyes widened, riveted on Vyra's hands, ready to . . . but they were empty.

"This isn't your business," Crystal Beth said to her, pulling herself into a sitting position next to me.

"Oh, then he doesn't know?" Vyra said in a challenging voice, hands on her narrow hips, talking over my body like I was furniture.

"*That* isn't *his* business," Crystal Beth snapped back. "Why don't you go downstairs and I'll come and talk to you . . . privately."

"I like this better," Vyra said, stepping closer to the bed, eyes only on the other woman.

"I don't care what you like," Crystal Beth told her, climbing off the bed and walking around the end of it to close the gap between her and Vyra. "You're not in charge here. And your money doesn't change that."

Vyra took a quick step back. Her little fox face went feral under the makeup as her heavily lipsticked mouth twisted with soundless words. Crystal Beth took another step toward her, her nude body glistening with kinetic confidence. Vyra's left hand flashed against Crystal Beth's tattoo, a sharp crack in the silence. Vyra's mouth made an O, like she was shocked at herself. Crystal Beth kept coming, stepped right in to her, wrapping her arms around the skinny girl, holding her immobile. "Stop that!" she said. Vyra struggled in her grip for a few seconds. Then she started to cry.

Crystal Beth walked her over to the bed, arms still wrapped around her. She muscled Vyra onto the mattress, right next to me, holding her down with one shoulder, her hips over Vyra's thighs. "Stop it," she said again, kissing Vyra's cheek. "Just stop it, now."

Vyra went from sobbing to sniffling, then gulped a breath and shuddered down into silence. "Good baby," Crystal Beth said softly to her. "That's right."

I got up and started to put my clothes on.

Crystal Beth unbuttoned Vyra's blouse. Vyra sat up slightly so it could come off her shoulders.

I zipped up my jeans, grabbed my jacket off the back of the easy chair.

Crystal Beth whispered something to Vyra.

"I'll bet he can't," Vyra giggled, unhooking her bra.

Crystal Beth turned her face toward me. "Stay there," she said. Then to Vyra: "What do you want to bet?"

Vyra whispered something.

"No," Crystal Beth said. "This." And whispered something back to her.

I put one arm into my jacket.

"Please stay," Crystal Beth said, sweetly this time. "Just sit in the chair for a few minutes, smoke a cigarette, okay? Just watch us. Then we can talk."

I turned around and sat in the chair. Then I took my eyes out of focus and watched them through a soft filter as Crystal Beth helped Vyra undress. When it got to her shoes, Vyra put up a battle and they wrestled around for a while, but Crystal Beth finally wrenched them off and threw them across the room.

Then they made love, generous to each other.

It ended with Crystal Beth on her belly, face buried in a pillow, moaning softly, Vyra behind her, face buried in Crystal Beth. They let go at the same time, explosively. Then stayed softly locked together for a couple of minutes, just off the edge of passing out until . . .

Crystal Beth took her face out of the pillow and looked over her shoulder at Vyra. "I win," she said, a happy laugh bubbling in her voice.

"Sleepy," Vyra murmured, her face against Crystal Beth's broad hip.

I covered them both with the sheet and went downstairs.

"You know how much this weighs?" Herk asked me. He was doing curls with some setup he'd jury-rigged from the supplies we'd laid in—two pairs of two-and-a-half-gallon plastic jugs of water threaded together with insulated wire through the handles and anchored with a piece of wood he used as a grip. He had one set in each hand.

"About forty pounds apiece," I told him.

"How'd you know that, bro?" he asked, grunting rhythmically with each lift.

"Quart of water weighs about two pounds," I said. "Four quarts to a gallon. That's eight, right? Times two and a half is twenty. Double that and you got each hand."

"No. I mean, I can do numbers. That kind, anyway. How'd you know what a quart weighs and all?"

"I don't know, Herk," I said honestly. I know stuff, stuff I read, stuff I heard. It's all in there somewhere, mixed in so thick I could never separate it out.

"You know how big an acre is?" he asked me.

"About the size of a city block. The whole block, square."

"Yeah! *That's* the kinda stuff I gotta know too."

"For farming?"

"Nah. I ain't gonna be no farmer. Gardens, they ain't like farms."

"Because they're smaller?"

"'Cause you do it all with your hands, gardening. Remember when they asked old Dante if he wanted to be a trusty, work outside on the grounds?"

"Yeah."

"He wouldn't do it, right?"

"Dante was old-school," I said. "He thought all trusties were rats."

"Maybe. But that wasn't it," Herk said, not breaking the rhythm of his curls, banded muscle popping out on his forearms. "You know what he told me? They had nice gardens outside. Flowers and all. But they worked the beds with those little tractors. Dante, he wouldn't have none of that crap. He said, if you didn't work it with your hands, you wasn't a gardener, you was a farmer."

"I got it."

"He gonna go for it?" Herk asked.

I knew what he meant. Didn't know the answer. Shrugged.

"But if he don't, you got another plan, right?" the big man asked hopefully.

"Got a bunch of them," I promised.

"Knock knock." A woman's voice at the head of the stairs. Herk and I both turned in the direction of the sound. And the click of spike heels on the steps.

Vyra popped into view, all dressed up again but with her hair piled on top of her head and the makeup gone.

"Can you come—?"

She stopped when she saw Hercules. He stood bare-chested, his long hair matted with sweat, frozen halfway through a curl, the bandage white against his skin. Over his heart, where the swastika lurked.

"Crystal Beth didn't tell you to come downstairs, did she?" I asked mildly.

"She said to get you," Vyra said, a defensive tone in her voice.

Hercules just stared at her.

"She said to *call* me, right?" I told her. "Not to come down here."

"Well, it's too late for that, isn't it?" Vyra came back, standing with her hands on her hips.

I said *Fuck it* to myself. And out loud: "Vyra, this is Hercules. Herk, this is Vyra."

The big man carefully placed the water bottles on the basement floor, wiped his palms on the side of his jeans and walked over to where Vyra was standing. He held out his hand. "I'm pleased to meet you," he said.

"Likewise." She smiled.

"Those are beautiful shoes," Herk said.

Vyra looked down at her feet. At the iridescent green high heels with a tiny dot of gold at the toes. Kept her head down while she said "Thank you" in a little girl's happy-embarrassed voice.

I left them there.

"**N**ow you know," Crystal Beth said defiantly. As though she was expecting something bad. And was ready to deal with it.

"What is it that I know?"

"About me and Vyra. About what we . . . do."

"So what?"

"So that's what Pryce knows too. That's what he knows that would end everything for her."

"I don't get it," I told her, puzzled.

"Her husband. He would never . . . I don't know if I can explain it to you. Men have . . . boundaries. Different ones for different men. He knows Vyra has . . . relationships. But he would never—"

"How can you know that?" I asked her. "It doesn't make a lot of sense."

"They watch . . . movies together. Not movies, I guess. Tapes. Vyra picks them up. She picks everything up for him—he almost never goes out of the house. He doesn't much . . . It takes a lot to get him . . ."

"What?"

"Look, I'm not . . . comfortable with this."

"Just say what it is, Crystal Beth. Whatever it is, it's not yours, okay?"

"Okay," she said, drawing a breath like she was about to get a shot from the doctor. "He's not easily . . . aroused. The tapes . . . help him. And some of Vyra's . . . outfits too. As he gets older, it gets harder and harder. Whoops!" She giggled. "I didn't mean—"

"I know."

"Anyway, Vyra would get different tapes. She knows what he likes. Once she was talking to some other women. At some club she belongs to. And they all agreed, nothing turns a man on more than seeing two girls . . . make love. So she got a few of those tapes and brought them home. But when he saw the first one, he went ballistic. Told her it was the most disgusting thing he'd ever seen. He pulled the tape right out of the cassette. He told her, if she ever brought filth like that into the house again, he'd divorce her. Vyra said he looked like a maniac. It scared her."

"How did Pryce find out about you and Vyra?"

"I don't *know*," she said, voice cracking around the edges. "I don't know how he knows anything."

"He has photos? Wiretaps? What?"

"I don't think he has anything. Not like what you're talking about. But it wouldn't matter. Vyra is a lousy liar."

I knew how true that was, but I kept the thought to myself.

"**V**yra's *really* confused now," Crystal Beth whispered to me later in bed.

"What do you mean?"

"Remember when you were . . . watching us?"

"Yeah."

"You know what our bet was about? The one between me and Vyra?"

"No . . ."

"She said if you watched us you'd get turned on and . . ."

"And . . . ?"

"Want to join in."

"Oh."

"She's . . . been with you, she says. A lot. But she doesn't know you."

"And you do?"

"Yes," she said, turning to throw one thick thigh over the top of mine. "She doesn't understand how important self-control is to you."

"Meaning?"

"Vyra thought you would get turned on. And then you'd do something about it."

"But you thought—?"

"I thought you'd get turned on. But I knew you'd just sit there unless . . ."

"Unless what?"

"Unless we asked you to . . . join us. Did you want to?"

"I don't know," I told her.

"How could that be? Either you did or—"

"It's not that simple. Part of me, I guess, wanted to. But it also seemed like it wouldn't be . . . private, I guess."

"Privacy is important," she said solemnly. "I understand."

"You think so?" I asked her. "Me, I've been in places where there wasn't any privacy. None at all. Where you can't even be alone with your *thoughts*. I just wanted to . . . respect whatever you were doing. Even if I didn't understand it."

"You don't understand two women making love?"

"I didn't understand why you were . . . why you didn't want me to leave."

"Maybe I hoped Vyra would win the bet," she said in my ear.

"What was the bet anyway?" I asked her, stepping away from where she was going.

"Next time you come here, you won't recognize my place," she said. "Vyra has to clean it all. Top to bottom. Every square inch."

"What if you had lost?"

"I would have had to shine her shoes."

"That doesn't sound—"

"*All* her shoes," Crystal Beth said.

"Nah, you didn't want to lose," I told her, wrapping my arm around her neck to pull her down to me, pictures of her and Vyra together flashing on and off my screen.

By first light, I was on the roof with Pansy. She had greeted the assortment of cold cuts I'd picked up at the all-night deli with mixed enthusiasm, turning her nose up at the dark-edged liverwurst. I didn't think twice about trying it myself, settling for some rye toast and a few fresh celery sticks with ice water.

I dialed up Mama on the cellular. Nothing happening.

After we came down from the roof, I looked around the dump I lived in, thinking maybe I should have been in on the bet with Vyra. Then I spent a couple of hours cleaning, filled two thirty-gallon plastic trash bags before I was done. Pansy followed me around for a while, then gave it up when she saw it wasn't going to be any fun.

When I was done, we took a break. Pansy got a quart of honey-vanilla ice cream. I got a cigarette. She finished first, licking the bowl so hard she even took the smell off.

I put on the TV set for her, changing channels until she settled down. I wished I had cable. The only old stuff you can get on regular TV is crap like "The Three Stooges." I always hated that show when I was a kid. Fucking buffoons. They weren't partners, those guys. Not like Abbott and Costello. Or good criminals, like Bilko.

Around noon I went back over to Crystal Beth's. Called her first so she could let me in downstairs. She'd never offered me a key of my own. Sending me a message? Or maybe she'd figured out that the Mole had already taken care of it.

I spent most of the afternoon with Herk, rehearsing. Called Mama around five.

"Man come. With envelope. Two envelopes."

"White man? Tall? Broad shoulders, clean face, long hair?"

"Not long hair," Mama said. Meaning the rest of my description was on the money. I'd figured the messenger to be Mick, Pepper's man. But his hair was long.

"Can you open it, Mama?" I asked her. Like she already hadn't.

"Sure." After about ten seconds: "Paper." Meaning: not money.

"A lot of paper?"

"One, two, three . . . seven pages," Mama said, taking her time. The only thing she speed-counted was cash. "And picture."

"Anything else? In the other one?"

"More paper. Writing. Say 'Call me.'"

"That's all? No signature?"

"Say 'Call me.'"

"Okay, Mama. Thanks. I'll pick it up later."

"You working, right?" Meaning: doing something against the law. For money.

"I'm working," I assured her.

During the drive to Mama's, I reached out for Wolfe on the cellular. Left word where I'd be, thinking how it was time for our crew to change numbers—the Prof was picking up a fresh set of cloners from the Mole.

The pay phone at Mama's was ringing as I came through the kitchen.

"You got my package?" Wolfe asked as soon as she heard my voice.

I hand-signaled to Mama, who brought the two envelopes over. I leafed through the contents quickly, holding the phone against my shoulder with my head. "Yeah."

"The picture is . . . the subject. From his employment application."

"Thanks."

"There's . . . enough there," she said. "To make the connection. Be sure you look through the thick one first."

"Got it."

"Listen, that envelope you wanted dropped off?"

"Yeah."

"There is no Mr. White at that address. Mick was insistent—he had the apartment number, remember? So they showed him the place. It's the model suite—the one they use to attract tenants. Nobody lives there."

"Okay."

"Anything else?"

"No. Thanks. Hey, did Mick cut his hair?"

"All part of the job." Wolfe chuckled. "A small sacrifice."

The security guard's photo showed a man in his thirties, black hair cut fashionably short, generic European face with an unprominent, slightly bladed nose, staring straight into the camera, unsmiling. Nothing there.

He was born on Long Island. Mother's maiden name was Wallace. On the birth certificate, someone had placed one of those red plastic pull-off arrows that say "Sign Here"—the kind lawyers attach to contracts they want you to sign in a half-dozen places—next to the name. Why? I kept looking. High-school graduate. Unremarkable military career. Associate-of-arts degree in criminal justice from a community college. Employed steadily, but he changed jobs a lot. Process server, credit-collection agency, store detective. All quasi-cop "investigator" stuff. Almost three years as an auxiliary police officer. That fit—authority freaks gravitate to stuff like that.

Credit report showed him as slow-pay. Not enough to discourage a sizable loan on a 1991 Corvette, bought used in 1995. Arrest record was clean, attached to his application for a pistol permit. Must have been before his short stay on Rikers Island—I guess the security-guard companies don't do periodic rechecks. Once he got the piece, his pay had gone up to $9.50 an hour. Married a few years ago. Divorced. No children.

His medical scanned normal, except for asthma. Attached was a photocopy of a printout from a fertility clinic. He and his wife had been trying to have a baby some years back. Genetic counseling was checked on the form. That was marked with one of the red plastic arrows too.

I went to the second envelope. Just two pieces of paper. The first was an exact duplicate of the birth certificate, only this version had an official certificate embossed into the lower right corner and a stamp on the back indicating it was a "true and accurate copy." I followed the red arrow—now his mother's maiden name was Wasserstein.

The other page was a duplicate of the fertility-clinic stuff. The red arrow took me to the genetic counseling section—now it said: SCREEN FOR TAY-SACHS. The substitute papers were beautiful work, impossible to distinguish from the originals. Wolfe was more outlaw than I'd thought. And she had access to some fine forgers too.

I removed the red plastic arrows, substituted the new pages for the old and sat down to reread the new, unified version.

The death warrant.

I've heard that plenty of women clean house in the nude, but I'd never seen one do it in lipstick-red four-inch heels. When Crystal Beth showed me into her place, Vyra was wrestling with the vacuum cleaner like it was an artifact left behind by aliens, muttering to herself, her pale skin shining under a thin sheen of sweat. She saw me, bent to find the cut-off switch, a puzzled look on her face. After a minute of hunting around, she ripped the cord out of the wall in one mighty tug, then looked up in triumph.

"I didn't want to mess up my outfit," Vyra said to Crystal Beth, nodding her head in the direction of the bed, where a couple of thousand dollars' worth of red and black and white silk stuff lay in a confused jumble. "Anyway, I'm almost done."

"Almost done?" Crystal Beth laughed. "You only started a few minutes ago."

"Well, what else is there?" Vyra demanded, crossing her arms under her breasts. She always did it that way. For the lift—I think she knew they were way too big to look good without a bra.

"There's the baseboards, the shelves, the bathroom, the—"

"The bathroom? I'm not cleaning anybody's—"

"Yes you *are*," Crystal Beth said, advancing on her. "You lost fair and square."

Vyra turned away from the onslaught, walked over and sat down on the arm of the easy chair, crossing her legs and arching her back as though a camera lurked. "Well, I wouldn't have lost if you weren't such a wuss," she said to me.

"Sorry," I said.

"Yes, well, it's not you that has to do all this work. It's your fault—the least you could do is help."

"And miss a chance to watch you? No way."

Vyra flashed me a smile, taking it as a compliment. But she didn't go back to work.

"I've gotta go talk to Herk for a bit," I told Crystal Beth. "Let me know when Vyra's done."

"*I'll* let you know," Vyra said.

"Better put some clothes on first," I told her. "It's drafty down there."

"This is like in the joint, huh?" Herk said to me.

"The joint? This place is fucking Paradise compared to—"

"I didn't mean . . . this," Herk said, making a sweeping motion with his arm. "I mean . . . talking, like. Remember, in there? The Prof was always tryin' to explain stuff. Like how to do crime good and all?"

"Sure."

"Well, this is like that. You been explaining to me, right? How I gotta act and everything."

"That's right."

"Only it's different this time, Burke. Real different." He took a deep breath, thought showing on his face, the heavy bone structures prominent under the flesh. The white flesh. Part of the passport he'd use to slip past a checkpoint very soon. "In there," he said, "the trick was, like, not to come back, you know what I mean? We was *gonna* do crime, right? All of us. We was thieves. So we made plans. This time it's different."

"How?" I asked him.

"This deal here, it's my last crime, Burke. I swear to fucking God. We pull this off, it works like you say, I'm done. And you know what else?"

"What, Herk?"

"This ain't like before. This time I'm listening real good."

"You don't like my shoes?" Vyra asked Hercules, standing at the foot of the stairs, one red spike heel on the floor, the other propped one step up, posing.

"I didn't notice 'em," Herk said, moving past me toward her, standing close. "That first time, the shoes was the first thing I seen. Coming down. This time I was looking at you."

"At me?"

"At your eyes," Herk told her. "I never seen a color like that."

Vyra's eyes were an everyday brown. She clasped her hands under her breasts, cocked her head, said "Really?"

"Yeah. They're the same color as . . . Ah, you wouldn't understand. It wouldn't sound so good to you."

"Tell me," Vyra said, taking her foot down to stand in front of him, looking up from under her eyelashes.

"Peat moss," Herk told her shyly. "You know peat moss? Like for growing roses? It's so . . . rich. Rich and strong. That's the color."

On my climb upstairs, I figured out how the amorous fool got away with stuff like that. He meant it.

"If I had lost the bet, I would have shined every last one of her damn shoes," Crystal Beth said ruefully, waving her arms to indicate the pitiful cleaning job Vyra had done.

"I believe you," I said.

"Ah, that's Vyra." She laughed. "She has no discipline."

"And no purpose?"

"You're not . . . making fun of me?"

"I wouldn't do that."

"Sometimes people . . . tease. They don't mean anything by it, but it still . . . hurts."

"Crystal Beth?"

"What?"

"Would you do me a favor?"

"Sure, honey."

"Go sit down. In that chair."

She did it, a questioning look on her upturned face. I walked over to the bed, sat down myself. "Now get off your fat ass and come over here," I told her.

She giggled, bounced over to where I was sitting.

"What?" she asked, laughter in her eyes.

"It's never really the words," I said softly. "Not the plain words. It's what they mean. I make a crack about your fat ass, it doesn't bother you, right?"

"Well, I *am* at my winter weight. . . ."

"Cut it out, girl. It didn't bother you because you know I think you're beautiful. If you *really* thought I was making a nasty crack about your weight, your feelings would be hurt, wouldn't they?"

"Yes," she said seriously.

"That's the difference. I know it and you know it. And I would never rank on you about your purpose. You're sure I think you have a great butt. . . . You're not so sure I take you seriously. That's it, right?"

"I didn't mean—"

"Right?"

"Yes," she said, head down.

"I do, little bitch. I swear."

"Oh, Burke. I know. . . . But you're wrong about Vyra. She doesn't have a purpose, but she's looking for one. That's more than most people ever do."

"It's more than I ever did," I told her.

"Come here," Crystal Beth said softly, opening her arms.

Lightning tore the sky that night. It was about nine. Pansy and I were watching TV, some show that had a dog in the cast. One of those perky, cute ones that get to talk in a human voice. Like "Baywatch," I guess. Across the bottom of the screen, a string of words crawled: SEVERE THUNDERSTORM WARNING IN EFFECT IN SUSSEX AND UNION COUNTIES UNTIL 8:30 P.M. DETAILS AT 11:00. Even Pansy sneered at it.

I found one of those trash-news shows. They had an interview with some money-for-pussy slut telling the world that she'd written her book about how her politician boyfriend liked to dress up like a French maid and clean her house because she wanted all her fellow Americans to be aware of what kind of man was making important decisions about their lives. The hardest trick that whore ever turned—coming up with a pious reason for selling secrets. Probably her pimp's idea.

I didn't like the idea of that politician much either. Who wants a government official dumb enough to trust a whore?

Then they did another "exposé" of strip bars invading middle-class communities. Devoted about three minutes to shots of anonymous thonged buttocks and beyond-genetics boobs, then about fifteen seconds to the winter-dressed picketers outside. I wondered, if surgeons could do brain implants, would anybody get them?

The show closed with some geek who writes incest-torture comic books shrieking that he's the new John Peter Zenger.

Sure wished I had cable.

T he cellular rang just before midnight.

"It's me," Crystal Beth said. "He just called."

"He wants a meet now? Don't say where on the phone. I'll be—"

"No. Tomorrow afternoon. Can you—?"

"I'll be there before twelve," I promised her.

A s I patted Pansy before I took off the next morning, I felt a tremor. Didn't know how it was transmitted, from her to me or the other way around. But I felt it, and I trusted it.

So I stashed the Plymouth on Houston. Leaned up against a building to kill some time. Lit a smoke. A woman in a loden-green wool coat with fancy horn buttons down the front walked by, making a sour face at my cigarette. The after-trail smell from her perfume was enough to gag a coroner.

A few minutes later, I took the subway to Bleecker Street. I couldn't set up a box for any meet with Pryce. Not a tight one, anyway. If he smelled it, he'd disappear. But I could make it hard for him to do the same to me.

On the subway I watched a man with his arms folded inside a dirty white sweatshirt, seeking the comfort of the straitjacket he remembered so fondly, his face going insanely serene when he found just the right position. Like the way a newly sprung convict moves into a one-room apartment even if he can afford more. There's something soothing about the familiar, even if it's ugly.

"**W**here's he want to meet?" I asked Crystal Beth as soon as she let me inside.

"He didn't say," she answered. "He's going to call at three and—"

I nodded, cutting her off. And felt myself relax. That's what had been spooking me—no way a man like Pryce tells you the address of a meet fifteen hours in advance unless he has enough personnel to keep the place under watch all that time.

As we walked past the second floor, I heard a door open behind us. I didn't turn around.

"Where's Vyra lurking?" I asked when we got to her place.

"She doesn't come every day. Sometimes I don't see her for a week or so. It depends."

"I wasn't trying to get into your business," I told her. "I just wanted to know if she was going to make one of her appearances."

"You could, you know."

"Could what?"

"Get into my business. You're already in my . . . life. Don't you want to know about . . . me and Vyra?"

"No."

"It was my . . . idea, I guess," she said, as though I'd answered the other way. "She's not gay. Well, I guess I'm not either. She's not bi—I was the first time she ever . . ."

"It doesn't—"

"I love Vyra. She's not what you think. What you *might* think, anyway—I don't know what you think. She's . . . lost. I wanted to help her find . . . herself, I guess. It's a natural thing."

"Why are you telling me?"

"Because you didn't ask, I guess. That's the way I am. I don't like secrets between . . . friends. But if anyone tries to *make* me tell . . ."

"I wouldn't try and make you do anything," I said. *No, little girl*, I thought, *you can't be muscled into stuff. You have to be tricked*.

"Vyra's fun. You'd think I'd know more about fun than she would, the way we were raised. So different. But that's not true. Maybe because I have a purpose . . . I don't know. I have a pair of shoes like hers. She made me buy them. I mean, she paid for them, but she made me go with her and get them. You want to see them?"

"Sure."

Crystal Beth walked barefoot to her closet and came out with a pair of hot-pink spikes with a little round black dot inset on each toe. "Four-and-a-half-inch heels," she said, grinning. "They make me really tall."

"They're, uh . . . remarkable," I said, struggling for the right word and missing it.

"I can't imagine where I'd wear them. Or what I'd wear them with. Vyra says I'm lucky. That I have such small feet."

"Is that genetic too?"

"I think so. My mother had tiny feet. Not my father, though. You want to see how they look?"

"Sure."

She slipped the shoes on her feet and paraded around a bit, pulling up her slacks at the ankles so the shoes could be displayed. "Do you think they look silly?" she asked me.

"It's hard to tell this way," I said, scratching my chin, deep in thought. "Try it with the pants off," I advised her solemnly.

It was almost four when the phone rang. This time it was an address on West Fifty-sixth. An office building, if I remembered the block right. I scooped Herk out of the basement and we hiked west to Eighth Street near NYU. Then we grabbed the N train to Fifty-seventh, and walked over to the address Pryce had given me.

There was an attendant in the lobby, but he didn't pay any attention to us as we walked toward the elevator. I quickly scanned the tenant directory, but I couldn't see anything next to 1401. We rode up anyway.

The hall carpet had been fresh when you could still buy a De Soto in a showroom. The walls were a dingy shade of layered nicotine. The overhead lighting alternated between pus-yellow and missing as we moved along the corridor. The office doors were a uniform dull brown, identified by the remnants of gilt decals displaying the numbers. We found 1401 just past a right-angle turn in the corridor, standing alone next to a window overlooking an air shaft. The window was the kind of stained glass you don't see in churches.

I rapped lightly on the door. The man who opened it was a little taller than me, with thinning light-brown hair and watery blue eyes. He raised his eyebrows like he expected me to say something. I didn't.

"You're—?"

"Yeah," I told him, moving past him into the office. Herk was right on my shoulder. I heard the door close behind us.

We were in what once had been a waiting room. The back wall was a receptionist's booth, complete with a sliding-glass window cut into the wall. Both empty. I opened the door beside the receptionist's window. Pryce was in the next room, seated behind a wood desk in one of those green vinyl swivel chairs they gave typists in the Fifties. He stood up when we walked in.

"Let's get started," he said.

We followed him to another room. It was small and square, with a nausea-colored linoleum floor and a single window that had been painted over with that silver stuff they use on bathroom glass. The only furniture was a knock-down card table with a clear glass ashtray on it and four black metal folding chairs. The walls were bare, painted an off-white that years of neglect had degenerated into just "off."

Pryce gestured for me to pick a chair. I took the one with its back to the window, nodding at Herk to sit on my right. Pryce sat with his back to the door, leaving Lothar to face Herk.

I handed him photocopies of the printouts I'd gotten from Wolfe. He scanned through them, eyebrows going up slightly when he came to the substituted pages. He handed the dead man's photo to Lothar without a word.

Lothar looked at the photo and nodded in recognition. Then he said the dead man's name.

Damn.

"Did you know him well?" I asked Lothar quickly, keeping my face calm.

"Only met him a couple, three times," Lothar said smoothly, looking at Pryce for approval. "That was the way we worked it."

"And when do you get the word?"

He looked at Pryce, who said: "Tuesday, there'll be a message at the drop. From Hercules. You'll turn it over—not the physical message, you'll destroy that—to the others. Offer to meet with Hercules yourself. They'll tell you to bring him someplace. Or they'll tell you to go there alone, but they'll be there too."

"They might—"

"No they won't," Pryce cut him off. "They'll *have* to find out. It's too close. Now, what you need to do is spend the next couple of hours together. Get familiar with each other, like I told you. This will be the last chance you get."

"How about a beer?" Lothar said to Herk, standing up.

"Okay, brother," Herk replied, following him out of the room.

We sat in silence until I heard the sound of a door close somewhere to my right. Then I leaned forward and dropped my best card on the table, my one shot at getting Crystal Beth out of the line of fire.

"We don't have to do this anymore," I said.

"What do you mean?"

"The threat to you is Lothar getting busted when he comes in on the divorce thing, right?" I asked, keeping my voice so low Pryce had to twist his head to turn his ear toward me—no chance they could hear us in the next room. "But if we just *wait*," I told him, "it all fixes itself. And I can get that done now."

"Explain," he said, voice even lower than mine.

"The woman doesn't go in. I don't care if it's all set up or not. She just doesn't go in. Not now. Her lawyer gets an adjournment, whatever. How long is this gonna take, anyway? Another two weeks, three weeks?"

"I don't know. I told you, I don't know the date that they intend to—"

"Whatever. It won't be long, you know that much. All we have to do is wait. Why do we need all this undercover stuff now? I can *guarantee* you the woman will wait. And that's all she has to do. When this thing they're planning goes down, *then* she makes her move. And Lothar, he just defaults—doesn't show up at all. They can issue all the warrants they want for him—he'll be underground, right? Gone for good. And that'll get her everything she wants. Once he disappears, she's free."

"How can you make that guarantee? You don't even know the woman's name," he said, watching my face. "Or, even if you do, you don't know where she is. You may control that . . . other woman, but not the one that counts."

"Wherever she is, she's *dependent*," I said. "She's not going to be able to do this by herself. She needs the others. That's the way it works. There's a whole support system. Not just money—she needs emotional support too. She's safe where she is. Her baby too. It may be a little tense, but it's not dangerous. She can wait. When this started, you wanted the whole thing called off. Well, we don't have to call it off, right? All we have to do is delay it. For as long as you want."

"It's not that simple," Pryce said. "Too much time has gone by. He—Lothar—is getting nervous. Not about the others—he's very confident there. About me. He wants something from me. A show of strength."

"What's that got to do with—?"

"He wants to see his son."

The weather changed in the room. The baby. I felt little dots of orange behind my eyes. My hands wanted to clench into fists. I pictured my center. Saw it start to fracture. Pulled it into a latticework, holding it with my will. I turned the blossoming rage into ugly green smoke, let it pass through the lattice. To somewhere else. Tested my voice in my head until it sounded calm, all the jagged edges rounded into smoothness. Then I let it out.

"That doesn't make sense," I said, checking the audio on my voice to be sure it was calm and peaceful. "He can't take the kid into the cell. Even if he has someone who'd take care of the baby, he'd never get him back once the wheels come off."

"He doesn't want to take him," Pryce replied. "Not now. He just wants to *see* him."

"To be sure you can deliver?"

"Yes. He knows I can handle the . . . other part. After all, we need his cooperation, so he can expect to be treated very well. But the . . . government doesn't know where his wife and baby are."

"And neither do you," I said, getting it for the first time.

He shrugged, as if it were a minor problem. One he could expect to have solved sooner or later.

"And that's what the threats were all about, huh? It was never about delaying some scam divorce. That was the deal you made with him—that you'd find his kid. And maybe—yeah!—and deliver the kid when he goes away. Hand him right over."

He shrugged again.

"But if he brings Herk in, he's skewered. You'd have your own source. If he rats Herk out, he goes down too."

Another shrug.

"Very nice," I told him, meaning it. "But I can get what I want without doing anything now. You might have threatened Crystal Beth into getting the woman to drop the divorce thing, but you know you don't have enough horsepower to make them give up the baby. Let's go back to where we started. Forget the divorce. It's not gonna happen, okay? Lothar won't come in. He won't get busted. You play out your own string."

"It's too late for that," Pryce said. "I have to have that baby. For an hour. Two hours, tops."

"Can't do it," I told him.

"You said you had total control of—"

"It doesn't matter anymore. Everyone has limits. That would be hers."

"I don't care about hers," he said quietly. "Only about yours. We have a deal. What you get is your friend Hercules. Vanished. With full immunity."

"That'd be good. But we can live without it."

"There's no statute of limitations on murder."

"What murder?"

He idly fingered the photo of the dead man, not saying a word.

"That's a guess," I told him. "Not an indictment."

He looked up at the ceiling, like he was seeking divine guidance. "Everybody's been lying to you, Burke," he said. "When you see your girlfriend, ask her about Rollo's."

"What about Rollo's?"

"You think she was a stranger there? They're all part of it."

"Part of what?"

"Her network. This Mimi, the one who runs the place. Her. The bouncer, T.B. Rusty, the big guy who sits in a corner and draws pictures. Even her husband."

"Crystal Beth has a—"

"Not her, Mimi. Her husband is the owner of the place. He never goes there, but he owns it. And half a dozen others like it, all around the country."

"So he owns a few bars, what—?"

"Not bars. Nerve centers. He's one of the bankrollers, like this Vyra person. But it's Crystal Beth who's in charge. This stalking thing, it's out of control. So many people just living in terror. It was only a matter of time before they banded together. Your friend Crystal Beth, she's running a lot more than you think."

"So she's a liar," I said. "So they're all liars. It doesn't matter.

I'm out of this now. Why should I help you get your hands on that baby?"

"This immunity thing, it's really quite wonderful," Pryce said smoothly. "You can always trade *up*. Give prosecutors a homicide, they'll give you a pass on a whole bunch of other stuff."

"So?"

He picked up the photo of the dead man again, held it like it was a delicate shard of spun glass. "So it's all a chain. But I hold the link that can snap it. If you don't believe me, maybe you should ask Anthony LoPacio."

"Who the hell is Anthony LoPacio?"

"Ah, that's right. You probably know him by some other name. Try 'Porkpie.'"

lit a cigarette to buy time, not surprised that my hands didn't tremble—I was dead inside. My brainstem felt clogged with all the messages. Only one came through clearly, acid-burning all the others out of the way.

Murder would fix this.

A pair of murders. Right here. Right now.

I looked up at Pryce, feeling my eyes go soft and wet. My eyes were Wesley's now, watching prey. I was born a motherless gutter rat. And when I'm cornered . . .

He saw where he was walking. His Adam's apple bobbed a couple of times. The muscle jumped under his eye. "There's another way," he said softly, playing for his life, putting his hands flat on the table, palms down. "We can be partners."

listened to every word he said, pushing killing him and his boy Lothar behind a door in my mind. But I left the door ajar. Then I went over the deal. Again and again.

Summed up:

Even if he was telling the truth, even if he was the only one who was, he'd walk away with all the cards.

And he could always come back and play them again.

"Why should I trust you?" I asked him.

"Because you know what *I* want . . . and because I'm the only one in this whole thing you can say that about," he told me. "The rest of them all have their games. Whether they want to save the world or destroy it, what difference? You and I, we're professionals. I can't do this without you, okay? And you can't get what you need done without me either."

I kept his eyes, but my mind went walking. Years ago, I did time with an Indian. He had some tribal name, but he never used it Inside. We called him Hiram. He told me a lot of stuff, and I always listened. Hiram told me that there was no separate Chickasaw tribe—"Chickasaw" was just the Cherokee name for "once were here, now are gone"—those who chose war as a way of life. The last to fall to the white man's guns—but the first to "adapt," which was why the BIA began calling them one of the "Civilized Tribes" as they walked the Trail of Tears. But Hiram said they were just biding their time then, waiting.

And some of their children's children still were.

Hiram told me there was no tribe called Seminoles either. That was just a name laid on them by Andrew Jackson . . . before he shipped them out to Oklahoma, where they could join the survivors from the Trail of Tears. What they really were was part of the Creek nation Jackson drove down into Florida from the Georgia border.

He said some of their children were still waiting too. Maybe, if the tribes hadn't warred with each other, if they'd ever joined forces, the whole thing would have come out different.

Hiram told me something else too. He said the badger and the coyote sometimes hunt together. In the high Northwest, in winter, when game gets scarce. The coyote has the better eyes, but he can't penetrate the rock-hard ground. And the badger can only see close-up. So the coyote would spot the prey, and alert the badger. Then the badger would dig it out, and they'd share the kill.

And go their separate ways, until the next time.

A temporary alliance of predators.

I had called Pryce a lone wolf, and he hadn't argued. But professionals never correct mistakes you make about *them*. And what had Wolfe called him? A bounty spotter? Maybe . . .

I kept his hands pinned to the table with my eyes, waiting.

When he couldn't wait any longer, he said: "And then there's the money."

"Which you can't front," I responded, back to where I was.

"How *could* I front it? I work on spec. All the risk is on my end. There's no contract. Strictly COD. You know how that works. It's all on the come, but I'll go fifty-fifty when it shows. What could I do to convince you?"

"I don't know."

"Name it and it's yours," he said. "But I have to have that baby."

"Any surprises?" I asked Herk. We hadn't talked all the way down on the subway, but now we were in the Plymouth. Heading north.

"Nah. He's a weak little punk, Burke. All that stuff about being a warrior and dying for the Race. His fucking 'brothers.' Like I don't know he's gonna give them all up, right?"

"Yeah."

Silence after that as the Plymouth ate up the miles.

"You ever know any of them?" he asked suddenly.

"Nazis? Sure. When I was in—"

"Not them. Jews. You ever know any Jews?"

"Herk, for Chrissakes. Who do you think put that tattoo on your chest?"

"Oh. Yeah. I wasn't—"

"Vyra's Jewish," I told him.

"Vyra?"

"Yeah, Vyra. The girl with the shoes."

"*She's* Jewish?"

"Sure. What's so—?"

"I dunno. I never thought about . . . I mean, listening to that

Lothar and all. Reading them books you got me. I never thought about *girls* being Jewish."

What do you say to that?

"**C**an you do it?" I asked the Mole.

"It wouldn't be precise," he said calmly.

"But you could make it look like this?" I asked, pointing to a sheet of graph paper on which I'd roughed out a sketch. "And it would work?"

"Yes," he said, giving me a look of mild surprise.

"What's the matter?" I asked him.

"It's very . . . intelligent," the Mole said.

"**W**hat's this?" Pryce asked, taking the thin flesh-colored wrap from my hand. It was three days after I'd gone to see the Mole.

"It's an ankle cuff," I told him. "The latest thing. Weighs less than a quarter of what the old ones did. Space Age plastic with titanium wire. For monitoring pedophiles in those outpatient programs. You put it on, I seal it, it stays on until I take it off. If you have it cut off yourself, that'll break the signal."

"And you expect me to wear this?"

"That's the deal," I said. "You wear this, I know where you are. Not precisely, but close enough." He couldn't know how much of a lie that was. The major dope cartels use satellite tracking systems that can show the precise location of a tiny boat in hundreds of miles of empty sea. But they have the millions to hire Silicon Valley whiz kids to write the software, and billions' worth of product to protect. Me, what did I have?

He thought it over for a minute. "And what good would that do you?" he finally asked.

"If you try and run with my money, I'll know it. And I'll find you easy enough."

"How do I know you won't just—?"

"Take you out when you deliver the cash? I don't expect you to trust me either. You can mail it. I'll give you an address. The cash shows up, you're off the hook."

"But you'll still be able to track me."

"Only for about thirty days—that's all the battery's good for. You can have it cut off as soon as you've sent the cash. The transmitter doesn't have that much of a range. I'd know you ran, but I wouldn't know where to."

"But in the interim . . . ?"

"I *already* found you," I reminded him. "I found you tonight. Every time we've been alone, it's like I found you, right?"

"So I wear this bracelet and you give me the baby?"

"You wear this bracelet and I let Lothar *see* the baby."

"Yes."

"And one more thing."

"Which is?"

"I need an address."

"Yes?"

"Porkpie hasn't been around lately," I explained it to him.

"Once Hercules goes in," he said quietly. "And Lothar sees the baby."

"Deal."

He took a breath. "You don't expect me to put this on now?"

"Why not?"

"You're not an engineer, are you?"

"No."

"Well, neither am I. It isn't that I don't trust what you said, but I'd like to have this . . . device examined before I put it on."

"Take it with you," I told him.

"See the baby?" Crystal Beth said. "No way."

"It's the *only* way," I told her. "Lothar won't be able to snatch the kid—we'll have him covered. But without that card, he's not gonna play. And if he doesn't, then Pryce . . ."

"You believe he'd do it?" Vyra asked me. "Bring everything down?"

"Yeah," I told her. "I do."

"I don't trust him," Crystal Beth said. "I'd *never* trust him. He doesn't have to do this. He's a pig. A filthy, lousy pig."

Vyra stood up. Walked near the window, bending her left hand at the wrist so the afternoon sun would fire the big emerald-cut diamond on her hand. She admired it for a minute. Turned to Crystal Beth like I wasn't in the room. "That's the only way you get truffles, honey," she said.

Crystal Beth walked over to where Vyra was standing. Put her hands on Vyra's neck and pulled her close. Whispered something.

Vyra walked to the door, swinging her narrow hips hard. She slammed it behind her.

Crystal Beth left the window and plopped on the bed, face up. She patted the covers for me to lie down next to her. I did it. She tugged at the back of my head. "What?" I asked her.

"I want to tell you a story," she said, guiding my head into her lap, twirling her hands in my hair. I closed my eyes. "When I was a little girl," she said, "I was afraid of heights. Not great heights, like in a city. There wasn't anything all that tall on the land we had. But we had a shed. For storing machinery. It was probably only ten feet off the ground, but I was afraid to go up there. On the roof, I mean. We were playing, and the ball got stuck up there. It happened all the time. We took turns going up there to get it. But when it was my turn, I wouldn't go. I was afraid. . . .

"Nobody made me go. But I felt bad. On the farm, everybody had to take turns doing stuff. But climbing that shed, I could never take mine. I never told my parents. I was . . . ashamed, I guess. Anyway, one day, one of the other kids teased me about it. And my mother heard.

"So she made a jump pool. Like a swimming pool, but out of blankets. And mattresses. And some bearskins she had. It was *huge*. It took hours and hours to make it, everything piled so high and soft. Then she got a ladder. I went first. She was right behind me, arms wrapped around me so I couldn't fall. Then we just sat up there. Everybody was watching. My mother told me we could sit up there as long as we liked. She told me stories. The kind I loved. About polar bears and sled dogs and seals and whales. And after a while, it was time to jump.

"We stood up and we held hands. My mother said we would be polar bears, jumping into the water from a little cliff. She was the mother bear and I was the cub. We did it, holding hands. *Everybody* cheered. It was so great. I was never afraid of heights after that."

"Your mother knew how to do it," I said.

"I thought that too. For a long time. Then my father told me the real story. My mother was afraid of heights herself. Where she was raised, it was all flat. Going up scared her. My father said she didn't even like to go in elevators."

"She had a lot of guts."

"Enough to give me some. I know how to jump into things now," she whispered.

Then she reached down and tugged at my hair, pulling me up to her.

"**G**ot him," the Prof's voice barked over the cellular.

I cut the connection. Pryce was about four blocks away, rolling toward the meet in the same white Taurus he'd used at the airport. I'd told him the meet was coming a couple of days ago, told him to have a cell phone handy and to get me the number. I rang him an hour ago, asked him how long it would take to get to an address in East Harlem. He said to give him an hour. We had a spotter up there too. I rang in on his cellular as soon as the Taurus turned into the street I'd given him, told him about the change of plans. It was just a short hop over the Willis Avenue Bridge to the new address, twenty minutes ETA.

Finding an abandoned warehouse in the South Bronx is no great feat. Securing the premises was another matter, but we'd had people in place since noon the day before, thirty-four hours ago.

From my vantage point on the second floor, I could see the white Taurus pull up. Pryce was all-in now—he couldn't know this wasn't a hit, but he couldn't get to the baby unless he ran the risk. One of the Cambodian trio stepped out from the shadows and walked toward the Taurus, right hand in his coat pocket. He motioned with his empty hand for the window to come down. It did. He walked right up to the driver's side, leaned in and said something. Pryce and Lothar got out. The Cambodian slipped behind the wheel and the Taurus took off.

I looked over to where we'd rigged a pool of light, using a generator to drive a single hanging overhead fixture. The floor had been swept in a ten-foot circle. Two milk crates were the only furniture in the artificial island. One of the Cambodians came up the stairs first, nodding to me to indicate the speed-search had gone okay—no weapons. Then Pryce. Then Lothar. Then the third Cambodian. "That's for you," I said to Lothar, pointing at one of the milk crates.

"I thought you were gonna take us someplace to see my—"

"Just sit down," I told him. "Be patient."

Max the Silent came out of the darkness. With a baby in his arms.

"**G**erhardt!" Lothar yelled, reaching out for the infant.

Max shifted his body, throwing his shoulder as a barrier.

"Sit down," I told Lothar. "We'll hand you the kid, okay?"

Lothar looked at Pryce. Getting the nod, he took his seat. I made a motion to Max. He closed the gap, handed the baby down. From his shoulder, Max unslung a blue cloth bag, placed it at Lothar's feet. Lothar held the child at arm's length, as if examining him for defects.

"He looks thin," he said to no one in particular. "That cunt had better be . . ." He turned to face me. "Where is she, anyway?"

"That wasn't the deal," I told him. "You wanted to see the kid, there he is."

"I thought—"

"Nobody gives a fuck what you thought," I told him, hardening my voice. "That's your kid, right?"

"Yeah," he said resentfully. "But I thought—"

"It's what you asked for," Pryce said to him, like he was a pizza-delivery guy. You asked for anchovies, you got anchovies. You changed your mind, too bad.

"I want to be alone with him," Lothar said. "I don't like all these . . ." He left it blank, but I didn't need a translator. ". . . standing around watching me."

"It doesn't matter what you want," I told him, no-flexibility ice in my voice. "I had to make some promises in order to borrow the kid for a few hours. One of them was that you wouldn't be alone with him. And I keep my promises."

"A promise to a cunt don't mean—"

"I drove for almost six hours to set this up, and I got a long ride to take him back," I lied. A professional habit, planting barren seeds. "And I made a deal too. You're not getting off that box. In that bag there's a bottle with some formula, a clean diaper, everything you'll need. And everybody'll step back, okay?" I waved my hand and Max did just that. Lothar's eyes swept the room, but the harsh overhead lighting kept him from seeing anyone. Even his wife, not thirty feet away, probably holding her breath.

I tugged gently at Pryce's coat, drawing him back deeper into the dark. He came along without protest. We moved along until I found the stairs. Then I went up one flight, Pryce right behind.

We had the next floor lit too. One room, anyway. Another pair of milk crates with a plank across them made a little table. On that table, a bowl of tepid water, an aerosol can of shaving cream, a thick white hotel towel, and a disposable safety razor in plastic shrink-wrap. Plus a half-dozen maroon-and-white sealed packets marked CORTABALM on the sides.

"Your turn to deliver," I told him.

"What's the other stuff for?" he asked.

"You have to shave the ankle before you attach the cuff. Like you would before you'd tape it up to play football, same thing. Otherwise you can sweat under there, the itch can be awesome. That's what the cortisone patch is for. It keeps the area fresh and clean for the whole thirty days."

He took the monitoring anklet—the one I'd let him take with him the last time—from a coat pocket. Without saying another word, he pulled up a cuff on his dark slacks, took off his shoe and sock and wet the ankle thoroughly. His hand was perfectly steady as he shaved.

No reason for him to be nervous. He'd had plenty of time to have an expert look at the cuff, tell him that there was no thread of Semtex wound through it. And that the wafer-thin battery would be damn lucky to last the thirty days.

When he was finished shaving, he toweled off the area. I handed him one of the cortisone packets. He tore it open. "Make sure it's flat," I told him. "Once this cuff gets clamped on, any bumps are going to stay there until it comes off."

The white cortisone pad was thin and moist. He smoothed it down with the fingers of both webbed hands. "Okay," he said.

I locked it on.

Fifteen minutes later, Lothar was done. The baby was getting antsy—he knew his mother was close and he wanted that comfort back—and Lothar finally figured out the kid's only response to anything said to him was to gurgle a few times.

Besides, Lothar had shown the cunt who was boss. He wanted to see his kid—he saw his kid. He handed the baby back to Max. The warrior's face didn't change, but I could feel his contempt all the way across the room.

It was as lost on Lothar as Max's *ki* had been.

"Tomorrow you get the letter in your box," Pryce told him. "There'll be a number there. Pay phone. You call. Meet with Hercules. And then you bring him in."

"I know, I know."

"Go downstairs with Alexander," I told them, nodding toward one of the Cambodians. "He'll stay with you until your car gets brought back around."

"Alexander?" Lothar said. "What kinda name is that for a gook?"

"It's a secret society," I said to him quietly. "They always take the name of the last man they kill. This is his fifth one."

Lothar looked at me, started to open his mouth. Shut it. He glanced over at the Cambodian, who showed him a brilliant smile. Half his teeth were the color of lead. The rest were missing.

They went downstairs. I watched as the white Taurus came up the street, watched the first Cambodian get out. They climbed in and took off. I didn't insult Pryce's tradecraft by writing down the license number.

The phone buzzed in a minute.

"Moving off," said the Prof.

"**H**e said black hair was okay," the baby's mother was telling Crystal Beth as I came back to the second floor. "He hated it at first. He wanted it to be blond. Aryan. But later he said that Hitler had black hair."

"He's gone now," Crystal Beth said to her.

"He scared me," the woman replied. "Even here. With all these . . . people around. You don't know him."

"I know him," I told her. "You won't see him again."

"Are you sure?" she asked, tension wire-taut in her voice.

"We're sure," Crystal Beth promised her.

"What's the kid's real name?" I asked her.

"Huh?"

"His real name. Lothar called him Gerhardt. Is that what you named him?"

"Oh! Yes, that's what Larry named—oh, I see. You mean, I could name him . . ."

"Whatever you want," I told her. "Starting right now."

"**H**ow long do I have to—?"

"This is for you too, right?" I told Vyra. "You can't just go back to your life the way you usually do. Part of this deal was to get you off the hook, remember?"

"Fine, I remember. But how long—?"

"Two weeks, three maybe. What's the big deal? This joint is beautiful," I told her, glancing around the hotel suite. "You can handle the time easy enough."

"But I can't stay *inside* for that long. My husband would—"

"You don't have to stay," I said, thinking how long I'd stayed—*lived*—inside places smaller than this joint's bathroom. "You got a private line there. When you go out, forward the calls to your cellular. When Herk calls, you're *here*, understand? Make sure you talk that way on the phone. Then call me. And get your ass in gear so you can be back before he shows up."

"But what's the difference whether I'm here or not? It's just so you can meet with him. . . ."

"Yeah. That's right. But we don't know who's watching."

"I thought you had Pryce—"

"It's not Pryce we're worried about now, Vyra."

"Oh, all *right*." She sighed dramatically, snapping open one of the four suitcases she'd brought with her.

She found a pair of magenta pumps and slipped them on. That seemed to make her feel better. Then she sat on the padded arm of a chair in the living room and watched as I made a full circuit of the place, checking.

"You think I'm a hypocrite, don't you?" she asked. But the tone of her voice made it clear she was accusing me of something.

"Huh?"

"What word didn't you understand?" she demanded, getting to her feet. "Okay, I'm stuck in this. Because of that . . . man. Pryce. And his nasty little threats. But that business with . . . Lothar, or whatever name you call him. You know I drive a Mercedes. . . ."

"So?"

"So I'm a Jew. You know that. I never made a secret of it. That's me, right? A Jewish American Princess. With big tits. And a rich husband. That about sums me up, doesn't it?"

"You tell me."

"And I drive a German car," she went on like I hadn't spoken. "What does *that* make me?"

"It makes you a person with money," I told her. "What the hell are you talking about? Nazis didn't build your stupid car.

The Germans today, they're just . . . people. Like us. Americans, I mean. Hell, we probably got more Nazis here now than they do."

"But their ancestors—"

"Don't mean a fucking thing," I cut her off. "Nobody's ancestors mean anything. People are what *they* do, not what someone else did."

"But you think I'm . . . weak, don't you?"

"Vyra, what is this?"

"It's still about money. My husband would dump me if he found out about me and . . . Crystal. He told me that once. He thinks when women . . . it's the most disgusting thing in the world. That's the only threat to me—money. It's different for the rest of them."

"That's the way it is," I said. "You wouldn't be in this if you hadn't put money into Crystal Beth's operation. And you did that because you . . . well, for whatever reasons you had."

"*Good* reasons."

"Okay. Whatever you say."

Vyra walked away from me. Sat down on a straight chair facing a corner, sulking. I left her there, went back to checking the place for problems.

"Are you still mad at me?" she finally asked. Not turning around—talking over her shoulder.

"Mad at you? For what?"

"For Crystal? For what we—"

"That's your business," I told her.

"You were with her too."

"Okay."

"That's it? 'Okay'? What does that mean?"

"It means I don't want to argue with you. Not now. When this is all done, you can throw a fit if that's what you want."

"What do *you* want, Burke?"

"I want this to be done."

"Me?"

"What?"

"You want me?" she asked, standing up and turning around.

"You want me to take my clothes off now? This is a hotel room, isn't it? That's us—you and me. That's what we do."

"Not now."

"You mean not ever, don't you?"

"I don't know. I haven't thought about it."

"Well, you *better* think about it. What happens after—?"

"Vyra, this isn't the way to do it, putting pressure on me."

"You think she's better than me, don't you?"

"Who?"

"Don't be such a swine. Crystal! Because she has that . . . purpose she's always talking about. Me, all I do is spend money, yes? Maybe, if you listened to me once in a while, you'd hear something. I'm a person too."

"I played square with you," I told her. "I never hustled you, never scammed you, never took your money, nothing."

"Yes," she said quietly. "Nothing."

"It's too late for that now."

"You're not getting another chance," she said, unbuttoning her blouse to play what everyone had been telling her was her trump card since she'd been thirteen.

"Whoever does?" I asked her. Then I walked out the door.

"Just be yourself," I told Hercules for the fiftieth time. "Don't get fancy. Don't get cute. They're not *gonna* ask you about the other guys in your cell. Anyone does that, you just pin him. With your *eyes*, okay, don't chest him. Like, why the fuck would he be breaking security with a question like that, understand?"

"Yeah, I got it."

"Your life, Herk. Whatever it was, that's what you say. The truth. You went to the kiddie camps, you went to the joint, you went . . . wherever. Don't change *anything*."

"Okay."

"This guy you took out. You did it because he . . ."

". . . was a Jew. A secret Jew."

"You think he was with ZOG?"

"Nah. He was just a wannabe, you know?" the big man said, slipping smoothly into the party line. "He wanted to be with us. But he couldn't be. None of them ever can. It's blood. They was born different, they gonna die different. A whole *lot* of them gonna die soon."

"Good! Now, look, all we know for sure is that they're in the area. Manhattan, Queens, Brooklyn, I don't know, but close. What you're doing, you're breaking camp, all right? They're gonna find you a new place to hole up. Understand?"

"Yeah."

"They can't be keeping that tight a rein—fucking Lothar seems to be able to go out whenever he wants. Besides, you got the big ticket—you're a certified life-taker, they're all gonna know that. They're not geniuses, but they know undercover cops don't kill people just for front."

"Just be myself, tell the truth," Herk muttered, working his mantra.

"You get to a phone, you call Vyra," I told him. "At the number I gave you. You know where the hotel is. Whatever time you can get away, you meet her there. Don't ask her, *tell* her. That's *your* bitch, understand?"

"Yeah."

"That's where we'll meet, you and me. No place else."

"Okay."

"You got money?"

"I think—"

"Herk, how much cash do you have, exactly?"

It only took him a minute to count it. "Twenty-seven bucks."

I gave him eight hundred in various bills and a few subway tokens. "That'll hold you," I told him. "Take this too." I handed him a roll of quarters. He squeezed it experimentally, then tested the clenched fist against an open palm, nodded an okay to me.

"Don't get caught carrying anything heavier," I said. "You get popped, Pryce is gonna think we did it on purpose. Then the dime goes down the slot. And we don't have Porkpie yet."

"I ain't no shooter," he said.

"No shanks either," I warned him.

He nodded again, unhappily this time.

"It's us and them, brother," I said, dropping my voice like we were back out on the yard. "They got their plans, we got ours."

Then I told him ours.

"**A**ll we can do now is wait," I told Crystal Beth.

"How long?"

"I don't know. That piece is out of my control. But it's down to weeks, not months."

"I don't know if I'm strong enough for this. How do you tell?"

"Tell what?"

"If you're strong enough."

"You're as strong as you act," I told her.

Wondering if I was.

"**H**e's in." Pryce's voice on the phone. I glanced down at the receiver the Mole had given me. It looked like one of those mini-TV sets. When I thumbed it on, the screen showed a hollow black circle on a gray background. Inside the circle, a blinking dot, like the cursor on a computer. Wherever Pryce was, he was within range.

"You sure?"

"They left together." Meaning Lothar and Hercules. The meet had been set for the bookstore where Lothar worked, a porno joint in lower Manhattan. "I won't know any more until I've had a chance to debrief."

"I'll be here," I told him.

I didn't know if I had hours or days to wait. I felt like a convict who just got a parole date. Not the good part, the go-home part. No, the part where you had to walk real soft, stay out of trouble, turn away from challenges. One slip and it's all gone. And every other guy in the joint knew it.

So I didn't go back to my old grounds. Even stayed away from Mama's. Waited at Crystal Beth's.

That's when the tour started. I didn't ask her why she'd wanted me to come along, figuring it was a way to kill some time. And maybe make some money.

The young woman was wearing a tan cashmere sweater under a matching blazer of a slightly darker shade, nervously fingering a string of pearls as if she knew they were too old for her. "It started with letters," she said, pointing at an expandable wine-colored leather portfolio sitting at her feet.

I pulled one out. It was on heavy stock, pale blue with marbled veining running random throughout. The writer's name was engraved at the top left, small black lettering, all lowercase. At the bottom right: address, phone, fax and e-mail. The text was typed: justified margins, a heavily serifed font.

You have such beautiful boys. I can't resist them. They are so seductive, so entrancing, I find myself drawn to them. But I assure you, my pedophilia is purely intellectual, a never-to-be-realized urge of which I am in full control. Please help me understand the objects of my love. Vital statistics would be such treasures to me. Their birthdays, their heights and weights. And I want to know them too. I already know Jonas loves model airplanes and Lance keeps tropical fish, but I want to know more. Please indulge me. Fantasies don't hurt anyone. But the pain of not knowing more about your perfect boys is real indeed. Thank you for understanding.

It was unsigned.

"Jonas and Lance were heroes," the woman said to me. "They saved a puppy from drowning. They got their pictures in the local paper. That's when it started . . . when he started writing to me."

"Did you ever answer him?" I asked her.

"Oh no. I was . . . terrified. I took his first letter right to the police. But they said he hadn't committed a crime."

"And the letters kept coming?"

"Yes. Not just to me. He wrote to the boys' school and asked for copies of their report cards. The school turned his letter over to me. They never answered him either. He wrote to the newspaper, to the reporter who had interviewed the boys, and asked him for information too. He wrote to everyone."

"But he never made contact?"

"He . . . Oh, I see what you mean. Not . . . direct contact. I've never seen him."

"You have . . . financial resources?"

"Yes of course," she said. "I know all about . . . him now. He's never been arrested. He doesn't work. Has some sort of private income. This kind of . . . thing." She shuddered, then gathered herself. "It's his 'hobby,' that's what he told the investigators we hired. It's not against the law."

"So why did you—?"

"Run? He posted a reward. For information about the boys. Especially pictures of them."

"Posted?"

"On the Internet. To one of those pedophile boards. I don't know how he did it. I never saw it. But one of the bodyguards we hired for the children caught a man taking a video of them at a soccer game. He told my . . . investigators that there was a reward for the pictures, and he was just trying to make some money. That wasn't against the law either."

"And you figured it was just a matter of time before he . . . ?"

"Yes. I'm only here temporarily. We have . . . resources. As you said. But I found out where he got his money, and that . . . ."

"The private income?"

"No, not that. He's done this before. And one of the boys'

fathers . . . one of the other boys, I mean, the ones he . . . watched before . . . I really don't know all the details . . . but he . . . the boy's father . . . had this . . . man's address and everything, and he went to his house and . . . hurt him, I guess. Beat him up or something."

"I'm still not . . ."

"The man—the boy's father, not the . . . man. He went to jail. For assault. And the . . . person who writes these filthy letters, he sued the boy's father. And he got money. A lot of money. I can't imagine why a jury would ever . . . but . . ."

"And you think that's what he's doing? Setting himself up for enraged parents to go after him so he can sue?"

"Yes! He lives in this little town. His whole family does. They're very prominent. They've lived there for over a hundred years. And the police *will* protect him. They already have. There's nothing I can do about . . . him. So we're leaving."

"You're going to get new birth certificates for the kids, change everything just so he can't find you again?"

"The only thing we're going to change is our address," the woman said firmly. "I know he could find us again. So we're leaving . . . America. We're going to live overseas. My husband already has a job . . . there. And my family will help us too. We're going where he can never hurt my boys."

"I—"

"Crystal Beth said you knew . . . these kind of people. *About* them, I mean. Would you feel safe? If it was your children?"

"No," I told her honestly.

"My husband just wants to *kill* him, he's so angry. But if he beats him up, we already know what's going to happen. And nobody's going to actually kill someone for writing letters."

"I'm sure you're right," I told her, lying as calmly as a mouse-watching hawk.

They didn't all have children. They didn't all run for the same reason. But they all ran from the same thing.

"I was walking home," the woman said, her voice crackling

like cellophane crumpled in a clenched fist. She had lovely skin, apricot flaring under cream. And long, lustrous light-brown hair, almost beige in the floor-bounced shine from the inverted goose-neck lamp. I couldn't see her body—she was so wrapped in layers of clothing that it disappeared. But her eyes were pinwheeling with pain as she talked. "I don't mean home exactly. To the bus. The bus stop. It wasn't that late. Maybe nine o'clock. It was summer. Last summer. And it wasn't even dark yet. Not really. I was tired from work—we had this big project to close and everyone had to stay late. The lawyers get to go home in limos—the clients pay for that. So they can discuss the case in the back seat or something, I don't know. But the secretaries, we have to just . . ."

The thought to get her back on the subject hadn't reached my lips before Crystal Beth warned me off with her eyes. I went back to waiting. It wasn't long.

"There were two of them," the woman said. "One was in a car. A dark car. The other came up right behind me. At the bus stop. The car stopped, the door opened, then the one behind me pointed a gun at me and made me get in.

"I thought they wanted my money. I mean, they *took* my money. And my watch. And a ring, not my wedding ring, just a costume ring. It wasn't worth anything. When they found the ATM card in my purse, they drove me to one. Then they went with me and made me empty it out. It was only a few hundred dollars. Then they had some kind of argument. Between them, I mean. I couldn't really understand it. I was in the back seat with one of them. While we were driving, he made me . . . He held the gun right by my face and he made me . . ."

I didn't move a muscle this time, feeling Crystal Beth next to me even though we were a couple of feet apart, watching the woman on the couch until she started again.

"When he was . . . finished, he said something to the one in front. Or that one said something to him. I don't remember. It was all so . . .

"They found a place to park. By the water, that's all I could tell. Then the one in front got in back. And he raped me."

I sat quietly, knowing the end to the story before she was into the second paragraph. Predators' footprints were all over the narrative, as stylized as a religious ritual. No way that was the first time those maggots had done that number. But why was she with Crystal Beth? The rapists weren't anyone she knew.

I waited for the rest.

"It took me hours to get home," the woman said. "I was a . . . mess. And petrified they would come back. I walked and I walked. I didn't have money for a cab. I should have called the police. But all I wanted to do was to get home.

"When I got upstairs, my husband was there, waiting up. It was after midnight, but he wasn't mad. I work late a lot. And the overtime's good. But as soon as he saw me, he knew. I wanted to take a shower. A long, hot shower. And a bath. I wanted to boil them right off me, make the dirt go away.

"But he wouldn't let me. He wanted to know what happened. I told him. I . . . think I told him. But he was so angry, I don't remember exactly. His face was so red, like the blood was going to break right through. He asked me, were they niggers? I didn't understand what he meant. They were . . . rapists. I didn't look at their faces. I didn't want to. And they told me not to, or they'd hurt me more.

"I told him everything. I didn't want to, but he kept slapping me and shaking me and *screaming*. I was so . . . humiliated. I was sure the neighbors could hear him. He made me tell him. Every single thing they did. And what I did. That's what he said, 'Tell me what *you* did.'"

"You didn't—" I started to say, but Crystal Beth cut me short with a chopping motion of her hand.

"He ripped my clothes off. My dirty clothes. From those dirty men. Then he shoved me on the bed. Face down. 'At least they didn't get this,' he said. Then he . . . Oh God, it hurt. Not just the . . . He killed me when he didn't care. When he blamed me."

The woman tried to take a deep breath. Failed miserably, soft sobs shuddering.

"After that, it was never the same," she finally said. "That was the only way he would ever . . . do it. And when I told him I wanted a divorce, he said I couldn't leave. Because I owed him. For what I did. And I couldn't go until I paid it off."

"**I**'m not ashamed of it," the auburn-haired woman said, her eyes hidden behind amber-tinted glasses even though the only light in the living room came from a deep-shaded lamp in the far corner. She was sitting on a straight-backed armless wood chair, knees together, hands in her lap. The room was furnished in heavy dark pieces bordered in ornate woodwork. The walls were eggshell, a framed print of a fox hunt over the fireplace, where a trio of small logs burned steadily. One corner of the big room was empty of furniture, waiting. She turned her head in that direction, turned it back to me, a question in her gesture.

I answered it with an affirmative nod.

Crystal Beth wasn't in the room. She was somewhere on the upper floors of the East Side townhouse, packing the woman's clothes. Some of them, anyway.

"It's the way I like to play," the woman said. "Hanky-spanky. Games, that's all. Foreplay, if you like."

I didn't say anything.

"It wasn't like you'd expect," she continued, judging me as I wasn't judging her. "No progression. No *Nine and a Half Weeks* scenarios. He did it the way I wanted. My rules. I like to be spanked, all right? Paddled, sometimes. Even the crop, if I feel especially . . . It doesn't matter. But when it's done, so am I, understand?"

"Yes."

"I was done. Not with . . . what I like. With him. That's all. People break up. They get tired of each other. Bored. Whatever."

I didn't say anything, watching the amber lenses watching my eyes, knowing mine were even flatter.

"But he got it confused. He thought, if I went over his knee, if I called him 'sir' and stood in the corner when he was finished . . . he thought that I belonged to him. I don't. I belong to me."

I shrugged my shoulders.

"He took it calmly when I first told him. It isn't like we were in love or anything. I met him through . . . an ad. In a magazine. After we broke up, there wasn't any trouble. I never knew where he lived. He always came here for . . . our meetings. But after I told him it was over, I . . ."

She went silent then, bowing her head. It lasted so long I realized I wasn't being tested. She couldn't finish the sentence.

So I did. "You put another ad in the same magazine. And he recognized it."

Her head came up. I could feel her eyes behind the amber lenses. "Yes! That's when it started. That's when he said if I ever . . ."

"It's all right," I told her. "You're leaving here today. He won't know where—"

"He said he owns me. I'm not allowed to . . . or he'll . . ." She took a deep breath. "I'm not going to . . . He can't make me give up my . . ."

"I know," I said. "It's what we'll use."

"I don't understand."

"You're going to move, okay? He won't know where. But he will know where to *look*, right?"

"You mean—?"

"Sure. Another ad. Change it around enough so it'll look like you're trying to disguise yourself. He'll answer it, do the same thing. When it comes to the meeting, it won't be you he finds."

"That'll make him so—"

"No it won't," I assured her. "It'll make him forget about bothering you anymore. The only thing you'll be giving up is those personal ads. There's other ways to find people to play with, right?"

"The scene is pretty . . . closed," she said dubiously. "The same people. The same places. It's hard to—"

"Get to know them first," I told her. "Sharing a fetish isn't a credential. First get close, *then* tell your secrets."

"That could take a long time."

"Safety costs."

She took off the amber glasses. Her face was heavily made up, dark eyes glinting with intelligence. "Do you know why I need . . . that, sometimes?"

"Guesses," I told her. "Varies, right? It may turn you on, but it also soothes you. Makes things right. Adds some balance. Pays the debts."

"What debts?"

"Guilt. Bad guilt. The kind other people give you. The kind you never deserved."

"How do you know so much?" she asked.

"I was looking for somebody else," the plump girl with the granny glasses and frizzy hair said softly, her back to me. Her eyes were locked onto a computer screen. A large one, vibrating with the brilliant colors of the advertisements they made you wade through before the Web browser she was using started to work.

"On one of the Survivor boards?" Lorraine asked.

"No," the plump girl said, still not turning around, Crystal Beth, Lorraine and me all standing in a fan behind her. "I was trying to reach a . . . warrior."

"You wanted something done?" I asked her, playing her for a battered wife, looking for a hit man on one of those wannabe mercenary boards.

"No! I wanted to . . . talk. About what . . . happened to me. I thought he'd . . . understand. I thought he'd talk to me."

"And he turned out to be . . . ?" I prompted her gently.

"It wasn't him," she said. "It was . . . I don't *know* who it was. But it wasn't him."

I spread my hands in a "What-the-hell-is-she-talking-about?" gesture to the women standing on either side of me.

"He pretended to be someone else?" Crystal Beth asked.

"Not the one I was looking . . . I mean, I don't . . . He read my posting. And he e-mailed me that he was a fighter. Against . . . them."

"People like your . . . ?"

"Father. Yes! Okay? My father. He had his own Web site. All kinds of stories about him from different magazines and stuff. How he rescued . . . girls. Little girls. He was a hero."

I got it then. The real danger of the Internet isn't just kiddie porn, or Lonely Hearts killers or race-hate filth or wacko conspiracy theories. Ever since the Polaroid camera and the videocam, once criminals saw the commercial possibilities, kiddie porn has flourished. People were lured into fatal meetings with correspondence lovers a hundred years ago. The race-haters would always have their shortwave networks and fax chains. And loonies never needed electronic assistance.

No, the seduction is of a whole generation of young people who affect that oh-so-blasé cynicism about anything that's in the newspapers or on TV, but lose all skepticism once it comes up on the Sacred Net. They never heard of fact-checking; they don't even understand the concept of sourcing. Any freak can create a "magazine," become a "journalist" and write an article about himself. Then he can post the article on some topic-related Web page, provide a link to his site and, bingo—he's whatever he wants to be. Instant credibility with the latest class of volunteer victim . . . cyber-chumps.

"Leave us alone," Lorraine said to me, pushing hard against my chest. I stepped back, toward the door to the plump girl's bedroom. When I had almost reached the threshold, Lorraine made a "Stay there!" gesture. Then she moved close to the plump girl, dropping one hand onto her shoulder. "Did you ever meet him?" Lorraine asked.

"No. First I had to . . ."

"Tell him . . . ?" Lorraine left it open.

"Yes. Tell him. Everything. So he could help me."

"And then?"

"Exercises."

"Like a kata?" Crystal Beth asked.

"Huh?" the plump girl replied, clearly confused. Lorraine made a traffic cop's motion with her hand, telling Crystal Beth to shut up. "A re-enactment?" she asked, voice so low I could barely hear her.

"Yes. He said it was to . . . give him information. So he could understand. He said he was going to . . ."

Nobody said anything. The plump girl stared at the screen, her hand playing with the mouse, moving it around on the desktop, clicking it on and off randomly as the screen jumped in response.

We stayed silent, watching her search. I didn't know what she was looking for, but I knew she'd never find it.

"I did it," she finally said. "But nothing happened. To my . . . father. I did everything he said. Everything. I did it all again. Even the . . . pictures. But nothing happened."

I kept waiting for her to crack. To break down, cry, smash her fist against the desk. Anything.

All she did was click the mouse and stare at the screen.

"Anyone can make up stuff on the Net," Lorraine said. "You have to—"

"I checked him out!" the plump girl said sharply. "I e-mailed other girls . . . that he helped. And I saw this story they did on him and everything."

"Anyone can have a few different e-mail addresses," Lorraine told her gently. "Anyone can—"

"I *know*," the plump girl interrupted. "Don't you think I know that? But I know there's heroes out there. Just waiting for me."

"You open that modem, you're spreading your legs," Lorraine said harshly. "It's too easy to go in disguise. Cyberspace is full of identity thieves. Web sites can be cloned. They can pretend to be anyone they want—you'll never know the truth. And 'e-mail'"— Lorraine's voice now venom-coated—"what the fuck is *that*? You think it's so 'intimate,' don't you? But it's not *private*. Every keystroke is recorded, don't you understand? It goes from you to a central bank to the other person. There's people with keys to that central bank. And people who can intercept even while you're online."

"I—" the plump girl started to protest.

"There's people who can help you," Lorraine said. "*We* can help you. Just stay off the Net, okay?"

"I can't," the plump girl said.

"**B**attered woman's syndrome," the black woman jeered, red square-cut fingernails grasping the front of the bar she was standing behind as though it were a lectern. It was a half-hour after closing time, and the joint was as empty as a senator's heart. "What a joke."

"What do you mean?" Crystal Beth asked her. "I thought it was a real . . . I don't know . . . advance. Something women could use in court to—"

"Why you say that? Because every year some governor cuts the sentence of a couple of women who're doing life for murder instead of walking around free behind self-defense? Bullshit!"

"But if society starts to under—"

"*Society* ain't close to that, girl," the black woman said. "And *society* ain't shit either. *Society's* all about control. Male control."

"It was the women's movement who got those laws passed," Crystal Beth said, using her "Let's-all-be-calm" voice.

"The women's movement? You mean my *sisters?*" the black woman replied, sarcasm clogging her throat. "Pack of stupid bitches, chumped off again. Let me tell you something, baby. This whole 'battered woman's *syndrome,*' that's just another way of saying we crazy, that's all. Man kills someone trying to kill him, only question is . . . was it gonna go down like that? Understand what I'm saying? Only thing the jury got to believe is that the other guy was gonna do it, just got beat to the draw, right? What we need some fucking *syndrome* for?"

"So a jury can understand how—"

"Oh just *stop* it, okay? Your man beats on you enough times, *hurts* you enough times, you know when he's gonna do it again. Could be the way he starts talking, could be as soon as he's had a few beers, could be a phone call from his goddamned mother . . . could be the way he starts *breathing*, all right? Point is, you *know*. Only thing is, that ain't enough. Not for the cops, not for no DA and damn sure not for no jury. Man says: 'Motherfucker went for his pocket. I know he always packs a piece, so I drilled him before he could get me.' Now, *that* sounds righteous. *That* one will fly. Woman says: 'Every time he start talking about how dirty the house is, I know, next thing coming, he's gonna start beating the shit out of me.' Now, *that* one's worth nothing, see? Nothing at all. Your man tries to kill you that first time, you kill him right then, you might be okay. But if you let him do it a *few* times, then you stuck. You let him beat on you and beat on you and . . . one day, you know you can't take another one. You *know*, soon as he wakes up from that drunken sleep, you're gonna get hurt so bad, you just . . ."

"I underst—"

"You understand *shit*, girl. You ever sit in on one of those lame-ass groups? You know, like for battered women? I did that, once. Fucking fool stands up and says, like, he used to beat on his woman, but that was 'cause he used to get drunk. So now he ain't no alcoholic, and he don't whale on his wife no more. Everybody applauds, okay? Big fucking *insight*, right? Let me tell you something, Little Miss Liberal, my old man, he used to beat me half to death and *then* he'd have himself a few drinks to celebrate, see?"

"I still think people would understand," Crystal Beth said quietly. "We have good lawyers. We could—"

"Only thing you can do for me is what you promised," the black woman said, her words just for Crystal Beth, talking past me like I was a piece of furniture, same way she had since we'd walked into the empty bar. "A new set of ID and enough cash to get in the wind," she said, eyes hard and committed. "I done time before. Short stretches. But some of those girls in there were doing the Book. For what I done last night. Sooner or later, they gonna find him. Right where I left his dead ass. You take your fucking *syndrome*, honey. Me, I'm taking the Greyhound."

There were more of them. Some staying in Crystal Beth's safe-house, some stashed in apartments around the city. Others all around the country, she told me. All races, all ages, all social classes.

"Why did you want me to hear all that?" I asked her later, upstairs in her room.

"So you would know. It's not just battered women. Stalkers are . . . all kinds. It's not just a matter of hiding out. Or even fighting back. *We* have to . . . change."

"Change how?"

"That's as individual as the victims. But I know it works. It's worked for me."

"When did you—?"

"I change all the time," she said gently. "But when you showed up in my life, that's when it really started."

"I never even *met* him," the woman said, striding back and forth before a wall of bookcases, talking like there was a much bigger audience than just me and Crystal Beth, never looking at either of us. Her long pewter-colored skirt was slit to mid-thigh, flesh flashing every time she moved.

I didn't say anything—I knew the drill by then.

"I wrote a book," the woman said. "About my life as an actress."

I knew what kinds of movies she'd made: mid-range Triple-X. Straight-to-video, paid-by-the-day, no-script, fuck-and-suck, basement-studio stuff. But she'd had a following, been a star in that world.

"I appeared on a few talk shows. You know, just to promote the book, right?"

I nodded like all of that made perfect sense.

"First he wrote a fan letter. Not to me—he never had my address—to the publisher. I didn't even answer it. That happens all the time. They just send autographed pictures back. I never even read the mail."

She shook her platinum-blond curls. A wig, as top-of-the-line as her dress and shoes. "He kept writing. Angrier and angrier. What did I think, I could just break off with him? I mean, I was never *with* him. He just got crazier and crazier. Here, take a look. . . ."

The letters were in chronological order, all photocopies. She went from "goddess of perfection" to "filthy fucking cunt" as time went along.

"My shrink said it was 'erotomania,' whatever *that's* supposed to mean."

"It means he idealized you," Crystal Beth said, "and then he constructed a—"

"It doesn't matter," the woman said, making it clear this wasn't going to be about anybody but her. "My lawyer said you had a program. I don't need a program, I need protection. Is that what *he* does?" she asked, still not looking at me, just pointing in my direction with a long fingernail as plastic as her chest.

"**H**e's crazy," the olive-skinned woman with the prominent nose said, looking up at me from the edge of the bed where she sat. Crystal Beth was next to her, their shoulders touching. The little room in the back of the waterfront restaurant was quiet, the factory-thick walls blocking the noise from up front.

We'd ridden over on Crystal Beth's motorcycle. "You want to drive?" she'd asked me.

"No way," I'd told her. I'd ridden bikes as a kid, even had one once, an old Harley 74, but I spent more time on the pavement than the tires had and I'd given it up.

"Come on," she teased. "It'd be fun for you."

"I'll have more fun holding on," I told her, watching that lovely smile flash in the streetlight's pitiful attempt at illuminating the murky alley.

But there was no smile on this woman's face, dread mixed in her voice like water in whiskey. "If he ever finds me . . ."

"Why do you say he's crazy?" I asked her. Not to know, to hear the rest of the story Crystal Beth wanted me to hear.

"He only wanted a daughter," she said. "For the son of his best friend."

"I'm not sure I—"

"His best friend has a son," the woman said, in that patient tone you use with people who aren't too bright. "So his daughter was going to be his best friend's son's wife."

"How old was the best friend's son?"

"Five. Almost five."

"So this wouldn't happen until . . ."

"... they were grown," she finished for me, like I'd finally seen the light. "First, he made sure I *could* get pregnant. I had to have tests. Then he kept me locked in the house for weeks. So nobody could have another shot at me, that's what he said.

"For months, we didn't have sex. I mean, not like ... the way you make babies. Just ... And when he was sure I wasn't pregnant, he said we could get started. Then we had sex over and over again. And I got pregnant. He checked the amnio—but it was going to be a boy. He took me for an abortion, and then we had to start over. After he beat me up."

"When did you run?" I asked her.

"When I got pregnant. I was afraid it would be another boy."

"Was it?"

She giggled, harsh and nervous—a discordant sound, no juice to it. "It wasn't anything," she said. "I wasn't really pregnant. I just thought I was. One of those home test kits. I ..."

"So why don't you—?"

"Oh, he's going to kill me," she said. Not a prediction, stating a fact. "When he finds me, he's going to kill me."

"**H**ow come it's only women?" I asked Crystal Beth later.

"What do you mean?"

"All these ... people you wanted me to talk to, they're all women. That's all you deal with, right?"

"It is now," she said. "It wasn't always that way. Men are victims of stalkers too. It's even harder for some of them, I think. You tell your pals some jealous woman is haunting you, threatening to kill your new girlfriend, they think it's cool. Women can be just as obsessive as men, just as vindictive."

"Just as dangerous too."

"Sure. We had one woman here, a lesbian. It was her lover, her ex-lover, who was after her. And *that* woman was scary, believe me. But most of the time, people don't see it that way. Women stalkers are cute. Or pathetic. Even when they cross the line, the public sees them differently. Remember that Betty Broderick woman? The one who—"

"Blew her husband and his new wife away right in their bedroom?"

"Yes. She had been stalking him for the longest time, but nobody ever stopped her. And even after the murders, the first jury actually hung. . . . They didn't convict her."

"Next time they did."

"I know. But that's not the point. If she had been a man, if the situation had been reversed, the first jury would have only been out fifteen minutes. And what about that woman judge, right here in the city? She stalked her ex-lover for *years*, did all kinds of horrible things to him, even got confidential court records on his wife. And what happened to her? Nothing! They didn't disbar her. Didn't even suspend her. She got 'censured,' whatever *that's* supposed to mean. Well, *I* know what it means—the rules are different."

"But if you think male stalking victims get even a worse break than women, how come you don't—?"

"It . . . didn't work out. The mix wasn't right. It got too . . . complicated, keeping men and women in the safehouses. There were . . . relationships."

Like you and Vyra, I thought.

"And when some of *those* didn't work," she continued, "it affected—maybe 'infected' is a better word—the whole process. We can't help everyone. Not even all the women. Or children. So we decided to stay narrow, keep a tight focus. One . . . of us was always saying that. Focus. That's where power comes from."

The kenpo guy? I thought. *T.B., the bouncer at Rollo's. Want to tell me about that too, you sweet-voiced little liar?*

"And there is one difference," she continued around my thoughts, "between men and women when it comes to stalkers."

"Which is?"

"The women always think it was their fault, somehow. They *always* think that. Even when they didn't contribute to the . . . ugliness in any way, they blame themselves. 'What was it about me that made him pick me out? What did I do to set him off?' That's one of the hardest things to overcome."

"Women always blame themselves?"

"I think so. In some way. I never met one who didn't."

"I'll bet Lorraine doesn't," I said.

Crystal Beth's eyes snapped, ready to rumble. "Because she's gay?"

"No. But she hates men, doesn't she?"

"She does. But if you think she doesn't blame herself for that too, you don't know her."

"So there's no role for men in your . . . movement?"

"Of *course* there is," she snapped. "If you knew some of the things . . . some of them have done for us . . . But they need their own movement, men. For stalkers. They need to band together too."

"So why did you show me all this?"

"So you'd like me better," she said, her voice solemn.

"This is how it went down," the man said, gesturing toward a chest-high stack of yellowing newspapers in the corner of the L-shaped studio apartment. I measured the place by moving around, casually touching things. A good burglar knows his own measurements better than a fashion model: I can stretch out my arms like I'm reaching for something, take a few strides, spread my fingers on a table, sit in a chair . . . and I'll be able to come back and do your place in the dark.

"What?" I asked him, not caring, but needing him to talk.

"Nineteen eighty. If Carter rescues the hostages from Iran before the election, he wins in a walk, okay? Now, who's cutting the defense budget? That's right . . . Jimmy Carter. And who's gonna give the military everything they could ever want? Sure, Ronnie RayGun. So what happened? The generals got together and crashed that copter in the desert. What's a few American lives compared to the military's greater good?"

"Uh-huh."

"They never tell you the full story. In the newspapers. How

come they always say 'raped and sodomized'? What does that really mean? Did she have to blow him or did she take it up the ass? You see what I mean?"

"Yeah."

"So, you said you had a message for me. From Lydia?"

"It looks bad," Crystal Beth said. She was standing next to the easy chair, one tiny high-arched bare foot on the padded arm, my right hand on a folded towel she'd laid across her knee. "I think there's some bone showing," she muttered, looking through a rectangular magnifying glass she held in one hand.

I tightened my fist. The pain shot through all the way to my shoulder.

"Hold still," she told me. Her voice was calm, but her forehead was beaded with sweat. She swabbed the knuckles of my hand with alcohol. I felt it burn clean. "I think I can . . ." she muttered, delicately picking at my hand with a pair of stainless-steel tweezers. "Yes!"

She held up a tiny white chip.

"I have to look under it now," she said softly, going back to my hand with the tweezers. "Just hold on."

The pain wasn't bad enough to let me go somewhere else. I concentrated on the rise and fall of her breasts under the white T-shirt. On the roundness of her bare arms. On her smell.

"It's clean," she pronounced. "And it's only flesh, not bone. It must have been a piece of tooth you got stuck in there."

"That makes sense," I grunted. Thinking about the freak opening the little closet and showing me his invention. An oblong length of wood, maybe a yard square and two inches thick, with U-shaped metal hooks screwed in at the corners. A length of heavy chain was anchored to the front with a massive eyelet screw. "This is for her punishment," he told me, eyes foamy behind the reading glasses he was wearing, showing me how the collar would fit over Lydia's neck, how the chain would go all the way down her back to between her legs and loop underneath, where it would be re-attached to the eyelet screw. "I can make it as tight as I want," he hissed, pointing to a ratcheting knob on the front of the board. "After she spends a couple of hours in this every day, she'll never disobey again."

The next thing I remember, he was on the floor, strange sounds coming out of the red-and-white mess that had been his mouth.

"This won't hurt," Crystal Beth said, holding a clear plastic spray bottle. She squirted some reddish mist all over the raw wounds across my knuckles.

"What is that stuff?" I asked her.

"Fibrin sealant," she said. "Biologic glue. It's made from proteins found in blood. Stops the bleeding real quick. It helps heal too."

"I never heard of it."

"It's not available here. They use it in Europe. The FDA is holding back on approval. It's made with blood. . . . I guess maybe they're worried about AIDS."

The spray was turning to a kind of jelly right before my eyes. Damaged tissue. Merging. Coming together. Healing wounds. Protecting. I looked at my damaged hand. And saw my family.

I didn't say anything.

"You don't have to worry about it," she told me. "This isn't European stuff. It's made right here. Lorraine makes it."

"Where does she get the blood?"

"From me," Crystal Beth said solemnly. "Now you have some of mine."

"He's coming," Vyra whispered into the phone. "Now."

I got there first. Dressed like a lawyer hurrying to an afternoon cocktail with his mistress before catching the 6:09 out of Grand Central to Westport. Nobody in the hotel lobby looked at me twice. And if the security people had questions, I had the answer in my pocket—a key to a small room on one of the lower floors. That gave me a place to duck into if I needed it. And another way into the hotel, through the underground parking garage.

Vyra was wearing one of those simple black dresses that would cost a workingman a month's pay. A long thin gold chain around her neck. Plain black patent leather spikes with a tiny row of gold rivets up the back of each heel.

"You going out?" I asked her as I walked through the door.

"Why? You think I look nice?"

"You look great," I told her. "Like you put on some weight."

"That's a *compliment?*" she wanted to know, hands on her hips.

"Sure."

"It's my butt, right?"

"Huh?"

"My butt. It's . . . flat. You like them when they stick way out. Like . . . hers."

"Huh?"

"Oh stop it! You know who I'm talking about."

"I never really . . ." I said lamely.

"Sure. Well, it doesn't matter. Different men like different things."

"And women don't?"

"I don't think so," she said seriously. "I mean, not as much, anyway. I never met a woman who only liked blonds, the way some men do."

"What do you like, Vyra?"

"I like . . . fun. At least, I thought I did. Fun. Whatever that is." She sounded sad.

"Look, maybe—"

A rap at the door. I motioned for Vyra to answer it, stepping back into the hall.

"Hey, baby!" It was Herk. Two big hands around Vyra's waist, picking her up in the air, kissing her hard. Vyra bent her legs at the knee, sticking her feet straight back, arms around his neck. If anyone was watching, they'd see what they were supposed to see.

Herk stepped inside, closed the door behind him, still carrying Vyra, walking deep into the room. When he finally put her down,

I stepped into sight, held my finger to my lips, pointed to the living-room couch. Herk walked over there, Vyra at his side. They both sat down. I made a "yap-yap" gesture with my fingers. Herk looked puzzled, but Vyra got it and started chattering away, asking Herk where he'd *been*, anyway. I took a position to the side of the door and waited.

I gave it five minutes. Nothing.

Vyra never stopped talking.

I stepped away from the door and walked to one of the back bedrooms, motioning for them to follow. Vyra said something to Herk about putting on a fashion show for him. Then they both came down the hall. The bedroom had an adjoining bath. I positioned two chairs on either side of the bathroom door, then turned the shower on full-blast. When I turned around, I got my right hand up just in time to stop Herk from putting one of his bear hugs on me.

"Whoa! What happened to the hand, bro?"

"I forgot the rules," I told him.

"What rules?" Vyra put in, noticing my hand for the first time.

"Hard to soft, soft to hard," Herk explained. "You clocked someone in the teeth, huh?" he said to me.

"Yeah. Sit down. How much time you got?"

"Got? I dunno. We ain't got a meeting until tomorrow night."

"Start at the beginning," I told him, shooting Vyra a look so she'd leave us alone. She ignored it, perching herself on the bed.

"Lothar and me had a meet. At that place where he works. He's got a back room. Anyway, nobody was looking at nobody else, you know those kind of places."

"What kind of places?" Vyra asked.

"Shut up," I told her softly. "We're not playing. This isn't a game."

"I'm in this too," she said.

"Yeah, you are. So do your piece."

"You mean, just sit here?"

"For now."

"I don't want—"

"Vyra, you can sit there nice and peaceful. Or I can use this," I said, taking a Velcro tourniquet out of my pocket.

"What's that?" she asked, as suspicious as a crackhouse door-man.

"It works just like handcuffs," I told her. "And I got a nice clean handkerchief for your big mouth too. Is that what you want?"

"You—"

"Yeah, I would," I promised her.

Her mouth snapped shut so hard flecks of lipstick flew off.

"From the beginning," I said to Herk again.

"Anyway, I had to stay there until—"

"There?"

"In the back room. Of the porno joint. Lothar gets this message from me, right? At his P.O. box. Then we talk on the pay phone, right? Then we meet, I tell him what I had to do with . . . that guy, okay? The Jew. He had to tell the others, the guys he was with. He couldn't bring me to them until he cleared it. So I had to stay there. Where he works. Overnight. It was weird, Burke. Being in that place all alone."

"At least you had plenty to read."

"That stuff? I tried to. . . . I mean, I looked through it and every-thing. But it's all the same, you know what I mean?"

Vyra took an especially deep breath, as if to remind him that it really wasn't. But she didn't say a word.

"Yeah, I do," I told him. "What happened next?"

"In the morning, before the place opens, he comes back. I had to stay for his whole shift, until it got dark. Then I went with him."

"To . . . ?"

"This place they got. A house. Just the other side of the Fifty-ninth Street Bridge."

"You got the address?"

"Nah. What happens is, you go to this bar, okay? Then you make a call from the pay phone over against the wall. There's all kinds of clicks on the line, like it's switching back and forth. You wait there. One of them comes by and picks you up. You get in the back of this van. No windows. Then you ride for a while. When you get out, you're in this garage, like. There's a doorway cut right into the house. I can tell from the way it's set up, the house is sup-posed to be all closed up. You can't even see outside."

"But when you want to leave . . . ?"

"You got to tell them. Then they take you. Through the garage and all."

"They take you wherever you want?"

"Nah, they ain't no taxi service. They drop you off near whatever subway you want. Or a cab stand. But I know they gotta drive that van a good half-hour before we get to the house from the bar."

"So they could have followed you here?"

"I guess . . ." he said, puzzled.

I shrugged it off. If they had, they wouldn't have learned much. Especially if they had monitored his calls to Vyra. "How many in the crew?" I asked him.

"There was like maybe six of them there. Not counting Lothar. He wasn't there when they talked to me. What they did, they asked me a bunch of questions. Just like you said."

"Any problems?"

"Nah. They mostly asked me about . . . the guy. How'd I do it and all. How'd we find out he was a Jew. Everything else, I just told them what was . . . what was true, I mean. About it. They told me about it, so I said I'd do it. Do *him*, I mean. Like you said."

"Did one guy ask you all the questions? Was there a leader?"

"I don't . . . think so. I mean, they was all talking. Most of the stuff they asked me, I didn't know the answers."

A warning bell went off in my head. "Like what?"

"Like what they was up to, the guys that was supposed to be with me . . . the guys I was supposed to be with. In my cell, like? Understand?"

"Yeah. What else did they want to know?"

"Like, what Lothar said about them. Stuff like that. I told them the truth . . . nothing."

"Herk, they never searched you?"

"Oh yeah," he said brightly. "They did that. Just like in the joint. Finger-wave and everything. Before they started talking. One of them, he asked me where I got the tattoo."

"What'd you tell him?"

"I told him an old Jewish guy gave it to me."

"Jesus."

"They thought that was real funny. They was all laughing at the guy who asked me."

I took a long, shallow breath, looking deep into Herk's eyes. They came back innocent, like the big damn kid he was. "Herk, did they say anything about what they were planning?"

"Nah. You know what? I don't think they *gonna* tell me either. It's like, I got to stay there, close anyway, 'cause they don't know 'xactly what they gonna do with me. But they didn't say nothing . . . uh, specific-like. Just . . . something's gonna happen. I mean, everybody knows that. Knew that, I mean. In my crew. The one I was with that told me to—"

"Yeah, okay, I got it." I took a deep breath, making sure I had the big man's full attention. "Listen close now, Herk. What's Lothar's weight? Can you tell?"

"He ain't no boss, Burke, I can tell you that. I don't mean he's like a flunkey or nothing, but he ain't the big cheese, that's for sure."

"Herk, *think* for a minute. Close your eyes. Try and put yourself back there. Just . . . listen, okay? We're not looking for the *boss*, we're looking for the *brains*, understand?"

"Bro, when it comes to the brains in a crew, all I know, it ain't never gonna be me."

"They all asked you questions, right?"

"Yeah. I guess."

"Were any of them like . . . hostile? You know, on your case hard?"

"Nah. Well, maybe this one guy . . . Kenny. But you could see he's weak. You know how their voice gets a little . . . I dunno, jittery? No matter how hard they talking?"

"Yeah."

"Well, that's Kenny. It *ain't* him, that's for sure."

"And it's not Lothar?"

"No way, man."

"Herk, listen real close now," I said urgently, lighting a cigarette. "I—"

"Can I have one too?" Vyra asked me.

Herk shot her a disapproving look.

"What did I do?" she asked, innocently, looking out from under her false eyelashes, her hands clasped in her lap . . . but squeezing her elbows to emphasize the cleavage.

"That stuff'll kill you," he said. "That's why you don't put weight on, all them cigarettes."

"You *too*? You think I should—?"

"I think you should shut the fuck up," I told her, turning back to Hercules, but handing Vyra a cigarette. "Now, listen," I said again. "You know the difference between feelings and facts?"

"I . . . guess."

I took a deep nose breath, drawing the oxygen all the way down to my groin, centering. If I couldn't translate it down for Herk, I was lost. "Listen to these questions, okay?" I said, holding his eyes. "One: when did you go to the joint the last time? Two: was it worse than the time before? Three: what was the charges? Four: was your lawyer any good? All right?"

"Yeah."

"Now answer them. One at a time. Concentrate."

"Okay," the big man said, brow furrowed. "I last went down in '91. For A and R. That's assault and robbery," he said in an aside to Vyra, who was still holding the cigarette I gave her, unlit. "It *was* worse the last time. 'Cause none a you guys was in there with me. But it wasn't that bad. I mean . . . you know how it is. I got crewed up quick. And . . . and . . . oh yeah! My lawyer fucking *sucked*. Miserable-ass weasel they give me in the court. He had me pled out before I could draw a breath."

"Good. Now: which of those was facts, and which was feelings?"

"They *all* facts, bro. The stone truth."

I had a piercing headache.

Vyra got off the bed and stood next to Herk, one hand on his shoulder, the other holding the still-unlit cigarette. She bent her face close to his. "Is true love a fact?" she asked him.

"Huh?"

"If you love someone, a true love, that's a fact, yes?"

"Sure."

"But it's also a feeling, right, Hercules? Love is what you *feel*, isn't it?"

The big man sat there pondering, Vyra's perfectly manicured hand sitting on his hyper-muscled shoulder like a butterfly on a boulder.

I didn't say a word.

"Yeah," he finally said. "It is. Sure."

"Did any of them ask you what it was like in prison?" I asked him quickly, trying to catch the ripple from the rock Vyra had dropped into the pool.

"Oh yeah, bro. Like, they was *all* interested in that. I figured it was 'cause none of them been—"

"What about the other questions? *When* you went down, what you went down for?"

"Nah, they was . . . Wait a minute. Yeah! One guy. Scott, that was him. He was the only one asking me about that fact stuff. Yeah! When I went in. Even what joints I was in. And—"

"—and your date of birth?" I cut in, smelling blood. That's the key to a criminal-records search, the foundation stone that unlocks all the data.

"Sure did, bro! I ask him, what's he want to do, send me a fucking birthday present? Couple of the guys laughed, but Scott, he still wanted to know."

"You told him, right?"

"Sure. Why not?"

"He's the man, Herk."

Vyra gave him a big wet kiss on the cheek. "You figured it out, honey!" she said.

Herk grinned broadly, Vyra's lipstick mark clear on his face. I made a grunting noise and his eyes swung back to me. "Whatever you do," I told him, "don't ask any questions. Keep your nose out of things, understand? They wanna tell you something, you listen. They don't, that's it."

"I got it, bro."

"Yeah. I know."

"Burke?"

"What?"

"It's gonna be all right, ain't it?"

"Yeah it is."

"You just tell me what to do and I'll—"

"I know. You got your own place yet?"

"I'm staying with Lothar. Right in the porno store. Only upstairs. He got a whole apartment up there. You can't even tell from the street. Pretty slick, huh?"

"Yeah. Lothar try and make conversation with you?"

"Just bullshit. Not about business. Well, not about . . . I mean, he got business of his own. Burke, did you know there was Nazi porno?"

"Nazi porno?"

"Yeah, like Nazis raping a girl. And torture stuff. Wearing those uniforms with what I . . ." He touched his chest. Where the tattoo was.

"Lothar's into that?"

"*Big*-time," Hercules said. "I think . . . maybe . . . ah, never mind—I'm too fucking dim to be playing Sherlock Holmes and all."

"What?" I asked him, leaning forward, putting my damaged hand on his thick forearm. "Come on."

"It's just a . . . feeling, like," he said, glancing over at Vyra. "But I think Lothar was doing that stuff first. I mean, the porno. And those other guys . . . one of them, anyway . . . comes in the shop, or he hears about what Lothar's got, I dunno. I mean, one of the guys from his first cell, not the one he's in now. The one I was supposed to be . . . Anyway I think he wasn't like . . . *with* them first. He's not a guy with guns or bombs or nothing. He used to write stuff. . . ."

"What stuff?"

"I dunno. About the Jews and niggers and all."

"You get the impression he's being cagey? Like maybe they got a bug in his apartment?"

"Man, I *never* know when someone's being cagey. That's what the Prof always says. Me, I'm thick. I mean, I never knew him before, so how'm I gonna know if he changed, right?"

"Right."

"When this is over, I'm going away," he said quietly.

"It's a long way from over," I warned him.

"And it's a long way I'm going, bro," Hercules said. "Either way, I'm gone. Live or die, I'm done with this."

I left Herk there. Told him to hang around a minimum of a couple of hours. Watch TV or something. Vyra still hadn't lit the cigarette.

I took the stairway to my room. Ducked inside. The message light wasn't blinking on the phone.

Good.

I called Mama. Nothing.

Even better.

I know what happens when there's too many loose threads—somebody weaves them into a noose. Panic was my enemy, but I knew how to deal with it: Aikido. In my head. My spirit against the enemy.

I stripped down to my underwear and closed my eyes, watching the loose threads dance on a tiny 3-D screen.

A movie. Only I wasn't just a spectator. Or even an actor. I was the director.

Working on the final cut.

No point trying to call Davidson. He doesn't trust phones and he'd go so elliptical that it'd take him an hour to say hello. I went over to his office, told his receptionist that I had an appointment. She couldn't find it on her calendar, so I told her to ask him, gambling that he wouldn't be in with a client first thing in the morning.

"You in trouble?" he asked without preamble as I closed his office door behind me.

"Not me. Maybe not anybody, if you can do something for me."

"Something in court?"

"If it goes right, it never goes to court. Some . . . negotiations."

"With . . . ?"

"I don't know the name of the AUSA. I'm not coming in at that end."

"And I'm not following you."

"Here it is," I told him. "I got a friend. A good friend. He's about to do something for the *federales*. Something big. The promise is immunity. For everything."

"Everything he's going to do? Everything he's already done? What?"

"Everything everything. He's not a rat. This is kind of an . . . undercover thing. All I've collected so far is a pack of promises."

"From the government?"

"From a guy who says he can get that done. A free-lancer."

"Oh," Davidson said quietly, a cubic ton of suspicion compressed into that one syllable.

"Yeah, I know. That's where you come in. My friend needs a lawyer. Somebody to drive the nails home. What I want, I want this guy, this free-lancer, to put up *now*. I want him to take you to someone—whoever—who can grant the immunity. And I want it. In writing. A cooperation agreement. Rock-solid, no loopholes. And the deal has to include a new ID."

"And a relocate?"

"Yeah, we can say that. But my friend, he's gonna walk away, sooner or later. The deal isn't for protection, it's for a new everything—name, face, Social Security, work history. And no testimony."

"No testimony? He's going to access them to the kind of evidence that stands on its own?"

"That's the deal," I said. "You can do it?"

"I can do it if this free-lancer you're talking about can deliver. If he really has that kind of influence. I understand what *you* want, but I don't know what I've got to bargain with to get it."

"How about if I tell you?" I asked, lighting a cigarette.

I left ten grand with Davidson, with the other half to come when the deal was done. He hadn't said anything about cutting his price once I told him what was going on, but his whole posture shifted behind the big desk. Davidson was a stand-up guy with the best credentials you can have in our business—a track record. And he was a hell of a lawyer. Most of the time, I hold back some of the truth when I talk to him. But he'd lost relatives to the death camps, and I knew what the truth would do this time. I wouldn't want to be the government lawyer who tried to get in his way.

Back at my place, I tried to think it through.

Mousetrap. Box. Closed-end tunnel. It all came up the same on my screen.

Pryce had me cornered. He had too many pieces on the board.

My mind ached with the strain from trying to slip out of the maze. My face hurt—sharp, spiking pain in the nerve cluster below the cheekbone. I couldn't figure out what was going on until I realized how tightly my teeth had been clenched. When I finally fell asleep, fever-dreams snapped me wide awake.

I knew what to do then. Stared at the red dot on my mirror until I fell into it. Stayed down there, safe and dissociated.

When I resurfaced I was calmer.

But still trapped.

"Are you afraid?" Crystal Beth asked later, lying next to me in the dark.

And that's when I knew what was wrong. Why I couldn't think my way out.

I wasn't afraid.

The first thing I remember about being a baby is terror so total that fear became my one true friend. Always with me, never leaving my side. Warning me, keeping me vigilant. Distrustful. A layer of protection between the terror and me—the little tiny bit that was me then.

Fear never abandoned me. I took it with me everywhere I went.

Everywhere they sent me. The State—my true parent—sending me to surrogates who continued its vicious work. The orphanage. Foster homes. Reform school. Prison looming as inevitable in my future as college was in the lives of the privileged.

Fear came there with me too. A friend I internalized so deep the wolf packs that ran wild through the joint couldn't smell it. That's because it wasn't *on* me, it was *in* me. I cherished it, nurtured it, encoded it into my own DNA. My face flattened, my hands stopped shaking. My heart went slow and cold.

I came into prison with a life-taker's rep. They test reps in there. I kept mine. It cost a lot, but it wasn't me who paid.

I got to where I never broke a sweat. My voice stayed within a tight, narrow range. I could stare down a cobra. But the fear-bolts always roamed loose in my body, firing off bursts whenever danger was around.

In prison, I lived in danger, adrenaline crackling through my synapses like turbo-boosted cocaine. It kept me alive.

My one goal, then.

Out in the World, I kept the fear. But I played it different. I learned to show the fear when it would do me some good. Trained myself to act, role-playing along the tightrope of survival.

Fear never left me. Until now.

I felt abandoned all over again. Deserted. Without my old friend, I couldn't plot, couldn't plan.

So why wasn't I afraid? I was boxed, all right. Couldn't see a way out. So why . . . ?

"Burke! Burke, wake up. Are you all right?"

Crystal Beth, shaking my shoulders, gentle but serious. I opened my eyes.

"Are you all right?" she asked again.

"I'm fine," I told her. "I must have drifted off, that's all."

"Drifted off? You were . . . not here. I mean, you weren't actually sleeping, I could tell. Just . . . zoned out or something."

"What's the big deal?" I asked her, wondering why she didn't recognize the same thing she did herself.

"It's been *hours* you've been like that," she said, answering the question she didn't know I'd asked. "I didn't want to . . . disturb you. I didn't know. But then you finally fell asleep. And I got scared."

"I'm fine," I told her again. "It happens to me sometimes. When I have to think."

"My mother said the shamans . . . Oh, I don't mean you. . . . I mean, you were . . . in a trance, like. Awake, but not here. One minute we were talking, the next you were gone."

"Can I have a glass of water?" I asked her, more to shut her down than because I was thirsty.

"Sure, baby."

She came back with a cone-shaped paper cup. The water was cold and clean. "Thanks," I said.

"You want anything else?"

"A cigarette?"

She lit one of mine, handed it to me, not saying a word. I smoked it all the way down in the darkness, my spinal cord crawling with snake-twisty nerves. Alive now.

Alive with fear.

Where I'd gone, it had come to me. I wasn't afraid of Pryce. I wasn't the target. He couldn't really hurt me. Yeah, he might know some stuff I wouldn't want shouted around the town, some old ID might be blown, crap like that. But there was nothing in it for him to try for me. If he knew enough to hurt me, he knew enough to know that he wouldn't live long if he did.

Maybe that was the difference. In prison, it's not how tough you are that keeps you safe, it's your capacity for revenge. Prison is icy hell. Feelings are the enemy. Showing them is a crippling ill- ness—sometimes a fatal one. You get raped, you're a cunt. And every con in the joint is free to use you like one. You kill the rapist, you're a man. Everything squared. Vengeance is the only true reli- gion in there. And if you have backup, even killing you won't make the killers safe . . . so they step off.

The first time I went down, it was for a good, high-status beef. Shooting a guy. Attempted murder, they called it, and they were right on the money. I did it because he scared me, but that wasn't how I profiled it once I was inside. In my version, I did it because he disrespected me.

It helped protect me. I watched plenty of others who couldn't stay safe. It was ugly, what happened to them. But even before I crewed up, the predators stayed away. Everyone knew—Burke would get even. Next to me, elephants had Alzheimer's.

If Pryce knew so much about me, he had to know that. He had to know that, whatever I was, I wasn't alone. I'd die for that, and that would die for me.

So I was safe from him.

But Herk wasn't. He was hung out to dry. Without the immunity, he was barbecued beef. Without the immunity, he was going back Inside. He'd never be a gardener. Never be a person, like he wanted so bad.

Doc, the prison shrink—I was his inmate clerk, a real sweet spot—told me once that the only thing that really distinguishes a sociopath from the rest of the world is that the sociopath lacks empathy. He feels only his own pain, cares only for his own needs. Selfishness squared. All sexual sadists are sociopaths, but not all sociopaths are sexual sadists. All sociopaths *are* the same thing, but they don't all *want* the same things. Take politicians—the way they breed is to fuck the rest of us.

All sociopaths are encapsulated. Always have every feeling they need right inside themselves. Nobody else counts.

The plague of the Nineties isn't AIDS, it's self-absorption. Sociopaths always crank the revs right to the redline. And keep the hammer down.

Amateurs think prisons are full of sociopaths. A pro would tell you the truth—the only sociopaths in prison are the failures. The rest of the population is all the result of the "Just Us" system. Flops and fools, weasels and weaklings. Lazy lames. Most of the convict population today is in there for drugs.

It's like we learned nothing from Prohibition.

I was safe from Pryce and Herk wasn't. So what?

I knew the answer to that: Herk would die for me.

That's an easy thing to say, but I knew it for true. A feeling *and* a fact. Herk had only been down with our crew for a few weeks when it happened. I was rat-packed in the long corridor between D Block and the commissary. Four black guys, three with shanks, one working lookout. It wasn't me they wanted. Not me in particular. A race war had been raging inside for almost a week. When that happens, color is the only target.

It wasn't a heist. They weren't looking to rough off some commissary goods. No, the next white convict who walked into their trap was going to die. They wanted a body. Any body, so long as it was the right color.

That was me, that day.

If it had been years earlier, when I was still on my first bit, when my image was more important than my life, I would have done it different. But that day, as soon as I spotted the first two, I turned and ran. That's when I saw the other one, sharpened rat-tail file wrapped in black electrical tape held low against his hip, moving in. He was the hit man—the others were carrying steel too, but they didn't look as professional, just there to drive the prey onto the killing ground.

I was unarmed. And out of time. I rushed the hit man, charging at his chest. He came up to meet me. I twisted my right shoulder like I was going to try and slide past on his right, exposing my back for a second as I planted my right foot and spun quickly, flattening my chest against the opposite wall away from his knife hand, firing my right elbow at where I thought his face would be as I scrambled crab-style toward safety. I almost made it. I felt the shank punch through my denim jacket and take me just below the shoulder. I went down, rolling away as fast as I could. Heard the pounding footsteps as the other two charged, knives held high.

That's when Hercules hit them from behind like a runaway train, taking them both into the wall. The lookout shouted something. I kept rolling, covering up as best as I could, kicking out at the hit man every time he got close. Guards piled into the corridor, the riot whistle blowing loud. Sweeter than church bells on a wedding day.

One of the hacks clubbed me right where the hit man's shank had gone in. When I came to in the prison hospital, my head was bandaged too.

If you can get to the hospital in prison, they can probably save you—the docs there have plenty of practice. Herk took almost seventy stitches, but they were slash wounds, not deep. I got a heavy tetanus shot, then they cleaned the wound out and packed it. Told me how lucky it was that it hadn't been lower—if he'd gotten a kidney, I was gone.

They did a prison investigation. Which means a body count. This one was zero, so they called it off. Herk and I told the same story. We were walking down the corridor and got jumped. No, we didn't see who did it. No, we didn't know if they were black or white—they had masks and gloves on. No, we didn't know how many of them there were.

The black guys told the same story.

The shanks were somebody else's. No prints . . . if they even checked.

Herk and I got thirty days' keep-lock. The black guys got six months in the bing. Except for the lookout. They cut him loose. An innocent bystander.

When the hit man died from eating a rat-poison-laced candy bar in solitary, the Man put it down to the race war. That had been Wesley's work, although I didn't know it then.

The other two sent word to me that there had been nothing personal—they'd mistaken me for somebody else. I was okay with them. Sorry about what happened. How about if they send a few crates of smokes over to my wing, make it up to me?

I sent word back: Sure. No hard feelings.

A couple of months later, the race war was over. For then—the only way it's ever over in there. One of the two guys who'd sent me the smokes was watching a softball game on the yard when someone came up behind him and played a one-swing game of T-ball with his head.

The hacks figured it for debt collection—the black guy was a known gambler. Like always, they got it about half right.

Less than a week later, his partner went off a high tier all the way down to the killing concrete floor.

The investigation was quick. After all, a lot of suicides don't leave notes.

The lookout was the sole survivor. He smelled the wind, took a voluntary PC. Refused to eat any food that the hacks didn't taste.

Which meant he was starving to death. He became convinced microwaves were being sent to give him cancer. Heard voices telling him he was going to die. They gave him medication—held him down for the needle. It calmed him, let him relax. After a while, he started to trust again, so they switched to oral meds. He always took them, no complaints. It wasn't so bad in there for him after that. He got tranquil, started to eat again. But he never came out of his cell.

That's where they found his body, burned to a crisp. If he'd screamed, nobody had heard.

Herk would die for me.

He was my brother.

My brother was in a box, not me.

But my family *is* me. My brother was in danger, and I was afraid. For him, for me. Same thing.

I had my old partner back. Fear was in me, alive.

And it would keep my brother that way too.

I guess I'll never qualify as a sociopath. But you don't have to be a sociopath to act like one.

I started to plot.

"Are you okay?" Crystal Beth asked me again. "You keep . . . going away."

"I'm back now," I told her.

In this city, some of the rats have wings. There's parts of Brooklyn where pigeon-racing is a bigger sport than baseball. And if you're tired of having your house covered in pigeon shit, professional exterminators will lay a covering on your roof to solve the problem. It's really a carpet of tiny little face-up nails—pigeons can't land on it.

But starlings live in this city too, and they need places to roost. For their tribe to survive. So what they do is they carefully gather twigs and paper and other stuff, drop it on the carpet of nails and then stand on *that*.

I don't know how they do it in other countries, but in America, people call themselves "friends" and it means about as much as when they sign their letters "Love." *All* their letters.

Down here, it's different. I have no friends. There's people I know, people I wouldn't hurt if I could help it. There's people I like, and maybe they like me. But it really comes down to Us, Them . . . and non-combatants.

Us is the deepest blood of all. And it only takes volunteers.

In your world, you ask a friend to get something for you, he'd probably ask what you wanted it for. And then he might say yes and he might say no.

When I asked Clarence to get something for me, he didn't ask me what I wanted it for.

And he didn't just say he'd get it for me—he asked if he could use it himself.

"What's the point?" Pryce asked.

"I don't want to say on the phone. Especially without a land-line," I told him.

"You want to meet, I can do that. But why does . . . my friend have to be there too?"

"I learned something," I said. "It could change the game, understand? Change everything."

"I still don't—"

"Change *everything*," I said, letting an organ-stop of pressure into my voice.

He was silent for a minute, but the cellular's hum told me he was still on the line. "The last time we met, it was all yours," he finally said. "This time, it has to be mine."

"Time and place," I said. "You call it."

"I can't just reach out and—"

"When you have it, let me know," I said. "But there isn't a lot of time."

"You trust me?" I asked Hercules in the bedroom of Vyra's hotel suite.

"All the way, brother," he said, no hesitation.

"Up to now, they been the players, we been the game, got it?"

"Yeah."

"We're gonna change the game," I told him.

Two days later. Three-thirty in the afternoon. Rain banging against Crystal Beth's dark window.

"You know where River Street is?" Pryce's voice, over the cell phone.

"What borough?"

"Brooklyn."

"I can find it," I told him. Lying. I know River Street. It only runs for a couple of blocks, parallel to Kent Avenue, right off where the East River flows under the Williamsburg Bridge.

"Go there now," he said. "You'll see my car parked."

"I'm moving," I promised.

"Are you inside?" I asked Vyra. Meaning: Are you in the suite, not the street?

"Yes." Her voice over the cell phone was clipped, precise. Not like her.

"You alone?"

"No."

"Your car is there?"

"Yes."

"Do this now. You *both* meet me at the Butcher Block. Now."

"I don't know where—"

"Your friend does. Now."

I cut the connection.

I spotted the burgundy Mercedes 600SL coupe coming down the block, moving slow. I stepped out so they could see me. "Get in my car," I told Hercules.

"What's going—?"

"Tell you later," I cut Vyra off. "Go back to the hotel. *Stay* there, girl, no matter what. If you don't hear anything in a couple of hours, call the number you have for me. Tell whoever answers that I went to meet Pryce. And I didn't come back."

"Why does Hercules have to—?"

"Not now," I said, turning my back on her and moving off to the Plymouth.

"It's gotta be this way, huh?" Herk asked me.

I took the Brooklyn Bridge to the BQE, heading toward Queens. Exited at Metropolitan Avenue and swung back toward Brooklyn.

"Yeah. When you play cards, the ace is boss, right?"

"Sure."

"We need the king to be boss, Herk."

He nodded soberly, watching the miserable weather. The sky was turning prison-gray.

"Burke?"

"What?"

"Vyra. Are you . . . like, with her?"

"With her? Like I'm with you? No. She's not one of—"

"Nah, I don't mean that. I never say things like I mean them. I mean, I say them straight, but they don't come out the way I'm thinking. You understand?"

"Yeah, I do. What do you want to know?"

"You and her. She was . . . like your girlfriend, right?"

"No. She was never my girlfriend. We . . . got together once in a while. That's all."

"You like her?"

"I don't know what I think about her. Never thought about it at all, I guess."

"I like her."

"You mean you'd like to fuck her," saying it bluntly to take the edges off.

"Nah. I mean . . . I would. I mean . . . I already . . . Burke, I really like her. She's real smart. And real sweet. I can talk to her about things."

"Like what? Shoes?"

"Man, you don't know her. She's really a . . . good person."

"Okay."

"What's that mean?"

"It means: okay. Whatever you want to do, it's up to you. But, Herk . . ."

"What?"

"She's got herself a real good gig where she is, you know what I'm saying?"

"Her husband? He ain't—"

"He's rich. Major-league rich. Remember what the Prof told us about women once? 'Some play, some stay.' Vyra, she's a player, all right?"

"You don't know her," the big man said, sullen and stubborn.

I shrugged my shoulders, concentrating. It wasn't time to worry about Herk being such a sap—we were a couple of blocks from River Street.

The white Taurus was parked on the street. No other car was close, but the block wasn't deserted: People walking around, maybe from the change-of-shift at some of the nearby factories, maybe locals. Cars crawled by too.

I pulled in behind, leaving myself room enough to drive away without backing up first. "Let's do it," I said to Hercules.

Pryce must have been watching us in the rearview mirror. The back doors of the sedan popped open as we walked toward it. We climbed in, Herk behind Pryce, me behind Lothar. Pryce put his right arm along the back of the seat, turned to look at me. Lothar stared straight ahead.

"All right, let's hear it," Pryce said.

"I want Herk to have his immunity now," I told him. "Before this goes another step."

"That wasn't the—"

"That's the deal now," I said. "I got a lawyer in place. You say when, he'll come downtown, you'll put the whole thing together."

"You can't expect to have that sort of deal in front," Pryce said in an annoyed tone. "You know better than that. Everybody will get taken care of at the same time."

"I think Lothar's *already* taken care of."

"That's different," Pryce said in the flat officialese they teach you in FBI school. "Lothar is an undercover operative of the United States government."

"So's Herk now."

"But they don't *need* him," Pryce said in a patient voice. "They don't even know about him yet."

"But you can do it?" I asked him. "You got that much juice with the feds?"

"Guaranteed," he said. "But what does this have to do with Lothar?"

"How do I know you're going to come through for Hercules?" I said, ignoring his question.

"I've done what you wanted, haven't I? You're just going to have to trust me."

I sat there quietly as a woman trundled past, pulling one of those little grocery carts behind her. Then I took out the fat tube of steel Clarence had gotten for me, said "Lothar?" and, when he turned sideways to listen, put a nine-millimeter slug in his temple.

It didn't make much noise, even in the closed car.

"You got it wrong," I told Pryce. "You're going to have to trust *me*."

Lothar's head slumped forward, his body held in place by his seatbelt. I grabbed a handful of his hair and pulled him backward so it looked like he was just sitting there. There was no blood, just a round little black dot on his temple—the opposite of a birthmark. Some of the powder had been removed from the cartridge to keep the sound down—the bullet was still somewhere in Lothar's brain.

"You—"

Pryce cut himself off, out of words.

I wasn't. "Now we're gonna find out," I told him, watching his hands in case we had to do him too. If it came to that, Hercules would have to snap his neck from behind—I didn't have another bullet. Clarence's connection made custom pieces—this one was a one-shot derringer with a thick core of silencing baffles. "Look," I said, my voice as calm as a Zen rock garden, "Lothar was stalking his wife. That's a fact, well documented. There's an Order of Protection. You know that too. Well, what happened was that he got spotted breaking into his wife's house. She isn't there anymore, but he didn't know that. He had implements with him—handcuffs, duct tape, like that. He was gonna kill his wife and kidnap the baby. Or both of them. Who knows? The cops came on the scene, and Lothar decided to shoot it out. Gunfire was exchanged. There's the result, sitting right next to you. That's the story that needs to get in the papers. So the others will see what happened. It won't surprise them either—they knew Lothar was a torture-sex freak with a major hate for his wife. Okay, that leaves Herk. He's your inside man now. And he needs that immunity. Or the faucet gets turned off."

"You're insane," Pryce said, looking through the windshield. The street was quiet.

"People could argue about that," I told him. "Nobody's gonna argue about Lothar being dead."

"You expect me to drive around with a dead body and—"

"I don't care what you do. I know people can't see through these windows from outside. You want cover, I'll drive point until you get clear. To wherever you want—we can stay linked on the cellulars. But I don't think you want me to see where you're going.

"It's time to prove," I told him. "If you're the real thing, if you're down with ZOG, you can do this. If you're not, it's all over. You got no more cards to play. You thought you knew me. Now you do. You take down Crystal Beth's network, you dime out Vyra to her husband, you turn Porkpie loose on Hercules, you're done, pal. You'll never find all of us. And one of us will find you."

"Get out of the car," he said in a tight, controlled voice. "Get out now. I'll call you."

We watched the white Taurus drive away. Smooth and steady.

I crossed the bridge into Manhattan. Pulled up to a deli on Delancey. A Latino in an old army field jacket was leaning against the wall, just out of the rain. He walked over to the Plymouth. Herk rolled down his window. The guy stuck his head inside, nodded at me. He went into the deli, came back with a paper bag full of sandwiches and a couple of bottles of apple juice. I glove-handed him the empty, wiped-down steel tube and five one-hundred-dollar bills. He pocketed both and walked off.

Herk dialed Vyra from a pay phone on the street. Told her he'd be there soon.

Back in the car, he turned to me. "Burke, I'm with you, okay? No matter what. I mean, I don't gotta understand why—"

"You know what happens when a raccoon gets his leg caught in one of those steel traps, Herk? You know what he's got to do, he wants to live?"

"Bite the leg off?" the big man said.

"Yeah. There's two kinds of raccoons get caught in those traps. The ones with balls enough to do what they gotta do. And dead ones. A bitch raccoon gets in heat, she wants a stud that's gonna give her the strongest babies, understand? You know what she looks for? Not the biggest raccoon. Not the prettiest one either. A smart bitch, she looks for one with three legs."

"I get it, bro. Okay, we got three legs now. I'm in. But . . . we got a problem. I think, anyway."

"What?"

"There's a meeting. Tonight."

"Damn. Why didn't you—?"

"I forgot. Until just now."

"Jesus, Herk. Even if Pryce goes for it, he can't make it happen right now. He's gonna need a day or so, minimum. The best we can hope for is the newspaper story. I thought we'd watch— he makes that happen, I believe he can do the immunity thing. And then I was going to have this lawyer I hired go in and tighten that up for you. But if you go to that meeting and Lothar isn't there . . . "

"He wasn't *supposed* to be there, right?"

"Huh?"

"I mean, he's supposed to be stalking his wife, right? And he gets smoked doing it, okay? No way I know about that. Or any of *them* either. Unless it's on the news. Why shouldn't I just go on? It ain't like me and him was supposed to be cut-buddies anyway."

"Herk, that's *if* Pryce goes along. That's *if* he can do it even if he wants to. That's *if* he hasn't already decided to cut his losses and down the whole fucking crew. If you know about the meeting tonight, Lothar did too. And he probably told Pryce."

"What else am I supposed to do?"

"You could jet," I told him.

"I was gonna do that, what'd you take Lothar off the count for? I ain't that stupid. I know what you was talking about. Lothar was the ace, right? Now I'm the top card. The only one that cocksucker Pryce's got. I thought we was gonna play this to win."

"I should have asked you about the next meeting."

"I'm going in there," he said. "And if that little motherfucker Porkpie dimes us out, I'll take the weight. For everything. I did that guy in the alley, I did Lothar, what's the difference? Life is life."

"I thought you said you weren't going back."

"If it was just me, I wouldn't," Hercules said. "But if it goes bad, the only way I can take the heat offa everyone is to stand up, right? So I'll do it."

"If that happens, I'll get you out," I promised him. "Not through the courts, over the wall. It'll take some time but—"

"I'll have the time, brother," the big man said, down but determined. "Now I gotta go say goodbye to Vyra."

"Did I do something to make you angry?" Crystal Beth asked meekly. Lying on her stomach, her body picking up bronze highlights from the candle's flame.

"Why'd you ask me that?"

"Because you . . . hurt me. When we made love. You were so . . . rough. Storming in here. Holding me down. Pinned down. I felt like I was in a steel vise. I couldn't move. And you didn't . . . wait for me. You just—"

"I'm sorry. I wasn't paying attention."

"Not to me, anyway."

"I said I was sorry, Crystal Beth. I . . . got something on my mind."

"Pryce?"

"Pryce is a dead man," I snapped at her.

She gasped.

"I mean, if he doesn't come through, he's dead," I said quickly. "It's really tense now, little girl. I shouldn't have . . . done what I did. To you, I mean. I'm sorry. If there's any way I can make it up to you, I'll—"

"We could try it again," she said softly, a little smile playing around her full lips. "From the top."

Where are you going?" she asked later.
"Out."
"Why can't you just stay here for the night?"
I could have told her I had to get back to take care of Pansy, but it would have been a lie. I have it all set up so Pansy can get food for herself when I'm gone. Not the food she loves—just dry dog food— but if she got hungry enough, she'd eat it. And a fresh water supply too. With the plastic garbage bags I'd laid out for her, she was good for a nice long time, although it wouldn't smell too great when I got back. And if I didn't come back, Max knew what to do—there was always room for one more mutt in the Mole's junkyard. I told Crystal Beth the truth. "I need a TV set. And you don't have one."
"Yes we do," she said. "Right downstairs. The one you had for Hercules. It's still in the basement. It's just a little portable, not cable or anything. But we could plug it in and—"
"Go get it," I told her.

It was the lead story on the eleven o'clock news. The male anchor read the copy as the camera panned over footage of a lower-middle-class house surrounded by yellow POLICE tape, using that ponderous tone they all go to when they think there's a chance anyone will mistake them for real journalists.

A Queens man long sought by the authorities for violation of a court Order of Protection has taken his own life after a shoot-out with police. Lawrence Bretton, age thirty-six, an unemployed printer, apparently invaded the home of his estranged wife and infant son, unaware that she had been living at another location.

The camera switched to Lothar's mug shot, probably from when he was first arrested for domestic violence.

Bretton was armed with a nine-millimeter automatic pistol and several clips of ammunition. He also had a pair of handcuffs and a roll of duct tape with him, leading to speculation that he planned some sort of kidnapping or torture. According to police sources, Bretton had threatened his wife with death on numerous occasions and was considered extremely violent.

The camera switched to a copy of the Order of Protection, with Lothar's true name in the caption.

When ordered to surrender, Bretton fired upon police at the scene and attempted to barricade himself in the house. Reinforcements were called in as well as the Hostage Negotiating Team, but a brief telephone conversation ended with a shot from inside the home. Ironically, Bretton was wearing a bulletproof vest, but he took his own life with a single shot to the head rather than surrender. Details of this astounding case, so emblematic of the domestic violence which has infected this city for so long, are still coming in. Stay tuned to this channel for . . .

"Oh my God," Crystal Beth said quietly. "That's him, isn't it?"
"That's him all right. But it's not over."
"It is for Marla," she said. "And the baby."

There was more at eleven-thirty. A beautifully woven web of lies, with such a heavy marbling of truth that digesting the whole meal wouldn't be a problem for any media-watcher. They threw in a whole lot of lovely professional details . . . including an excerpt from one of the wiretapped calls Lothar had made to

Marla. Even with the profanities bleeped out, it was explicit enough to make the hairs on your forearm stand up.

I watched the show with Crystal Beth sitting next to me. Knowing Pryce could get it done now, knowing he had the juice.

And wondering who he really was.

The phone didn't ring all night long.

In the morning, I went back to my office. Exchanged a half-pound of boiled ham and a plump custard cream puff for the present Pansy had left for me to clean up.

The joint where I'd gotten the ham also sold cooked stuff—mostly chicken and beef, spinning on a rotisserie. I had bought a nice-looking hunk of medium-well steak, planning to split it with Pansy, but it was as tough as a Philadelphia middleweight, so she got all of that too.

I settled for some toasted stale bread and a bottle of ginseng-laced soda, wishing I hadn't duked the cream puff on her so quickly.

Soon as I was done eating, I tried Mama's. Drew a blank.

I remembered I'd never gotten Porkpie's address from Pryce. And realized it didn't matter anymore.

The day crawled. I went out to get the newspapers. More of the same. Except for the hostage team at the scene, it wasn't that big a story in New York. Man abuses woman. Woman—finally—leaves man. Man swears if she won't have him she won't have anyone. Court issues Order of Protection. Man beats the crap out of her. Back to court. Man is given low bail, if he qualifies . . . which means: woman not hospitalized or media not paying attention. Another Order of Protection issued, this time with a pompous warning that impresses only the autoerotic judge.

Sooner or later, woman is found dead, with that useless piece of paper in her purse. Man nearby, dead by his own hand. Happens all the time. Only this time, the intended victim had flown the coop before the fox broke in.

If the papers had gotten hold of the Nazi angle, it would have been front-page for days. But not a word of that slipped out. The usual round of neighborhood interviews, ranging from "I can't believe it" to "I knew he'd do it." Pious editorials about "junk justice" and the need to get tough on domestic violence. Somebody who didn't want to be identified said it was a terrible thing all right, but he could understand a man being driven crazy by not being allowed to see his own child.

And the usual always-good-for-a-quote collection of exhibitionistic "experts"—every TV producer worth his sleazy job has a Rolodex full of them.

The papers ran a bunch of teasers like: "The whereabouts of Bretton's wife and son are unknown," but nobody took the bait, even when one of the slime-tabloids offered a hundred grand "reward" for "the whole story." And without a victim the media could wring their hands over, the whole story would be as dead as Lothar in a couple of days.

I slapped a fresh battery pack into the cellular and hit the streets, looking for the Prof. Left word in a few places for him to call Mama's.

I rang Vyra from a pay phone down the street from the hotel. She was in.

When I walked in the door to her suite, she was barefoot, wearing a big white fluffy bathrobe, her face scrubbed clean but bloodless and haggard. "Have you—?" she asked.

I shook my head no, sat down in one of the plush chairs, placing the life-line cellular carefully on the arm. She sat on the couch across from me, hugging herself inside the robe. "I'm scared," she said.

"Me too," I told her. "But all we can do is wait for word now."

"Did you have to make him . . . do that?"

"Do what?" I asked her.

"I don't *know*," she almost wailed. "He wouldn't tell me. But I know it was very dangerous. I begged him not to, but he just . . ."

"It all had to be done," I told her. "All of us, whatever we did."

"He said . . . he said you were all doing it for him."

"And . . . ?"

"And I know better, don't I?" she said, eyes snapping at my face. "It's not for him. Not *just* for him, anyway."

"So?"

"So I'm one of them, aren't I? I'm one of the people he's . . . doing it for. Me. If anything happens, I'm responsible too."

"What was the choice?"

"For the . . . for the network, for Crystal, I don't know. For the women, I don't know. For me, I know. The rest of them, it was to protect their . . . lives, or their children. Or something important. Me, it was to protect my spoiled little ass. My . . . money."

"And now you feel guilty?"

"You're a miserable person to talk to me like that," she said bitterly.

"I'm not downing you, Vyra. It's way too late for petty bullshit like that. Herk said I misjudged you. Maybe I did. I never got to know you, and—"

"—now you never will," she finished for me.

"No, I never will," I agreed. "And if that's my loss, I'll have to carry it."

"I never got to know you either."

"That was no loss," I promised her.

"Oh God, I wish he'd call," she said softly.

Vyra finally agreed to go take a nap after I swore I'd wake her as soon as her phone rang. But it was my cellular that buzzed first.

"Have your lawyer go to the Southern District tomorrow, first call. Tell him to go to the fourth floor and just wait. Tell him to wear a carnation in his lapel."

"What color?"

"This time of year? He'll be the only one wearing a flower, don't worry. Tell him to just wait. Somebody will come and get him."

"And make the deal?"

"Yes."

"You sure there's anybody to make a deal for?" I asked him.

"No," he said. And hung up.

The buzzing of the cell phone had woken Vyra, and now she wouldn't go back to sleep.

"He's so different," she said. "I never met a man . . . I never met anyone like him."

"Yeah, Herk's one of a kind, all right."

"You don't understand a word of what I'm saying, do you?" she said sadly. "He told me about his life. His whole life. From when he was a little boy. You never told me anything like that. I've known you for years . . . and you're a stranger to me. And he *asked* me about my life too. You never did that. Burke," she giggled, "you know what he said?"

"How would I—"

"He asked me about growing up. What it was like for me. I told him I was a JAP. You know what he said? He said: 'I thought you was a Jew.' Can you believe it?"

"From Herk? Sure."

"You don't get it," she said, peat-moss eyes alive in her made-up face. "Okay, he didn't know what 'JAP' means. So what? Where he was raised, he'd never heard the term. But the thing is, it didn't make any difference to him. It's me he likes. Not my money. Not just my . . . tits," she said, flicking her hand against her breasts like she was dismissing them.

When she started to cry, I told her a shower might make her feel better. Naturally, she argued, but I made the same promise I had when she took her nap, and she finally went along.

When the hotel phone rang, I hit the bathroom on the first ring. I pulled the shower curtain away, held my fist to my ear like it was a telephone. Vyra leaped out of the shower covered in suds, hair wet, a loofah in one hand. She ran to the phone, snatched it up.

"Hello."

She held the phone slightly away from her ear so I could listen, but I didn't move . . . just in case.

"Ah, you *promised*, honey," she cooed into the receiver. Then she listened for a minute before she said: "All right, baby. Whatever you say. You're the boss. I'll wait for you, okay?"

Whatever he said in return was real short. Vyra whispered, "I love you, Hercules," and hung up.

Then she started to cry, hands over her face. I stepped to her, gently held her shoulders, standing at arm's length to keep her breasts off my chest. "What?" I asked her.

"He's all right. He's all right," she sobbed.

"So why are you crying?"

"Because I'm *happy*, you moron!"

"What did he say?"

Vyra walked over to the bed and sat down, oblivious to the instant puddle she created.

"He said he couldn't keep our date. For tonight. He told me I was his bitch, and he'd come when he could. And to shut up and do what he told me," she said, a sunburst smile turning her little face lovely like I'd never seen it in all the years I'd known her.

I went down to my own room in the hotel and called Davidson, gave him the word.

"Wear a *carnation*?" he squawked. "Jesus, are these guys for real?"

"Oh yeah," I told him. "No question."

"Then consider it done," he said. "Give me a call tomorrow night. Anytime after six."

"**Y**ou heard from the Prof?" I asked Mama.

"Right here," she said. "You come now, okay?"

"I'm rolling," I told her.

It wasn't just the Prof at the restaurant. Clarence was there too. And Max. And Michelle.

"What's all this?" I asked them.

"Grab a pew, Schoolboy," the Prof said. "We need to sound what's going down."

"With . . . ?"

"With that fool Hercules. And you."

I sat down. Had some soup while the others waited, their faces masks of patience. Whatever it was, it wasn't enough for them to try and take on Mama.

Then I told them. Everything.

"You capped a guy? In front of a fed?" the Prof asked, an angry-puzzled look on his face.

"I don't think he's a fed," I said. "Not like any fed I ever heard of, anyway. Wolfe says he's an outlaw. Me, I don't know. He got stuff done. . . . I don't know how a free-lancer could pull that kind of weight."

"I fucking *knew* it," the little man said. "This was a hoo-doo from the get-go. I thought you was done with guns, son."

"I am. Or I was. I . . . There was no other way to do it, Prof. Without the immunity, Herk was just a piece of Kleenex to this guy Pryce. Use him and throw him away, right?"

"Why didn't we get together, figure something out?" he wanted to know.

"This one's mine," I told him. "Herk was with us Inside, but it's me who owes him. Then the whole thing with Crystal Beth's safehouse. And the women . . . I wasn't gonna drag everyone else in it with me."

"I don't feel a thing for most of them," Michelle piped up, dismissing all the women under Crystal Beth's protection in one fell swoop. "They don't protect their babies, they're not real women in my book. They're stupid or they're cowards, makes no difference to me. Some of them would go on a date with Ted Bundy and leave John Wayne Gacy to babysit the kids."

She drew a deep breath, steadying herself. "But this isn't about them. What's *wrong* with you, baby? Okay, you made a mess. Got yourself in a jackpot. It's not the first time. Not the first time for any of us. You know how to work my boy, don't you? Say 'Nazi' to the Mole, and he's in. And Clarence got you . . . what you needed for that job, right? You've kept us all on the edges, and it's not right."

"You said it yourself, Prof," I reminded him, looking for backup. "About Clarence."

"That was before—"

"It wouldn't be right to bring Clarence in, that's what you said. And you," I said, turning to Michelle, "you're right. . . . I did look for help, okay? But I never brought anyone right down next to it. This could blow up, honey. And you wouldn't like prison."

"Don't you even *think* about patronizing me," she snarled. "I was Inside too. When I was just a girl. Before I had the . . . before I became myself. You try doing time in a men's prison when you're a woman. I stood up there, I can stand up now."

"I'm sorry," I said. "I—"

Max reached across and tapped me on the chest. It felt like the wrong end of a crowbar. He pointed at me. Made the sign of fists holding prison bars. Then he pointed at himself. And made one of the signs we use for the Mole, open-circled fists held up to the eyes to mime the Mole's Coke-bottle glasses. He bowed his head. Reminding me of that time we'd gotten trapped in a subway tunnel trying to sell a load of hijacked heroin back to the mob. We'd been ratted out, and the tunnel was full of police. I'd held them at bay with a pulled-pin grenade while everyone else made it out the other end. Reminding me of his debt.

"If we don't know, we can't show," the Prof told me, eyes locked on mine. "This ain't the usual choice. It ain't between bail or jail. We want to do right now, we got to play live-or-die—only a punk plays for the tie."

"I am with my father," Clarence said, his hand on the Prof's shoulder. "Always."

"It's a done deal," Davidson told me on the phone. "Can you come in, let me show it to you?"

And pay you the rest of your money, I thought.

"Sure," I said.

"They tried to fold some interlocking contingencies into the mix," Davidson told me in lawyer-speak.

"Meaning?"

"He gets immunity. But in order to get the new ID and everything, he has to come in."

"So?"

"So now we have two separate instruments," he said, smiling. "If your . . . friend decides not to come in at all, he won't have the new ID, he won't be in the Witness Protection Program, he won't get the plastic surgery or anything. But he'll still have the immunity. And even if he's dropped for anything *subsequent*—he's covered for the entire period past."

"What period?"

"Your friend has been a government agent—not an informant, Burke, a government agent, on the payroll—for almost six months. Well prior to the period when the . . . incident occurred."

"I never heard of—"

"Happens all the time," Davidson assured me. "The FBI had a

man inside the Klan car that killed one of the Freedom Riders. They had men inside the Panthers too. And just about everyplace else. People like that *have* to have ongoing immunity, risky as that is, otherwise they'd reveal themselves by refusing to participate in ... whatever."

"And there's no 'truthful-testimony' stuff in the deal?"

"No testimony at all. Not even a debriefing."

"Does he have a control?"

"That's this Pryce individual."

"You meet him?"

"I don't know. The AUSA identified himself. And there was a woman from ATF. A man from the FBI. Big Irish guy, good-looking—I've seen him around before. A Treasury guy too. But there were a couple of other people in the room that never spoke. And I couldn't see their faces—they were back out of the light."

"Sounds pretty intense," I said, sliding the rest of Davidson's money across the desk in a plain white envelope.

"I've been in worse," he replied. "This time, at least, I was representing one of the good guys."

T hree days later ...

"They said he was a hero," Hercules told me, sitting in the bedroom of Vyra's suite. The king-sized bed was wrecked. The room smelled of just-done sex. The shower was running, with Vyra inside it. "He died for the race."

"When did they find out?"

"It was on the news. Before the meeting, even. The way they figured it, he went after his wife. When the cops showed, he took himself out so's he wouldn't crack under torture."

"Torture?"

"Oh yeah, man. They said ZOG has got these brain things they put on your head. And chemicals they can inject you with, make you give up your own mother. So Lothar, he knew this. And he protected the race."

"They sound like a crew of real paranoids."

"Paranoid? You don't know nothin' about paranoid, brother. You should hear them. Always talking about black helicopters and shortwave intercepts and remote telemetric surveillance and a whole bunch of other crap I don't even listen to anymore. Jesus."

"They didn't say anything to you about Lothar?"

"To me? Nah. They was too busy talking to themselves. I just went along."

"You believe they bought the story?"

"I'm here, ain't I? Besides, Lothar told them he was gonna do somethin' like that anyway, someday. He had *plans* for that cunt, that's what he kept telling 'em. So they wasn't surprised. Maybe a little at him killing himself and all, but not even that much."

"Paranoid as they are, they didn't panic?"

"Well, not really. But we all had to stay together for a couple of days. At least that's the way it ended up. They said they couldn't be sure Lothar didn't have something on him that would trace back to us, so some of them wanted to split up. But the others wanted to stay. I dunno if it was 'cause they was scared to be alone or they wanted to watch everyone or what. But Scott said we had to hang tough. Nobody went out. They got enough stuff in the basement there, you could live for *years*, man. All kindsa dried food and water in bottles. And guns . . . man, they got *boxes* of fucking guns."

"What did you do, all that time?"

"Watched TV. Worked out. Listened to them going on about the race."

"They say anything about their plans? Or a date?"

"April thirtieth. That's the one they was gonna use. You know that's the day Hitler killed himself in his bunker? To keep from being taken alive. Just like Lothar, that's what they said."

"April thirtieth. That's still a long—"

"Not no more," Hercules interrupted me. "See, everyone don't have the date. I mean, there *is* no date, like."

"I'm not following you."

"The cells. They ain't in touch. With each other. Soon as one starts, the others go right behind them. But it's this one—this cell—that gets to start. And they want to get on with it now."

"You know when?"

"They ain't decided yet. But I know the place they're gonna hit. Twenty-six Federal Plaza."

"Federal Plaza? On lower Broadway?"

"That's the one. It's perfect, bro. You know what's in there? The FBI. IRS. And Immigration too. Everything they hate. All in one place. And it's only a block away from the federal court too."

"That building's a monster. They'd never get a truck close enough to—"

"Bull*shit*," Herk cut in. "It ain't that tight. They showed me—it was in the papers—this fucking loon got on the goddamn *roof* there. Said he was going to off himself, take the dive. People standing around on the ground, yelling up at him to jump and all. You can't get into the underground garage, the way they did at the World Trade Center, but you know what? You can park cars all *around* the place. On Broadway, on Worth, on Lafayette, and on Duane. They ain't gonna use no dumbass rental truck, like Oklahoma City. They *bought* the stuff. A *lot* of stuff. For years, they been buying the stuff, just waiting. Got legit plates for the rigs and all. There's seven of us. That's more than enough."

"You're getting to be a real pro at this terrorism stuff, huh?"

"Oh man, it's just jive-talk. You know, like in the joint—we call things different names than they do out in the World. This Federal Plaza goes up, we don't need no communications—the media'll do it for us, that's what they said. Soon as it's on the news, the other cells take the word. And it all goes up. You know what else? They said all kindsa stuff is going up just from copycats. Like with the nigger churches."

"What are you talking about, Herk?"

"Ah, I didn't mean it, man. I been down with them, I talk like them. You know how I feel about the Prof. I wouldn't never—"

"Not about words, Herk. The churches. What about them?"

"Oh, yeah. Well, the way they explained it, see, they *used* to firebomb colored churches. In the South, right? A long time ago. To stop the spooks from voting and all. Okay, so, like, it's started again, right? You see churches going up all over the place. Only it ain't just the Klan and all. It's, like, *everyone*. Motherfuckers see it on the TV, they want to do it too. You got kids painting swastikas—like I got," he said, tapping his chest—"all over the place. And they ain't Nazis or nothing. Some of them, they're, like, mud people themselves. You know, Pakis and Koreans and all. They don't know nothin' about the Jews, they just follow the pack. Go along. That's what's happening with the churches, that's what the guys say. You know what? They even got colored guys burning down colored churches. So when we blow the building, it ain't just the other cells gonna do it, man. Everybody's gonna be jumping on."

"Fuck! And they have everything they need already?"

"Sure. They was pulling jobs. Bank jobs. And armored cars. Before I got there. To raise money for all the stuff they got. That came up, once."

"Huh?"

"That I was the only one who hadn't . . . I mean, even Lothar, he went along on a couple of the jobs. I was the only one who didn't do none of the robberies."

"So what happened?" I asked him, suppressing my frustration at the big man rambling through a mine field.

"Well, this guy, Kenny, he tried to like get in my face, you know? It'd never happen Inside, a punk motherfucker like that trying to aggress *me*. But I guess maybe he felt safe, I dunno. Anyway, you not allowed to ask anyone what they did—in their own cells, I mean, that's the rules—but he asked me if I knew what it felt like to stick a gun in a Jew banker's face and take his precious money."

"And . . . ?"

"And I asked him if he knew what it felt like to stab a motherfucking Jew in the heart and stand there and watch him die." He laughed.

"What's so funny?"

"These guys better not go Inside, bro. At least, not this Kenny punk. I wanted it, he woulda given me his ass right then."

"Yeah. Okay. But you don't have the date, right?"

"I'm telling you, Burke. *Nobody* got the date. I ain't no genius, but I got this much figured out. Once they got the date, ain't nobody leaving. We're all gonna go together. In separate cars. Then we go to the scatter plan."

"What's that?"

"This ain't a real cell, okay? Like, they all come from different ones. The scatter plan is we all go back where we came from. I mean, ZOG's gonna be down on us like white on rice soon as this thing blows. It's every man for himself. Every cell's supposed to have something set for each guy. When he comes back, understand?"

"Yeah," I said, thinking it through, looking for the hook. "You're sure it's Federal Plaza?" I asked him.

"It's what they *say*, bro. And they ain't saying nothing else. They say everyone's gonna blame the Arabs first. There's a bunch of them went down for the World Trade Center, right? And they— the Arabs—they supposed to of sworn they was gonna do more. I guess they—the guys in the cell—talked over a lot of spots. Before I came in, I mean. But this is the only one they talk about now. They got maps, big blow-up maps so you can see every little building on the street. They got all the lights timed. They wanted to do it on a Saturday—d'you know that's like the Jew Sunday, where they go to church and all? Anyway, they can't do it then, 'cause the area's too packed."

"That whole area is empty on Sunday mornings," I said.

"Yeah. That's when it's gonna be. That's what they said."

"Damn! Why didn't you tell me—?"

"I don't know *which* Sunday, bro. I thought you meant when they was gonna—"

"Never mind," I told him. "Herk, did you ever see the cars they're going to use?"

"Nah. But I know it ain't just cars. They got one of them private garbage trucks. Not from the city, you know the ones I mean?"

"Sure." Private carters handled most of the commercial trash collection in Manhattan. Seeing one parked in the early-morning hours wouldn't make a cop look twice.

"And they got a semi too. From one of the moving companies."

"Jesus. They're gonna pack all these with explosives?"

"Yeah. I dunno what kinds, but I tell you this for sure, man—it ain't no puny dynamite. The stuff they got, they say it's gonna fucking *level* that building."

"It's Twenty-six Federal Plaza," I told Pryce.

"It can't be," he said. "It has to be a diversion of some kind." The muscle jumped under his eye. "Or they made Hercules . . . they know he's a plant."

"I don't think so," I said, maybe more hope than analysis.

"Your friend's not a genius," Pryce came back, a trace of something like sadness vibrating at a low register in his thin voice.

"He's got an education," I told him quietly. "Not your kind of education. Mine. Maybe he wouldn't score so high on an IQ test, but he was raised in places where you had to know when they were coming for you if you were gonna survive."

"Maybe, but—"

"—he's as smart as that piece of shit Lothar," I cut him off. "If they didn't make him, they're not gonna make Herk. Besides, I think they're in too deep now. And remember, he's got that credential. One none of them have. If they bought Lothar, they'll buy Herk."

"Sunday morning adds up. It would minimize the loss of life, but that's not such a bad thing from a public-relations standpoint. Oklahoma City angered even some of the extremists—so many dead children from that day-care center. . . . And any other time, they couldn't be certain they could get enough vehicles close enough. But . . ."

"What?"

"You know anything about explosives?"

"Not much. But I know people who—"

"They could not significantly damage a building of that size without getting much closer than the street," Pryce said in a tone of finality. "Unless . . ."

"What?"

"Unless the explosions were linked, somehow. Unless there

was one single detonator for all of it. Maybe if they hit it from all sides . . ."

"He said they were gonna—"

"I know. And he said it wasn't dynamite either. No homemade stuff. But they don't have the technology to go nuclear. We would have picked that up on the wire way before this."

"You ever look closely at one of those giant garbage trucks?" I asked him. "You got two, three of them—*and* a goddamned semi—packed to the rafters with plastique . . ."

"Burke," he said, leaning forward, putting his webbed hand on my forearm, gripping tightly, "does Herk know who's going to be holding the detonator?"

"He didn't say. It's not gonna be him, that's for sure."

He was quiet for a few minutes. I didn't say anything. You could almost *watch* him think. Finally, he leaned back against the seat cushions of the Taurus and closed his eyes. "I don't think Lothar is going to be the last of them to die for the race," he said.

W e sat in silence as I left his mind and tried to go into theirs. Be a race-hating beast. It only came up one way.

Herk was going to die.

After all this, Herk was going to die.

"The leader, the one with the detonator, he's going to blow them all up," I said. "That's the way you see it too, right?"

"What else could it be?" Pryce asked me. He reached in the side pocket of his jacket, pulled out a street map of lower Manhattan. With a yellow highlighter, he drew a box around Federal Plaza. "Let's say they park the rigs here. And here. And here. All right? Maybe half a dozen drops in all. One man to each vehicle. Each one of them has park-and-run orders. The detonator man is waiting, probably in a van of some kind—maybe the same one they use for transport from that bar—not far away. They each park their individual vehicles, get out and just walk away. When they're all assembled back at the van, it takes off. Then the detonator man hits the switch."

"Only he's not gonna wait," I said.

"No. Waiting increases the risk. On all counts. And if any of them is captured, he could bring down the whole deal. Leaderless cells only work but so far. Whoever was captured, he'd know *something*. And the plan is to create anarchy—taking credit for the bombing would work against that. One Nazi in custody blows that whole deal."

"Then it's time to take them down?"

"How can we do that? Hercules doesn't know the address where they're holed up. Just that bar you told me about. I doubt we could stake it out—it sounds like the whole place belongs to them. Probably some of the surrounding property too. And if they're really close, I don't think he's coming out again anyway."

"But if we don't—"

"We couldn't risk planting a transmitter on Hercules," he said, intercepting my thoughts. "If they found it, they'd just cut and run."

After they killed Hercules, I thought.

"But if we could find the place *without* using a transmitter—"

"Without the explosives, we don't have a case anyway," he cut in. "Lothar's gone," he reminded me. "So we don't have any conspiracy testimony either. Hercules wouldn't be much good to us even if he decided to go on the stand—yes, I know," he said, holding up his hand in a don't-interrupt gesture—"the agreement says he doesn't have to. But even if he did, we have to be able to take them *with* the goods. And alive, if we can."

I wondered if he was really that stupid. Or thought I was.

"Oh," Vyra said when she answered the door to the suite, disappointment clear in her face.

"Has he called?" I asked, no preliminaries.

"No. Have you—?"

"Nothing. Listen, Vyra. If you give a damn about Herk, listen as good as you ever did. I *need* to talk to him. It's worth his life, understand? If he calls, if he shows up, you got to let me know *right then*. No playing around, no grabbing a few minutes for fun . . . right then. That fucking *second*, you understand me?"

"Is he—?"

"I don't know," I told her. "I don't know anything. He may not be able to come out again. We're getting close. This is Thursday. It could be as close as this weekend. But if he does get a call to you . . ." The next thought hit me so hard I had to sit down, think it through. Then I said: "Vyra, did you give him anything when you saw him?"

"Give him anything?" she demanded, an undertone of hysteria slipping in. "I gave him my—"

"Listen to me, you stupid bitch," I said quietly, grabbing her by the hands and pulling her down next to me. "This isn't about pussy. It's about a man's life. My brother's life. Now, answer my question. Did you give him anything? A watch? A ring? A shirt? Anything."

"Why do you—oh, don't!" she squealed, holding her hands in front of her face. "He wouldn't take any . . . I . . . oh my God, I *did* give him something. A scarf. My pink chiffon scarf. He wanted it. He said it smelled like me. He took it with him when we last . . ."

"Yes!"

"Burke, what's wrong with you. Why does it—?"

"Vyra, baby, I'm sorry if I scared you. I wasn't trying to. Just to make you see how important this is, all right? Now listen to me. Are you listening?"

"Yes. I swear."

"If Herk calls, if he's on his way to see you here, you call me immediately, got that?"

"Yes."

"But if he calls and says he can't get away for a while, or *anything* like that . . . if he's not coming for a while, you tell him this, okay? Tell him: Wear your scarf. Tell him you miss him, and he should wear your scarf. For you. So you can be with him. You understand?"

"I . . . do."

"Vyra, forget everything, okay. *Everything*. There's no yesterday now. You have to get this right. I'm counting on you." Then I bent and kissed her on the cheek.

"I promise," she said.

How many Nazi bars could there be within thirty minutes of the other side of the Fifty-ninth Street Bridge? Astoria, maybe? It was a mixed neighborhood with a lot of small local joints. Long Island City had everything from warehouses to topless bars and artists' lofts. Maybe they were even over near the waterfront, past the Citibank Tower. But . . . if I asked around, if word got back to them . . . that could do it for Herk too.

So all I had was Vyra's promise. Vyra, the liar I'd always known her to be.

Herk had to get out, or get to a phone one more time.

And he had to be right about Vyra.

Crystal Beth put her head down and took another experimental lick. I was dead.

"Did I do something?" she asked, tilting her head to look up my body toward my face as I lay on my back, eyes open, staring at the ceiling. Seeing the cellular phone in my mind, willing the goddamned thing to ring.

"No," I told her, wondering for the hundredth time if the batteries were still good, if I shouldn't have gotten a backup clone to the same number from the Mole, if I shouldn't have told Herk the last time to . . .

"Did I *not* do something?" Crystal Beth wanted to know, still not moving.

"It's not you," I said. "It's me."

"You're worried about—?"

"Yeah," I cut her off, thinking what an inadequate word "worried" was for what I was feeling.

"Do you want to talk about it?"

"No."

"Why not, honey?"

"Because it's not yours, Crystal Beth. Not anymore."

"What do you mean?" she asked in a challenging voice, propping herself up on one elbow. "I've been in this since—"

"Whatever happens now, it's not going to be you. Or any of your stuff. Pryce isn't going to rat you out. You or Vyra or your network. Nothing."

"But you got yourself into this for—"

"For my brother. For my family. Not for you."

"But you love—"

"Them."

"And you love me too," she said aggressively, her hands on my shoulders, hauling herself up so her nose was right on my forehead. "Me too. Don't you?"

"Crystal Beth . . ."

"It's not what you say, it's what you do, remember?" she whispered against me. "Why can't you be honest with me?"

"Like you are with me?" I asked, pushing her away so I could sit up. And watch the cellular, sitting there across the room plugged into the portable charging unit, smirking its silence at me.

"What. Do. You. *Mean?*" she asked, each word a bullet in a cocked revolver.

"You're so *honest*," I said sarcastically. "Such a good hippie, you are. All peace and love and truth, right?"

"I would have told you about Vyra if she hadn't—"

"And about Rollo's?" I said quietly.

She got off the bed and walked to the black window, her body glowing in the faint light. She bowed her head, clasped her hands in front of her. Like a child being punished, made to stand in the corner.

I watched her thick, rounded body. That gravity-defying butt. *Belle* jammed across my mind. Not as a word, or even an image.

Just a . . . flitting . . . gone. I felt the flashback coming and put it *down*. Away from me now. But not gone, I knew. Never gone. That big girl. Going out to die . . .

I . . . stopped. Focused on Crystal Beth's pigtails standing out stark against her shoulderblades. But it was like watching a hologram—the image shifted, and now it was Herk's face against her back, framed by the pigtails, trusting.

Crystal Beth turned, breaking the spell, and came back to the bed.

"Do you want me on my knees?" she asked.

"I told you, it's not you. I can't—"

"Not for *that*," she interrupted, her voice hushed and delicate. "To apologize. I wronged you. I had good reasons, once. But they . . . I don't know. It doesn't matter. I want to tell you. Do you want to listen?"

"Yeah."

She went to her knees, looking up at me sitting on the bed. "I didn't tell you about Rollo's because it wouldn't be right to endanger the others. I had people to protect. We're all part of the same . . . I don't know how to explain it to you. The network, that's one thing. There's a lot of us in it. But there's something smaller. Closer. Family. Like yours. Mimi and T.B. And Rusty."

"Rusty?"

"The big guy, the one who's always drawing."

"Oh yeah, him."

"There's others too. Cash—you didn't see him, he wasn't in that night—he does the . . . marketing for us. Gets the word out so people know where to find us, make the connections. We even have a radio station . . . well, not really a station, but we've got people on the air—Bad Boy and Autopsy—they broadcast out of Salt Lake. There's a code we use. On the Internet too. Mimi's sister Synefra set it up. . . . Look, we're . . . one. I wasn't trying to trick you. Or . . . maybe I was, I don't know. I'm not good at it. Vyra said you were . . . someone who could help us."

"Vyra's in your family?"

"No. The others don't . . . I love Vyra. She's really a sweet, wonderful girl. You don't know her."

"That's what Herk said too."

"He's right. Sex doesn't mean you know someone. But once you . . . did what you did—for us, I mean—I could have told you. I should have told you. I apologize for that. I don't want secrets from you."

"What difference does it make now?"

"Families can . . . merge," she said softly. "Families can come together. No matter what you say, no matter what you *said*, anyway . . . you have a purpose. You have a purpose now."

"So?"

"My mother and father were from different tribes. But they . . . merged. They were . . . partners. I want to be your partner."

"Come here," I said, holding out my hand to her.

When she came to me, I told her what it would cost to be my partner.

When Pryce walked in the front door of Mama's restaurant, he instinctively held his hands away from his body. Whatever he was, he had a pro's nose—he knew he was one wrong move away from an unmarked grave.

He walked the gauntlet, past Mama's register, past Clarence and Michelle sitting in one of the front booths, past Max the Silent wearing a waiter's apron, past the Prof, although he couldn't have seen the little man unless he looked under one of the tables. If he had, he would have seen the double-barreled sawed-off that was the Prof's trademark back in his cowboy days.

They had his face now. Had his walk, his webbed fingers, the skull beneath his skin. Had him all, every piece of him. And soon they'd have his voice. They could pick him out of a crowd even with the best plastic surgeons in the world doing their work.

And he knew it.

But he kept on coming, right to my booth in the back.

Mama kept her position at the register. I'd already had my soup. And she didn't serve it to outsiders.

He sat down. The muscle under his eye jumped. I knew by now it wasn't an anxiety tic. Probably the last plastic-surgery job had gone a little wrong, damaged some of the nerves in the area. I wondered why they'd never fixed his hands.

"I know how to do it now," I told him, no preamble. "But now it's time to find out who you are."

"What does that mean?" he asked, even-toned.

"You ever wonder," I asked him, "if it's only terrorists who have enough balls to drive a truck loaded with explosive?"

"I don't get your meaning."

"I've got a plan. But it needs something I don't have. Six heroes."

"Heroes?"

"Six men—six people, I guess they don't need to be men—willing to drive trucks loaded with death."

"You don't mean—?"

"It's the only way it can work," I said, watching my unsmoked cigarette burn in the glass ashtray. "Lothar ever tell you who was in charge?"

"No. He said it was a collective. Everyone equal."

"I think it's this guy Scott. But it doesn't really matter. It's got to be the way you figured it. Six of them drive the rigs, plant them around Federal Plaza. The last one, he's in the van, waiting for the pickup. Only thing is, there isn't going to *be* any pickup. Soon as he knows they're in place, he's going to hit the switch. There goes the building. And the evidence."

"So we have to interdict—"

"No. Sure, they're going to have to convoy it—in case one of the rigs breaks down or something. And they have to *all* be in place before they detonate too. But what makes you think everything's parked right near where they're holed up? Odds are they don't want to be bringing trucks over the bridges at that hour. Trucks aren't allowed on the Brooklyn Bridge anyway. They got to have at least some of them stashed in Manhattan. Or just the other side of the Battery Tunnel—there's plenty of warehouses around there. And the van, it has to be close by, right on top of the action. I don't know the range of the radio detonator they've got, but it can't be that far, especially with all those tall buildings around.

What we need to do is take them down as soon as they park and separate. And we have to do it *quiet*. If the guy in the van hears shots, he's gonna hit the switch and book."

"But if the detonator man doesn't hear anything, he's going to wait a little bit and—"

"And blow it up. I know. That's where your heroes come in. Some people say you're a bounty hunter. A free-lancer working for cash. Maybe that's true. I don't know. But you had enough juice to make the cops and the media play along with the Lothar thing. So I figure you're something else."

"Such as?"

"Such as a . . . I don't know a name for it. But every government needs people who can work outside the law. And I figure, that's you."

He didn't say anything. The muscle jumped in his face a couple of times, then went as quiet as he was.

"There's only one thing that'll absorb that much explosive without killing everyone around," I told him. "Water. You need to clear a path. Right to the river. The Hudson's the closest. It's only a few blocks. You need to take out the drivers. No gunshots. No noise. And you need six people to drive the rigs right to the river. Right *into* the river, it comes to that."

"Six people to drive trucks loaded with explosive? Knowing that any second they could just vaporize?"

"That's about it."

"And what about the man in the van?"

"He's the only one who we don't know where he'll be, right? He'll be close, but that's all we can count on. The way I figure it, he'll probably wait until the first one of them comes back. That's the only way he'll know they're all set up. Or maybe he'll just have some time limit of his own."

"It would have to be volunteers. . . ."

"Sure it would. You got that kind of people?"

"Yes," he said, no inflection in his thin voice. Not saying anything about the hard part. Anyone who's served in the military knows the U.S. government will let you die. They watch soldiers die all the time . . . for some general's ego or some country's oil. But there was only one way to stop all the Nazi drivers without making noise. And if that went wrong, it wouldn't just be expendable soldiers who lost it all. Whoever gave *those* orders . . .

"I need something else," I told him.

"More than . . . ?"

"Yeah."

"What?"

When I told him, he didn't say anything.

"It's time to lay them all out," I said. "Face up. You got a handkerchief on you?"

He took a clean white one out of the side pocket of his suit jacket, not saying a word.

"Stand up," I said. "Put your right foot on the chair over there."

He did it. I took out the key to the ankle cuff and twisted it. The white patch was underneath, undisturbed. "Take the handkerchief," I told him. "Peel that off. Carefully. Wrap it up tight. Don't touch it."

He did that too. At a gesture from me, he sat down again.

"When you get back to wherever you're going, get that to a lab."

"What will they find?"

"You know what a Nicoderm patch is?" I asked him.

"Yes, a time-release dose of—"

"That one is too. Only it's not nicotine it was dispensing. You left that one on for thirty days, you'd be a dead man."

He didn't say anything, but the pupils of his eyes deepened.

"We're all in now," I said. "No more bargaining. No more threats. We're a unit now. A hunter-killer team. I don't know your game, but you know mine—I need Herk out of there. Alive."

"But we can't—"

I leaned forward and told him how he could.

And wished I had a god to pray to that I was right.

F antasy haunts prison. At night, inside the cells, if you could see the pictures playing on the screens inside men's heads, you'd see everything on this planet. Other planets too.

Some convict fantasies are sweet. Some are freakish. Some are beyond lunacy. But some are so common they've become classics. And if my old cellmates could see me . . .

Lying on my back on a king-sized bed in a luxo hotel suite, a beautiful naked woman on either side of me.

But they were holding hands across my chest, giving each other comfort in the presence of a man who had none for either of them.

Late Saturday afternoon.

Hard darkness outside. Soft darkness in the room.

When I tuned out the words, their girl-talk was soothing. My eyes were closed. I tried to drift into their mingled scent. Lose myself.

Time stood there, laughing at its joke.

Like when I was Inside.

Was my brother already gone? I was back in the foster home, waiting for my mother to come and take me away from the terror. Knowing inside me she never would and . . .

The phone rang.

Vyra sprang from the bed like a tigress, grabbing the receiver before the first ring was done.

"Hello?"

A split-second pause, then: "Oh, honey, am I glad to hear from you! When are you—?"

This time she listened a little longer before she said: "I'm sorry, baby. I didn't mean to—"

He must have told her to shut up, because she went quiet for a long minute. Then she took a deep breath and said softly: "Hercules, will you do something for me? Some little thing, just 'cause I miss you so much?"

He must have said okay, because she came right back with: "My scarf? You know, my pretty pink scarf? The one you said smelled like me? Would you wear it?"

The next words out of her mouth were: "No, I mean, wear it *anywhere*, darling. Just so I know it's *with* you, okay? Then I'll feel like I'm with you too."

I don't know what he said to that. Vyra replied, "Me too. I . . ." and put down the phone. "He hung up," she said to me and Crystal Beth, her voice cracking around the edges.

"This will be hard for me, mahn," Clarence said. "It would be better if I did the—"

"Well, you *can't*, baby," Michelle said, honey and steel intertwining in her perfect voice to form an implacable ribbon.

"It is not right," the islander said, trying to push his will past hers. "It is my job to . . ."

"What?" I asked him, trying for edgeless calm. We were too close to the flashpoint now to play around.

"I am the man," Clarence said. "And Michelle is—"

"What?" she asked this time, the honey gone from her voice.

"My sister," he said quietly. "My little sister. Who I love so much."

Michelle stood up. Walked around the side of the booth and kissed Clarence on his ebony cheek. "Little sister's gonna be just fine, baby," she said calmly. "You just show me how to do it, and I'll make you proud."

"If I knew the frequency, I could jam it," the Mole told me, standing next to Terry in his underground bunker.

"But we don't have—"

"This is a scanner," the Mole said, holding up a box with a few rows of square LEDs. "I think I know the type of transmitter they must be using. If the range is narrow enough, maybe . . . but he has to have it armed. If he waits to arm it until the last second, there is no chance."

"We can't risk it," I said.

"But Michelle . . ." the Mole said softly, fear driving the science from his voice.

"What is Mom gonna—?" Terry asked, picking up the Mole's fear like it was forest-fire smoke.

"It'll be fine," I told the kid.

He ignored me, looking to the Mole.

"She will," he promised.

"I have to be there," the boy said. Only it wasn't a boy speaking anymore.

I looked at the Mole. We both nodded.

Max was as angry as I'd ever seen him. No matter how many times I explained it, he chopped the air in a violent gesture of rejection.

"You know how it's got to go," the Prof said, agreeing with me. "We only get the one toss. We need a natural. And you can't roll snake eyes with three dice."

But when I signed that over to Max, his nostrils flared and his face went into a rigid mask of resistance. He wasn't buying.

We went round and round. The mute Mongolian wouldn't budge. Finally, he made a complicated series of gestures to Mama. She bowed and went off. When she returned, she had a stalk of green in her hand, some kind of plant I didn't recognize. Max pulled out a chair, set it in the middle of the restaurant floor, pointed at it for me to sit down.

I did it. Mama licked the back of the green stalk and pasted it to the front of my leather jacket, right over the heart.

I sat there. Max walked up to me. I watched him carefully. Nothing happened.

Max held up the green stalk in his huge hand . . . the hand I'd never seen move. Making his point.

I held out my hand for the stalk. Gave it to Mama. "Put it back on me," I told her.

She licked the stalk again, slapped it down over my heart.

I motioned for Max to step back. Further. Further still. Until he was at least ten feet distant. Then I made the gesture of rolling up a car window. Sat looking through the imaginary glass. Made a "Now-what?" gesture.

The warrior's eyes narrowed to dark dots of molten lava, but he couldn't penetrate the problem. And he knew it. If Max could get close, he was as unstoppable as nerve gas. But if they saw him coming, it was over.

He bowed. Not to me. To the reality we faced.

"**W**e can't bring no outsiders in on this. Family only," the Prof said in his on-the-yard voice. "That means we ain't got but three ways to play. The Mole don't jam, you got to slam, School-boy. Otherwise, Michelle's gonna—"

"I know that," I told him.

"You got to be the monster, my brother. Wesley's gotta be there, you understand?" Telling me there would be no El Cañonero this time—he wasn't family.

"I won't miss," I told him.

"You do, we're all through," the little man said, hand on my shoulder.

It was chilly on the roof, but I was colder inside. Sunday morning, three hours past midnight, the sun still a couple of hours short of Show Time. The primitive part of my brain pressured me to check in—howl at the moon just to hear the return cries and assure myself that my pack was close by—but I kept my hands away from the cellular in my coat. No traffic on the street, no traffic over the airwaves—that was the deal.

I made myself relax. Fall into the mission. Slow down. Think of something warm. Last contact with the other world: Crystal Beth, chasing Vyra out of the hotel bedroom with a hard smack to her bottom, giggling at Vyra's squeal. Then coming over to me.

"It's time," she said. "You can do it now. I want you. Before you go, I want you."

"I—"

"You *can* do it, darling. Hercules is alive. You know it now. I want . . ."

"What?"

"Your baby. I want your baby. I want your life in me no matter what happens. I swear to you, Burke. Listen to me: This is a holy promise. I will be a wonderful mother. I will protect our baby with my life. Our house will always be safe. Please, honey. Come on. No matter what happens, your child will have your name. You'll never die."

"Crystal Beth, you—"

"Two names on the birth certificate. *Two.* Yours and mine. We are mated. I'm not trying to change your mind. You have your purpose, and I wouldn't stand in the way. But leave me this, yes? A baby. Your name. And my love."

"I—"

"Maybe your baby's already there," she said softly, patting her slightly rounded belly. "Condoms don't always—"

"I can't make babies," I cut her off. "I had myself fixed. A long time ago."

A tear dropped from one almond eye down her broad cheek. "But you can still make love," she whispered. "And that's where babies are meant to come from, right?"

I t was four-forty-five when the cellular throbbed in my chest pocket. I was alone on the roof, but I'd disabled the ring, just in case.

"Got 'em." The Prof's voice.

"All of them?"

"Full cylinder," he said, ringing off.

A full cylinder was six. Where was the detonator man? Where was he? Where was this man who threatened everything sacred to me on this earth? The man who would burn my safe house to the ground? Where was the filthy motherfucking . . . ? Wesley called to me from beyond the grave and I filled in the blank: where was the . . . *target?*

Dehumanizing the enemy.

Icing up.

It wasn't a man I had to kill, it was a thing.

A hateful, malignant, evil thing.

Not "him" . . . "it."

The coyote had spotted the prey—time for the badger to do its part.

In the winter we'd made, food was life.

And only death would harvest it.

Now that he'd called in, the Prof would bail, but he was on foot and he couldn't get far. Terry was down there someplace too, looking like a teenage boy with spiked hair, stumbling home from one of the clubs. Carrying homicide in the side pocket of his long black coat. No way to stop him from coming. No way to stop him at *all* if he spotted the creature who would hurt his mother. The Mole had dropped him off a good distance away, but if the kid picked up the scent . . .

Max the Silent was down there too, somewhere in the shadows, raging and lethal. We couldn't keep him away either. And if he saw the van first . . .

It had to be me. And we only had a few—

"On Hudson, between Jay and Harrison." The Mole, soft voice throbbing through the phone.

"You sure?"

"Gray Ford Econoline van. Driver only. Says 'Benny's Kosher Deli' in black letters on the sides."

"Can you jam—?"

But he was already gone.

I hit the speed-dial switch, said "Go!" as soon as it was picked up. I dropped the phone into my pocket and ran across the roof, holding the night-vision scope in both hands, willing Wesley into me.

There it was. Maybe four blocks away. A good spot—Hudson pulled plenty of commercial traffic even that early in the day—nobody would look twice at a van.

The clock high on the steeple corner at Worth and Broadway chimed five times behind me. I swept the area with the scope. No sign of Terry. I knew I'd never see Max even if he was down there. Not much time now . . .

A pearlescent white Bentley coupe came west up Leonard Street, heading for the T-turn on Hudson just north of where the van was parked. The big car moved with slow confidence, a rich rolling ghost. It pulled to the curb and a slim black man climbed out. He was wearing a Zorro hat and a calf-length white fur coat. A woman got out the passenger side. A white woman with long blond hair wearing a transparent plastic raincoat. I could see them talking. Saw the man's hand flash against the woman's face. Then he shook her, hard, and wrenched the raincoat off her body. She was standing there in red spike heels and dark stockings, covered only in a tiny white micro-mini and a skimpy black top. She walked a few feet away. A little purse slung over one shoulder banged against her hip. Hooker's kit: just big enough for a few condoms, some pre-moistened towelettes, a little bottle of cognac, maybe a tiny vial of coke. And the night's take.

The pimp waited until she looked back over her shoulder, then he pointed his finger warningly and climbed back into his ride, holding the plastic raincoat in one hand. The Bentley took off, making the left onto Hudson and moving right past the van.

The hooker stood on the corner, shivering but hipshot, waiting. A delivery truck passed. She made a "Hi-there!" gesture with one hand. The truck pulled over. She sashayed toward it, waving her hips like a flag. Leaned into the cab of the truck. No Sale. The truck pulled away.

A dark Acura sedan turned the corner. The hooker waved, but the car never slowed.

I snapped the tripod together, positioned the heavy rifle and spun the set-screw to tighten the rig. I nestled my cheek against the dark wood stock, starting to connect. The rifle was bolt-action, unsilenced. It would have to be a one-shot kill or it was all over anyway. I wondered where the target's hands were. If the detonator wasn't armed, we had a window of safety. But then the Mole couldn't find it to jam it and . . .

Dejectedly, the hooker started to walk up Hudson in the same direction the Bentley had gone, arms wrapped around herself for warmth. Cold comfort. I cranked the scope up to full magnification. The van driver was barely visible, just a dark blot in the side window. I prayed for him to be a smoker, but the interior stayed dark.

I had watched Wesley work. That clear-skyed night when he took a mobster off a high bridge, working from a dinky little island in the East River, I was standing right next to him. I knew how to do it.

Breathing was the key. I slowed mine way down, knowing I had to squeeze the trigger between heartbeats. Ignoring the pain in my damaged right hand, my finger on the unpulled trigger, caressing, probing for the sweet spot. So hard to shoot *down*, calculate the drop. My eye went down the barrel, finding the cartridge. I looked past the primer into the bullet itself. Full metal jacket—I needed penetration, not expansion. It had to be a head shot. Blow his brain apart, snap the neuron-chain to his hand. The hand on the detonator.

I became the bullet. Seeing into his skull. Locking the connection with my spirit before I sent death down the channel.

To keep my house safe.

My heart was a clock, every tick an icepick in a nerve cluster. How much *time?*

The hooker walked right past the van, not giving it a glance, looking over her shoulder at the wide street, hoping for some traffic. Suddenly, she stopped, turned to stare right at the van, hands on hips. I could see she was saying something. No reaction from the van—it was as dark inside as I was.

Except for that white blob. The target.

The hooker walked over, nice and slow, giving the detonator man a real eyeful. Nothing. She came right up to the van, rapped on the window like it was a door. The window came down. The hooker's left hand was on the sill, her right hand dropped down to her purse. I saw a whitish face in the scope, wearing a dark base-ball cap. Zeroed in until I was one long, thin wire of hate—my mind to my finger to my eye to the slug to the target.

I caught the rhythm of my heart. Started the slow squeeze on the trigger in the dead space until the next beat, the electrical impulse already launched along the wire. The whitish face exploded in fire. A split second later, the sound of the shot echoed up to where I was perched. My finger was still locked on the unpulled trigger, frozen.

The wire snapped.

A motorcycle roared into life. A low-cut racing bike flowed around the back corner like liquid over a rock. The hooker yanked the tiny skirt up to her waist as the bike slid to a stop. The rider was dressed in a set of racing leathers, face hidden under a black helmet and visor. The hooker jumped on the back and the bike rocketed away so fast the front wheel popped off the ground. The blond wig flew off.

I tracked them through the scope in case they needed cover, but they faded from sight long before the bike's raucous exhaust stopped echoing through the concrete canyon.

I worked the bolt, ejecting the unfired cartridge. It hit the rooftop with a dull thud and I dropped to one knee, pulling an infra-red micro-beam out of my pocket. I found the cartridge, scooped it up and pocketed it.

As I got to my feet I heard a rumble down below and my heart stopped. I looked over the parapet. It was a giant semi with ALCHEMY TRANSPORT SYSTEMS painted on its side, heading right past me. Toward the river. Behind it, a panel truck, a dump truck, the carting-company rig and a pair of station wagons. Convoying together.

Ground Zero, moving.

Past me. Then past a dead crumpled target in a van.

I disassembled the sniper's outfit in seconds, threw everything into a felt-lined carry-all. I slung the wide padded strap over my shoulder and took the stairs all the way to the ground floor, hoping that Pryce's fix held and I didn't run into a security guard, a silenced semi-auto in my right hand in case I did. When I saw the broad back of Max the Silent on the bottom step, I knew that last part was covered no matter what Pryce had done.

We were in the Plymouth, rolling toward the West Side Highway, when Max grabbed my arm a split second before the ground shook and the Hudson River shot straight up into the air, a skyscraper of white foam.

Then the sky behind us lit up with battlefield gunfire, tracers razor-slashing the night.

It wasn't the detonator," Pryce told me thirty-six hours later. "It was armed, all right, but he never got his finger on the button before . . ."

I didn't say anything. The detonator man had wanted to blow up the world . . . and the last thing he saw was it happening to him.

"We got all of them down the ramp and into the drink but the last one," Pryce continued. "He must have put a timing device in that one . . . just to be sure."

"How many—?"

"We lost four," he said quietly. "The driver, and the three closest on the perimeter."

"Your people were fantastic," I told him. Not knowing a better word for heroes. Wishing I did.

The news reports said all six neo-Nazis had resisted. Five had gone down in a blaze of gunfire. No word about the silencer-equipped snipers who had taken out each of the drivers as soon as they were in place. Or how all the gunfire was for show, way after it was really over. The fire-team would have waited until they got the all-clear, counting on their backup to seal off the area. But the explosion on the river had told them they were out of time.

"Seems the van driver took Lothar's way out," Pryce replied dryly, telling me that was going to be the story for the press.

"I never thought you'd be able to use tranquilizer darts," I said. "At that distance . . ."

"It was the only way," he told me. "Even with that pink flag flying from the antenna to tell us which vehicle had your man inside, we couldn't risk being wrong."

So the whole gang had been alive when the river blew. But only one had survived to the end.

One plus Hercules.

"And the one we captured," Pryce continued, "once we explained the true plan to him, once he realized the detonator man was going to take them all out, he started singing like a canary on crank. We took down almost a hundred of the others all around the country before the media even had the explosion on the air. And there's more to come."

Not a word from him about Clarence the pimp. Or Michelle the hooker. Or Crystal Beth the getaway driver. They'd all passed through the sealed cauldron like some vague rumor, leaving it to the whisper-stream to tell the story.

And not a word from me about how Herk and one of the lucky Nazis had gotten tranquilizer darts and nothing else . . . while the rest of them went down in a hail of lead thick enough to shield out X-rays. The others got it easier than the detonator man—they were already asleep, never saw it coming. Pryce had to have been right there—he was the only one who could ID Herk.

"I'm gone," he told me quietly, holding out his hand for me to shake. "None of the numbers you have for me will be any good after today. And I won't have this face much longer either."

I took his hand, wondering if the webbed fingers would disappear too. Watched the muscle jump under his eye. I'd know that one again.

"I'm gone too," I said.

"**Y**ou're really going?" I asked Vyra, unable to keep the surprise out of my voice.

"Yes." A lilt in her usually waspish voice. "We are." She was standing next to Hercules, who was vainly trying to cram another pair of shoes into a monster pile of suitcases.

"I've got . . . people still in Oregon," Crystal Beth said. "That'll be their first stop. Or, if they like it there, they can—"

"It doesn't matter," Vyra interrupted her. "We're going to be together. From now on."

Hercules stood up. He was bare-chested, sweating with the strain of "helping" Vyra pack. On his chest, the black swastika was now a murky Rorschach blot only a warrior could read. Or could be entitled to carry. His eyes were wet.

"I never fucking doubted you for a minute, man. I knew you was too slick for those lameass motherfuc—"

"It's done now, Herk," I told him.

"We never gonna be done, brother," the big man said.

Crystal Beth and Vyra kept hugging and crying.

I stepped away from it.

"**A**re you going to stay?" Crystal Beth asked me late that night.

"Tonight? Sure."

"With me? And not just tonight?" she asked.

The time for lies was done. "I don't know," I told her.

An excerpt from

CHOICE OF EVIL

by **ANDREW VACHSS**

soon to be available in hardcover from
Alfred A. Knopf, Inc.

I nosed the Plymouth carefully around the corner, checking the street the way I always do when I'm heading home. The garage I use is cut into the closed-off base of an old twine factory which had been converted into upscale lofts years ago. Above the designer-massaged floor-through apartments is what the yuppie occupants think is crawl space. That's where I live.

A pal had tapped into their electricity lines and installed a stainless steel sink-and-toilet combo. A fiberglass stall shower, a two-burner hot plate, a duct to the heating pipes below . . . and it turned into my home.

I've lived there for years, thanks to a deal I made with the landlord. His son got himself into a jackpot—an easy enough feat for a punk who thought ratting out his rich dope-dealing friends was a fun hobby—and ended up in the Witness Protection Program. I stumbled across him while I was looking for someone else, and I traded my silence for a special brand of rent control. Didn't cost the landlord a penny, but it bought his punk kid an anonymous life. And safe harbor for me.

Some of my life is in that building. And when I saw the pack of blue-and-white NYPD squad cars surrounding the back entrance, I knew that part of it was over.

I just sat there and took it. The way I always do—fear and rage dancing inside me, nothing showing on my face. I've had a lot of practice, from the hospital where my whore of a mother dropped me—dropped me out of her, I mean—to the orphanage to the foster homes to the juvenile joints to prison to that war in Africa to prison again and . . . all of it.

It didn't matter anymore. Nothing did. Somebody had dimed me out. And the cops would find enough felony evidence up there to put me back Inside forever once they connected it up.

I watched the cops carry Pansy out on a litter, straining under the huge beast's weight. Pansy's my dog. My partner, not my pet. A Neapolitan mastiff, direct descendent of the original war dogs who crossed the Alps with Hannibal. I had dreamed of having my own dog every night in prison. They'd taken my beloved little terrier Pepper from me when I was a kid, that lying swine of a juvenile court judge promising me there'd be another puppy in the foster home they were sentencing me to. I remember the court officer laughing then, but I didn't get the joke until they dropped me off. There was no pup there, and I had to do the time alone, without anyone who loved me.

I never saw Pepper again, but I did see that court officer. It was more than twenty years later, and he didn't recognize me. When I was done, nobody would recognize him either. That's the way I was then. I'm not the same now. But I've only changed my ways, not my heart.

I'd raised Pansy from a pup. Weaned her myself. She would die for me. And it looked like she had. Standing up all the way. She'd never let another human being into my place when I wasn't there.

I said goodbye the way we do down here—promising her vengeance. I was using the little monocular I always carry to get a close up when the screen shifted focus: I saw Pansy stir on the litter. She was still alive. The cops must have waited for the EMS unit— they carry tranquilizer guns. So I didn't need the badge numbers of the cops anymore—I needed my dog back. I U-turned the Plymouth slow and smooth and aimed it toward a place where I could make plans.

"**H**oney, I called around for hours. We know where she is," Michelle said, her lustrous eyes shining, reflecting the pain in me. She's my sister—my pain is hers.

"Where?"

"The new shelter. The one in Hunter's Point, just across the river? In Long Island City."

"Yeah, I heard about it. It's private, right? Part of the fucking Mayor's giveaway plan."

"Baby, relax, okay? Crystal Beth ran over there the second I called her. It could get a little stupid . . . Pansy's got no license, no papers . . . but Crystal knows how to act. Just sit tight, and—"

"When did she leave?"

"Honey, stop. You're *scaring* me. She's been gone almost . . . three hours now. You don't expect her to haul that monster on the back of her motorcycle, do you?"

"I don't care how she—"

Michelle put her hand on my forearm, willing me to centered calmness, reminding me of all the years I'd invested in learning the path to that place.

"Can you get Max for me?" I asked Mama. She'd been hovering nearby since the minute I'd come in.

"Sure. Get Max. Come soon, okay?"

I just nodded.

"Burke, you don't need *Max* for this," Michelle told me. "Jesus! It's not like they're gonna care, right? So she doesn't have a license. So Crystal Beth has to pay a fine . . . or what*ever*. It won't take long. . . ."

I stayed inside myself, waiting. Felt Crystal Beth's small hand on my shoulder before I heard her approach. Smelled her orchid-and-dark tobacco scent. Didn't move. She came around the table and sat down across from me.

"Burke—"

"What happened?" I cut into whatever she was going to say, already knowing it was bad.

"The . . . license thing wasn't a problem. Just like Michelle said. They were willing to let me take her. But they wouldn't bring her out —they said I had to go back and get her myself."

"And . . . ?"

"And she was in a cage. A big steel cage. Like a tiger or something. There was a sign on it, in red; it said: DANGEROUS! DO NOT APPROACH! The . . . attendant, he told me she wouldn't take food. Even when they shoved it into the cage, she wouldn't eat. He warned me not to come near her, but I did anyway, and she . . ."

"What?"

"She tried to kill me. She lunged at the bars, snarling and snapping her teeth, and . . ."

"They don't know the word," I said, half to myself. I had poison-proofed Pansy when she was still small. Unless you said the right word, she wouldn't touch food, no matter how hungry she was. I had a friend who ran a little auto parts joint. He had a Shepherd, a real nice one. He used the dog to guard the place at night, so nobody could help themselves. Some degenerate tossed a strychnine-laced steak over the fence. When the dog helped himself, he died. In pain.

I'd trained Pansy so that would never happen to her. And I should have known she wouldn't walk out with anyone but me.

They try and get dogs adopted at the shelter. If they can't, they gas them. Who was going to adopt a sixteen-year-old, hundred-and-fifty-pound monster who could bite the top off a fire hydrant? But Pansy wasn't going to be gassed . . . she'd loyal herself to death first.

Not a chance. I owed her at least what I'd always promised myself. That I wouldn't die caged.

"Michelle, go find the Prof for me," I told her.

A few hours later, I was with a piece of my family, waiting on the rest.

"I can't scam her out," I told the women. "I mean, I could go there myself, and she'd come with me. But if I show up . . . the cops know where they got her from, and they might be expecting that. I'm surprised they didn't try and follow Crystal Beth . . ."

"I was on my bike, honey," Crystal Beth said, her face calm with assurance.

I knew what she was telling me. There wasn't a cop car made that could keep up with Crystal Beth on that motorcycle of hers, especially with the steady rain that had been falling for days. For the first time, I noticed what she was wearing—a full set of racing leathers.

"But how were you gonna get Pansy on—?"

"We had a car too, standing by. If I got her out, I was just going to load her in there and—"

"Whose car?"

"I don't know, Burke. The Mole lent it to us. Some big dark thing. He made me a new license plate for my scooter too. Even if the cops saw it, they won't make anything out of it."

"The Mole was gonna drive? Jesus, I—"

"Not the Mole," Michelle interrupted. "Terry."

"He's not— "

"Yes, he is," she said, a trace of sadness in her voice. "My little boy's almost a man now. He doesn't have a license, but he can drive."

Terry. Had it really been that long since I'd pulled him away from a kiddie pimp in Times Square? Since Michelle took him for her own? Since the Mole had raised him in his junkyard? Since . . . ?

Then the door swung open and the Prof walked in, Clarence at his heels.

"What's the plan, man? I got the word, came soon as I heard."

"We have to get her out before they—"

"I said the *plan*, fool. You know I'm down with the hound. So gimme the four-one-one, son. They gonna be laying in the cut, waiting on you to make your move. We gotta be quick, but we also gotta be slick. Otherwise . . . "

"Let me think," I told the only father I'd ever had: the one I met behind the Walls.

"**E**verybody got it?" I asked. It was almost nine o'clock at night by then, more than sixteen hours since my life had been torn apart.

Everybody nodded. Nobody spoke. I looked over at the big circular table in the corner, now piled high with what we needed.

"You sure they're open twenty-four hours?" I asked Michelle.

"That's what they *said*, honey. But I don't know if they'll actually open the doors, even if you say it's an emergency. It's not a medical place. All they do there is keep the dogs and . . . "

"Kill them," I finished for her. "It doesn't matter anyway." I turned to look at Crystal Beth. "You got the floor plan?"

"Right here," she said, unrolling it on the table in front of me.

"Mole," I called, summoning him over. Then I started to explain what I needed.

"There *have* to be women there," Crystal Beth said, standing to one side of the table, little hands on her big hips, face tightened against any argument.

"Look, this is—"

"You say 'man's work' and I'm going to—"

"No, girl," I said soothingly. "I wasn't saying that. It's just you don't have any experience with—"

"With what, hijacking?" Michelle interrupted. "That isn't the way to do it. You and the Prof, sure. I know you even got Max to go along sometimes on that crazy stuff you used to do, but if you think—"

"I am going too, little sister," Clarence said in his dignified island voice, blue-black West Indian face set and resolute. "You are not to blame Burke for this. Yes, I would follow my father, wherever he walked. But I love that great animal too. She is not going to die," he said softly, his hand caressing the 9mm semiauto that was as much a part of his wardrobe as the peacock clothing he draped over his lean body every day.

"That's not the *point*. I don't want—"

"Michelle, I am going," the Mole said. Soft and gentle, like always. But not, like always, deferring to her. "Not Terry. You are right. He is my boy too, not only yours. And he is too young to risk . . . whatever there is."

"Will you morons fucking *listen* to me?" Michelle yelled standing up so suddenly she knocked a bunch of glassware to the floor. She walked over and stood next to Crystal Beth.

"This isn't about what you imbeciles *think* I'm trying to tell you. It is *not* a hijacking, even with all those . . . guns and things you have.

It's still a scam, right? And they are *not* going buy it unless you have a woman doing the talking, understand?"

"Girl's telling it true," the Prof said. "We don't work it right, they ain't gonna bite."

The Mole nodded, slowly and reluctantly.

"Yeah," I said, surrendering.

I t was near 3 a.m. by the time we were ready to ride. Michelle and Crystal Beth were both dressed in military camo-fatigues, complete with combat boots. Max and I went for the generic look. Crystal Beth in the front seat right next to me, her left hand on my thigh, transmitting. Max and Michelle were in the back, Michelle yammering a nerve-edged blue streak, the mute Mongol warrior probably grateful he couldn't hear. I had decided the Plymouth wasn't much of a risk—I always keep the registration on me, and the car got a fresh coat of dull cream primer last night.

I waved across to where Clarence sat behind the wheel of what would pass for a Con Ed truck unless you looked too close. If you did, you'd be looking at the wrong end of the Prof's double-barreled sawed-off. Somewhere in the back of the truck, the Mole was preparing his potions.

We caravaned along until we got to the pull-off spot on the FDR. I pointed to a white semi-stretch limo with blacked-out glass. "That's yours," I told Crystal Beth. "The rollers won't look twice at a car like that this time of morning. It'll look like someone's coming home from clubbing. Besides, it'll hold everyone."

"I'm staying with you," she said.

"No, you are *not*, girl," I told her. "Max can't drive worth a damn, and the Mole would crash it for sure. Clarence is the best wheelman we got, but we need him in the truck. We're *leaving* the truck when we're done, and everyone can't fit in this car. You just park it where I told you to, and we'll all meet up before we hit the place."

"Burke, I—"

"Crystal Beth, I swear I will throw your fat ass out of this car right now, no more playing. Drive the limo or we'll do this without you."

She punched me hard on the right arm and got out. She walked over to the limo, opened it with the key I'd given her. I waited until I heard it start up, then I took off.

The Animal Shelter was freestanding—a long, low concrete building, T-shaped at the back end. I pointed out my window for Crystal Beth to pull over. She parked the big limo perfectly, left it with the nose aimed straight out. When she got into the front seat of the Plymouth, I said: "They're going to take the truck around the back. Mole'll stay with it. The Prof and Clarence will meet us out front. Then we do it. Ready?"

Everybody nodded. Nobody spoke.

I parked the Plymouth just around the corner, out of sight from the front door. We all got out. The Prof and Clarence slipped around the corner and linked up with us.

"How we getting in, Schoolboy?" the Prof asked. "Scam or slam?"

"Slam," I told him, showing the handful of Semtex I was holding. "Me first. Stand back."

I walked up to the door. Put my ear to it. Nothing but a few random, doleful barks—the Captured Dog Blues—no sound of human activity. I patted the Semtex all around the knob and the lock, then made a long seam tracer for the door's edge. I jerked the string loose and ran back around the corner.

The second the door blew off the hinges, we all charged, faces covered with dark stocking masks, hands gloved. I was first in the door. The attendant was at his desk, face slack with shock. I showed him the pistol.

"Touch the phone and you're dead," I promised him.

Max slid past me, unslinging the huge set of bolt-cutters from over one massive shoulder. The Prof stepped into a corner, his scattergun weaving, a snake looking for a passing mouse. The lights flickered, then went out—the Mole saying he was on the job.

Crystal Beth stepped up, shoving me aside, shining a halogen flashlight in the attendant's face.

"This is a message from the Wolfpack Cadre of the Canine Liberation Front," she proclaimed in a perfect liberal-twit revolutionary's voice. "You may no longer imprison our brothers and sisters without fear of consequences!"

"Look, I—" the attendant started to speak.

"Silence, lackey!" Crystal Beth snarled at him. "This is a jailbreak, not a debate."

A soft explosion rocked the back of the building. Then another.

The attendant moved his lips like he was praying, but no sound came out.

I walked past him. Saw Max's broad back bent over as he severed the heavy lock on the door to the cage area. Then we both popped the cages open, one by one. The dogs milled about uncertainly, until one spotted the gaping hole in the side of the building. He ran for it, and the others followed.

Pansy was there, her cage standing open. On her feet, daring Max to come closer.

"Pansy!" I called to her. "Come here, sweetheart!"

The big beast's head shot up. She bounded over to me. "Good girl!" I told her, patting her huge head. Then I gave her the hand signal to heel and we merged with the river of dogs flowing to freedom.

As soon as she saw the car, she knew what to do. I popped the trunk and she jumped inside and curled up on the mat next to the padded fuel cell and looked up expectantly. I handed her a giant marrow bone, whispering "Speak!" at the same time. I closed the trunk lid, knowing the air holes I'd punched in it years ago would let her breathe just fine. And if anyone heard her pulverizing the bone, they'd just think the old Plymouth had a bad differential.

Even with us working the wrong side of the river, some citizen could have called the cops by then. We had to move fast. I stepped back inside the front door just as Michelle was taping up a cardboard stencil warning the world against the unlawful imprisonment of dogs. Clarence sprayed the blood-red paint with one hand, the other holding his pistol steady.

"Don't think about the phones after we're gone," I told the attendant, just to get his attention. As he looked up, Max materialized behind him and did something to his neck. He wouldn't be making any calls for hours.

"They all out?" I asked Clarence.

"All gone, mahn. Every one."

"Scoop the Mole—he's back there somewhere. Then get in the limo and fly. I'll be right behind you."

I tossed a smoke grenade into the back of the joint and dashed for the Plymouth.

I read all about it in the afternoon paper, Pansy stretched out next to me in Crystal Beth's apartment. On the top floor of her safe-house.

BOOKS BY ANDREW VACHSS

"Vachss is in the first rank of American crime writers."
—*Cleveland Plain Dealer*

BLOSSOM

Two things bring Burke from New York to Indiana: a frantic call from an old cell mate named Virgil and a serial sniper whose twisted passion is to pick off couples on a local lovers' lane.
Crime Fiction/0-679-77261-8

BLUE BELLE

With a purseful of dirty money and the help of a hard-bitten stripper named Belle, Burke sets out to find the infamous Ghost Van that is cutting a lethal swath among the teenage prostitutes in the 'hood.
Crime Fiction/0-679-76168-3

BORN BAD

Born Bad is a wickedly fine collection of forty-five stories that distill dread down to its essence, plunging readers into the hell that lurks just outside their bedroom windows.
Crime Fiction/0-679-75336-2

DOWN IN THE ZERO

The haunted and hell-ridden private eye Burke, a man inured to every evil except the kind that preys on children, is investigating suicides among the teenagers of a wealthy Connecticut suburb and, along the way, discovers a sinister connection.
Crime Fiction/0-679-76066-0

FALSE ALLEGATIONS

A professional debunker specializing in "false" allegations of child sexual abuse has stumbled across the case of his career—the real thing. What he needs now is a man who knows how to find out the truth, a man like Burke.
Crime Fiction/0-679-77293-6

FLOOD

Burke's newest client is a woman named Flood, who has the face of an angel, the body of a high-priced stripper, and the skills of a professional executioner. She enlists Burke to follow a child's murderer through the catacombs of New York so she can kill him her bare hands.
Crime Fiction/0-679-78129-3

FOOTSTEPS OF THE HAWK

As Burke tries to unravel a string of sex crimes, he is caught in the cross-fire of two rogue cops who are setting him up to be the next victim.

Crime Fiction/0-679-76663-4

HARD CANDY

In *Hard Candy*, Burke is up against a soft-spoken messiah, who may be rescuing runaways or recruiting them for his own hideous purposes.

Crime Fiction/0-679-76169-1

SACRIFICE

What—or who—could turn a gifted little boy into a murderous thing that calls itself "Satan's Child?" In search of an answer, Burke uncovers mechanisms of evil even he had not imagined.

Crime Fiction/0-679-76410-0

SHELLA

At the heart of this story is a natural predator, Ghost, searching for a topless dancer named Shella, who has vanished somewhere in a wilderness of strip clubs, peep shows, and back alleys.

Crime Fiction/0-679-75681-7

STREGA

The implacable Burke has a new client, a woman who calls herself "Strega" (Italian for an erotic witch)—and a new assignment that leads him into the deepest oceans of the twisted city.

Crime Fiction/0-679-76409-7

THE TALENTED MR. RIPLEY
by Patricia Highsmith

Tom Ripley is sent to Italy with the commission to coax Dickie Greenleaf back to his wealthy father. But Ripley finds himself very fond of this prodigal young American. He wants to be like him— exactly like him. Ripley will stop at nothing to achieve his goal—not even murder.

"[Highsmith] has created a world of her own—a world claustrophobic and irrational which we enter each time with a sense of personal danger."   —Graham Greene

Fiction/Crime/0-679-74229-8

THE CHILL
by Ross Macdonald

A distraught young man hires Archer to track down his runaway bride, but no sooner has he found her than Archer finds himself entangled in two murders, one twenty years old, the other so recent that the blood is still warm.

"The American private eye, immortalized by Hammett, refined by Chandler, brought to its zenith by Macdonald."
—*The New York Times Book Review*

Fiction/Crime/0-679-76807-6

THE KILLER INSIDE ME
by Jim Thompson

Lou Ford is the deputy sheriff of a small town in Texas. The worst thing most people can say against him is that he's a little slow and a little boring. But then, most people don't know about the sickness.

"Probably the most chilling and believable first-person story of a criminally warped mind I have ever encountered."   —Stanley Kubrick

Fiction/Crime/0-679-73397-3